S...

Runaway Billionaires: Arthur Duet, Book 1

By: Blair Babylon

Genevieve is a lawyer, not a babysitter, and certainly not a dog trainer. She is just about to become a full barrister, a British litigating attorney, when her law mentor dies unexpectedly. She is shuffled off to another barrister, one who's nothing at all like her kind and decent former mentor, and then she is assigned the office's worst case: Arthur Finch-Hatten, six-feet and four-inches of ripped, loaded, hot English nobleman who is wasting his life and his inherited estate so audaciously that his younger brother is suing him for control of their family's earldom. There is a darn good chance that Arthur will lose everything, even his crazed, badly behaved puppy.

Unless he shapes up.

Her new boss hasn't been able to convince Arthur to mend his ways. His uncle's lectures haven't had any effect on his depraved debauchery and lavish lifestyle.

The only way for Genevieve to make partner is to win Arthur's case, and the only way to win his case and save his earldom is to keep him from spending his days hungover in bed and his nights pouring Cristal on naked, drunk women before flying off in his private jumbo jet to the next party.

Arthur is enough to make any woman need a stiff drink.

PRAISE FOR STIFF DRINK

"I love walking blind into a Blair Babylon book because only then can I really appreciate all of the emotions, nuances, and life that you will encounter. Each of her amazing characters are completely and deliciously complex to their very core. There is nothing easy about her storylines either. They make you work, suffer, and sweat right along the characters every step of the way. **These books become a part of you.** Even if you don't want to acknowledge that fact, it is still so very true. Blair Babylon has forged a true masterpiece! **She has taken a wonderfully wicked storyline, infused it with some fantastically stunning characters, and then molded it with spectacular twists and turns** that gives you a truly extraordinary and wonderfully epic adventure. With this incredible powerhouse of an addition to her fun and quirky new series, I am absolutely on pins and needles to see what she creates next! **This is one author that NEVER fails to deliver,** and when what she delivers is pure bliss wrapped in utter perfection." — *Goodreads reviewer*

"So much danger and mystery surrounds Arthur. When Genevieve is appointed as Arthur's barrister she needs to do more than win his case. This was filled with great chemistry, a building friendship, issues dealing with Genevieve's painful past and also Arthur's job. I cannot wait for Book Two of their story as book one was enjoyable to read and I need to see how their story ends. Huge fan of this author!" — *Goodreads reviewer*

"Any time a book has Blair Babylon's name, I'm going to read it. And, more often than not, I'm going to love it. This is no exception." — *Goodreads reviewer*

"This book will provide you with lots of lawyer jokes, machinations of unknown (yet) level, and **scorching chemistry that will keep you entertained and intrigued for hours!!!** Blair Babylon's characters just keep getting better and better! These are the characters that you wouldn't want to let go of, soon. And **their story will replay in your mind** as you lay imagining at night." — *Goodreads reviewer*

PRAISE FOR BLAIR BABYLON'S BOOKS

"The book oozed heart and passion from every page, it was as if it was traveling through my fingers to touch my very soul - I'm gobsmacked at how I feel about it! It showed more than I thought I was going to get it gave me *love and passion in absolute bin loads and moreover it was full of desire, hope, longing, honesty and devotion* - not just from the characters but from the author also because her devotion to her craft was clearly evident in this book - she nailed it!!" -- *Books Laid Bare Blog, (Every Breath You Take, Rock Stars in Disguise: Xan)*

"*Every Breath You Take* was an absolutely stunning and creatively passionate exploration of two lost and lonely people finding the missing part of their heart and soul in each other. What a breathtaking journey filled with unwanted hope, unwavering love, and unexpected devotion! This series is continuing with such a brilliant depth of heart and soul that I just can't get enough of. I am definitely looking forward to more of these ground-breaking stories." --*Shadowplay Book Blog, (Every Breath You Take, Rock Stars in Disguise: Xan)*

"This book brings together two of the author's series, Billionaires in Disguise and Rock Stars in Disguise. Prior to this book, the two were entirely separate. If you haven't yet read any of the books in these series, then what are you waiting for? **You do not need to read them to understand this book, but reading them will give you a broader understanding of the incredible canvas Blair is using as her background. She has basically created these worlds and characters from scratch, and what a world it is."** ~*Fictional Men's Page for Book Ho's*

"This was one incredible story. I can't wait to continue with this series." ~*Books and Beyond Fifty Shades*

* * *

"Let me first say WOW... I am seriously addicted to Blair Babylon's books her imagination whether it be Crime, Rockstar or Billionaire. **She creates a world where you are immersed with colourful and diverse characters and situations that you don't want to escape from."** *~Kat's Book Promotions*

"What a pair! This story had me clutching my chest. **I loved Tryp. His damaged and broken soul tugs at your heart strings.** His need to spiral down into the darkness to escape his past will have you wanting to comfort him and just whisper sweet nothings in his ear. The unlikely friendship was definitely the perfect route for this story. It takes a special kind of person to handle all of Tryp's darkness. Elfie definitely proved herself worthy and I loved her determination and strength even though she has a past of her own that she is desperately trying to run from. **Blair Babylon delivers a truly emotional story that had me on one helluva emotional rollercoaster.** I am definitely looking forward to reading more from this series." *~Jennifer's Book Obsession, (Somebody to Love, Rock Stars in Disguise: Tyrp)*

"Just believe me when I say you DON'T want to miss this one." *~Jo's Book Addictions (Somebody to Love, Rock Stars in Disguise: Tyrp)*

"There is much more to this story than just a ROCKSTAR ROMANCE - but heck its that and more." *~Kat's Book Promotions (Somebody to Love, Rock Stars in Disguise: Tyrp)*

"This was my first Blair Babylon book and I was on a rollercoaster. **Tryp and Elfie need to read by all, a raw story of friendship and love.** Truly only the strong survive. I want more of these two."*~Romance Bytes (Every Breath You Take, Rock Stars in Disguise: Xan)*

"The chemistry Wulf and Raegan have is amazing and

the fact that they are both so stubborn makes their relationship funny at times. The series covers everything from finding out about the good, bad, and ugly of each other to meeting the family. There are raw emotions in these books." ~~*Random Musesomy Book Blog*

"Blair Babylon knows what she is doing. **This is some of the best romance I have read, hands down.** It's got a little bit of everything, for everyone....the story was so well written, infused with sex, humor and drama, that **I would gladly read it over and over again."** ~*Contagious Reads Blog*

"If I could give 10 stars I would! I adore this book, I have read it two times completely and many times parts of it." ~*Katrina's Books Blog*

"AWESOME! When I first started reading this book I thought it was going to be your regular romance book and I thought, what kind of spin could possibly be put on this kind of relationship. Don't get me wrong, I am the first person to admit that I love a good relationship. I think it's hot but I was still waiting for a new refreshing spin on romance novels, and this was it for me. So of course you still had the typical kind of damsel in distress and then that sexy as hell man coming to save her. **Well the twist is something that you wouldn't expect....** Wulf also has a secret, and when I mean secret, it's a big secret. No, it's nothing that you might be thinking, like he is married or he is gay. **I mean huge, I was in complete shock when I found out.** That is one of the things that I loved most about this novel, **everything that I thought was completely wrong and it kept me intrigued the entire time.**" ~*Fictional Book Ho's Blog*

"The writing was great! Her characters are extensively developed and **I loved the way the author "peeled away" the layers** of them and let us really get to know them gradually. I loved the mystery in the characters' backgrounds and personalities. **I loved the suspense and action thrown in the story also!"** ~*Sammy's Book Obsession*

Also By Blair Babylon

Working Stiff (Runaway Billionaires #1, Casimir)
Stiff Drink (Runaway Billionaires #2, Arthur Duet, Part 1)
Hard Liquor (Runaway Billionaires #3, Arthur Duet, Part 2)

Billionaires in Disguise: Rae, Complete Omnibus Edition
"An Extravagant Proposal (Billionaires in Disguise: Charley)"

Falling Hard (Billionaires in Disguise, Lizzy #1)
Playing Rough (Billionaires in Disguise: Lizzy, #2)
Breaking Rules (Billionaires in Disguise: Lizzy, #3)
Burning Bright (Billionaires in Disguise: Lizzy, #4)

"Alwaysland" (A Prequel to Rock Stars in Disguise:Xan)
What A Girl Wants (Rock Stars in Disguise: Rhiannon)
Somebody to Love (Rock Stars in Disguise: Tryp)

Every Breath You Take (Billionaires in Disguise: Georgie)
Wild Thing (Billionaires in Disguise: Georgie)
"Skiing in June, A Rae and Wulf Epilogue #1" (Billionaires in Disguise: Rae)
"Kidnapped, A Rae and Wulf Epilogue #2" (Billionaires in Disguise: Rae)
"Rae and Wulf: At the Hospital"
Lay Your Hands On Me (Billionaires in Disguise: Georgie)
Nothing Else Matters (Billionaires in Disguise: Georgie)
"Montreux, A Rae and Wulf Epilogue #3" (Billionaires in Disguise: Rae)

The Rock Star's Secret Baby (Rock Stars in Disguise: Cadell)
"Dream On" (Billionaires in Disguise: Georgie, Epilogue #1)
"Keep Dreaming" (Billionaires in Disguise: Georgie, Epilogue #2)

Runaway Princess Bride (Billionaires in Disguise: Flicka)
Stiff Competition (Runaway Billionaires #4, Maxence)

STIFF DRINK

Runaway Billionaires: Arthur Duet, Book #1

Blair Babylon

Malachite Publishing LLC

First Print Edition: March, 2017

Printed in the United States of America

STIFF DRINK

RUNAWAY BILLIONAIRES: ARTHUR DUET, BOOK #1

Crows Fighting Over Crumbs

Genevieve "Gen" Ward stood in the conference room of Serle's Court Barristers, a London law firm, eyeing dozens of manila folders strewn across the long table.

Her black, high-heeled shoes still bore traces of cold graveyard mud and shed dried flakes onto the rug, even though she had tried to wipe it off. Her cheeks felt starched-stiff from grinding her teeth during Horace Lindsey's funeral. Weeping at a funeral was so American. Horace would have been so disappointed in her if she had cried in front of all the other lawyers.

The folders on the table held the summaries of Horace's law cases that he had been fighting when he had died. Gen's future as a British trial lawyer, a barrister, rested on which of them she might be assigned.

Just not the case of Lord Arthur Finch-Hatten, the Earl of Severn, she prayed to the capricious gods of the court. *Any case but that one.*

Outside the conference room's long windows, a fountain spouted water amid the formal garden's winter-dead lawns, as prim as any palace's grounds. The tall spires and walls of Lincoln's Inn—an antique, Gothic building that housed lawyers' business offices—surrounded the garden and blocked out the skyscrapers and honking cars of central London.

Inside the conference room, the sixty-odd other senior and junior barristers crowded around the table, craning their necks and shouldering each other for a better look at the labels typed on the folders' tabs.

Everyone was dressed in mourning black, and the gathered lawyers resembled vicious crows, ready to do battle over crumbs.

They would not, however, make a move toward the folders.

The Head Clerk, Celestia Alen-Buckley, stood at the head of the table, her short arms braced on the dark, carved wood as she glared at the folders strewn between the rows of hovering barristers.

The Head Clerk would decide who would be assigned to which case. Her dark eyes narrowed, watching the barristers, sizing each of them up even though she had known them all for decades. With just a glance, the lawyers shriveled under Celestia Alen-Buckley's gaze. Without her formidable power stretching over the table, the barristers might have leapt onto the table to melee for the cases, each worth many thousands of pounds and mostly completed.

All the black-clad lawyers and staff had just returned from the funeral of their esteemed, learned colleague Horace Lindsey, one of the most senior barristers in chambers. The kindly, grandfatherly man had taken a special interest in Gen. Her multiple disadvantages—having spent her formative years in America, retaining an abominable Texas accent despite her best efforts, her lack of the benefits of the British independent school education like most of her colleagues had enjoyed, and of course, her unfortunate appearance—had provoked his pity.

Her mother had assured Gen of her lack of looks her whole life, telling her that she had to be especially smart and diligent to make up for her long, horsey face and too-big teeth.

Her whole life.

Gen liked to think that she had grown into her face and teeth when she had stretched to a towering five feet and ten inches, but her mother had continued to harp on Gen's thick waist, her thunderous thighs, and her cankles.

So Gen worked like a demon dog to make up for all her disadvantages.

Horace Lindsey had noticed Gen working late—all the other pupil barristers had left for the pubs and an evening of socializing and drinking—because Horace was still at his desk, too. They drank tea while they worked, and he had imparted the little bits of lore and advice that, as an outsider, she had sorely needed. Horace had thought of her as an up-and-comer, a grinder, despite all her disadvantages. He had been the first senior barrister to make a cup of tea for Gen, one late evening while they were listening to streaming music while they worked. She had practically fallen in love with him and his sparse, white hair when he had presented her with a hot cup of tea and a wry, wrinkled smile. He had become her pupil master for the first six months of her internship, called a pupillage.

Horace had suffered a heart attack at his desk just a few days before, late at night, a few weeks after Christmas. Gen had called the ambulance while he had clutched his chest, and then Gen had told Horace's partner, Basil, that his last words were of him.

They weren't, of course. Horace's last words had been instructions on his cases. Gen had taken notes with one hand and held Horace's meaty fist with the other while he gasped, suffocating. He had been desperate to leave those final instructions on his cases, and she had printed out every word and stapled them into the manila folders littered on the conference room table.

And now all the senior, junior, and pupil barristers in chambers hovered over Horace's folders, nudging each other as they peered at the labels, ready to pounce on the most prestigious cases or the ones most easily won or settled.

Genevieve was a lowly pupil barrister, the lowest rung on the barrister ladder, still in her first six-month term of law practical training, only recently speaking for clients in court with Horace looking over her shoulder the whole time. The Head Clerk would assign her the dregs of Horace's cases to write the briefs for a new pupil master.

If she got any at all.

Just not Lord Severn's case, she prayed again.

Lord Arthur Finch-Hatten, the Earl of Severn, had been one of Horace's most difficult cases. His younger brother, Christopher Finch-Hatten, was suing him for possession and control of the family's earldom and several estates. For any other defendant, this would have been designated a frivolous lawsuit that would have gotten the filing lawyer assigned costs or disciplined by the Bar Council.

Except that the defendant was The Right Honorable Arthur Finch-Hatten, the twenty-fifth Earl of Severn, the notorious and incorrigible scoundrel, *damn it.*

When Lord Severn deigned to grace the law offices with his presence to discuss the lawsuit against him, he strutted through chambers, the walking incarnation of privilege and sin. His deftly tailored suits were cut close to his muscular body as if he had been carved from dark marble. His strong cheekbones and square jaw were the pinnacles of centuries of beautiful women bred to powerful men to produce stunning gentlemen and ladies in the next generations. His ancestral tree was studded with several kings of England and Scotland, several more and farther back than the current heir to the British throne could claim.

As Lord Severn strode through the chambers, his silvery-blue eyes surveyed the female admins and junior barristers as he decided which of them to tempt into a night or a week of exuberant debauchery. Dark hair fell across his forehead, and the subtle scent of some hideously expensive cologne—warm spices and clean musk—wafted from him as he passed Gen, who always seemed to be caught out of her tiny office when he arrived. She would rather have barred her door against his influence.

Lord Severn usually left the barristers' chambers with a

young woman hanging on his arm and smiling up at his arrogant face, and then Horace had scoured the gossip websites with trepidation until the woman came back to work, shame-faced but oddly exuberant and dripping with new jewelry. His superficial relationships never lasted longer than a few weeks.

Lord Severn was a silver-eyed, silver-spoon-fed, silver-tongued billionaire, which was absolutely everything they needed him *not* to be.

Gen prayed that she would not have to deal with Horace's most problematic case.

The tan file folders splayed across the table.

Gen waited quietly, her hands clasped in front of her.

The other barristers did the same.

Celestia Alen-Buckley examined each file and made her pronouncements.

Some folders, she perused the stickers and pursed her lips, deliberating, her eyes picking out a few barristers as possibilities, before she handed them off.

Some folders only received a cursory glance and a deliberate throw to a senior barrister.

Evidently, some considerations had already been made behind the scenes.

Damn it. Gen should have lobbied to be assigned the Lombardi case. With Horace's wise and gentle instructions, it should settle soon. Gen needed a few wins in her docket.

She needed court wins *a lot.*

Tenancy offers—an invitation to set up shop as a "tenant" within the chambers, essentially a job offer to be a litigating lawyer in the law firm—would be made nine months from then, at the end of September. If the senior barristers didn't offer tenancy to Gen, it would destroy her career just as it had officially begun. No other chambers would take her on. She would have few options to salvage her career, and they were all bad.

Gen's new boss, Octavia Hawkes, stood across the table

from Gen, eyeing the manila folders littering the dark wood table. Octavia's blond hair was tightly coiffed into a French twist, as it always was on court days. Her black suit clung to her slender body. Her tailor came to her home once a month to adjust any suit that wasn't a perfect fit.

Yep, glamorous, successful Octavia Hawkes was Gen's new boss and her competition for Horace's best cases.

Gen needed to snag *several* of those cases or at least one really good one.

Most pupil barristers were in debt, of course, unless they had wealthy parents who had ponied up the cash for their education. Gen sure as heck hadn't had that advantage, either. The bar course had cost thirty thousand pounds for the year-long session. Thirty thousand pounds of debt, and Gen owed that money to her mother.

And her mother needed it back *now*.

Not in five years. Certainly not in ten.

Right *now*.

Celestia Alen-Buckley divvied up the cases.

The Lombardi folder whisked across the table to James Knightly, one of the other first-sixers who was vying for a tenancy offer. James had brought a caramel macchiato to the funeral and handed it to Celestia Alen-Buckley, and now James had the Lombardi file.

James played the barrister game exceptionally well. His father was a judge.

Gen mentally kicked herself again for not cozying up to Celestia Alen-Buckley yesterday and this morning. She ought to have known better.

File by file, Celestia Alen-Buckley made her pronouncements, her dusky hands flipping the folders across the table to be grabbed by their intended recipients too fast for Gen to keep track of them.

Finally, only one folder remained on the table.

Please, not Arthur Finch-Hatten. Please, God. Not Arthur Finch-Hatten.

Celestia Alen-Buckley picked up that last folder and looked straight at her.

Gen tried not to shrink under the woman's stare.

Celestia Alen-Buckley whipped the folder down the long tabletop, the paper whispering on the wood the whole way. It skidded to a stop right where Gen stood.

"Here, Genevieve," Celestia said. "You're ambitious. If you can win it, you'll make your name here."

Gen was reaching for the folder when she saw the label, a blur of black ink on white with three capital letters sticking up: an *A*, an *F*, and an *H*.

Damn it.

First Meeting

Gen's first meeting with her new client, the scandalous Lord Arthur Finch-Hatten, the Earl of Severn, was scheduled for eleven o'clock the next morning.

Her handwritten notes covered the inside of his manila folder:

Call him Lord Severn, My Lord, or Your Lordship. Not Mr. Finch-Hatten. Certainly not Arthur or Hey Hottie Sugar-Buns.

Don't offer to shake his hand. You're a barrister for God's sake, and barristers don't do that.

Don't stare at him. Act like a damn professional.

The meeting was not to be held in her cubby of an office at Serle's Court Barristers. In her office, her pupil desk was hardly larger than her laptop and couldn't have held even a fraction of the documents that she needed to go over with him.

Instead, Gen had reserved the smallest of the conference rooms for the all-important first meeting. The windows looked outward from the building over the winding streets of central London, lined closely with brick structures like a medieval city. The other side, the *good* side of the building, faced the courtyard garden.

In the conference room, the heavily carved table seemed ridiculously ornate to Gen, but she had grown up in America. Her bourgeois tastes ran more to clean lines and modern furniture rather than the trappings of wealth and history that were the norm in British barristers' chambers. She needed to get used to this kind of thing.

She waited in the conference room for Lord Severn to show up.

By eleven in the morning, Gen had made good progress on her work for the day and had drunk several all-important cups of coffee.

That morning, she had also prepared several more cups of coffee for her new pupil mistress, Octavia Hawkes, who took her coffee at a piping-hot one hundred eighty degrees Fahrenheit, which is eighty-two centigrade after Gen converted it in her head from the American stuff to the British thing. Octavia also required exactly one quarter cup of half-and-half that Gen purchased twice-weekly from the market on her way to work and no sugar. Gen made Octavia's coffee perfectly five times per office day, or else Octavia's crimson-painted lips retracted into a red dot of anger on her face.

Gen didn't want to see the red dot of anger. Every time it appeared, Gen's chances to obtain tenancy in the law chambers dropped a little.

Pupil barristers always made and served coffee for their pupil masters or mistresses. Gen had made Horace's tea during her first six, though after the first month, they had been making tea for each other.

The student lawyers also wheeled in the silver tea service and chocolate cookies at high tea every day at four-thirty, and they served the drinks at the chambers' occasional cocktail parties. It was a very British way of putting baby barristers in their place: making them serve their betters like actual servants.

But that morning, Gen waited in the conference room, fiddling with a pen, shuffling the stacks of papers associated with the Finch-Hatten case, and drinking her third cup of coffee. The cookies over on the sideboard called to her, even though they were the plain biscuits that they served to clients, not the chocolate ones that the barristers reserved for themselves at tea.

Lord Severn was late.

The lazy libertine had struck again. He had probably been out carousing and womanizing until the wee hours of the morning, perhaps a belated New Year's party, and had only just gotten his privileged arse out of bed. When Horace Lindsey had arranged meetings with Lord Severn, Horace had joked that he always set the meeting for half past the hour in his own schedule, but he had told the rascal Lord Severn to be at the offices on the hour and started charging him then.

She did her best not to grind her teeth. It was all billable hours, after all. Lord Severn was paying her to wait for him.

But twenty-five minutes was excessive.

Gen's pupil mistress, Octavia Hawkes, would have said, "Tardiness robs us of opportunity and the dispatch of our forces," one of her quotes from Machiavelli. Octavia liked *The Prince* and Sun Tzu's *The Art of War* a little too much.

As she had control over Gen's entire future, Gen studied both books so she could hold a coherent conversation with Octavia.

Horace Lindsey had preferred Shakespeare, and his quotes were still marked on some of his clients' file folders.

Like all lawyers who were waiting for a scheduled meeting, Gen busied herself with yet another case and billed that client for her time, too. Racking up the billable hours was another way to distinguish herself from the other pupil barristers who were competing for a tenancy offer.

Of course, everyone was doing that.

Gen needed to do something *smart*, something *exceptional.*

Something besides waiting for Lord Severn to show himself.

Even Horace's death from overwork hadn't shamed the irascible Lord Severn into mending his ways.

Gen straightened the stacks of papers on the table. She had read over and taken notes on all of them over the last few days, even though it should have been an easily winnable case.

Honestly, the Finch-Hatten case should never come to trial. No solicitor nor barrister should have touched the complaint.

Lord Severn's parents had died in a car accident when he and his younger brother had been small children. As was customary, they had not divided the earldom and properties but had left the vast majority of the estates to the eldest son, Arthur. They had bequeathed only enough money for an excellent education and a nest egg to his younger brother, Christopher. Preserving the great estates in this manner was still common practice.

There had been no way for Arthur's parents to know that Arthur would become a lascivious wastrel, while his brother, Christopher, would become an upstanding doctor with ties to Doctors Without Borders and do *pro bono* work in the most disadvantaged parts of London.

But even if they had known how their two sons would turn out, it probably wouldn't have made a difference.

After their parents' deaths, the younger brother, Christopher, had gone to Eton and other very British independent schools to prepare him for an excellent career because he would have to work for a living.

Arthur Finch-Hatten had been raised in one of the world's most expensive boarding schools in Switzerland, *Institut Le Rosey*, where the very wealthy dumped their inconvenient children.

No wonder the poor sod had turned out so badly, Gen mused. He hadn't stood a chance. Everyone at that hoity-toity school probably had the work ethic of a sloth with a Quaalude problem.

Arthur had grown up among the offspring of Saudi sheiks, deposed European royalty, African and Latin American dictators, politicians and businesspeople from every continent, and Russian mobsters. The joke was that Le Rosey held their parent-teacher conferences in conjunction with the World Economic Forum that took place in January in Davos, Switzerland because many of the parents were in town that week, anyway. "Davos" is the annual event where the world's twenty-five hundred most powerful people gather to discuss their world domination and to ski. Some of the world's most effective security forces, supplemented by elite mercenaries, kept back the conspiracy theorists and anarchists who protested outside and at a considerable distance.

Her phone screen read eleven-thirty.

Gen shuffled the papers, checking over her notes.

Maybe, like Horace, she should have just assumed that Lord Severn would be at least half an hour late and scheduled other clients' appointments in the meantime.

She whiled away the hour, her professional meter ticking off her ever-increasing fee, staring at the pages of the brief in her hand and wondering why the case had even gotten this far. It seemed that any judge should have thrown this out.

The parents had written their will.

It was a legal will.

It was aligned with the laws and customs of England.

The estate had been settled twenty years before.

Gen didn't see how Christopher could even contest it.

Except that the defendant was the notorious rake, Lord Severn.

She was still staring at the paper when Miriam, one of the junior clerks, opened the conference room door and leaned inside, giggling. "Your client is here," she practically sprayed.

Miriam never *sprayed* anything. The clerk was the soul of decorum and took care of Gen's fees with the utmost professionalism.

Miriam withdrew, and the door gaped wider.

Gen steeled herself for battle. This client who was a walking waste of oxygen wasn't going to put one over on her.

Lord Severn strolled into the room, his long legs covering the carpet at a quick pace even though he walked leisurely.

Gen had seen Lord Severn before, of course, but she had dodged behind other people and scurried back to her office while he had met with Horace. A nobleman with such an outrageous fee always commanded the attention of the most senior barrister in the office.

When he strolled in, Lord Arthur Finch-Hatton, the Earl of Severn, was still staring straight ahead at the window that overlooked the crowded streets of central London, so Gen's first look at him was his profile.

Morning sunlight streaming in the window clung to his golden skin. His cheekbones were hard slashes, and his jaw was a sharp right angle above the crisp, white collar of the dress shirt and black business suit he wore. His lush lips curved in a smile, as if looking over London from such a prestigious advantage suited him. The subtle lift of his chin and roll of his broad shoulders suggested that, had history been different, he might have ruled the land that spread beneath the window.

He turned to survey the rest of the room and caught Gen sitting at the table, gaping at him.

Oh, God. She was *staring.*

He always caught her staring.

She was staring at the black curls of his dark hair that stroked his ears and the back of his neck, and she was staring at the way his very precisely tailored suit skimmed his strong shoulders and the rounded biceps of his arms and then narrowed at his waist and hips, and she was staring at his extravagant height and his long legs and the way his head tilted with amusement as he caught her staring at him *again.*

Gen's brain turned to goo.

Damn, Lord Severn was one gorgeous man.

No, no, no.

No, Gen was a highly trained barrister, not a silly schoolgirl meeting a good-looking man for the first time. She had seen lots of handsome men.

Lots of them.

Lots.

Lots-lots-lots-lots-lots. The goo in her mind grew fuzzy tendrils, and cotton candy filled her skull and stopped up her ears.

Her thoughts slowed as she met his eyes.

My God. His *eyes.*

His eyes weren't blue or gray or any color that she had ever seen on a real human being before.

His eyes shimmered with an unexpected delight and intelligence.

They narrowed when he smiled that good-natured, natural smile that beckoned to her.

And most of all, his eyes sparkled *silver* and were bounded by a dark blue ring.

They changed color depending on the light, from baby blue to silvery-gray and all the shades in-between. Gen saw all the variations as he turned his face from the sunlight toward her.

They were beguiling, magical, unearthly.

That was not damn *fair.*

Gen had heard about peoples' knees weakening, but she was already sitting down. Still, her bones turned to soft clay, and she grabbed the sides of her chair because she was in danger of slithering out of it and onto the carpeting under the conference room table.

Lord Severn walked toward her.

It was customary for barristers to stand when greeting a client.

She should stand up. *You really should stand up.*

Stand up, dammit.

Gen gripped the sides of her chair and pushed with her arms to lift herself to her feet.

Even though too-tall Gen was wearing blunt, two-inch heels, Lord Severn was still *inches* taller than she was. At least four inches. Which meant he was at least six-four.

Blathering. Her brain was *blathering.*

His tie was the same azure-silver as his eyes but glimmering silk.

Goddamn it. She had seen Lord Severn before, *several times,* and he *always* had this effect on her.

Her and pretty much *every* person who was sexually attracted to men. One of the clerks, Roland, had actually fainted after Lord Severn had left chambers one time.

She should have gotten immune to him with subsequent exposures, *right?* This crazy reaction should have worn off by now, *right?*

Dizziness spun her head, and she gasped for air because she had forgotten how to *breathe.*

At her stupid sucking sound, Lord Severn smiled, though it was a sad smile like he regretted that his mere presence was overwhelming her so.

He pulled out a chair on the other side of the table. "I was terribly sorry to hear about Horace Lindsey's untimely death. He was an excellent barrister and a family friend."

Even though it was only eleven-thirty in the morning, Lord Severn's breath carried a faint whiff of whiskey under the mint, like he had just come from a gentleman's brunch.

Gen's mind searched for words.

Any words.

Wut arrre werdz.

She gathered her brain together and squeezed something out.

"Yes, it was a great loss to us all," she managed.

Lord Severn nodded. "He spoke highly of you. I'm pleased that you will be taking over my case."

"You *are?*" she blurted. Oh, good grief. Could she be any more junior-high school? "I mean, Mr. Lindsey did a great deal of work preparing for this case. I'm honored to argue it in his stead."

"Horace and I always discussed my case over a liquid lunch at my club. Why don't you skive off work for a few hours and enjoy my hospitality?"

"Oh, I couldn't," Gen said. "I'm due in court with Ms. Hawkes this afternoon."

"When?"

"Three o'clock."

"I could have you back by then."

"But I have to read the briefs that the solicitors sent over so that I know what I'm arguing." Her native Texas accent broadened in her mouth. "What use is a hired gun if they don't know whom to shoot?"

Lord Severn tilted his head. The corner of his lips twitched up. "Horace didn't mention that you were American."

Damn. Gen had been living in London for several years. Surely, most of her American accent should have faded away. She was trying like the Devil to enunciate, but evidently, she was still garbling her marbles. "I was raised in the States until I was seventeen, when my mother and I moved back to London."

"So you're a British citizen?"

None of Gen's other clients had worried about what color passport she presented at customs. "Yes, I was born here. I have American citizenship, too, because when I was a kid in Texas, my dad made sure of it. I still travel with my US passport sometimes."

Lord Severn leaned his elbows on the table and watched her. "And why would you use an American passport when you travel?"

The laser-like focus of his silvery eyes blinded her, and Jesus, he had *dimples* when he smiled.

Gen stuttered, "Masochism?"

Lord Severn laughed and adjusted his tie. The silver silk flashed in the sunlight, and his eyes took on a metallic sheen. "There's something you won't hear a barrister admit to every day."

"Yes, well, barristers don't admit to a lot of things."

"Do tell." His voice was warm with amusement as if he liked her.

"Oh, I couldn't say. Professional courtesy."

"Said the bishop to the actress."

"Quite." She laughed at him. Her laugh didn't sound like a nervous cackle, either, which was a small miracle.

"I can only imagine what those other barristers do," he said, and his eyes *twinkled.*

Jesus, Lord. How did he get his eyes to *twinkle* like that? They practically *glittered* with white-hot sparks, and Gen felt herself leaning forward and swaying her back like a broken-down mare to push out her boobs, two of her few decent physical assets. She admitted, "Sometimes, we play games in court."

"What kinds of games?" he asked.

Go ahead, his voice implied. *Say something outrageous, something unprofessional, something sexy.*

Gen giggled. "One judge plays online poker all day while hearing cases, so we find him online and take his money while we're arguing the cases."

Lord Severn's jaw dropped a little. "Does he know that you're playing against him?"

"Oh, heavens, no. But if you win the case and the money from him, then the losing barrister has to buy a round for the pub that night."

Lord Severn leaned in. "Are there any others?"

Gen whispered, "Like, we give each other a list of words that we have to work in during arguments."

He asked, "What kinds of words?"

In his high-bred, arch English accent, his open-ended question couldn't have sounded dirty, and yet there was just the suggestion that, if she said something naughty, he would be even more amused.

"Anything. Last time, the words were encumbered, rectitude, and nabob."

"Oh, you barristers and your vocabulary. Horace said that he admired your wit."

"He did not," Gen said.

"Oh, yes. He was quite taken with you, in his own way, of course."

"Of course."

"He thought that you would make an excellent QC or a judge."

Gen blinked, trying to process that Horace thought she could rise so high. "That's more than I could hope for."

"And yet he saw it in you." Lord Severn leaned back in his chair and crossed one leg over the other.

His pant leg rode up above his ankle.

The precisely tailored suit that he wore was soft black, as were his shoes, but his socks were *teal.*

Shockingly *teal.*

His ankles were a flash of Caribbean-sea color in the very conservative English barristers' chambers.

Nothing that Gen was wearing had anywhere near that kind of color. Her pale gray blouse, black suit, pearl earrings, and beige-toned stockings and underwear were all respectable.

It wasn't every day that someone wore teal socks into a trial lawyer's office. Most clients were in a battle for their lives. They might lose or win a great deal of money or be sent to jail at the end of their trials. Most people wore their somber, Sunday best into her office to discuss the strategy and their odds.

The vibrant color of Lord Severn's teal sock was so unexpected, so *careless,* that Gen felt like a Victorian matron offended by a glimpse of a table leg that should have been covered by a modest lace skirt.

Oh, Lord. She was staring at his ankle, a trim ankle that led up his leg to a swell of calf muscle.

She had to stop.

Stop looking.

Gen snapped her eyes up to his face.

Lord Severn's smile grew. "Something amusing?"

"*No.*" She pointedly did not look near his foot.

He did, however. "My socks amuse you?"

"*No.*"

"A barrister wouldn't wear anything so whimsical, would they?"

"Of course not. A judge might actually take offense, thinking that the barrister was flaunting the dignity of the court."

Lord Severn said, "Because you're in the professions. A man matches his socks to his pants. A gentleman matches his socks to his mood."

Gen steeled herself not to ask how he chose his underwear. "I can't imagine what sort of mood you're in to choose such an—" she didn't look down at them, "—unusual color."

"I'm a creature of many appetites, it's true." Though he was still smiling, his gaze didn't waver from her eyes as he said this.

And right there, with Lord Severn's words and his sultry glance that turned his silver eyes molten, their conversation went from casual banter, a pointless conversation that meant nothing to either of them, to something heated and with the suggestion of an offer, an implied extension of his hand to go wherever he might lead her.

Gen stared down at the paperwork she was holding, trying to steady her hands. "We need to go over this information," she said. Her voice sounded thin in her own ears. "Is this contact information correct?"

He took the paper from her outstretched fingers, and she snatched her hand back as if his touch might burn her.

He held the paper pinched in his fingers as he scanned the list. "This next-of-kin bit is Christopher's information, my brother who is suing me. Quite honestly, we weren't raised on the same continent. The last time I saw him for any length of time, he was seven, and I was ten years old."

"Are you estranged?" she asked, unsure how to put that politely.

Lord Severn laughed. "Estranged doesn't begin to cover it. Let me add a few contact numbers." He snagged one of the several pens rolling across the conference room table and wrote in neat block letters in the margin of the paper. "If I'm ever in trouble or in hospital, call these two: Casimir van Amsberg and Maxence Grimaldi. These are their private numbers. Max is often out of cell phone range. Leave a message for him. It will take both a while to get to England, so plan for that. If I die, and *only* if I die, call this last number, too."

"Oh, I'm sure *that* won't happen." She paused. "You aren't sick or anything, are you?"

"Healthy as can be. I plan to die in my own bed of advanced old age, preferably by being stepped on by an elephant." He cleared his throat, as if he usually added something else to that sentence but hadn't.

"An elephant? In your bedroom?" she asked.

"It's as likely as anything else."

Gen glanced at the paper and read upside down. "Elizabeth? No last name?"

"Yes, ask for Elizabeth, and then tell them what happened to me and answer any questions they have with all the information you know."

"Is she your family solicitor? Or the estate's?"

"I'd better write them down, too." He did. "This is the number for my groundskeeper at Spencer House. He could handle the day-to-day functioning until the estate is settled."

That seemed like a lot of information for just a barrister to have. "Are you sure you're not planning to die?" she asked.

He looked up at her, grinning. "No one plans to die, and

yet so few people truly *live.*"

"I'm sure most people live for quite some time."

Lord Severn laughed, a ringing, joyful sound. "Not like me. Every day, every single day, I *live.*"

Yes, and they needed to talk about how he *lived*, too.

"Now," he said, leaning in, "let's talk about getting you out of this cubicle and onto my plane to the continent tonight. I know a guy who thinks he's a rock star. Perhaps we can see his show from backstage and disabuse him of the notion, afterward."

Partying with rock stars was absolutely part of the problem. "Mr. Finch-Hatten—"

"Lord Severn," he said.

Gen glanced behind her, looking to see if someone was standing there.

"No, *I'm* Lord Severn," he said. "I'm a third-rank peer of the realm. One uses 'Lord' and my title as the Earl of Severn. I sign letters and documents as Severn, rarely with my surname."

"I'm sorry." Her hands fluttered over the paper in front of her, where she had written that note *right there* to call him that.

"It's perfectly all right, just something you should know."

"I'm *so* sorry. I hope you aren't offended." She grabbed the table to keep her hands from flopping off like brain-damaged bats.

"No offense taken," *Lord Severn* said. His hand lifted and hovered across the table, gently falling toward where her hands were braced against the dark wood.

Gen pushed back from the table, scooting the chair across the thick carpeting. "I think we should begin to discuss your case by going over some of the depositions. I have transcripts. The transcripts are right behind me, in the files. I'll just get one of the transcripts so we can discuss your case."

She bolted out of her chair and scrambled for the table,

pretending to sort through a file folder while she fought herself.

Her hands tingled. She shook them, flicking her fingers to try to fling the crazies away.

Spidery nerves crawled up her arms.

Not now, not now. She knew Lord Severn hadn't meant anything by their conversation and certainly not about being *a creature with appetites.* A little harmless flirting never killed anyone.

He wasn't flirting with her anyway. No one flirted with horsey-face Gen unless they wanted something, or it was a dare, or they were a predator with a taste for the weak and stupid.

Deep breath, deep breath.

Her skin stilled, and her body quieted. The panic drained away, a small blip in her day that would have no effect on the afternoon or the rest of this meeting, she resolved.

Time to get back to work.

Gen walked her fingers through the tabs sticking out of the block of files in the box. "It's in here somewhere. Do you want me to ring up the clerks and have some coffee or tea delivered?"

She *felt* him standing at her back rather than having heard him move.

The skin on the back of her neck heated, and a smoky shadow loomed up the white wall in front of her like an evil poltergeist trying to break through the centuries-old plaster.

His voice, whispering near her shoulder as he bent down, was low in his throat. "Or we could go back to my apartment for a liquid lunch. Or perhaps to Majorca for the weekend, to become better acquainted as barrister and client."

He trailed his fingers over the outside of her upper arm, the merest suggestion of a caress.

Training kicked in.

Gen jabbed with her elbow, striking backward as hard as

she could.

Her blow was deflected sideways before she connected with his solar plexus.

She spun and kicked.

Air. No contact.

She flipped around as her kick whiffed through the air and stumbled backward, banging her hip on the table.

Lord Severn stood several paces behind her, angled sideways, his arms up and ready to block again. His hands were balled into loose fists so he could either strike or block. His steady gaze was serious over his fists.

He said, "I'm sorry. I misunderstood our banter, earlier."

"Don't touch me," she said, and the crazy shaking filled her hands and spread up her arms. "Don't *ever* touch me."

His voice was solemn. "As I said, I misunderstood. I won't approach you again." It sounded like a promise. "Are you all right?"

Gen leaned against the table with the boxes of file folders. The air felt chunky in her throat as she tried to breathe it, choking her. "I don't like that sort of thing."

"As I said, my mistake. I didn't mean to cause offense, and I won't presume again. I apologize for my error."

She was still breathing too fast in panicky gasps. *Damn.* Krav Maga lessons for two years, and she hadn't landed a blow when it had mattered. "I'll bet you're not used to women telling you no."

"I'm not used to misreading signals." Lord Severn lowered his hands, though he kept them near his waist and in front of him.

She had gotten caught up in the moment. She should have shut down any sort of invitation, fast. Her heart pounded in her chest, vibrating down her weak legs.

"I'm not used to men hitting on me," Gen admitted.

"Why not?"

She stared at him, at that gorgeous man with his testosterone-molded cheekbones and geometric jaw and those silvery eyes lined with dark lashes. He had probably never felt like the fat, ugly, lumbering giant in the corner of a party where everyone else was a pretty little elf. *"Look at me."*

Lord Severn blinked and lowered his hands to his sides. "You're funny and smart and attractive. Horace doted on you. He said once that he would adopt you if he thought you would stand for it, which was his highest praise. I quite imagine that men are all over you."

A laugh caught in her throat and turned into a snort.

Oh, that was sophisticated. Way to complete the image of the horsey, designated fat friend. She didn't even have her pretty girlfriends around to make her seem like the good-natured buddy.

She tried to cover up the snort by saying, "Uh, no. The men are *not* all over me."

And the thought of men being *all over her* made her legs shake.

Lord Severn said, "Their loss, then."

She tried to breathe more slowly, holding her breath between inhales, but fear still drowned her. "You probably only date beautiful duchesses and models and actresses and stuff."

He chuckled and took another step backward, putting more blessed space and air between them. "I've dated a few daft beauties. I had to measure every word I said lest they tattle to everyone they knew from lack of common sense. Handling women as if I'm manipulating a toddler to behave in public is tiresome."

Gen shook her hands to flick the heebie-jeebies out. She still wanted to scamper up the wall and cling to the ornate crown molding, shrieking curses down like a rabid spider monkey until Lord Severn left. "That sounds difficult."

Lord Severn walked around the table and sat in his chair. He gestured to the papers spread over the table. "Can we resume our discussion of my case?"

Gen nodded and drew a deep breath. She didn't like saying this. She felt like a wuss. "I just need to find that deposition. Could you remain seated while I turn my back, if you would be so kind?"

Lord Severn patted the arm of his chair. "I won't move."

She gathered every ounce of her willpower and pivoted, turning her back to him, and started walking her fingers through the files. "I can call for coffee or tea."

"I would appreciate a coffee." His voice came from across the room and on the other side of the table.

Good.

The air around her seemed to thin, and Gen breathed more easily.

The papers under her fingers drifted into focus, and though she listened for any scuff of his chair moving or his tread on the thick carpeting, she only heard Lord Severn clear his throat a few times and rustle some papers, all on the far side of the table.

When she turned around, clutching the depositions, Lord Severn was leaning back in his chair, studying a piece of paper, entirely at ease.

He smiled at her. "Did you find the deposition?"

She nodded. Her neck felt stiff, like she was holding herself ready for him to assault her.

Gen dropped the papers on the table, letting the *swoosh* cover up her deep breath. She shook out her hands again.

"Okay, so let's talk about winning your case for you." She tapped the pile of papers in front of her with her pen, covering up that she was still flicking her fingers. "There's no mention of a jury strategy. It seems that Horace was preparing your case for an appeals court or magistrate instead of a trial."

Lord Severn shook his head. "Oh, no, no. We won't be going before a court at all. Matters of peerage are always heard in the House of Lords."

Gen grabbed papers, trying not to look like she was

reading frantically. "Did Horace *say* that?"

"We discussed the case rather than the venue, but I assumed."

"Nothing is tried in the House of Lords anymore. Not since the Supreme Court was created in 2009. The last trial of a peer in the House was in 1935."

"But this is a matter of peerage, not a criminal case to be tried in the special court for nobles. The House of Lords always hears cases concerning peerage claims."

"But they never try cases anymore. They disbanded their court years ago. I think it was in 1948. The Law Lords aren't even members of the House of Lords anymore."

"But Horace said that we should appeal directly to the sovereign to throw it to the Lords."

Yes, yes. Gen could just remember from her university days that the Crown was the fount of all honor, and thus the Crown was entitled to decide all questions related to peerage disputes.

In practice, the sovereign referred all disputes about who got to be the duke to a committee in the House of Lords—Gen wracked her brain—the Committee for Privileges and Conduct, and then the committee told the sovereign what to do in the case.

But the committee didn't even have Law Lords anymore, not since 2009. Surely, a bunch of stuffed shirts who weren't even barristers or solicitors couldn't decide such a contentious case based on law and precedent and honor without even Law Lords to advise them.

"Are you a member of the House of Lords?" she asked Lord Arthur Finch-Hatten, the Earl of Severn, just in case.

"Egads, no. My grandfather held his hereditary spot until the reform in 1999, but neither he nor I ever stood for election. I'm far too busy with other priorities."

Yeah, she just bet he was.

"I need to look over these depositions," Gen said, trying to come up with something to say that would not let on that she was entirely out of her depth.

"Quite," Lord Severn said drily and stood.

Oh, yeah. He knew.

"I just have to study this." She clutched the papers to keep her hands from shaking. "Give me a few days, and we'll meet again to discuss your case."

He brushed some non-existent lint from his suit jacket. "I'll find some way to occupy my time."

"No, you mustn't." Gen stood and let the papers in her hands flutter to the table. "Horace told me about your escapades. Every time you went on a bender, he watched the gossip sites for days, fretting that you might have given your brother yet more ammunition. The only reason this case has gotten this far is because of your atrocious behavior. For anyone else, anyone who acted with an ounce of decorum, such a stupid claim would have been dismissed immediately."

Lord Severn flicked his fingers in the air. "My actions don't matter. This is all a matter of peerage and privilege. My parents bequeathed the earldom and Spencer House to me."

"Your brother is getting the National Trust involved. Horace thought you might lose when he was fighting this for you."

"And now *you're* fighting it for me, so you see to it that my 'escapades' don't influence the case."

"Ms. Hawkes and I can't win your case if you're doing everything you can to sink it!"

Lord Severn sighed and looked out the window. "Be careful about that fiery American temper. The House of Lords won't like that."

"*Nothing* is ever tried in the House of *Lords!*"

His sultry glance down at her was laced with pity and derision, and Gen felt like a lower-class biscuit aping her betters.

Class will out, she had heard more than once when certain

other pupil barristers had made unfortunate choices in alcohol quantities or sleeping arrangements. They had lost the respect of the senior barristers in chambers, and thus their chances at tenancy, with a single miscalculation.

But Lord Severn's stare made her feel all sorts of new levels of inferiority.

When he spoke, his cut-glass, upper-crust British accent clipped the words, "You need to do your homework."

Lord Severn turned on his heel and strode out of the room, his long legs covering the plush carpet in just a few steps.

Gen sank into her chair, holding her head in her hands.

Between her panicked freak-out and lack of understanding about Lord Severn's case, this meeting could not have gone any worse.

The only things worse than throwing the case to someone else was getting fired by the client or losing it in court.

And she had just increased the odds of both of those.

Disaster.

Chambers High Tea

CHAMBERS high tea was held at precisely four-thirty every day in the largest conference room. Pupil barristers brewed the tea in the enormous, Victorian-era silver tea set and served it in bone china cups to the barristers like waiters.

Outside the windows, the sun was already setting on the other side of the historic building that housed Lincoln's Inn, the wan winter sunlight barely able to crest over the roof and chimneys.

Gen poured a cup of tea for her boss, Octavia Hawkes, and added one lump of sugar, and then she poured another cup for one of the other senior barristers, David Trent, and another and another. The tea steamed sweetly, misting her cheeks with warmth and soft scent.

Beside her, fellow pupil barrister James Knightly poured tea for his pupil master, Leonard Boxster, and placed two of the chocolate cookies on the saucer for him. James blew across the top of the tea because Leonard Boxster liked his tea scandalously lukewarm. James said, "So I heard that you were *closeted* with His Lordship Arthur Severn this morning."

Gen grimaced at James's innuendo and poured tea for another senior barrister. "We had our first meeting to discuss his case."

James asked, "What's he like?"

Oh, that was a minefield. She couldn't say that Lord Severn was as hot as a blue brushfire in the Texas August sun, nor that he was funny, infuriating, and smelled like masculine devilry. "He's concerned about his case."

"That's not what I've heard."

"Then you've heard wrong. Of course, he's concerned about it. Who wouldn't be?"

"Someone who's too busy whoring and drinking his way across Europe."

Gen had left herself open for that one. "He met with me for a suitable amount of time, and we discussed his case. There was no whoring or drinking involved."

"How's he paying you? In cash or services rendered?"

What a smug ass. "His account was set up with the clerks when Horace Lindsey was his barrister."

"Must have been in services rendered, then."

Gen didn't bother scolding him. James had always been an arrogant, slimy asshole. Everything that came out of his mouth was a put-down or an outright lie. He was going to be an amazing barrister, and he was Gen's primary competition to get the one tenancy position at the law firm of Serle's Court Barristers.

She said, "Horace had better taste than Arthur Finch-Hatten."

James laughed and walked away, having gotten her to say something derogatory about a man who was better-looking and richer than he was.

And nicer.

Gen finally poured herself a cup of tea and sipped it.

Just a few more hours of work after tea time, and maybe she could go home for the day.

Unless the internet caught Arthur Finch-Hatten whoring and drinking his way across Europe again.

Arthur's Dark Mistress

Arthur and Elizabeth had walked out into the deer park behind Spencer House. Though it was January, the mild afternoon was cool on his face, and the air drifted through the thick sweater he wore.

Elizabeth—no last name given, and her first name was not Elizabeth—appeared to be in her late forties, judging from the broad streaks of silver that ran from her temples to the blond French twist on the back of her head and the beginning of softness around her chin. Arthur didn't trust his approximation of her age, amongst other things.

The formal gardens checker-boarded the earth behind them, but out there in the deer park, wild grasses and trees grew in thickets of dense brush. In the distance, over by a copse of trees, a herd of over a hundred deer gamboled and grazed in the late afternoon sunlight. The males still had their antlers, as they tossed their heads and bawled. Arthur had seen them lose their antlers as early as late January, depending on the weather, so the shed might be soon.

The soft dirt under his feet gave off a whiff of good earth with his every step, and a breeze crackled through the bare trees at the edge of the field.

"Of course you'll win this case," Elizabeth scoffed at him. "Primogeniture has never been successfully challenged. Your parents could have left the bulk of their estate to anyone they wanted, and the eldest son is the usual heir. Christopher doesn't stand a chance." Her Swiss accent sounded like German tones softened with French slurs.

Arthur had known Elizabeth for over a dozen years, but the sibilance of her Swiss accent still disconcerted him. They were in Britain. She should have a polished English accent. When they were in public, her accent remained crisp and British, but she dropped the pretense when they were alone.

She sounded so foreign.

Arthur said, "The courts seem concerned with fairness, lately."

"To hell with fairness," Elizabeth scoffed.

"My barrister is worried about some of Christopher's allegations. He's evidently persuading someone from the National Trust to testify on his behalf."

"Persuade them not to. You haven't been mismanaging your estate too badly, have you?"

"I've put good people in charge of it. I'm rarely here to manage it, personally."

"Blaming me for everything again, are you?" Her voice was light as she teased him.

He raised an eyebrow and one corner of his mouth. "You're a convenient target."

"Good thing our adversaries never agreed with you."

"Indeed. My original barrister died, you know. He was an old hand, knew all the judges and the currents that eddied. My new barrister is pessimistic about my chances. She thinks I'm a waste of a human being. Told me to curtail my 'escapades.'"

"Isn't she sweet." Distaste was evident in Elizabeth's rough voice.

Arthur said, "She is attempting to rein in my activities and contacts."

Elizabeth flipped her hand toward the sunlit trees. "You can't."

"She is adamant."

"So retain a different lawyer."

"A friend in those chambers has mentioned that all the

barristers feel the same way. My file was evidently quite the hot potato when the Head Clerk was assigning out Horace Lindsey's cases. No one wanted it, and a new lawyer might insist on my good behavior before taking my case."

"So promise them what they need to hear."

"And then they will remove themselves from the case when I don't follow through."

"I didn't think they could do that. They have a rule about taking cases that are offered, don't they?"

"In theory, but not in practice." His friend had assured him that the so-called cab rank rule was often discussed but never adhered to, nor enforced.

"So *cultivate* your lawyer," Elizabeth said.

"She's not a Russian mafia princess or a minor sheik. She's merely a London barrister who was given my case."

Elizabeth rolled her eyes, but subtly, just a flick of her eyelids and mascara-darkened eyelashes. She said, "Such sentiment."

"She's an innocent," Arthur mused.

"She's a lawyer. She's hardly innocent. Shakespeare would have had her first against the wall when the revolution came."

"It's unethical."

Elizabeth laughed. "When have we ever concerned ourselves with such luxuries?"

"I won't harm this woman."

"Do you *like* her, Arthur?"

His five seconds were ticking by. Gen's puckish sense of humor amused him. Her intelligence intrigued him. Her lush body aroused him.

He really liked that she hadn't shrunk away from him but had turned around swinging.

His training had saved him from a nut punch or a black eye, barely. She had obviously been attacked, perhaps even abused, and he wanted to stand in front of her to protect her and to wrap himself around her to heal her.

That wasn't like him.

Odd.

Arthur said, "She seems fragile."

"Of course she seems *fragile.* She's not one of us. I'm merely encouraging you to make certain that you win your case. Convince her. You're the best at it."

Arthur looked at the spongy sod beside his shoe. The grass was thin in spots, and the black soil marred the emerald green. "I'm not."

"You learned from the best."

"Certainly." He had been seventeen.

She said, "All my contacts are the highest performers."

"I may have poisoned that well."

"Makes the chase that much more interesting." Elizabeth drew a finger under Arthur's jaw, almost cradling his face in her palm. He wanted to lean into her touch, but he sure as hell didn't.

Elizabeth said, "You're useless to us if you're not the Earl of Severn. Cultivate her so that you get what we need, which is to win your case."

And so, Arthur would cultivate Gen, just like he always did.

Elizabeth withdrew her hand, stroking her fingers under his jaw. "I would hate to lose my best boy."

A Long and Flexy Mate

Late at night, in the quiet stillness of the barristers' chambers, Gen was leaning back in her office chair, reading the depositions for the case of that rascal Lord Arthur Finch-Hatten, the Earl of Severn. Her lamp cast a pool of light around her small pupil's desk.

Gen was lucky to have been assigned a tiny office of her own, though the room was about the size of a broom closet and smelled odd, like dust and old polish. Its small window overlooked the twinkling night of central London. A draft sneaked in the edges of the window, bringing with it cool night air and green grass scent from the courtyard of Lincoln's Inn. Her door opened to a small waiting room with couches and an admin's desk.

From the waiting room, the double doors to her pupil mistress's office loomed at the back, shut tightly now. Darkness leaked through the cracks around the heavy wooden doors.

No one had walked by her open door for forty-five minutes, though other pupil barristers rustled paper in the far offices, trying to appear more industrious, more earnest, than their peers. Gen was pretty sure that her two girlfriends from university, Lee and Rose, were still slugging away in their chambers where they were doing their first six-month internships, one floor down and a few windows over. Thank God they were doing their pupillages in different chambers, so they were not Gen's direct competition to obtain tenancy. The competition was cutthroat. Gen had heard that some people sabotaged their fellow pupils, making it look like they had done something unethical or illegal, to boot them out of the competition for tenancy.

So far, nothing like that had happened in Gen's chambers as far as she knew, but she was hopelessly naive. Even Horace had gently suggested that Gen might want to be a bit more conniving when the situation called for it. It was the British way.

Gen was so hopelessly American, believing that hard work and rigor would win others' respect and allow her to get ahead in life. Horace had despaired when she had talked about it.

The clock on her computer clicked over to ten-forty. Time for another refresh.

Gen tapped the glowing computer screen of her laptop on the search bar, hoping and praying that nothing new popped up.

The top return for "Arthur Finch-Hatten Severn gossip" was still dated a month before and was the same picture, thank the law gods. He hadn't managed to do anything gossip-worthy yet.

Damn it, the man was almost thirty years old. Maybe not all the way to thirty, but he was at least twenty-eight or so. Gen wasn't sure. In any case, Lord Severn needed not to sabotage his own damn law case and leave her to pick up the pieces.

Maybe Lord Severn had gone home to bed, *alone*, like a good boy, despite the defiance in his pale gray-blue eyes when he had left the conference room that afternoon.

Yeah, it could have happened.

Gen snorted at her own feeble hopes and hit the refresh button again.

The top story was still that grainy photo of Lord Severn escorting a leggy blonde into a VIP area at a nightclub and pausing for a moment for the cameras before he walked in after her. Gen read the caption for the thousandth time: *Earl*

Severn and Peony Sweetling out on the town, drunk and rumoured high on cocaine at the Tiger Bar.

Damn him. *Seriously.*

His brother, Christopher, was accusing Lord Severn of snorting both the estate's principal funds and the money provided by the National Trust for the upkeep of the family's palatial country home, Spencer House. Misuse of National Trust funds could land Lord Severn in jail.

This was intolerable.

Surely Gen had Lord Severn's cell phone number in his contact information somewhere. She would just ring him up and insist that he stay in for the few weeks or months before his case was tried before a judge.

And surely it would go before a judge. Octavia Hawkes would argue the case and oversee Gen, of course, because Gen was still a pupil. Octavia was ultimately responsible for the case.

Surely Gen wouldn't be thrown before the House of Lords while she was still a pupil. Maybe she should confer with her pupil mistress.

Octavia Hawkes would have to take over the case if it had to be argued before the House of Lords, of course.

Getting rid of the case and the responsibility for the naughty earl would be a huge relief, a metaphorical ton of weight lifted from Gen's shoulders.

Which meant that it was absolutely the wrong thing to do.

Passing off a high-profile case because she couldn't handle it would mark her as spineless.

Spineless pupil barristers did not receive invitations to tenancy.

No high-powered litigator wanted a sniveling, low-level lawyer in their office who thrust their difficult cases upon their betters. Barristers must contribute to the prestige and finances of the office, not hang around the necks of the other lawyers as dead weight that the others had to compensate for.

And so, Gen could not ask to be relieved of the incorrigible Lord Severn's case, not if she wanted that job offer, and she *had* to get that job offer.

It was not overstating the case to say that her mother's life depended on it.

The darkened office was eerily quiet at this time of night.

Gen sighed and hit refresh. Still nothing.

Somewhere down the corridor, a door slapped closed. High-heeled shoes clicked across the wooden floor outside.

Gen busied herself, positioning her hands on the keyboard and ducking her head in case Octavia Hawkes walked in.

The clattering of shoes resolved into two sets of footsteps, and Gen relaxed in her chair.

Her university friends Lee and Rose swung around the doorway and into Gen's small office. Both were slim, limber ladies, wearing business trouser suits as pupil barristers ought to. Rose Pennelegion's somber black suit was a few shades darker than her skin, and her hair was braided in a slick updo.

Lee Fox grinned hard and held up a plastic bag. "Thought you might want take away?" Her Cockney accent hollowed out her words because it was after eight at night. During the day, Lee carried on with an impeccable middle-upper-class accent, and no one but Rose and Gen knew that she had been born and attended government schools in the wrong part of London. She tossed her bright red hair behind her shoulder. The color was barely natural enough not to draw questions by the staid senior barristers but just bright enough to be fun.

Gen slapped her laptop closed and set it aside. "Oh, Lordy, you two are life savers. I thought I was going to have to eat my desk."

They giggled and dragged chairs from Hawkes's waiting room into Gen's tiny office. The legs screeched on the wooden floor, but none of the barristers were around to complain about the noise.

Rose crossed her legs and folded her hands on her knee, waiting primly.

Lee unpacked the boxes, and the complicated scent of Chicken Tikka Masala rolled into the tiny room. The boxes were stamped with the red logo from Mumbai Take-Away, their favorite place, even though Mumbai was liberal with the red chili powder.

Gen's stomach flopped over and growled so loudly that Lee and Rose laughed at her.

Within seconds, they were ripping apart the naan flatbread and sopping up sauce while they forked chicken chunks into their mouths. Gen liberated a few bottles of stout from the stash in the break room to cool the spice on their tongues. She was used to spicy food, having grown up eating Tex-Mex, but Lee and Rose were British to their Union Jack-wrapped hearts and couldn't handle the heat.

When all that was left were wiped-clean paper boxes and the smell of curry lingering in the air, Gen leaned back and grabbed her purse off the floor. She dug inside and held out a couple of notes. "That was so good. How much do I owe you guys?"

Lee waved Gen's money away. "Forget it."

"I've been keeping track," Gen said. "You aren't letting me pay my fair share. It's not cool."

"We're fine with it," Rose said, hunting in the plastic bag for mints. After the CTM, they all needed mints.

"Come on. Take a quid or two," Gen said.

Rose laughed. "It's so funny when you say 'quid' with that American accent. It's just all wrong."

"Take it," Gen insisted. Lee and Rose were also tens of thousands of pounds in debt for their degrees and courses. They couldn't afford it, either.

"No," Lee said, looking out Gen's small window. "Pay us back when we're all barristers."

"You won't want the money by then," Gen said.

"Have you got the money for your mother's home this month?" Rose asked, using a paper napkin to wipe every trace of curry from her burgundy-painted fingernails as fastidiously as a noblewoman's cat.

"Not quite yet, but I was going to do some devilling for Devereux this week. I'll get it. I'll be fine."

Devilling is the practice of a senior barrister farming out work to pupil barristers—writing briefs and drafting precedents—for a cut of the hourly rate. Violet Devereux was a master at it, with dozens of little devils running in and out of her chambers every day, exchanging paperwork for cash.

So many little devils traipsed through her door every day that some of the pupil barristers had christened her office the Devilhouse. Gen thought it was a stupid name.

Lee looked out the small window at the glittering London lights in the dark. "I do wish you would just let us pay for things for a few more months without all this conversation. Can't we be British about it?"

Oh, so that was it. Gen was being too American again. "I'm sorry."

"And we'll have none of that," Rose said briskly, standing and brushing her pants as if a crumb might have fallen from her ruby-painted lips. Even though Rose had eaten as much curry and naan as Lee and Gen, her lipstick was somehow perfect and glossy. "You can't be apologizing for everything like a Canadian, either."

Gen rolled her eyes at that. The British apologize for things even more than Southerners.

"How are you going to get an offer of tenancy if you're not British enough? It's up to us to teach you." Lee's accent rose to bitingly arch. "You must accept our well-intentioned gesture with grace and not mention it amongst us, lest it affront our pride."

Gen laughed. "If you insist."

She really should learn to be more British. At the most inappropriate times, her inner American, or worse, her inner *Texan* rose and ranted, usually when someone was doing something *wrong*.

The internet held all kinds of traps for her.

Oh, the internet.

Gen fished behind herself and propped her laptop on her knees.

"Don't mind us," Lee said. "We're just the people who brought your supper."

"Just a sec." Gen tapped the screen to refresh the news search. "I've got this new client, Arthur Finch-Hatten, and he sometimes goes on a wild drunk and ends up on the gossip sites. It's like he's *trying* to lose his case."

The same list repopulated on the computer screen with the Peony Sweetling picture at the top, and Gen blew out the air trapped in her lungs. Finch-Hatten hadn't done anything publicly stupid yet.

She looked up.

Lee and Rose were both staring at her. Lee's mouth had fallen open, and Rose had frozen with her hand in the air.

Lee asked, "Are you shitting me?"

Rose threw Lee a glare and asked Gen, "*You* got Lord Severn's case?"

Gen looked back and forth between her friends. "What makes you think I can't handle that ornery colt?"

"I rather think no one could handle him," said Rose.

Lee snickered, "Actually, *everyone* has handled him."

Rose ignored her. "Has he propositioned you yet?"

"No, of course not," Gen lied. That was more believable anyway.

"He will," Rose said. "He struts through the corridors and offices like—"

"—Like red hot man candy wrapped in a bow," Lee said.

"—as if he has his pick of women, and he does *pick*," Rose continued. "He's a predator."

Gen drew in a long, slow breath, trying to look casual and normal. They didn't know.

"He doesn't assault women, does he?" Gen asked. She might have to be alone with him, perhaps in taxi cabs or other conference rooms. She could arrange to never be in that position, but she had to make arrangements ahead of time to ensure her safety.

"No, I've never heard of him assaulting anyone," Rose said.

"He doesn't have to," Lee said. "The ladettes hand him their knickers."

Rose rolled her huge, dark eyes. "He's not a rapist and doesn't assault, but I've heard that he's very good at convincing women to do *things* that they might not do, otherwise."

The fear of assault drained out of Gen. Indeed, that was exactly her experience. Lord Severn had backed off and stayed backed-off as soon as she had said no.

Gen asked, "Like what kind of things?"

"Oh, I couldn't say," Rose said.

Ah. Rose was a vault that a lot of people confided in. Gen knew better than to push. Anything that anyone had told Rose in confidence, she would take with her to her grave unless there was a damn good reason. At university, Gen had stayed up with Rose one night while she had rambled about an ethical dilemma, whether it was better to break a confidence, and in the end had gone to the authorities because a child was in harm's way. Gen had known that Rose would make the moral choice in the end, but it was going to take some angst to get there.

"So, he's harmless if you tell him no," Gen said, just to clarify.

"Yes, that's what I've heard," Rose said, nodding.

"But who wants to turn 'im down?" Lee asked, her hands rising to the corners of the room. "He's a long and flexy mate, 'e is."

Long and flexy? "Is that literal?" Gen asked.

"No, berk. It just means he's nice looking. *Sexy.* I haven't had him."

"Oh. Okay." Gen rolled her eyes at Rose, who grinned.

"I haven't!" Lee nearly shouted.

Rose pursed her lips.

Gen motioned for her to shut the office door.

Rose leaned back in her chair and flicked the door closed with two burgundy fingernails.

Now that they wouldn't be overheard, Gen said to Rose, "The lady doth protest too much, methinks."

"I do *not* protest too much!" Lee said. "If I'd've had Lord Severn, when I was finished with him, he'd need an IV drip, an ice pack, and therapy. I'd tattoo it backward on my forehead in diamonds so I could read it in sparkly things every morning: *I thumped 'is Lordship Arthur Finch-Hatten, the Earl of Severn.*" She held her scarlet hair away from her face. "Is it written on my forehead in diamonds? Well, is it?"

Gen and Rose had to admit that Lee did not have a booty call confession tattooed on her forehead in glittering gems, so it must not have happened.

Lee asked Gen, "Have you boinked him yet?"

"God, no. I've only had one quick meeting with him," Gen said.

Lee and Rose looked at each other, and an eternity of debate passed between them.

"What!" Gen said.

Rose asked, "So, what's he like?"

"Yeah, did you drop on your back on the conference table and beg him to bang you hard?" Lee asked.

Gen almost stood up. "No!"

Lee told Rose, "I'll bet she did."

Rose asked Gen, "So what did you talk about?"

Gen sighed. "At first, very little." She gathered herself to spill the beans to her girlfriends because that's what had to be done. "Up close, he's *stunning.* Like, *literally* stunning. It was like I'd taken a Taser to the frontal lobes. My mouth would not work for several minutes."

Rose nodded, "Those *eyes.*"

Lee added, "That *arse.*"

Rose's loud sigh at Lee's coarseness was audible even over Lee and Gen's laughter.

Rose asked, "And then, what was he like?"

"Well—" Gen picked around her little freak-out and considered the rest of the meeting. "—He was funny."

Rose gasped. "He was *not.*"

"He was. He was asking silly questions about the games that we play in court. Like, you know, the word game Stannis insists on playing, where you have to work certain words into the arguments?"

"Oy, I hate that one," Lee said.

Rose shrugged. She'd read English poetry at Oxford. Gen had yet to go up against her, but she bet that Rose would be very, very good at that particular game.

Gen said, "Or playing online poker in Judge Germaine's courtroom. James had to buy a round at The Collared Dog that night because I won twenty quid from the judge online and won the case."

"Nice," Lee said.

"But the weird thing is," Gen said, "it seemed like he was really *listening* to me. It wasn't like mere flirting, not like he was hanging on my words because he wanted to get into my pants, but that he was genuinely interested in what I had to say, like maybe I had something important to tell him."

"You were telling him whether or not he'll be keeping a whole, filthy lot of money," Lee said, "and whether you can save his noble arse."

Gen shook her head. "No. It was more than that. Different, somehow."

Rose pursed her lips. "And then what happened?"

"Nothing, really." *Nothing to speak of because Gen didn't speak of anything about that.* "We discussed his case a bit, and then he left."

Lee asked, "So are you buddies with 'is Lordship? Have you friended on social media and declared that you're in a twittership with him, yet?"

Gen rolled her eyes on that one. *Honestly.* "Uh, *no.* Indeed, I don't think he likes me very much. I had to tell him to quit carousing and chasing skirts. I told him that judges and juries didn't like it and he was going to lose the case if he kept carrying on. He didn't take kindly to that."

Lee and Rose looked at each other again with one of those looks that held an entire conversation, a long and sad conversation.

Gen opened her hands, begging, *"What!"*

"You have to be more subtle, Genevieve," Rose said. "You have to bring them around to it. Let him understand it rather than be so direct."

"Because he's a man and I'm just a woman?" Gen asked. "Because of chauvinism and sexism?"

"No, dear." Rose set her beer bottle on Gen's tiny desk. "Because he's British, and because you're British, too."

Oh. Gen had been too American again.

Dagnabit.

She admitted, "Yeah, maybe I could have done that better."

"There's always a next time," Rose said briskly.

Lee piped up, "I propose a toast." She held up her beer bottle. The light shone through the empty glass bottle. One drip slid down the inside to the dry bottom. "That's unfortunate. Good thing I have this." She snagged a flask from her purse.

"And what have you got there?" Rose asked her.

"Good Irish whiskey," Lee said. "Here, pour some in that empty bottle of yours."

"I think Patrick would have words if he saw the abomination of good whiskey being polluted with a dirty beer bottle." Rose held out her empty bottle.

Lee tipped the flask and dribbled whiskey into Rose's bottle. "Gen? You up for it?"

"Hell, yeah. Fill 'er up," Gen said, holding out her empty bottle for a shot.

Lee added at least a triple shot of whiskey to Gen's bottle, and they held their drinks up in salute. Lee's metal flask clicked against their glass bottles. "To 'is Lordship Arthur Finch-Hatten, the Earl of Severn, and his tight arse."

Gen giggled, getting a little tipsy, and they all drank to the Lord Severn's butt.

The whiskey burned Gen's throat, and she caught her breath afterward. This was awful. It was horrifically unethical to treat a client so, even in private. "I should not be drinking to my client's butt."

"No jury with ladies on it would convict you," Lee said.

Rose tittered behind her hand and sipped the whiskey from her bottle.

Lee and Rose finished their drinks and left Gen's office, saying that they would see her the next day for lunch.

It was well past midnight. Gen should go home, too. She had to be back at work in just a few hours to get Octavia her first cup of the morning at seven.

Gen sat alone in her dark closet-slash-office, alternately staring at the paperwork in Lord Severn's case and then at her computer screen. She drained the last sip of whiskey from her beer bottle during her vigil, waiting to see if Lord Severn was indeed at a sordid nightclub somewhere or if he had gone home to a lonely bed.

Ha. As if.

She refreshed the computer search again, but the top result was still the same grainy pic of Lord Severn and Peony Sweetling.

That *had* to be a stage name. Peony Sweetling. *Sheesh.*

She should call His Lordship Arthur Finch-Hatten, the Earl of Severn, and she should tell him to stay home like a good little earl and not screw up her case because judges and juries totally hated that kind of gallivanting about.

She really should.

Should.

How many beers had she had with the CTM? Three?

Probably three.

Maybe four.

And then the whiskey.

It was an excellent idea to call His Lordship Arthur Finch-Hatten the Earl of bloody Severn and tell him a thing or two.

It didn't feel very British to be so direct. It felt very American, and it felt so very *right.*

Yep, Lord Severn's cell phone number was right in his file.

That made it easy.

As Gen reached for the office phone, her wrist brushed the trackpad on her computer.

The browser refreshed itself, searching again for any news, gossip, incriminating photographs, or other dreck posted about "Lord Arthur Finch-Hatten OR Earl Severn AND gossip."

The top photograph, that infuriating one with the blond bimbo and intimations of cocaine, floated down the screen, leaving white space.

Oh, God.

No.

Another picture materialized out of what must have been Hell.

His Lordship Arthur Finch-fucking-Hatten, the Earl of fucking Severn, was sitting on what looked like an infernal throne with *three* twenty-something women snaking around him. His suit was rumpled, and his silvery tie was askew. A bright red lip print marked his neck.

Even through the graininess of the telephoto shot, his pale eyes were obviously glazed over, and he was listing to the side as if he were half-dead.

The caption for the picture was "Lord Severn-and-Seven Drunk Again. Which of these Three Tarts is a Drug Dealer?"

Ah, bloody hell.

DRUNK-DIALING THE EARL OF SEVERN

GEN snatched up her office phone from the table behind her and dialed the number in the file.

Ringing chattered through the phone, and a man's deep voice asked, "Yes?"

"Lord Severn—" Gen started, her voice a little screechier than she had meant. She was too wound up, too drunk.

"Oh, it's you." Lord Severn's voice lightened a little as it came from her phone. "The contact listing said that Horace Lindsey was calling from beyond the grave."

She tried to lower her voice, "It's Genevieve Ward." Still screechy. And a little slurred.

"Yes, Ms. Ward, I know." He chuckled, a deep, low laugh. "If this were Horace, I would have to say that you've reincarnated extraordinarily quickly and as an attractive woman, you should know. Perhaps this time, I'll take you up on your kind offer."

She bulled over his words even though her tongue was numb and heavy in her mouth. "Someone saw you out carousing and took pictures of you with three women tonight. *Three!* Are you deliberately trying to sabotage your case? Do you not want to be the Earl of Severus anymore?"

"Severus? Ms. Ward, have you been drinking?"

"It doesn't matter if I've been drinking. There aren't any pictures of *me* up on gossip sites, half-unconscious and with women hanging all over me!"

"I'm flattered that you called me when drunk-dialing. Are you at your office?"

How could he know that? "How could you know that?"

"The contact identification shows Serle's Court Barristers. I thought it was Horace Lindsey calling." His voice was warm and gentle. "Remember?"

"I am not drunk but you are and you need to go home and quit letting those assholes get pictures of you when you're *drunk*. You're going to blow out your liver or something."

"How are you planning to get home?"

"None of your business."

"Is there anyone there with you?"

"None of your business."

"Ah, I see how this game is played." Some mumbling. "Don't go anywhere. I'm on Chancery Lane, nearly at your office, now. Luckily, I happen to be quite close."

"You're drunk, too. You shouldn't be driving."

"I'm not driving. I have a lady who drives me around, and I never get drunk."

"Dude, I saw the pictures. You're probably crawling around on the floor of that car and vomiting on your way to the next bar."

"I was on my way home to my demon-possessed dog, but I thank you for the vote of confidence." He still sounded amused.

"Dude, I saw the pictures!"

"Don't believe everything you see on the internet. I'm driving past Lincoln's Inn now. Where is your office?"

"None of your business."

"Ah, yes. There are only a few lights on. Those are the law library," he mused. "Are you in Horace's office?"

"No. When he died, they assigned me to a new pupil mistress, Octavia Hawkes."

"So you're in her office?"

"I have a little office right next to hers."

"Is that in the same chambers as Horace's office was?"

"Two doors down, past the clerk's suite."

"Splendid. You're doing so well, helping me find you."

A warm glow touched Gen's cheeks. "S'alright."

The growl of the car motor in the background of his voice died away. He said, "I've arrived. I'm coming up. Don't go anywhere."

"You don't have to do this."

"It's entirely in my self-interest to make sure you get home all right. If my barrister dies of alcohol poisoning, I'll definitely lose the lawsuit."

"There are over sixty lawyers in this office. Someone else would take your case." She wasn't sure that was true.

"Horace wanted you to take it."

"No, he just had me write a Shakespearean quote on it while he was dying."

"And that was?" Gen could hear the smile in his voice and the tapping tread of his steps on the marble staircase.

While he lay dying, Horace had instructed her to write: *Though I, once gone, to all the world must die: The earth can yield me but a common grave, When you entombed in men's eyes shall lie.*

She told him, "Sonnet eighty-one."

Silence grew over the phone as his footsteps stopped. Lord Severn asked, "That one?"

"Yes. I thought it was odd. What do you think he meant by it?"

The footsteps resumed clacking in the background of Lord Severn's voice. "I'm almost there."

"It was weird that he wanted me to write that. He knew he was going to die, didn't he? It's so sad that he died. I miss him a lot. I think about him every day, and it's hard to keep from crying when I find his handwriting in files. Does that mean that he wanted me to take his case?"

"I suspect he did. Horace was a wise man and a good friend."

"It took forever for the ambulance to arrive. I called them right away."

"Of course you did." His voice echoed from the phone

and from down the hallway. "I'm sure you did everything you could. Where are you?"

"The only lamp still burning in the office because the industrious little American has to prove her worth."

"I see your light." The footfalls quickened. "Are you all right?"

Gen wiped her eyes. "I didn't cry at his funeral."

"Of course not. Horace wouldn't have wanted it any other way." Lord Severn rounded the corner of her doorframe and held on, his phone still pressed to his ear.

Gen mashed her eyes to dry any tears that might be still in them and looked up.

Damn, Arthur Finch-Hatten was gorgeous even when he was wearing jeans and a rumpled dress shirt instead of a tailored suit. The denim clung to his long legs, accentuating the lean muscles underneath. His dark shirt had one button open at the throat, no tie, just a peek of his collarbone. Without a suit jacket covering him up, his shoulders looked even broader, and his chest, more rounded under the thin fabric. He had a trim waist, narrow and tight, with the suggestion of hard muscles wrapping his body.

Gen's brain turned to alcohol-soaked goo.

She hung up the office phone in its cradle.

Lord Severn stuffed his phone into a back pocket and walked into her cubby of an office. "Let's get you home."

Gen braced her arms on the desk. "Why would you come here?"

"It's important to me that you arrive home safely," he said.

"And why is that? I'm nothing to you," Gen fretted. Drinking made her surly, sometimes.

"That's not true. You're my barrister who is going to save my earldom and a great deal of my money."

She shrugged. "Barristers are a dime, a dozen."

"Horace recommended you. I trusted him with my fortune and my title. I trust what he said about you."

"Horace didn't give me your case. The head clerk assigned it to me for absolutely no good reason. It was dumb luck for me, and it was bad luck for you."

He shook his head. "I'm sure Horace Lindsey left instructions, or perhaps he had discussed the matter with my solicitors and they made the recommendation. On several occasions, he said that you would be his second at the table during the hearings. He told me that if anything happened to him, I should make sure you handled my case."

Gen scuffed her shoe on the wooden floor under her desk. "I don't know why he would say that."

"Because he trusted you. He thought that anyone else in your chambers might not understand how best to handle it."

Horace had been overly sentimental, sometimes, even though he had that polished British reserve.

She said, "I think someone else should handle your case. I'm just a pupil barrister. I've only been arguing cases for a few months, and always with Horace making sure I knew what to say. I'm not qualified. You need a senior barrister, probably a QC, someone with a lot of experience and who understands the British legal system better than I do."

Lord Severn smiled at her under the light cast from the single ceiling bulb in her office. "Now I'm sure that you're too intoxicated to see yourself home. A barrister would never say such a thing, otherwise."

"Maybe it's because I'm not a good barrister."

"Horace thought otherwise, and I trust his judgment."

"You're drunk," she said.

Lord Severn laughed. "Perhaps, but you're worse off than I am. Let's get you to the car. You're far too drunk to be walking around, giving away your cases."

"You should listen when I tell you to dump me. I gained a first at Oxford. I'm smart."

Lord Severn glanced around her tiny office. "Do you

need anything? Should you take your laptop or lock it up for the night? Do you have a jacket? It's chilly out there, even for January."

She scooted her chair back from her tiny desk and grabbed her jacket off the back of it. "Everything stays here. Just need to lock my office door."

"All right. Let's go." He held out his hand, palm up.

Gen recoiled from his grabbing hand. "I can walk fine. I don't need help."

Those silvery-gray eyes of his tracked how she swayed as she held onto her desk, and even in her drunken state, she could see that he didn't look drunk at all.

Not at all.

Not even a little.

Why not?

The high heels on her shoes felt broken, and every time she walked, her ankles flexed like she was going to fall over. "I don't need help," she repeated, wobbling around her desk.

"Of course not," Lord Severn said. "But I'm here if you would prefer a hand."

Gen snagged her purse off the floor and stumbled past him and out of her office. "I don't usually get drunk like this."

"I should expect not." Lord Severn followed her out and watched her twist the metal key in the knob. He tilted his head, examining the outdated lock set on her door. "Is that the only lock on your door?"

"I'm very junior here. Not much is kept in there."

"Merely my personal phone number and contact information, copies of my passport and credit history, and my friends' private information, amongst others."

"Oh, yeah. I should do something about that." The floor wiggled under Gen's feet, so she leaned against a wall to steady herself.

"I'll send someone over tomorrow to upgrade that.

Come, now. The car is waiting."

Gen staggered down the hallway beside Lord Severn until they reached the staircase. The offices upstairs had been remodeled with modern furnishings like any law office anywhere in the world.

Dang it, they had already passed the elevator, and going back would make her look weak and drunk.

Marble stairs stretched down to the ground floor: long, imposing, centuries old, and slick as satin.

Gen gripped the banister so hard that her knuckles inside her hand groaned.

"You could hold my elbow." Lord Severn jutted his elbow out to the side as if to assist her down the staircase at cotillion.

She said, "I'm fine. Don't grab me."

"I wouldn't dream of it," he said. "Last time, you tried to pummel me."

"And I'll do it for realsies this time."

Yet, Gen eyed his arm. Merely an elbow offered as a handle didn't seem as threatening as a hand grabbing at her and ready to shove her down.

Lord Severn stood with his elbow akimbo. "Shall we?"

Gen might fall headfirst downstairs because she was so stupidly wobbly.

The other option was to hold onto his arm. Not him holding her, but her holding onto him.

She was as skittish as a thunder-spooked colt. Ridiculous.

Falling down the stone stairs and dying was not the best alternative, though.

She had to find a way over, around, or through things, unless she wanted to live her life like a gun-shy gopher.

Without looking, she curled her fingers under his arm.

His arm tightened against her hand, pulling her to his side.

Gen didn't let go.

She was fine. She was just hanging onto him. He wasn't

grabbing her.

It was different.

She told herself that again.

It was different.

Under the fine fabric of his shirt, Lord Severn's biceps muscle twitched, a tremor in the hard globe of his upper arm. Against the backs of her fingers, muscular cords wound around his side.

He must have a lot of spare time to hit the gym.

Lazy noble jerk.

Warmth filtered through his shirt to her hand, and a hint of cologne that smelled like apple pie spices and warm wood clung to him.

"Shall we?" he asked.

Gen nodded. She walked down the stairs, trying not to fall on her face and crash down the steps nor accidentally mash her body against his.

Her hand shook on Lord Severn's arm, no matter how hard she tried to steady herself.

Damn.

Lord Severn looked around the dark wood of the staircase as they walked down. "My grandfather was admitted to the bar in Lincoln's Inn."

"Your grandfather was a barrister?" Gen concentrated on breathing slowly and not hyperventilating.

"Of course not," he scoffed. "My grandfather was an earl."

Oh. Right. "Why was he admitted to the bar?"

They were about halfway down the staircase.

Lord Severn said, "We wolfish earls must have something to do with our free time. My grandfather read law at Oxford and served on certain committees in the House of Lords."

"I read law at Trinity College at Oxford."

"Trinity is an excellent college. Everyone seems to love it. I did."

"You were at Trinity? Did you take a degree?"

"Oh, yes. A while ago, a few years ahead of you, I'd wager. But it doesn't matter."

"Of course, it matters. What course did you take?"

He shrugged, and his arm under her hand rose. "Modern Languages."

"That must have been hard. I barely passed French."

"I read Spanish and Russian."

"That's interesting."

"Not particularly. There were quite a lot of classical books to read in the course. I rather thought that we would speak the languages, but uni is an education in many ways, isn't it?"

"Oh, yes. Many ways." Gen felt herself laugh and almost choked on it.

Wow, Gen was impressed with herself, that she could hold onto Lord Severn's arm and laugh at his jokes and not freak out or climb up on the banister like an overweight, ungainly spider monkey to get away from him.

Maybe she should have been impressed that Lord Severn was so skillfully distracting her.

Well, he was a party animal. Everything was just fun and a great time had by all, right? He was probably very good at getting people to relax. That's why people flocked to him.

That's why *women* flocked to him.

She asked him, "So are you doing anything with your degree?"

With his other hand, he patted her fingers that were wrapped around his arms. "Nothing to speak of."

"Then why did you go to university?"

"As I said, we wolfish earls must have something to do with our free time. I went to university for a few years before embarking on my depraved and debauched lifestyle."

"Oh, yeah. That's right. I'm supposed to be lecturing you about the deplorable ways you spend your time and money."

"It appears that I've taken up rescuing damsels in distress

tonight. Is that more to your taste?"

Somehow, they reached the bottom of the stairs and the safety of the ground floor.

Gen had made it. She hadn't freaked out or fallen or yanked her hand away and tumbled down the stairs.

Halle-freaking-lujah.

She caught her breath, and just as she started to drop her hand away from Lord Severn's arm, he settled his other hand over her fingers.

It didn't feel like he was intentionally trapping her, just steadying her.

She did feel a little trapped, but she didn't shake him off. She could handle this.

Gen considered making her fingers go limp and letting them slide out of his arm, but Lord Severn continued to talk about the history of Lincoln's Inn and his family's long connection with the law society, telling her about the history of the art that they passed.

His arm warmed her fingers, too. Gen's hands were always cold.

And, to be frank, Gen was holding onto the arm of one of the most notorious playboys and eligible bachelors in England. Every time Lord Severn looked at her or asked her something about herself, it was like he glowed from the inside, and she warmed from his light. Even now, with his fingers gently holding hers, when he smiled down at her as they walked through the antiquated building past the dark wood and stone of the lobby, she felt like he *liked* her.

Maybe he did.

Oh, she was being silly. Horsey-faced Gen wasn't in the same league as His Venerable Hotness, the Right Honorable Lord Severn.

She must be drunk.

But she could enjoy the moment.

Lord Severn rambled on about King Charles II as if he had known the guy while they walked through the lobby, out the front doors, and along the sidewalk.

Just outside the portcullis, a car was idling, waiting for them.

Lord Severn finally let go of her fingers, and she jerked her hand back to her side. She stood, fidgeting, while he opened the rear door for her. When she finally climbed inside, her high heel caught on the rim of the door, yanking her foot.

Somehow, she saved it and just sat down hard on the pillowy leather. Sprawling across the seat with her fanny in the air was totally par for the course, but not this time.

Gen's hand felt abnormally warm.

She held her fingers to her chest. Her hand had been trapped by his arm against his ribs for several minutes, and she hadn't panicked at all. Surely, this was some kind of a new record for her. Someone ought to be proud.

Lord Severn climbed into the other side of the car. "Unfortunately, I can't take you home with me. Your fellow barristers would talk. So, where shall I take you?"

"That might be the only way to keep you out of trouble, if I hung around you and hounded you day and night."

He chuckled. "Let's hope it never comes to that. All those ethics rules about barristers and their clients would surely get in the way."

"You know about those, huh?"

He winked at her. "It's come up once or twice."

Gen peered at him. "What's that supposed to mean?"

"It means you should read my file carefully. Horace wasn't my first barrister at your law firm."

Shock cracked through her. *"No!"*

"Certainly. I think that's why I was assigned to him." Lord Severn asked, "And what's your address, again?"

Had she told him her address to begin with?

It didn't really matter.

Gen rattled off the address to him. "In Islington. It's not too far off. About fifteen minutes."

Arthur told the driver, a lady in her sixties with short, gray hair visible above the seat back, to take them to the address. The car pulled away from the curb, rocking Gen back in her seat.

Outside the car, the night air in London was chilly but not bad for January. The buildings slipped by along the sides of the street. The ground floor shops were shuttered and dark, but lights still shone in some of the upstairs windows. Shadows flitted in the bright squares even though it was well after midnight.

The car's engine hummed in the quiet.

To be polite, Gen should make conversation with Arthur Finch-Hatten, who was sitting right over there on the other side of the back seat.

Right over there.

The car passed under a street light, and the blaze of light flared on his strong cheekbones and the dimples in his cheeks.

Damn, he was gorgeous.

Gen's brain fuzzed like radiation had turned all her radio signals to static.

She needed to say something.

Think, think, think, think, think.

Let's see: she could harangue him some more for his carousing.

No, she had harped on that enough.

She could talk about the weather or sports or something.

Gen didn't know much about sports and was rarely outside during the day except to travel to court. Most of the time when she was out, her face was stuck in paperwork while she rode in taxis or on the train, anyway. The weather was a mystery to her except for a few instances between vehicles and buildings.

She could compliment him on his incredible physique—the hard muscles around his torso and arm—that she had been feeling up while he had guided her drunken butt down the stairs. Maybe she could ask him to take off his shirt to show her just how ripped he was, just out of curiosity.

Awkward.

Topics of conversation, each more stupid than the last, vortexed in Gen's head.

Oh my God, she had to say something.

Now.

Talk *now.*

Gen blurted, "Those little white wigs that barristers wear in court really start to stink if you don't have them cleaned, and some people *never* do that."

Oh, no. Anything but that.

Lord Severn looked over at her, startled, his silvery eyes reflecting the bands of street lights that shone in the car as they drove, and his expression cracked into a huge grin. "Do tell."

"Um, yeah. They're traditionally made out of horse hair, so they last forever, but they're really itchy. Everyone hates them."

Lord Severn was still smiling that blast of sunshine that warmed her from the inside, out. He said, "I can only imagine."

"And the robes are hot. You have to wear them over a suit, and it gets really steamy. Some of the big guys sweat through them. The bands on the collar are stiff and poke the underside of your chin."

"Abominable," Lord Severn agreed.

"It's better to argue cases where you've never met the client but only taken instructions from the solicitors. It was kind of disconcerting to actually meet with you in chambers. I keep feeling like I should throw you back to the solicitors and have all of our communication go through them. It's traditional. The law is more pure when it works like that. I can concentrate on the case and the nuances of the law and the facts instead of—" She glanced over at Lord Severn, so beautiful with his brilliant smile and his gray eyes twinkling in the streetlights and moonlight "—distractions."

"Certainly," Lord Severn said, "but I like to know who is working on my case. Horace and I had lunch several times a month to discuss developments."

"He was charging you for his time for those lunches."

"Of course he was."

"He was charging you while you were at *your* club," Gen said.

"Of course. Otherwise, he would have billed me for reimbursement, too."

"And you're okay with that?"

"Of course." Lord Severn's smile turned a little puzzled, and he tilted his head as he looked at her.

"All right, then. If it's all on the up-and-up," she said.

"You're not going to charge me for this car ride home, are you?" Lord Severn asked, grinning again.

Damn, he was beautiful when he did that.

She laughed. "You should charge me cab fare, I suppose."

"I think we can agree that each would cancel out the other."

"Oh, I don't think you've looked at how much I'm charging you per hour," she said.

His eyes twinkled again. "Can you imagine how much it would cost to hire an earl to drive you around?"

"You're not driving," she pointed out.

"As a companion, then," he said. "I was auctioned off last year for charity to a very nice duchess in her late forties for thirty thousand pounds. Now if we do the math to arrive at a per-hour fee—"

Gen asked, "How many hours was it?"

"There was dinner, and the symphony, so that was a few hours."

"And you dropped her off at home at—"

He raised one eyebrow, but he was still smiling. "About ten the next morning."

"Oh! I don't want to know any more!" Gen was laughing

so hard that she grabbed her stomach. "But it does bring down your per-hour rate quite a bit if the date lasted sixteen hours."

He laughed. "Well, she did pay an exorbitant sum, and it was for charity."

"So it was a charity—" She couldn't finish the term.

Lord Severn shook his head, though he was still grinning. "Not at all. Our commitment to services for refugees might have brought us together, but mutual attraction ensured that we were not divided."

Gen laughed again. "That's a nice way to put it."

"I'm a nice man."

"I've heard a lot about what kind of man you are, Lord Severn, but 'nice' has never come up."

"Call me Arthur, not Lord Severn. What tosh. And don't believe everything you read on the internet."

The car coasted to a stop in front of Gen's place, a terraced house attached in a long row to the other houses that solidly lined the street. Delicate iron bars covered the dark windows. A bare bulb shone a glaring light above the white-painted front door and touched the red brick of the three-story building in the night.

"Home sweet home," Gen said. "Thanks for the ride."

She started to get out of the car, pushing open the door and trying to find the sidewalk with her foot, but Lord Severn was already out of the car. He appeared right beside her, offering her his hand one more time.

Politeness and fear scuffled in her stomach.

Gen tried to take his outstretched hand. She really did. She let go of the back of the seat and tried to move her hand forward, but it stopped in the air. Her hand fell straight down onto the soft leather of the seat. "I'm fine. Thanks, anyway."

Lord Severn dropped his hand, but in the wan glow of the dome light inside the black town car, Gen saw his smile turn soft. He backed up. "I'm right here if you need a hand."

Gen struggled her way out of the car into the cold, night air. Her high heels scraped on the sidewalk and slipped, but she saved herself. Lord Severn's hand hovered in the air when she bobbled, but he didn't touch her.

She stumbled up the sidewalk to her house with Lord Severn trailing behind her. "You don't have to come in if you don't want to. I'll be fine."

"It's quite all right. I'm worried about the state you're in." His hand grazed her elbow, turning her to face him. "I meant what I said before."

"About what? King Charles the Second being your homeboy?"

"About not molesting you. I would never force myself on a woman. I abhor the thought."

"I'm sure you wouldn't." She thought no such thing.

"I just want to see you inside."

Gen slid the key into the lock and jiggled the stiff lock. "Oh, all right. But I'm fine."

Lord Severn put his hands in his pockets.

Gen's key grated in the lock. The door knob wasn't an antique and distinguished like the one on her office door at Lincoln's Inn. This set was just as mundane as the building around it. Decades of dust had settled in the mechanism, making it hard to turn. She forced the key.

The lock clicked, and Gen pushed her front door open. Inside the vestibule, which was about the size of her closet-office, she set her keys in the empty bowl on the little table so she could find them the next morning.

Lord Severn followed her inside and waited.

She pushed open the next door, which led directly into the kitchen. Gen and her mother had just remodeled the kitchen a few years ago with stainless steel appliances and bamboo counters on two walls. Four tomato-red melamine chairs clustered around a small table of light wood over on the side wall.

With the two of them in there, the tiny kitchen almost felt a little crowded.

Gen said, "I'm inside. You can go now."

He nodded. "What's through there?"

"Just the reception room that leads out to the garden."

"Can I see it?"

He shouldn't be invading this far into her house. Her neighbors would talk, and his delicious smell would get all over her stuff. "Um, sure."

She led him through the door and stopped in the middle of the room. They hadn't redecorated in there yet, and it looked like they had jumped back in time to the nineteen-fifties. Chintz and ruffles wrapped all the furniture and draped over every available surface. French china stuffed a hutch in the corner. Her mother had shipped the blue rose-painted dishes from England to Texas and then back after Gen's father had died. A thick blanket was folded on the back of the couch.

Lord Severn glanced around the living room.

Arthur Finch-Hatten, the Earl of Severn, also called "The Right Hottie Lord Severn" by the press, was impossibly standing in Gen's apartment. Any red-blooded woman would have grabbed him by his shirt and kissed those lush lips until his gray eyes closed and his strong arms wrapped around her and carried her to the bedroom.

Gen bet that many women had done *exactly that.*

An impulse to also do *exactly that* seized her.

For the first time in months, Gen felt a wanting, a warmth, that made her feel stupid and excited at the same time.

Damn, it was like mind control. It was like she could smell his high-status-male hormones and wanted to jump him.

His cologne was scented with cinnamon and warm wood smoke.

Maybe that was the actual smell of money.

Gen glanced around her little house like she was seeing it for the first time. "Yes, I know. Nine hundred square feet that looks like it was decorated by a little old lady."

"I think it's perfectly respectable."

Gen said, "It's my mother's house."

"Does she live here, too?"

"No." She stared straight at him, unwilling to say more.

He gestured to a door on the other wall that led to the stairway. "Are the bedrooms upstairs?"

"Yeah, but I don't think that's appropriate." Under her feet, the floor slanted and she stumbled, grabbing the wall.

Lord Severn sauntered over to stand beside her, but he didn't touch her, just stood there with his hands outstretched in case she fell. "I want to make sure you're settled for the night."

Gen sighed, "I'm fine. Time for you to go, Lord Severn."

"Arthur," he said. "When we can be informal, call me Arthur."

"It seems unprofessional."

"I'm begging you to."

She looked at him, trying to focus her bleary eyes on the right angle of his jaw and those stunning silvery eyes. "Why?"

"Why not?" Lord Severn, *Arthur,* retracted his hand. "All right. My work here is done. Sleep well." He began to turn but looked back at her. His silvery eyes weren't sad exactly, nor wary, but there was a softness to them. He said, "Lock the door after I'm out. You can't be too safe these days, what with letting strange men into your apartment and all."

Her jaw dropped. "But you insisted!"

"Still, can't be too careful."

He walked out the door, his hands in his pockets, and Gen watched out the kitchen window as he walked towards his car. His butt was just the right amount of round in his snug jeans as he strolled down the short sidewalk. Just grabbably round.

The driver got out of the car to try to open his door, but he waved her off. Her slow walk and quick retreat suggested that they went through that charade often.

Lord Severn, *Arthur,* was just a nice guy, making sure that she got home safely.

Yeah. Right.

Visiting Momma

Early the next morning at the nursing home, Gen pushed open the door from the hallway to a small bedroom. Medical smells clogged the air of the room, irritating Gen's tender stomach. She rarely drank that much, and being this hungover was an altogether new experience.

No more whiskey after beer. *Never* again.

In the small bed in the corner of the room, a frail woman stared at the ceiling. Her gray hair was matted to her head, not dirty, just flattened bedhead because she never left the bed.

When Gen had been a child, her mother had loved or pretended to love helium balloons. Every time Gen got one, her mother confiscated it and tied the string around her own wrist, miming for hours that the balloon was pulling her hand into the air and almost lifting her off her feet if she stopped paying attention to it. The play-acting had made Gen laugh for so many years, all the way through the teenage times.

Now, IV bags leading to her mother's arms hovered over the bed like those balloons. Gen's heart broke some more.

"Momma," Gen said in her strongest Texas accent. "Momma? I'm here for a while."

The woman in the bed melted, the tension leaving her arms and body.

Gen went and sat in the chair beside the bed and took out her phone. "I can't read for long this morning, momma. I've got a case to argue later this morning at work. Octavia has me cross-examining and giving arguments right from the get-go, far more than Horace did. I loved Horace Lindsey, absolutely adored him, but being Octavia's pupil is trial-by-fire. Don't you worry, though. We'll get through at least a chapter before I have to go."

Gen began reading from a new mystery that she had downloaded a few days before.

The stroke which had incapacitated her mother six months before had been the massive, hemorrhagic kind. A blood clot had lodged in a vein in her mother's skull, and the blood vessel had blown apart. Gen had gotten a call at work from their next door neighbor, Esme, who had said that her mother had fainted in the garden. When Gen had arrived at the hospital, the doctors had said it was a miracle that her mother had survived at all.

They kept using that word, *miracle.*

Her mother's life—lying in a bed for six months, alternately shaking and sweating, grunting and groaning, unable to tell them if she was in pain, her blue eyes uncomprehending and staring at the walls or tracking things that were not there—did not seem like a miracle.

It seemed like she was in Hell.

Gen prayed for a real miracle.

She knew better than to pray for her mother to recover. The doctors had been imaging her brain and had seen no recovery, despite the physical therapy that the assistants were trying.

Every night, Gen prayed hard that a miracle would come in the form of enough money to keep her mother in this better nursing home here in London where Gen could visit her every day.

The administrators had first assigned her mother to a different nursing home, one much farther away and beyond the suburbs of London. Gen hadn't been able to visit during the week, only on weekends. It had taken three hours to take the tube to the suburb and hire a cab to take her to the nursing home.

Plus, that first nursing home had had something wrong with it.

Things were better, now, but they were far more expensive.

Her mother had little equity in the Islington house that she had bought when she moved back to the United Kingdom.

The health care facilitator had demanded to know where the thirty thousand pounds that had been in her mother's bank accounts two years ago had gone, so Gen had had to admit to the woman that her mother had loaned it to her to pay for the bar course over a year before her stroke.

The woman had demanded the money be put back in her mother's accounts immediately, which was impossible. The tuition to the college had already been paid. The woman then said that Gen could "top up" her mother's monthly nursing home allowance so she could be moved to the more expensive home in the city.

So Gen was doing that.

The office was paying Gen only a pitiful stipend during her pupillage. She couldn't pay the money back to her mother's accounts until she obtained tenancy in the chambers.

If she were offered tenancy.

She was one of six pupil barristers competing for exactly one job.

If she didn't get the job, she had few options.

There was a year-long solicitor's course that she could take to become the other kind of lawyer, but it cost even more money that she didn't have. Plus, she wouldn't be paid for that year she was taking yet another course, and then she would have to do a solicitor pupillage for a pittance, again. It would be over two years before she started earning money in any amount if she did that.

Hanging out her own shingle as a barrister wasn't an

option. Barristers who don't work in an approved chambers are severely limited by the Bar Council in what they are allowed to do. She wouldn't make enough money to pay her mother back that way.

She was too chubby and horse-faced to dance on tables, so that was straight out.

Nope, she had to survive the barrister pupillage and win the job or else her mother was going to be sent back to the other nursing home.

So Gen would do that.

Gen opened the book. "It takes place in America, Momma. Here we go. 'Angel Day focused the black tunnel of her gun sight and crosshairs on the man holding the shotgun, ready to shoot him.'"

THE GIRLFRIEND TACTIC

"WE have a problem," Octavia Hawkes said.

Gen fidgeted in her chair, which had been placed squarely in front of Octavia Hawkes's huge desk like Gen was a naughty schoolgirl brought before the headmistress. Hawkes had called Gen into the meeting as soon as she had arrived.

Octavia's lips had contracted into the red dot of anger on her face, frightening to behold.

Beside Gen, Lord Severn, *Arthur,* lounged in his chair, his long legs stretched out. He had been ushered into Octavia Hawkes's office right after Gen had and not glanced at her when he sat down. Instead of the jeans from last night, he wore a navy blue suit, and a whiff of soap and warm-spiced cologne had puffed from him to Gen.

The man smelled like cinnamon rolls, cleanliness, and sheer male power. No wonder women wanted to lick him.

He examined the end of his dark blue tie and dropped it to flop on his hard stomach.

Wow.

To be any more unconcerned, Lord Severn, *Arthur,* would have had to light a cigarette and sip a shaken martini.

Damn it. Gen needed to pick one of those names and run with it. Constantly brain-stuttering "Lord Severn, *Arthur,*" was driving her crazy.

She fidgeted on the hard chair, gripping the edges of the wooden seat, trying not to look like she had been caught out of bed after lights-out.

Octavia Hawkes spun her laptop around so that Gen and Lord Severn, *Arthur,* could see what she had been looking at. "What the living hell is this?"

Of course, her screen showed that damned picture of Lord Severn, *Arthur,* sprawled on the throne with the three women twining around him and that stupid drug dealer headline.

"I can explain." Gen had no idea how she was going to finish that sentence.

Lord Severn asked, "What of it?"

Hawkes stood and strolled around her desk while she spoke to him. "Horace spoke to you, *repeatedly,* about the fact that your *lifestyle,*" she spat, "might jeopardize your case. If you are going to behave in such an undignified manner, your solicitor will need to retain another barrister. You need adult supervision, you adolescent wanker."

"I assure you, I have no need to wank," Lord Severn, *Arthur,* intoned with mock seriousness.

Octavia wound up for a verbal punch. "We don't fight hopeless cases. I certainly don't, and Gen needs court wins in her column before the tenancy decisions are made at the end of September. We aren't Atticus fucking Finch, here."

She meant the honorable lawyer from the novel *To Kill A Mockingbird.*

All lawyers know that book.

All lawyers have read that book and, at one point, were inspired by that book.

Most senior lawyers laugh at that book, Octavia included. Now, Octavia went to Sun Tzu's *The Art of War* or Machiavelli's *The Prince* for inspiration and quoted them liberally.

"Hmmm, Atticus fucking *Finch,*" Arthur Finch-Hatten said. "Good name. Good, strong name for an idealist."

Gen spoke up, "I'm sure that if Lord Severn understands —"

"I understand perfectly," he said. "I understand that I will live my life as I please, and you will fight my case to the best of your ability. The law and tradition are on my side. We will prevail."

Hawkes leaned against the front of her desk and glared down at Lord Severn. "Judges and juries are capricious and unpredictable. You could very well scuttle this with an ill-timed indiscretion." She sighed. "We could sue that gossip website. Perhaps a court injunction."

"That would fuel the fire," Lord Severn, *Arthur,* said. "They would report on the injunction and imply that it must all be fact.

Hawkes scowled at him as much as she could, which meant that the sides of her mouth turned down around the surgical filler in her cheeks. Her forehead between her eyes didn't move at all, remaining Botox-smooth. She said, "You're close to the royal family. Can't their connections run interference with the press for you?"

He laughed. "They gave up on me years ago. Besides, it takes the spotlight off their downstream heirs if I'm caught behaving badly. I wouldn't be surprised if the official palace photographer is the one following me around and feeding these photographs to the tabloid sites."

"Libel?" Hawkes asked. "Defamation? Damages?"

Gen said, "The pictures back up their statements pretty well." She asked Lord Severn, *Arthur,* "They aren't photoshopped, are they?"

Lord Severn shook his head, and his dark hair fell over his forehead. "All genuine."

"Damn it," Hawkes muttered. "You must stop giving them ammunition."

Gen backed her up. "You can't get drunk and let them take pictures anymore, Lord Severn."

"Arthur, not Lord Severn."

Octavia's eyelids flared open, which meant that she was trying to raise her eyebrows at this breach of etiquette.

He flipped his fingers in the air. "I wasn't that drunk."

Gen said, "You were falling all over the place. And you can't do drugs, especially not in public."

"There are no photographs of me with drugs because I used none. I had a few cocktails, vodka and soda. What were you drinking last night?" he asked Gen.

Octavia Hawkes turned her over-waxed eyebrows toward Gen, but her face didn't move. Her lips remained contracted into an angry, red dot.

Gen admitted, "Stout. Then whiskey."

He said, "Wrong order. That's dangerous. Do be careful. There might not be such a harmless man such as myself around, next time."

"You were *with* him last night?" Hawkes glared at Gen, turning to stand between her and Lord Severn.

"No," Gen said, raising her hands, palms out. "No way. I was here, in the office, working. I put in billable hours."

Octavia didn't open her teeth when she spoke. "Then to what is Lord Severn referring?"

Behind Hawkes, Lord Severn, *Arthur,* was smirking. *Seriously?*

Gen said, "I needed a ride home from the office last night, and Lord Severn happened to be in the area and provided it."

Lord Severn interjected, *"Arthur."*

Hawkes frowned harder. "Why didn't you rein him in while you were about it?"

"The damage had already been done. The photo was already on the gossip sites. I found it last night while I was still here."

Hawkes's tone was acidic. "Maybe you can *prevent* the problem next time instead of going drinking with him afterward to celebrate."

"I didn't go drinking with Lord Severn!" Gen protested.

"Arthur!"

"Irrelevant," Octavia said. "How are you going to prevent this kind of thing from happening again? How are you going to prevent it *tonight?*"

Gen quailed. "I—I guess I could follow him around and keep an eye on him instead of working here. That's better than hitting refresh on the computer all night to see whether a photographer has already snapped an incriminating picture of him. You said yourself that he needs adult supervision. I'm an adult."

That last part might have been a little more bitter than Gen had intended, but dang it, that whole night had been one anxiety-fueled refresh after another.

Octavia Hawkes leaned toward Gen. "And how do you plan to do that?"

Think-think-think-think-think.

Gen looked over Hawkes's shoulder at Arthur Finch-Hatten, the Earl of Severn, the glorious scion of the British Empire—glamorous and gorgeous and strong and tall—who was silently laughing at her inability to keep him from destroying his life and her career.

Her hands clenched into fists. Gen said, "I just won't *let* him put himself in undesirable positions."

Lord Severn, *Arthur,* chuckled. "Good luck with that."

Time to rope that steer and hogtie at least three of his legs.

Gen lifted her chin. "We'll put it out there that I'm his new girlfriend. I'll stay with him every waking hour, and he'll stay with me. He's been caught by a woman, and so it's perfectly logical if he isn't drinking and whoring his way across London anymore. I will be his supervising adult."

Lord Severn stood and towered over both of them, panic widening his silvery eyes. "Wait a minute—"

"And if you don't behave—" Gen stood up, braced her hands on her hips, and stared nearly straight into his gorgeous, shimmering eyes. She almost melted but she sure as Hell didn't let herself get all gooey, "—then you can find yourself some new barristers, new ones who aren't tenants in these chambers. You can start all the Hell over with someone else."

Octavia Hawkes's head snapped up, and her overly plush lips stretched into a grin. "I think that's an exceptional idea, Gen."

Lord Severn straightened and smiled, smoothing his tie into his suit jacket. "It's unethical for a barrister to date a client. You would surely never be offered tenancy and probably would be dismissed from chambers."

Octavia chuckled and dismissed the problem with a wave of her hand. "I'll take care of that. Don't you worry about it all," she told Gen. "Just a few, well-placed whispers in the right ears will ensure that it's seen that you're taking one for the proverbial team. Indeed, it will increase your chances to receive a tenancy offer."

Gen turned back to Lord Severn, *Arthur*, and sucked in a fortifying breath. "So, what do you say? Am I your girlfriend, whom you're going to pretend to be head-over-heels for and spend every waking minute with, or are you going to call your solicitors and tell them to find someone else to fight your case? Someone whom Horace didn't *recommend?*"

Lord Severn didn't seem distressed by this development at all. Indeed, his face was utterly emotionless, and his silvery eyes turned icy. "So you're to be my girlfriend in *all* ways?"

That asshole was trying to run her off.

"Hell, no," Gen said, her Texas accent turning harsher than usual in her mouth. "You'll give me no lip and keep your hands to yourself."

"Or you'll punch me, I imagine." One side of his mouth curved up a little, but his eyes were still cold, even snakelike. He said, "If I indulge in a sham relationship, perhaps it will last longer than a month. And when is this charade to begin?"

Octavia butted in, "Immediately. You'll pick Gen up from work, and you'll see to it that she's safely home when you're ready to retire for the evening." She grabbed Lord Severn's elbow and pulled, turning him to look at her. "Gen is doing a pupillage, here. She gained a first-class degree at Oxford in law, and she did the European law track. She survived a grueling bar course and exam. She beat out four thousand applicants for one of three hundred pupillage spots and only one of six in these chambers. She needs to be on time for work, and she needs to be able to concentrate. Try to put your selfish appetites aside for once, and don't scuttle her chances."

"Ah," Lord Severn said. "Well played, both of you.

"What?" Gen looked between the two of them.

His face was rigid like a Greek statue, like the marble almost ready to soften into flesh, but not quite.

Octavia was smiling. Her Botoxed forehead was still as smooth as a snake. She said, "I rather think so. Gen will be finished with work around five. I trust you can keep yourself out of trouble until then?"

Lord Severn looked down at Gen. "There is a private social engagement that I'm to attend tonight. If you are to pose as my girlfriend—" His voice was flat, unfeeling, but at least he hadn't sneered that last word "—you'll need appropriate clothes. I'll have someone here at five for you."

"I've got clothes, Lord Severn," Gen protested.

Octavia's eyes widened like she would have raised her eyebrows if she could have.

He didn't look Gen up and down. If anything, his voice was gentler. "You'll need *different* clothes. Someone will arrive for you at five. And if we are to indulge in such a charade, you must start calling me *Arthur.*"

He strode out of the room, not looking back. The office door smacked shut.

Gen sank into her chair. "I shouldn't have suggested that. He's going to ditch me or make me look like an idiot at this party. This was a *terrible* idea."

Octavia shrugged and walked back around her desk. "It doesn't much matter either way. If he does anything wrong, we will remove ourselves as his barristers, and little will have changed. If he doesn't, you have a shot to win his case. It's quite a win-win situation for you."

"Do you think so?" Gen asked.

Octavia looked up, seriousness flickering in her brown eyes. "Chances are, we're going to lose Lord Severn's case. I don't believe that he will be able to refrain from his debauchery for any length of time. This last effort will emphasize that we went to extraordinary measures to continue with his case. It's just for show."

"Oh." Gen leaned back in her seat. "I'll do my best, then, at this party-thing."

Octavia pressed her lips together before she spoke, and her voice was lower when she said, "Use caution tonight. Sun Tzu said, 'He who wishes to fight must first count the cost.' Considering the clientele of this law firm and the circles that Lord Severn moves in, at least a few of our other clients and perhaps some of the solicitors who send business to us may also attend. To be frank, if you make a fool of yourself at that party and drive off clients from other barristers in chambers, you won't get a tenancy offer."

USB

In a small bedroom within his apartment, Arthur jiggled a minuscule USB drive as he inserted it into a slot of a desktop computer. It was a tight fit, but he manipulated it in.

Afternoon sunlight shone into Arthur's computer room through gauzy curtains hanging over the windows and French doors that led out to the rear balcony. Six floors below the terrace, London flowed over rolling hills down to the shining Thames River in the distance, a cubic carpeting of buildings and winter-dormant lawns.

A small, mostly white dog slept near Arthur's feet, still rolled over on his back in case Arthur wanted to resume rubbing his belly.

Empty coffee cups littered the desk. He would take the cups back to the kitchen when he had a chance. The smoky scent of good coffee hung in the dark air. Even inhaling in that room could give someone a caffeine buzz.

Six computer screens were staggered over the desk and a shelf above it. On one, a new window popped open from the USB drive, listing files.

Thin curtains cut the sunlight's glare, which Arthur preferred. Staring at the screens for hours sometimes gave him headaches. The monitors had been positioned so that the screens weren't visible from the windows, even though the windows were thoroughly silvered to make them opaque to even the most sophisticated surveillance equipment.

He had only a few hours to work before he was to meet

Gen for the evening's charity soiree.

The two of them had cornered him. The barristers at Serle's Court had been trying to curtail his lifestyle ever since the firm had taken his case. He'd gone through three different barristers, including poor Horace Lindsey, all of them haranguing him at every opportunity.

The pincer movement that morning had been technically beautiful, he had to admit. Arthur was quite the student of warfare tactics, though traditional military tactics were beyond what he usually studied.

Now, he had to spend hours every day with Gen Ward.

While most men would have been thrilled to spend hours of the day with the luscious Genevieve Ward, doing so without the prospect of seducing her would be torture.

Her body was all curves and softness, from her soft lips to her spectacular tits to the curving, lush globes of her ass. His hands felt empty even sitting there at his computer desk. He wanted to press her softness against himself and fill his hands and fingers with the flesh of her ass and long, curvy legs.

Arthur liked a nice ass on a woman.

A lot.

And tonight, he would stand beside Gen Ward for the evening, after she and Octavia Hawkes had outmaneuvered him, and try to do his damn job while Gen made every effort to ensure that he didn't.

Once again, the first layer of his job would be to convince everyone that he was a drunken degenerate who was trying to convince them that he wasn't one.

The deeper layers of his job were such that he couldn't discuss them with anyone except through the reams of paperwork he produced each week.

Paperwork filled his days and his nights, shoving aside his actual work.

Every evening's schedule was more tedious than the last. He would rather be at home with his dog, perhaps with his computer on his lap, taking down a government or two while he watched a movie.

Even that seemed hollow, sometimes.

Arthur refused to pity himself. He was a fantastically wealthy nobleman with a consuming life's work, plus he had a dog. It was enough. It was far better than most people's lot in life.

He bent and scratched the dog's hairy tummy. The dog's white tail thumped the ground, but he didn't wake up.

Arthur leaned in to read the list of files on the tiny USB that had been glued to the thigh of one of the women on the previous night. Her body had been drop dead gorgeous, but the woman herself was a dead drop.

The list read like alphabet soup.

STUXNET MOD 17ar9b

GAUSS Build 68en093

FLAME ver y73mel1007

DuQu Mod wbpp638a

Just random letters, odd file names, and some version numbers. To the vast majority of people, the file names were meaningless drivel.

To Arthur, they meant chaos. They meant cities burning and protestors rioting.

He reached for his keyboard.

Tea and Marriage Therapy

GEN poured tea in a china cup and added sugar for Linnaeus Grover, a member of chambers who had recently taken silk, which meant that he had applied for and been accepted as Queen's Counsel. It also meant that he was distinguished in his profession, could accept or refuse cases with impunity, and could charge truly exorbitant fees.

Grover's clerk had been ecstatic when his boss had taken silk. He had sharpened all his pencils and called all the man's solicitors, informing them of Grover's happy announcement and his new fee structure.

Linnaeus accepted the tea from Gen and smiled at her, craning his neck upward. "And how are you this afternoon?"

"Very well, thank you." No other comment was needed, Gen knew. "And yourself?"

"Quite well, quite well," Linnaeus said, holding onto his suit coat's lapel as if it were his new silk court robes.

Beside her, James Knightly asked Grover, "Biscuit, sir?"

Linnaeus patted his stomach as if he were about to refuse but then reached for the offered cookie and ate it anyway.

James Knightly said to Grover, "Such a shame about Fred Norquist's marriage being on the rocks." Fred was another of the pupil barristers competing with Gen and James to get the tenancy. "I heard that Fred and his wife are in couples counseling three evenings a week."

Gen wanted to roll her eyes. Everything that James said reeked of ulterior motives.

"Good that he's making a go at it," Linnaeus replied.

"Yes, but such a shame," James said. *"Three evenings a week."*

"Quite a bit of time to put in when you're a pupil barrister," Linnaeus said.

Gen almost sighed with how easily James had gotten Linnaeus to agree with him that Fred was taking too much time off, but she knew better than to be so dang obvious.

Linnaeus Grover said, "Some people just can't handle the demands of a career in the law."

And there it was: the death knell of Fred Norquist's career as a barrister.

Fred wouldn't be getting a tenancy, not with one of the senior barristers holding the opinion that he couldn't handle the demands of a law career. If Fred were lucky, he would get a third starvation-wage pupillage for six more months in another set of chambers where he *might* obtain tenancy.

If he didn't get a third six, well, then he had very few options.

All it had taken to sabotage Fred's chances was the wrong person finding out that he and his wife were in marriage counseling and using that against him.

Law chambers are snake pits, but they are full of lawyers. It was hardly surprising.

Practicing

Gen's black court robes hung in the corner of her tiny office. The hanger was hooked over a nail driven into the wall. Gen reached for them. The polyester fabric was smooth under her fingers as she took the flowing material off the hanger.

The robes were usually called a bar gown. If she were going to court, she would flip it around her shoulders so that the fabric draped around her like a loose jacket or a graduation gown, open in the front, and it hung precisely to her knees.

It had cost Gen over four thousand pounds for the set: the robes, a white powdered wig like she was living during the Revolutionary War, three shirts and collars, and six sets of the long, white tabs that hung down like a bow. Everything was second-hand. New robes and stuff would have cost half again as much, maybe twice.

But now, Gen twisted the robes into a thick bundle like a heavy arm, and she laid it over her shoulders.

It was just weight, not too heavy. It didn't mean anything.

She looped the fabric behind her from her shoulder to her waist and pulled it against her back.

It still meant nothing. It was just weight.

She held it there until she started breathing normally, and finally, she did.

She kept doing that, wrapping it around her, pulling it snug against her and letting it brush her clothes and her skin, until her smile didn't waver anymore, even if her hands still shook a little.

PICK ME UP

AT five o'clock, sharp, Gen was powering down her computer on her tiny pupil desk when Miriam, her clerk, called her on the office phone.

"Ms. Ward, you have a visitor." Miriam's voice was even and decorous, just like usual. Obviously, His Lordship Arthur Finch-Hatten, the Earl of Severn, hadn't come in person to collect Gen.

Gen told her, "I'll be right there."

She tossed her necessities in her bag, grabbed her coat, and locked her office, twisting her new key in the shiny new set of locks that a man had come to install just that afternoon.

Octavia Hawkes called through her open office door, "Good luck tonight!"

Gen quailed and considered taking the back staircase so she could escape from the building, but she waved to Octavia as she left and walked through the corridors to the office waiting room.

There, Miriam stood, waiting with another woman.

The other woman's dark pantsuit contrasted her short, gray hair. She smiled and extended her hand. Delicate veins ran along the back. "Good evening, Ms. Ward. I'm Pippa Coke, Lord Severn's driver."

"Yes, ma'am." Gen shook her hand. The woman had a gentle handshake. "I remember you from last night."

"Thank you, ma'am, and you needn't call me 'ma'am.' Please call me Pippa."

She smiled. "Thank you. Call me Gen?"

Pippa smiled and walked with her through the building and down the stairs to where the car was waiting.

And what a car it was.

Okay, so last night, Gen had been too wasted to notice that Lord Severn, *Arthur,* had poured her into a *Bentley,* and a midnight-blue, four-door Bentley at that. The back just had the discreet trunk ornament—a capital B with wings—and didn't say the model, but Gen had been hanging around very rich barristers for almost a year. She knew a Continental Flying Spur when she saw it because it was one of very few models of Bentley she had not seen up close.

None of the very wealthy senior barristers in her tony, highly successful law office could afford a Continental Flying Spur.

Bentleys are very British cars, refined, seeming to shout *I've made it!* to the world in the politest way possible.

When the driver opened the rear-seat door, Gen glanced at her, unsure if the woman was holding the door for her. Pippa's slight nod gave her permission.

All right, then.

Inside, the Bentley's beige leather was velvety, and pale wood trimmed out the doors and dash up front.

The door latched shut beside Gen, and the city noise that she hadn't even noticed out there *stopped.* The silence was so sudden that she felt like her ears were stopped up. She sniffed and breathed through her ears for a moment to try to clear them, but the car still insulated her from all sound.

Pippa opened the driver's door.

London groaned and growled and whined like fighting ferrets.

When Pippa shut her door, it all stopped again.

Wow.

Pippa turned over the engine, and a slight hum fluttered under Gen's feet through the deep, plush carpeting.

This thing sounded like it was even the twelve-cylinder

model—the expensive upgraded engine for the truly wealthy—and it probably sounded like a snarling bear to anyone outside.

Damn.

Pippa informed Gen, "Lord Severn has arranged for you to meet his tailor at Selfridges. He wanted me to convey his apologies for not meeting you himself, but time is of the essence today."

"Thank you?" Gen said, still unsure.

"Of course." Pippa pulled into traffic with the easy confidence of someone driving a car that could accelerate like a roller coaster if she needed it to, and she drove them through the skyscrapers and building-lined streets of central London.

When Pippa pulled the car up to the side entrance of the city-block-sized department store that is Selfridges, a lanky man in a slim suit was waiting at the curb and opened Gen's door. Traffic noise swarmed into the car. Hundreds of Ionic columns lined the five-story building that towered above her.

"Come!" the man holding the door ordered. "Out now, Ms. Ward!"

Pippa twisted around and told her, "That's Graham. I'll pick you up here when he calls."

"All right." Gen scooted out of the car and trotted after the man into the store and followed him up the escalator.

Way up the escalator.

Gen had never been that far *up* in the rarefied air at Selfridges before. She had always shopped on the lower, less expensive floors, and the escalator hummed under her feet as they rose through the floors into the ever-more-expensive areas.

The tailor whisked Gen through the designers' areas and into a dressing room, tossing gown after gown over the changing room door at her.

Blue satin wrapped around her head, and she struggled to free herself, ripping out strands of her hair that caught in the tiny beads. A lot of the dresses had beads.

With absolutely no input from Gen, Graham decided that a scarlet silk sheath, beaded with thousands of silvery grains, best highlighted her coloring and flattered her figure, such as it was. His long examination down his nose told Gen exactly what he thought of her figure.

He also grabbed some sort of cast-iron underwear that he stuffed her into with a clinical, disinterested demeanor before he wound a dressmaker's tape around her body like he was trussing her up to bake for Thanksgiving. The way that he handled her body felt mechanical, like he was pounding a dent out of her chassis and fine-tuning her engine's timing before a parade.

Gen kept her panic about being manhandled under control during Graham's disinterested, perfunctory procedure. He didn't even look at her most of the time, either examining the overall effect he saw in the mirror or staring at the dressmaker's tape and entering the numbers into his phone.

At the register, Gen reached her shaking hand into her purse for her wallet, not knowing how she was going to be able to afford to pay the bill for all those zeroes on the price tag.

Graham the tailor waved her off and told the clerk to put everything on his tab, including a small box of chocolates that he tucked in a bag for her. He winked and told her, "Lord Severn wants you to have a lovely time tonight."

Well, that seemed nice of him.

Less than an hour after she left work, Gen was hustled back to the curb and the waiting car. Pippa drove her home to freshen up while Gen tried to figure out what had just happened.

Half an hour after that, Graham dropped off the dress that he had altered to just skim her curves that were uplifted and tucked and smoothed by the corset.

An hour after that, Gen locked her front door as the

Bentley pulled up yet again. The insanely expensive car looked monstrous in this working class neighborhood, a noble lord striding among the peasants' hovels. The sedan looked larger than some of the row houses that closely lined the streets, and the paint shone darkly in the moonlight that showered the roofs and fences. Light from the corner street lamp splashed a cold glare over the car's rectangular grille.

Gen's brand-new high-heels wobbled on the rough cement as she walked the few steps to the sidewalk, and she clutched the dress's heavy fabric to hold the hem above her ankles. A small, matching purse dangled from her wrist, another surprise from Graham when he had delivered the altered dress.

She didn't feel like a princess.

More like a vandalized statue.

Yet she needed to blend in at the party to keep an eye on Lord Severn, *Arthur,* so she bobbled on her high heels to the waiting car. She had worn her work coat over it, a modest but tailored beige trenchcoat, which kept her warm in the near-freezing night. The weather had turned colder that day.

This time, when Gen slid into the back seat while Pippa held the door, Lord Severn, *Arthur,* was waiting for her. She said, "Oh. Hi?"

He said, "Good evening," and looked away, out the side window at the lit windows of the other houses across the narrow street.

Tonight, Lord Severn, *Arthur,* was wearing a suit-type tuxedo with a dark gray tie. Just as the dome light inside the car dimmed, Gen saw that the monochrome black and silver contrasted his eyes, and they looked pale baby blue.

He had thick, black eyelashes, too, the bastard. He really had won the genetic lottery: looks, a noble title, and untold wealth.

The man even *smelled* good. A trace of his cologne wafted through the car: spices and faint wood smoke.

Pippa slid into the driver's seat and pulled the car away from the curb, driving through the affordable section of Islington. Gen hoped they wouldn't get mugged in such an ostentatious car.

She started, "Um, thank you for the dress, and the shoes, and the purse, and everything." She couldn't quite bring herself to look at him anymore. Her brain might turn to goo from his gorgeousness, and he had spent thousands of pounds on the clothes she was wearing that evening. It was embarrassing. "I can pay you back."

"It's fine," he said, still looking away.

"No, I *will* pay you back. I didn't want to make a scene with Graham, but I don't want you to pay for all this."

He flipped his fingers, dismissing her thanks and her offer. "It's quite all right. You would have been within your rights to bill me for them, so I'm merely avoiding the hassle and billing fees."

She sucked in a shocked breath. *"I wouldn't."*

He turned slightly to look at her from the sides of his eyes. A streetlamp passing over the car flashed pale light over his face, illuminating his cheekbones and hard jaw. "You're a barrister. Of course, you would have."

"Just because I'm a barrister doesn't mean that I don't have scruples!"

"There are many professions where ethics matter less than results. The law is surely one of them."

"Look, I know how a lot of lawyers operate. My boss, Octavia Hawkes, quotes Machiavelli so much that I think she's going to launch a coup. I'm not like that. I won't compromise what's right."

When he laughed, he leaned back against the car seat. "Practicing for your QC application already, are you?"

"I'm *not.* I *believe* that."

"Perhaps, but you won't for long. And if you didn't bill me for the dress and your time tonight, Octavia Hawkes would."

"I wouldn't let her. I'd strike it out," Gen insisted.

"We've already taken care of the dress. Bill me for the hours yourself so that you won't get on the wrong side of your boss. I understand. I expect it."

"I can't believe that you think I would do such a thing!"

"I've dealt with many lawyers in my life. *Many.* You should do it."

"You don't know *me* well at all."

"I'm pretty good at reading people."

"You didn't 'read' me very well yesterday morning. Or maybe that was just your arrogance, thinking that all women want to fall on their backs and hand you their panties."

This time, he turned and looked straight at her. The inside of the car brightened as they sped through Knightsbridge, one of the poshest parts of London near Kensington Palace. Light shone out of the glass buildings and huge windows of the expensive apartment buildings, illuminating the street. He said, "I did misread you that afternoon, but I don't think that about women."

"Like Hell, you don't. I know guys like you, arrogant and full of yourselves. Let me tell you one thing, buster: I'm not like that. So you can just stop thinking that you can charm my panties off and stop being mad because you can't. I'm here because *you* can't keep *your* panties on. If you acted like a damn adult, we wouldn't be in this situation. Now you cowboy up and quit sulking."

Lord Severn, *Arthur,* had listened in smoldering, angry silence, and his eyes narrowed. "You don't know a damn thing about me." The car slid to a stop, and he was out of his door before she could say boo. The door slammed, and air puffed through the car.

Arrogant son of a— She turned to get out of the car and wrestled the beaded dress, which was too tight around the thighs when she was sitting to move comfortably, even though it looked perfect when she was standing. She reached for the door handle and just got a fingernail on it before it was yanked out of her grasp.

The car door opened. Whooshes and crunches of city noise rushed into the car with the cold night air.

Lord Severn, *Arthur,* was standing on the sidewalk, holding the door. A smile curved his lush lips and danced in his silvery eyes.

He asked, "Shall we, darling?"

First Party

OUTSIDE Gen's car door, Lord Severn, *Arthur,* stood, slightly bent, with his hand extended to help her out of the car. Behind him, people crossed the sidewalk, most wearing business suits or work clothes under their winter coats, hurrying home late.

Gen touched Lord Severn's, *Arthur's,* large, warm hand to steady herself as she got out of the car, and he grasped her fingers as she stumbled when her heel caught in the hem of her dress *once again.*

Damn it. Someone should prevent her from wearing high heels. She was too tall for them. With these silly shoes on, she was over six feet tall.

Gen stood in front of Lord Severn, *Arthur,* on the sidewalk in front of the tall building, so near to him that warmth rolled out of his suit jacket and brushed the bare skin of her neck. She could have turned her head and kissed the soft spot on the underside of his chin. He was even taller than Gen was.

She stepped back and dropped his hand. Her fingers felt cold.

"Come now," he said. "It's time to go."

Gen turned to take a gander at where they had ended up. She had been so distracted by arguing that she hadn't been watching where they had been driving.

Downtown London rose all around them, the buildings taller and finer than where Gen lived in the Islington area. She knew this street. They were near the British Museum, the Regent's Park, and not too far from Hyde Park in Soho. This part of town hosted the posh hotels for London's rich visitors—foreign royalty, movie stars, and people with more money than sense.

The hotel that towered above them, the Langham Hotel, had been the first grand hotel in Europe. Gen's mother had told her its story several times, beaming with British pride about it. When they had moved back to London, her mother had taken seventeen-year-old Gen around town to all the places where the rich people lived. Gen's mother had been a solid middle-class Brit before she married Gen's father, an exotic Texan from a far-off land, but she'd had a charity scholarship in a private boarding school where uppity people sent their spoiled children to be educated.

The Langham Hotel had always been one of their stops when they walked around London. Honey-colored blocks and creamy bricks rose many stories into the air. Every window—and there were many of them on the long and wide building—was arched as if it were a church. It was a kind of church, although it was devoted to the worship of money and prestige.

Lord Severn jutted his elbow at her again, offering her his arm rather than taking her hand.

She had been fine with holding onto him last night when he had helped her down the stairs. She should be fine with it this time.

Do it, dammit.

Gen looked up at the Langham Hotel and curled her fingers under his arm. She hoped that she sounded flippant when she said, "Are you taking me to a hotel for a reason?"

His warm smile was entirely at odds with his anger in the car. "The party tonight is in the grand ballroom and the courtyard garden."

"Someone's birthday?" she asked.

"It's a benefit supper and dance for a charity."

"Probably something I've never heard of, some sort of

esoteric, upper-crust dance company or classical music orchestra."

"The Rainforest Alliance is an established charity that preserves wildlife and their habitats all over the world."

Okay, so she might have heard of it. "Do you do these charity events often, or is this a new attempt to repair your reputation? I'm happy either way."

"Often," he said. "Several times a week, I eat rubbery chicken, mingle with snobby people, and throw money at good causes as fast as I can so that I may leave and do something fun."

Ah. Gen had seen the pictures of his idea of "fun" in the tabloids.

She climbed the white, stone steps holding his arm, but they separated to push through the revolving door. He waited for her on the other side with his proffered arm.

Inside the hotel, the decor was refined, understated, and British. Most of the room was monochromatic like a silver nitrate black-and-white photograph from some earlier age when everyone had exquisite taste.

White-painted wood moulding trimmed the walls and was wedged into every available seam and corner of the walls that stretched several stories into the air. However, instead of traditional wooden trim around the doors, black-veined, white marble slabs had been cut into the shape of moulding to embellish the openings.

Towering columns crowding the huge room were carved from this zebra-striped stone. Meeting rooms and restaurants that adjoined the lobby were closed off by black wrought-iron doors backed with glass, airy and yet imposing at the same time. The chandeliers at the ceiling glowed like suns and dripped crystal that had subtle touches of burnished golden drops.

The whole place felt like only old money was welcome.

The only splashes of color in the hotel lobby were the enormous bouquets of fuchsia and white flowers in a few niches. Their flowery scent flowed across the floor, tickling Gen's nose. Even nature was restrained from its usual, riotous expression.

Gen stopped, flummoxed as to where she should go.

Lord Severn laid his hand over her fingers that were still trapped in his elbow and gently pulled her forward.

They walked through the lobby and back to an enormous ballroom staged with white-covered tables. The three-story marble columns were alabaster and topped with pale gold finials, different than the ones in the lobby. The crowd milled around the tables, whirling and splashing among the furniture and through the doors like waves washing up around rocks.

As soon as they entered the doors, Lord Severn raised his hand in greeting and called out, "Hello, Bertrand! So nice to see you again."

The man who must be Bertrand turned around—a willowy man in his sixties—and saw them. A grin widened on his wizened face and he walked over with his hand extended to shake. "Severn! I thought you weren't going to make it!"

Wow, people did use *Severn* like it was Arthur's name.

Probably stuck-up people, but whatever.

As he approached, Bertrand's eyes strayed to Gen, and he glanced down to her toes and up to her eyes. His gaze lingered where her hand was tucked into Arthur's elbow.

Bertrand's gaze snapped up to Lord Severn's, *Arthur's,* face, and his grin widened further. "You old rascal. And who do we have here?"

Lord Severn shook Bertrand's hand and then patted Gen's fingers in the crook of his arm. "This is Genevieve, a *close* friend." His arm loosened and allowed her fingers to slip free so she could shake Bertrand's offered hand.

Bertrand's smile seemed awfully sly. "It's a *pleasure* to *finally* meet a close friend of Arthur's. Most of his *friends* don't make it past the two-week mark."

"Pleasure to meet you, too," Gen said, wary of what the hell he had meant. She was supposed to be posing as his girlfriend, but there seemed to be all kinds of subtext there. Was Lord Severn, *Arthur,* discreetly signaling to them that she was a prostitute or something?

They mingled some more. People seemed genuinely happy to see Lord Severn, not sniffy or anything. He must have a better reputation among the noble class than he did in the tabloids.

The third couple to whom he introduced her were Edward and Anne de Vere, the Earl and Countess of Oxford. Gen shook the Countess's hand and said, "Very well tonight, ma'am. How do you do?"

Lord Severn, *Arthur,* slipped his arm around Gen's back and rested his palm on her waist.

The warmth of his strong hand leeched through the thin silk of her dress, and his arm was firm across her back.

Gen's bones froze and locked.

The smallest part of her, a part that almost felt foreign or long-forgotten, wanted to lean against his side and seek more of his warmth and firm flesh.

But far more of Gen's body—her blood and bones—froze with fear.

The Countess was watching Gen's face with worried eyes.

Through an act of will, Gen forced her fingers to break the fearful frost and open, letting the Countess's hand drop.

The lady's slim eyebrows rose, and she glanced down at her shorter husband, a moment of connection to ask his opinion, but he hadn't seen and stared back, unblinking.

The Countess of Oxford asked Gen, "Are you quite all right, dear?"

"Yes," Gen ground out. Her voice shook, and she staggered a step away from Lord Severn.

He dropped his arm and continued as if nothing were wrong. "Lord Oxford is an award-winning author. Sadly, fiction writing is beneath his station, so he must keep it a closely held secret, which means absolutely everyone knows."

The Earl of Oxford beamed up at Lord Severn. "My scribblings are for my own amusement and my friends' mockery."

Lord Severn told Gen, "He is short-listed for every major prize in Europe this year, from the Booker to the Nobel."

Lord Oxford laughed and turned away. "Oh, you cad."

Lord Severn chuckled, and the diversion had given Gen enough time to breathe and laugh a little, too.

Damn it. She had practiced what to do if Lord Severn, *Arthur,* put his arm around her waist or shoulders by winding those court robes around herself, feeling what it would be like for him to reach around her and touch her so she would get used to it, but she had freaked out anyway.

Damn it.

She reached over and touched his hand, trying to apologize for looking like an idiot in front of his friends.

His fingers barely touched hers before he lifted his hand to gesture at someone standing over by the open doors that led to the garden. "Oh, Gen. There's someone else whom I want you to meet. So nice seeing you, Edward, Anne. Come with me, Gen."

Gen stumbled after him, still shaking.

He led her over to another couple standing just outside the doors. The cool night air blew in the doors as they walked out into the cobblestoned garden. Outside, instead of supper tables, a bar was set up near a dance floor. A string quartet played something soft and classical that Gen didn't recognize. For her, the music from the two violins, the slightly larger violin, and the cello blended.

She said to him, "I'm sorry. I didn't mean to—"

Lord Severn said over her, "Nigel and Daria, may I introduce Genevieve Ward, a pupil barrister at Serle's Court Barristers, and my close friend."

A middle-aged couple stood there, their heads canted

toward each other. Both of them smiled slightly crooked, British smiles.

The lady's smile seemed amused because her eyebrows were slightly raised as she regarded Gen.

The gentleman inclined his head. "A *close friend* of Arthur's? Exceptional. How do you do?"

"Oh, I'm fine," Gen piped up. "I got a little flustered just now, but I'm fine."

Neither one of them changed their somewhat kind and slightly interested expressions.

Arthur cleared his throat. "Gen, may I present Lord Nigel Appleby and Lady Daria Appleby, the Earl and Countess of Rosslyn."

Gen brushed her palm over her hip to dry it and held out her hand. "Pleased to meetcha. This is quite a get-up, huh?"

Uh-oh. She'd gotten all rattled and reverted to speaking Texan. Well, shucks. It probably didn't matter.

Lord Rosslyn said, "Yes, it certainly is an event."

"It's the first time I've been to a benefit for the Rainforest Alliance," Gen said. "It's really nice."

"That's a refreshing attitude," Lady Rosslyn said. "These things can be dull."

Lord Severn touched her elbow. "Gen, shall we get a drink? The bar is just over this way."

"If you've been to a lot of benefit suppers," Gen said to Lady Daria, "I suppose they might get old after a while. The hotel is really beautiful, right? All that marble, and those lovely chandeliers. I just can't get over them."

Lady Rosslyn said, "I thought them a bit overdone."

Nigel inclined his head, and his bloodless lips thinned. "And who is your pupil master at Serle's Court?"

"Octavia Hawkes," Gen said. "I like her."

"Hawkes is my barrister for the wealth management firm that I founded," Lady Rosslyn said. "Do you work closely with her?"

"Oh, yes," Gen said, nodding. Her hair, twisted up the

back of her head, flopped in its pins. "We work on a lot of cases together."

Lady Rosslyn smiled. "Oh, splendid."

Lord Severn, *Arthur,* held her elbow this time. "Gen, let's go get a drink. Nigel, Daria, pleased to see you again. Do drop by for a visit at Spencer House sometime. I'm there for weeks at a time, now. It was open for public tours during Christmas, so I stayed away."

"Oh, that's unfortunate. The National Trust demands so much for their pittance, even our homes at Christmas," Lord Rosslyn said.

"Yes, I'll only go out there for a few weekdays once visiting season begins in June."

"Oh, quite," Lord Rosslyn said. "Our country house is open to the public on weekends, too. It's such a good idea to move into town for the summer."

"I'm planning a few suppers for the spring, between visiting seasons. I'd be honored if you attended."

"We'd be pleased to come."

Lord Severn, *Arthur,* led Gen away.

At the bar, he asked what she wanted, which was "White wine?" He ordered a chardonnay for her.

"I don't know what I'm doing here," Gen told him. "I'm out of my league. I'm floundering. Lord Severn, you should take me home."

"Call me Arthur. Someone may overhear you."

He handed her the wine glass, a real glass glass, not a plastic fake-cup. *Dang,* they did everything upscale at these things.

He said, "Just breathe."

"That's the problem. When I breathe, I get enough air to say something stupid."

Lord Severn, *Arthur,* chuckled. "I'll smooth it over with them."

"But they're *clients.* Octavia specifically warned me not to say anything stupid around *clients!*"

He shrugged. "They were friends of my parents. That's what the Spencer House invitation was about, reminding them of our connections."

"I can't have you doing that, Lord Severn," she said, shaking her head.

"Arthur. Now we're going to practice. Call me Arthur."

"It seems wrong."

His voice dropped to a deeper, darker tone. "Say my name, Arthur."

Gen stared at her glass. "Arthur."

"Again."

"Arthur."

"Say something else, and call me Arthur."

"Arthur, I can't let you put yourself out for me, *Arthur."*

"Good girl." His voice rose half an octave to what was still a deep voice for a man, but closer to his normal tone. "These little favors that we pay each other, these little social gives and takes, this is the way the world works." Arthur received his drink from the bartender, something clear in a highball glass, and he clinked his glass against hers. *"Salut."*

"My boss would like that. She's got Machiavelli quotes framed in her office. It's creepy. 'The arms of others either fall from your back, or they weigh you down, or they bind you fast.' That one is her screensaver on her laptop."

He shrugged. "Machiavelli wrote *The Prince* as satire. Everything else he wrote was in favor of a free republic."

"Do you think so? That was the prevailing argument during the Enlightenment, but Octavia quotes it like Gospel."

He smirked. "Power-hungry dictators rarely see the humor in anything, let alone a work aimed directly at them."

She laughed. "You say that like you know it's a fact."

"I'm a hereditary aristocrat and courtier who attended a boarding school for the children of oligarchs and deposed royalty. Some of my closest friends are power-hungry dictators."

"Arthur, you slay me. I never know when you're kidding."

He laughed. "Perhaps I'm never kidding."

"I can't believe that."

He glanced over her shoulder and into the crowd. The smile fell off his face. "My brother is here."

Gen cracked up. "See? You're hysterical. You're kidding me right now."

His jaw bulged where he clenched it. "He's just seen us and is coming over. Don't say anything because he'll seize any opportunity to his advantage." He raised his hand and grinned. "Christopher! Such a surprise to see you."

The man who walked over to the bar was nearly as tall as Arthur was, but he had faded auburn hair and sharper features. He was still handsome as all heck, but he was a paler, slighter version of his brother. "Hello, Arthur. Fancy meeting you here."

So this was Christopher Finch-Hatten, the plaintiff—the British say *claimant*—the guy who was suing the wayward Earl for his inheritance.

He didn't look all that much like Arthur.

His eyes, though. Gen took a long look at the man's eyes. Christopher had the same pale, silvery eyes as Arthur did. Perhaps they were a little less steel-blue than Arthur's were, a little more dreary-day gray, but he had the same dark lashes and slightly almond shape that looked so sexy on Arthur.

Gen had to stop thinking things like that about her client.

Arthur said to Christopher, "I thought we divvied up the charities better than this."

"Yes, it's a pity that we had to run into each other, but Duchess Maria Shrewsbury is one of my patients." He turned to Gen. "I'm a physician, you know. I've made something of myself and done something with my life, unlike my waste of a brother, here."

Gen fell back on platitudes. "A pleasure to meet you, I'm

sure."

Christopher winked at her. "Yes, I'm sure, too. You seem like a nice girl. Why don't we have a drink rather than you wasting your time with Arthur? He'll break your heart after he's fucked you once or twice."

Sweet baby Jesus, Christopher was talking that way to her when she was supposed to be Arthur's *date.*

Gen looked up at Arthur, expecting him to be livid, but his smile hadn't changed. Arthur did sigh before he asked, "Is your lovely wife here, Christopher?"

Wife?

Oh, hell, no.

Gen lowered her eyebrows at Christopher.

"No, she's not," Christopher said, frowning that Arthur had played dirty at their little game. "Is this woman one of the three tarts in the picture with you last night? Is this the one who provides you with your cocaine?"

Arthur glanced across the garden and raised his glass to someone. "I see Maria over by the shrimp bowls. Has the duchess had melanoma, then, and that's why she retained your services?"

"Privileged," Christopher said, obviously pleased with himself at his privileged, personal information about the duchess, "but she has never been ill a day in her life."

Arthur turned to Gen. "That means the duchess had extensive amounts of cosmetic surgery, not skin cancer."

"Now, now!" Christopher said. "I said nothing of the sort."

"Of course not, Chrissy," Arthur said.Christopher

Christopher's tone grew more serious. "See here, now, Arthur. I've asked you not to call me that."

"I use that name in memory of our mother, who called you that when you were in your infancy," Arthur said, his tone light and amused.

Christopher frowned, his colorless eyes narrowed. "I don't remember that at all."

Arthur glanced at him. "Of course you don't, but I remember them."

This was a family spat, and Gen didn't need to be there. She started to step back, but Arthur grabbed her fingers to keep her there.

Christopher said, "I don't need to remember them. I had a perfectly respectable English home with Aunt Jayne and Uncle Peter here in England. I'm not some Swiss usurper, rolling in and snatching up titles from real Englishmen."

Arthur smiled at Christopher. His tone was convivial, even complimentary. "Yes, you're the one saving England, aren't you?"

"I'm saving one human life at a time," Christopher snarled, his eyes narrowing. "I devote much of my time to charity, taking on *pro bono* cases from poor immigrants from the East End and flying around the world to help people in poverty such—"

"—That you spoiled earls will never know," Arthur finished with him. "Yes, yes. I heard it at your wedding reception and every award ceremony for you that I have ever attended." His jovial tone didn't seem angry at all, more like he was indulging in an often-repeated joke.

Wow. Gen would have decked Christopher for saying something like that to her. Her fist closed like she still might punch him. Second sons of earls shouldn't mess with Texans.

The crowd was flowing past them from the garden back into the ballroom.

Arthur said, "I believe they are seating for supper. Do keep yourself out of trouble, Christopher, and give my love to Jacquetta and the girls, won't you?"

He led Gen off among the tables.

Arthur found their name tags on seats right up near the hostess's table. He greeted Duchess Somerset warmly and kissed both her tucked cheeks. Gen had been hanging around Octavia Hawkes long enough to be able to list the fillers and injectables that the duchess must be utilizing to stay so smoothly ageless, but she seemed like a nice lady.

Their table had a tall placard in the middle of the bouquet that read *Platinum Circle.* When she glanced at the back of the room, Christopher Finch-Hatten was seated near the wall, and his bouquet didn't have a sign on it.

Gen leaned over and whispered to Arthur, "Were you an actor or something?"

He shook his head and raised an eyebrow at her. "Never had a taste for it. Why?"

"I would have punched somebody who said that kind of stuff, family or not. Maybe especially family."

He chuckled. "I considered punching him when he came on to you. Other than that, he says things like that all the time. No use getting one's feathers ruffled over it."

"You certainly have a talent for acting. I would have believed everything you said to him."

Arthur looked off over the crowd in the ballroom. "I wouldn't have."

Supper turned out to be a choice of vegetarian, salmon, pheasant, or prime rib, not rubbery chicken at all. Arthur had the roasted butternut squash salad, she noted, and ate the greens and slices of barbecued vegetarian meat-like substance.

Gen had the prime rib, rare. She didn't get prime rib very often, or ever, actually. The last time she had had prime rib had been at her mother's birthday supper in Texas the year before her father had died.

The meat melted when she cut it with her fork and on her tongue, releasing roasted juices. She chewed every bite slowly, savoring it.

At the supper, Gen asked Arthur about the Rainforest Alliance, and he brightened when he talked about it. His silvery eyes sparkled more as he discussed acreage of Amazonian and other rainforests saved by the charity, just by buying it up rather than fighting with governments.

"You sound really enthused," she told him, "like this is really important to you."

"Me? Heavens, no," he chuckled. "I attend these charity balls and buy overpriced auction lots merely to prove my scant worth as a human being and save my immortal soul."

She laughed. "At least some good comes out of it."

"I prefer to do charitable work with some hands-on time." Arthur leaned his elbow on the table and ducked his head as he whispered, "Did I ever tell you about the time that I was a kitten socializer at a humane society?"

Gen couldn't imagine Lord Severn, the notorious slacker, voluntarily playing with kittens. "Were you really?"

He pulled his phone out of his pocket. "I think some friends may have taken some pictures."

There was even a video—played silently because they were in the center of a packed charity supper—where Arthur was laughing his head off while tiny balls of fluff climbed up his shirt and perched on his shoulder. A black puff of silk fuzz rubbed its wee face on his ear and cheek while he shook with giggles.

Gen asked him, "So how many women fall for this B.S. and sleep with you?"

"A surprising number, considering how easy this was," Arthur replied, one eyebrow dipping as if he were mystified. He confided to her, "I should do one with puppies."

She laughed, and they joked for the rest of the supper.

One of the stories he told ended with, "And there I was, trussed up like a mummy, hanging upside-down from a bridge in Budapest. I must have looked like a bat because villagers, actual villagers, were coming across the bridge, pointing and shouting, 'Vampyre!' They spelled it with a 'y.' You could hear the 'y' by the way they said it."

His stories all ended with him nearly murdered due to a misunderstanding or naked in public.

She cracked up at every single one of them.

Arthur could be absolutely charming when he wasn't

accusing her of inflating billable hours or educating her on the legal system of Britain.

He laughed at a stupid thing that she said about legal maneuvering, his silvery eyes flashing as he rocked back in his chair.

Yes, he could be absolutely charming.

She had the sugared strawberries for dessert, slicing the dark, sweet fruit into quarters and practically purring with happiness as she ate them. Gen liked chocolate, sure, but sweet, ripe strawberries were the food of the gods.

Arthur watched her as she ate them. "You like the strawberries?"

"Oh, my God, yes," she groaned, sucking another scarlet berry into her mouth and letting the juice wash over her tongue.

Arthur nodded and went back to his dish of melons and cheese.

The supper dishes were cleared away, and the string quartet out in the garden area struck up a waltz. Some of the pretty couples got up to dance, the women wearing vibrant dresses that must be couture and the men in tailored, dark tuxedos. Within seconds, they were whirling and waltzing over the dance floor.

She watched the gem-toned gowns and sharp suits move, trying not to look wistful.

Beside her, Arthur stood and opened his hand to her. "Shall we?"

Gen blinked. "Shall we what?"

He asked, "There's dancing. Would you care to dance?"

Outside, the upper-class lords and ladies spun and stepped neatly around the small courtyard. "I don't know how to dance like that."

"Come on. I'll lead." Arthur picked up her hand from the table, holding her fingertips gently in his, and tugged her a little. He grinned.

Arthur had such a devilish, carefree smile and they had

been having so much fun talking that Gen found herself smiling back at him and standing, even though she had no idea how to dance like those guys.

He led her through the crowd, their fingertips still touching.

Oh, no.

No-no-no-no-no.

Gen knew how people waltzed. She'd seen it a billion times on TV and in movies.

And yet it was only just then—as her high-heeled pumps wobbled over the rough cobblestones and they were nearly at the smooth surface of the dance floor surrounded by flame-topped heaters—that she realized, if she waltzed with him, he was going to have his arms and hands all over her, and she would be shoved up against him.

Nuh-uh. She was out.

Gen turned back toward the blazing lights of the hotel ballroom and whipped her hand away from his.

"Gen!" Arthur called.

Nope. Not going to happen.

Gen trotted away, weaving through the thick crowd that was streaming toward the music wafting through the air and the night sky. Fairy lights were strung over the garden, though larger lights illuminated the space and cast sharp shadows on the block wall surrounding them.

"Gen!" Footsteps clattered behind her, and Arthur dodged in front of her. "Wait."

"I'm just not comfortable with it."

"I know," he said gently.

"And I certainly don't want to talk about it."

"I wouldn't ask. I also won't grab you or grope you. It'll be just a nice, calm dance."

Over by the bar, Arthur's brother Christopher was watching them, his pale eyes almost white in the distance.

She couldn't make a scene. Christopher would use it somehow, if only to needle Arthur.

She said, "It'll be weird."

"It won't." Arthur was standing closer to her now, and he touched her fingertips again. "It'll be quick. If we're seen dancing a bit, we can make our farewells and leave."

Gen dithered. Leaving the party sounded *great*. "What are you planning to do afterward? Have some *fun?*"

Yes, her tone was sarcastic.

"No. I'm going home for the night." He raised his hands and wagged his head, grinning. "It's after midnight. I had a full day of picking out a suit to wear. I'll drop you off at your place and head back to my apartment."

"Promise?" she asked him, her hands on her hips.

He raised a hand. "On my honor."

Gen totally did not know how to interpret that one. Instead of confronting him, she admitted, "I'm a little shpilkes about dancing."

"I understand."

"I don't think you do."

"I think I do understand," he said. In the twinkling glow from the fairy lights, his eyes looked pale baby blue. "I dated a Catholic girl once," he said. "She went to a Catholic boarding school in France instead of the Swiss one that I attended. When we danced, she said that we should 'leave room for the Holy Ghost between us.' I thought it an amusing statement."

"Okay," Gen said.

"And I assure you, I would never clutch a woman or fling her around. At that Swiss school, they did teach us to dance *gently.*"

Arthur was really serious about this dancing thing. *Really* serious. He had promised to go home soon afterward, so if she did this, maybe she wouldn't have to worry about him for the rest of the night.

And she was in desperate need of some shut-eye. Drinking with Lee and Rose last night had been rough. That very morning had been rougher. *Far rougher.* She hadn't been hung over like *that* since university.

She could go home and *sleep.*

Gen said, "Okay."

Arthur smiled and turned back to the dance floor. Gen followed.

From across the garden, Christopher watched them walking back toward the dance floor. His colorless eyes didn't leave them the whole time. Gen finally looked away to follow Arthur through the crowd.

Arthur stood near the fringe of the dance floor, away from the crush near the center.

Gen stepped up close enough and looked up at his eyes.

He held up one hand. "Take my hand."

She lifted her right hand and gingerly set her palm in his. The flesh on her arm shivered.

He pointed to his other shoulder. "And here."

She rested her left hand on his shoulder.

He took his hand off her waist for a moment and adjusted the placement of her hand on his shoulder, which seemed odd but not threatening in any way.

"All right," he said. "Shall we?"

They were so far apart that her arm was nearly straight, and Gen was a tall girl.

He had indeed left room for the Holy Ghost.

And maybe a small elephant.

Arthur raised his other hand. "Ready?"

He was going to touch her body, her torso, practically her skin under the red silk and beads.

Get it over with.

Gen nodded.

Arthur slowly brought his hand around and rested his palm and fingers on her waist. His touch was so light that it hardly moved the silk of her dress, but the warmth from his hand filtered through the thin cloth to her skin.

He asked, "All right?"

She nodded because her throat was so tight that she

couldn't speak.

"One, two-three," Arthur said, and he guided her hand as he moved into the waltz.

Gen had not been demurring when she had claimed not to know how to waltz. She really didn't, but Arthur kept their steps small so when she bobbled, she wasn't far off track. Within a few moments, she glided more easily with him, which meant that the possibility of colliding with his strong chest and ending up with his arms caging her was fading away.

A few moments after that, she relaxed a little more.

"Good?" he asked.

"Yes, better," she said.

"Good." He looked over her head. "Bentley?"

Gen wondered if there were a car back there.

Behind her, a man's voice asked, "May I cut in?"

Arthur looked back to Gen, his blue eyes serious. "They're friends of my parents. They just want a moment of our time. Are you all right with this?"

Arthur stepped to the side so she could see the couple he meant.

The man was quite a bit older than she was, maybe around sixty. The gentleman had black hair salted with gray and dark eyes, nice-looking and trim.

The woman had silver and gold hair drawn up in a complicated knot on the back of her head and a polite smile. She was probably a few years younger than her husband, perhaps mid-forties, but the filler in her cheeks and her oddly smooth forehead made her look just around forty. In her form-fitting dress, she looked like she might be a runner.

Arthur assured Gen, "It's just for a moment."

Her mouth went dry, but she managed to stammer, "All right."

Arthur's hand left her waist. Using their joined hands, he spun Gen in a little circle and handed her off to the man,

Bentley, who took her hand very gently in his and barely touched her waist.

Maybe it was because Bentley was so much older than she was, over twice her age, or maybe it was because he was about the same height she was, or maybe it was the way he stood far back from her, almost as far as his arms could have reached, but after a few moments of figuring out where to put her feet, Gen relaxed.

Bentley smiled at her. Their eyes were just about level. He said, "So you're the 'close friend' of Arthur's whom we've been hearing about tonight. So pleased to finally make your acquaintance."

"Um, thanks. So you knew Arthur's parents?"

"Yes, they were friends of ours for years. So you're an American?"

"I'm a British citizen, but I grew up in the States."

"Lovely. Such an interesting accent."

He sounded as if he might mean that. "Um, thanks?"

"I've always liked a Western US accent. So firm. Ah, here come my better half and Arthur. Lovely to meet you, Gen. Hope you're having a good evening."

"Thank you? Nice to meet you, too?" Gen fretted that she had been stupid.

Bentley's hand left her waist, and he guided her back toward Arthur, who switched Bentley's wife back to him.

Arthur said, "Lovely to see you, too, Elizabeth. Yes, I'll ring tomorrow."

Gen moved back into Arthur's arms, and again, he barely rested his hand against her side and held her other hand.

She said, "That was weird."

"Oh, no. It's done all the time. Very nice that you got to meet Bentley. He's grand."

"Sure. Why is it important that I meet your parents' friends?"

Arthur ducked his head and whispered near her ear. His breath floated over her neck, warm from his lips just an inch from her skin. "If you're to pose as my girlfriend, it makes sense that I would introduce you around."

"Haven't you had girlfriends before?"

"I've always been casual in my relationships. None of them lasted more than a month. It's more fun for everyone that way."

"Hit and run, huh?" she quipped.

He laughed. "So to speak."

The dance finished, and Arthur led her off the dance floor. Her whole body sagged with relief when he dropped his hand off her waist.

Arthur glanced back, maybe feeling her deep sigh, but he didn't say anything.

At the bar, he ordered her another chardonnay in a real glass-glass and another vodka tonic for himself. They talked for just a little while longer, until Gen said, "So, we were going to call it a night?"

Arthur looked over her head. "Yes. I think we should." He broke a path through the crowd for her, nodding and saying goodbyes to the people he had introduced her to, and they made for the door.

Gen had drunk several glasses of water with dinner and a few glasses of wine on top of those. "I'm going to stop at the little girls' room on the way out."

"Of course." Arthur discreetly waggled his finger toward a set of doors over on the side. "I'll be at the bar."

"Because of course, you will."

"Because of course, I will," he agreed with her, laughing.

Gen made for the doors, used the facilities, and was washing her hands when Elizabeth, the woman who had cut in while she and Arthur were dancing, came into the ladies' room. "Oh, hi!"

The woman stood at the next sink over and unnecessarily smoothed her perfect gold and silver hair back into her French twist. Her smile seemed kind and amused. "So, you're involved with our Arthur."

Just a babysitter. Gen said, "A little. Kind of."

"He's quite a lad, our Arthur," Elizabeth said.

In the colloquial sense, that meant that Arthur was quite a player. Yeah, this was not news to Gen. "Sure."

"I wouldn't want to see you get hurt," Elizabeth said.

"I won't, but thanks." Gen knew better than to have any feelings for a guy like Arthur.

"I feel I should warn you off. Dating our Arthur could be dangerous."

She seemed so sincere that Gen felt like she should come clean that she was just keeping Arthur from making a fool out of himself for a month or so until his case settled. "It really is casual. I think we're just having a good time."

"Well, don't let it interfere with anything." Elizabeth touched up her lipstick with more dark rose color.

"Like what?"

"Heavens, I wouldn't know. You never know what that boy is up to." Elizabeth's dark eyes slid sideways, and she looked at Gen through the mirror. Her voice sounded kind when she said, "I wouldn't want a nice girl like you to get hurt."

Gen shrugged. "Okay, thanks. But there's really nothing between us, long-term."

"Glad to hear it, dear. Lovely meeting you." Elizabeth smiled at Gen and walked out.

Wow, if even his parents' old friends were warning her off, Arthur might be even worse than she thought.

Maybe something even worse than her girlfriends, Lee and Rose, had warned her about.

Maybe even worse than the tabloids had reported.

She chuckled at that. It was indeed a good thing that she wasn't really dating Arthur. Losing her heart to such a cad could only lead to heartbreak.

Gen glided out of the bathroom, secure in her knowledge that she was doing the right thing by protecting her heart, and looked for Arthur.

In the thick crowd, black tuxedos eclipsed flares of bright colors as the people shifted and mingled. The chaos of color disoriented Gen for a minute, and she squinted to look over the top of the kaleidoscopic hues to find him.

She finally saw Arthur over by the bar, standing with one elbow resting on the wood and holding a drink in his other hand. His easy posture and gentle smile looked like he was watching something soothing, maybe a sunset, but his brother Christopher was standing right in front of him.

Ruddy anger contorted Christopher's face, and the tendons in his neck stood out like ropes. From across the room, it looked like Christopher was speaking loudly, on the verge of shouting.

People standing around Christopher and Arthur shrank back and looked at each other, trying to figure out how to respond to this very un-British display.

Arthur rattled the ice in his glass, sipped, and then cracked a grin and said something to Christopher with one eyebrow raised.

Christopher shrank as if Arthur had decked him and slunk away into the crowd.

As the crowd began to turn away and fill in the space that had bloomed around the two men, Arthur turned and saw Gen standing by the bathrooms. He raised his glass to signal her and sauntered through the crowd toward her.

Damn. Gen wished she could be that cool in court when things got heated. Arthur was the dang Ice King.

She should ask him how he did that.

Polish Her Up

Gen waited up against the wall, fidgeting with her little purse and trying to straighten her red silk dress weighed down all those sand-sized beads while Arthur made his way across the room to her.

He dodged one last older gentleman, drained the last of what was probably yet another vodka tonic, and set the glass on the tray of a passing waiter in one, smooth move. In that impeccable British accent of his, Arthur asked, "Shall we blow this popsicle stand?"

Gen asked him, "Are you okay?"

"As right as rain." He offered her his elbow. "And as illuminated as a light bulb."

Gen laughed. "It's a good thing you're not driving, then."

"Pippa is quite aware of how indispensable she is. If you give her any more notions of grandeur, she'll insist that I hold the door for her. Now, away to the car."

Arthur walked perfectly steadily, even providing a steady support for Gen when her heel slipped on the steps.

She asked, "How many vodka tonics did you have?"

"Lost count."

"More than five?"

He laughed. "I had more than five *before* supper."

And then several more afterward with her. "That many?"

"Of course."

"No wonder you only ate salad for supper."

"I'm a vegetarian most of the time," he whispered. "Eating low on the food chain-type of thing. I don't advertise it."

"You sure don't *look* it."

"And how would you know how I *look?*"

Oh, God. What had she said? "I totally wouldn't. Never mind that I said that."

"It's forgotten. Or I'm having an alcoholic blackout. I can't tell which. Ask me tomorrow."

"I can't imagine how many calories you drank. I count every calorie I eat, even breath mints."

"I burn it off in other ways." He winked at her and then raised his hands, laughing. "I'm sorry. I forgot our arrangement. I'm not being a cad. Well, I was. But I've stopped."

"My God," Gen said. "You're a drunken, randy English nobleman named *Arthur.*"

"I am not. I am pure as the driven snow on the Alps in Gstaad." The Bentley rolled to a stop at the curb, and Arthur jogged around and held the car door open for her. "Besides, I was named that before my mother knew I was a drunken degenerate."

He shut her door and jogged around the car to get in the other side.

Gen mused aloud, "The only thing worse would have been if you had been named *Austin.*"

Arthur laughed harder. "Oh, but Austin Powers was a spy. I can't imagine having a real job and such. Sometimes, I wish I were a spy like Austin Powers or James Bond, even though being an MI6 intelligence officer is very different in real life than is portrayed by those fictional characters. Fewer car chases and diabolical villains. No secret island strongholds at all. More paperwork. So much more paperwork. More memorizing minutiae of who is at what party thrown by whom to report to one's masters. Mostly dinner parties where diplomats become sloppy after a few drinks and divulge indiscretions, especially around Christmas. Christmas is truly the busy season. But I'm merely an idle nobleman with no redeeming qualities." He smiled. "Certainly not a spy."

She laughed at his slightly drunken ramblings. "Oh, Arthur. You've got redeeming qualities."

"If I had any, Christopher's lawsuit wouldn't have gotten this far."

In the back seat of the dark car, driving through London, she slipped her hand under his arm. "I think you're funny."

"I think you're the only one."

"Elizabeth and Bentley seemed to like you."

He looked at her from the corners of his eyes. "Where did you hear her name?"

"You said it when we changed partners while we were dancing."

"Ah." He leaned back in his seat.

"Is she the 'Elizabeth' whom I was supposed to call if you die? Friends of your parents?"

"Yes. She is Elizabeth, but you can talk to anyone who answers that number."

"They seemed fond of you."

"Did Bentley say something while you were dancing?"

"Not much, but I saw Elizabeth in the ladies' room. She kept calling you '*our* Arthur.' I got the feeling that she likes you, even if she does think you party too much."

Arthur had turned in his seat while she spoke, and he leaned toward her. A streetlight passing over the car shone sallow light into the car, and the irises of his eyes were almost clear except for a dark ring around his wide, dark pupils. "You spoke with Elizabeth?"

"Yes, she thinks you're going to break my heart and leave me shattered. It's a good thing I'm just your barrister, huh?"

Arthur was leaning close to Gen, and he wasn't smiling. His handsome face had fallen into perfectly serious, very sober lines, almost like he had had nothing to drink at all. "Tell me what she said, her actual words."

"She said that dating you could be dangerous and that

she didn't want a nice girl like me to get hurt."

Arthur leaned back, and he was kind of looking down at her sideways. "Those were her words?"

"Yeah. Something like that."

"Well." Arthur poured himself a vodka from the mini-bar in the car. "That's altogether different now, isn't it?"

"I don't know what you mean," Gen said.

"Shall we take you home?" Arthur asked. "Pippa, are we on our way to Islington?"

The woman in the front seat said, "Yes, sir."

"Excellent."

"Home at a somewhat decent hour." Gen took her phone from her purse and checked it. "One A.M., anyway. At least I don't have anything at work until ten. I had a client cancel an appointment."

"Oh?" Arthur asked. "Why is that?"

Gen sighed. "Horace had a very posh client list, and Octavia Hawkes's is, if anything, even more so. Very upper-class. Even in the low-level cases that I've been assigned, no one wants to work with me. I'm too American, too uncouth, and too amateur. Even Horace kept saying that I needed to be more British. I keep trying to work on my accent, but it never comes out right."

Arthur patted her hand that was still tucked in the crook of his arm. She was almost getting used to him touching her like that.

Almost. Her arm still felt like spiders were running up her skin.

Arthur sipped his drink. "I hesitate to mention this, but Horace liked you, and I liked Horace. Some little things that might be beneficial to you in your profession and might help you retain some of those clients can be learned rather easily."

Gen paused. "Like what?"

"Oh, just some mannerisms. Inconsequential things. Subliminal things that will put people at ease."

"So like elocution lessons? I looked into those."

"Your Western American accent is the least of your worries. Some people will find it charming, and it makes you seem industrious and a little dangerous, always good qualities in one's barrister."

"You're going to make me into a lady?"

"Let's say I can make a few introductions, a few recommendations. Polish you up a bit."

"Like what?"

"It hardly bears saying," he said.

"No, seriously. Like what?"

He sighed. "The British are unflaggingly polite and do not enumerate faults nor prescribe actions for people. Perhaps I could nudge you in the right direction or make suggestions."

Another streetlight shone yellow glare through the back windshield, and the light dawned on Gen. "Just like that, right?"

"Yes, just like that."

"You're not going to put a book on my head and have me parade around in front of you, are you?"

"Splendid idea." Even in the dim light from the other cars' headlights and the tall buildings' bright windows, Gen could see Arthur's comic leer.

"Oh, Lord!" She started to pull her hand away from his arm.

Arthur patted her fingers around his biceps and laughed. "My plan was that I should observe you in court or around your offices, perhaps offer some advice. We are supposed to be dating. It would be perfectly natural if I attended some of your court appearances as moral support or took you to lunch. It would ease your job as dogwatcher. It would be a very English courtship, take you to certain events, be seen in the correct places, and make connections with the right people."

She smiled at him. "And you are very English, aren't

you?"

He chuckled. "I am more English than the princes of the realm, who until the current generation were far more Hanoverian Germans than English, at least genetically. Thank heavens for Princess Di and Duchess Kate for infusing some Englishness into our royal family."

"Oh, my. Not that anyone would say such a thing," Gen laughed.

Arthur laughed, too. "My bloodlines include both sides of the War of the Roses, the Scottish kings, and go back to the Anglos and the Saxons. I'm as British as King Arthur of Camelot and as English as the OED."

"King Arthur, huh? Maybe you should be on the throne."

He shuddered extravagantly. "God forbid, and a few centuries ago, that statement would have gotten us both killed. I'm far happier as just a wastrel earl, spending my estate as quickly as possible. I have earned my nickname, the Earl of Givesnofucks. I shan't lose it easily."

"Oh, my word. How am I supposed to defend you if everyone calls you that?"

"It's just a few friends, not the general public. Hopefully, you'll never have to meet them because if you do, it means that something has gone horribly, terribly wrong."

"Are those the two guys that I'm supposed to call if you're in jail? What're their names?"

"Casimir and Maxence, and yes, those two. Max and I had to go intervene with Caz just a few months ago, although we couldn't help the poor bugger."

"Was he in jail?"

"No, but he got a life sentence."

"I don't get it."

"Married. The poor bloke got married."

"Oh, well, you're in no danger of anything awful like that happening to you. You've even got me as a fake girlfriend now to fend off any matrimonial-minded women. Only the one-night ladettes will have any interest in you, now."

He straightened as if a light bulb of wonder had lit over his head. "This deception keeps getting better and better."

"Pleased to be of service, your highness."

"Ah, ah, ah. I'm only an earl, not a member of the royal family. The correct term of address is My Lord, Your Lordship, or Lord Severn. When I'm not about, you call me His Lordship. And we've started polishing you up already."

"This could be less painful than I'd thought."

"I can be positively delightful when I'm of a mind. Shall I observe you in court tomorrow?"

"You might make me nervous if you tell me things while I'm trying to work. I have to really concentrate when I'm in court because of the games that barristers play."

"You mean like working certain words into your arguments?"

So he remembered what she had said during their first meeting. "In this case, I meant the real games, head games, where they try to out-argue you about everything."

"I shall only watch, and then we shall adjourn to a private supper afterward to discuss the notes."

"That sounds okay." It sounded pretty nice.

"Splendid, and here we are at your house." The car rolled to a gentle stop in front of Gen's mother's house. Arthur held out his hand to shake. "Thank you for a lovely evening, Genevieve. I shall see you on the morrow in court. Don't be surprised if I just slip in."

"Okay! I'll see you tomorrow!"

Gen practically skipped up the short sidewalk to her house except that she was still being careful on those fragile high heels.

Everything was looking up. Without even rolling over on her back and spreading her legs, Gen had tamed the wild Earl of Severn.

Arthur was really a sweet guy, in many ways. It was really great of him to offer to "polish her up," and he hadn't made a drunken fool of himself tonight and offered clickbait to the paparazzi at all.

If he didn't feed the trolls, she could win his case, and he was going to make her more amenable to the firm's higher class of clientele, too. This would help her in her quest for tenancy. She would be able to pay her mother's nursing home bills.

Everything was going to be fine.

Gen locked her front door behind herself, cleaned up, hung the ridiculous, overpriced dress on a hanger for the night, and wrapped herself in a quilt to sleep on the downstairs sofa.

She slept well.

Better than she had in months.

Things were going to be all right.

The next morning when Gen got to the office, she flipped open her laptop.

The internet search for "Lord Arthur Finch-Hatten OR Earl Severn AND gossip" refreshed itself.

A new picture appeared at the top of the queue.

Oh, God, no.

Gen stared at the screen, unable and then unwilling to believe what she was seeing.

The date on the pictures was for the night before, and it sure as Hell wasn't at the Rainforest Alliance dinner. From the darkness in the background and the women's glittery pasties on their boobs, it looked like he had gone to a strip club.

She picked up her cell phone to call His Lordship Arthur fucking Finch-Hatten.

Needed Tonight

Arthur sat in the rear seat of the car, sipping his soda water, and watched Gen teeter happily up the sidewalk to the cozy house that she used to share with her mother before her mother's stroke six months before. Tragic, that. Reading about it in her background check had horrified him. She hadn't mentioned it yet, so he hadn't, either.

She went into the terraced house and closed the door. The door jiggled in the light from the bare bulb on the landing when she locked it.

Good.

Just one lock? He would call his lock man to add more locks to the doors and windows tomorrow. Perhaps an alarm system.

Pippa pulled the car away from the curb and drove toward downtown London. She asked, "Where should we go?"

"Find a place to park for a moment, if you would?" Arthur pulled his phone out of his pocket.

Pippa found a small parking area behind a shop, took a look around, and stepped out of the car. Yes, she knew the drill.

Arthur dialed a number on his phone that was not in the contact list.

A woman answered, "Yes."

Not hello.

Not her name nor his, though surely she had recognized the number.

Arthur could imagine lamplight glimmering on her silver and golden-streaked hair.

"What the Hell were you doing in the ladies' room with her?" he asked.

"We had a nice chat," the woman said. Her upper-crust British accent softened with each sentence, sliding toward French-like sibilance.

"That's not what she said."

"She seemed fine, not distressed."

"Only because she didn't realize what you were saying. She thinks that you were warning her that I would break her heart."

The woman laughed, a high, tinkling sound. She finally said, "How amusing."

"I don't find it amusing in the slightest."

"She's in no danger from us, dear heart. You know that."

Arthur hated that nickname and the history behind it, but he was British, so he gave no indication of it. "She has no need to know such things."

"That's true."

"Then why would you be sending cryptic messages to such a girl?"

"She's distracting you, dear heart."

"This lawsuit is distracting me." Arthur knew better than to suggest that something might be done about it. He wasn't a monster.

She said, "You shouldn't allow yourself to be distracted."

"I'm not. Not really."

"Excellent. You're needed tonight."

He listened to the details, hung up, and tapped the window for Pippa to get back into the car.

She glanced through the rearview mirror at him, her gray eyebrows raised.

Arthur said, "Luton."

Pippa navigated the car out of the car park and back into the snarling London traffic.

STIFF DRINK

Come to Jesus

GEN held her cell phone in her hand and started into Arthur the second that he said, "Hello? Gen?" in that maddening, drowsy voice of his.

She yelled, "What in the seven Hells do you think that you're doing?"

A rustling sound, like sheets being adjusted, rumbled through the line. "Sleeping."

"How in the Hell did you get to Paris and then get photographed in a strip club after you dropped me off at home last night?"

"I didn't want to keep you out late. You had to work in the morning."

"I swear to *God,* Arthur. *Paris.* A *strip club* in *Paris.* I swear to *God* that I will drop you and your case like you're an armadillo with leprosy."

"That's a pleasant image."

"How did you get to Paris and back so fast?"

"I have a plane," he said.

"You had to have filed a flight plan. Is that why you wanted to leave the charity thing early? So you could go get smashed with hookers in Paris?"

"I hadn't planned to go to Paris. It was a whim. I can leave within an hour of calling. Also, they were strippers, not hookers."

"Arthur, why, *oh why,* did you go carousing last night?"

"I was bored. I needed a diversion."

"From *what?* What on Earth could be so terrible about your charmed life of charity balls and sports and working out and traveling on a perpetual vacation that you *of all people* need a diversion?"

"That's none of your business."

"It *is* my business. Everything about you is my business because I agreed to take on your case and especially since I put my career on the line by pretending to be your damn girlfriend!"

"You're certainly acting like a real girlfriend. Can't a guy go to one strip club?"

"I don't care *that* you went there. I don't care *why* you went there. I care that your *picture* is on *five different gossip websites* with a French stripper who's sticking her tongue in your ear!"

"Five? That's rather more than I had thought."

"Yes, five, you son of a bitch!"

"Now, now. Such language. If we're going to polish you up—"

"You're not going to 'polish me up' because I am going to walk into Octavia Hawkes's office right now and tell her that I can't handle you. I will tell her that she has to defend your case because it's far too complex for a mediocre, stupid baby barrister such as myself!"

"That doesn't sound like it will help your chances for tenancy much."

"Losing your case will *murder* my chances for tenancy!"

"Hawkes is thinking about applying for the silk, isn't she?"

Gen wanted to reach through the phone and strangle that arsehole. "So what if she is applying to be Queen's Council? She's brilliant. She's worked hard her whole life. She deserves it."

"And she's giving you her unwinnable cases because she knows they're unwinnable and needs to get her stats up. In addition, she doesn't want to argue my case before a judge who might be giving her a recommendation."

But that wasn't how it had happened. "The Head Clerk

gave me your case, not Hawkes."

"Are you telling me that your Head Clerk had no guidance from the more senior barristers? That no one sought to sway his judgment?"

"Her judgment, and I'm sure that it was all on the up-and-up." Except that even caramel macchiatos had been legal tender for the crime of bribery of Celestia Alen-Buckley that afternoon, but Gen hadn't known it.

Arthur said, "Your boss is sabotaging you."

"She is not, and even if she is, she's my pupil mistress. I'll take her hopeless cases for her, and then she'll make sure I get a tenancy offer in return."

"Has she said that?"

"Well, no."

"Then it's not a binding contract, and it wouldn't be even if she had said it."

"It's never a binding contract. It's not in writing. And who's the damn attorney here, anyway?"

"I don't want to see you get hurt."

"*Then stop fucking around and making it impossible to win your case!*"

A moment of silence over the phone. "Score one for you."

"Hell, yes, 'score one for me.' I mean it. This is your come-to-Jesus moment, you drunken degenerate. If you don't stop going out, getting hammered, and ending up in the tabloids as nothing more than a joke about being a waste of oxygen, I swear to God that you and your solicitor can find a new barrister to argue your case!"

"You can't do that, you know."

"I can and I will!" Gen fumed.

Arthur said, "Cab rank rule."

His deep voice sounded ridiculously, infuriatingly smug. She snarled, "How do you even know about that!"

"My uncle is a barrister."

"I thought Christopher lived with him, not you."

"Everyone stayed at Spencer House for the holidays until I was nine. After that, Caz and I often went home with Max for holidays. Sometimes we went to Caz's place. Not often."

Dear Lord, Arthur hadn't had a home to go to for Christmas or Easter vacation from boarding school. Gen raised one fist in frustration. "I'm sorry."

"Don't be. Caz and Max are my family."

"They don't even live here."

"But they would be here if I needed them, in a heartbeat."

"As soon as someone thought to call them, and as soon as someone managed to get ahold of them."

"Well, yes, but they would almost certainly arrive just one heartbeat after that."

She didn't have the heart to argue with him. "I'm sure they would."

"But, back to the cab rank rule, you can't dump my case on someone else, and I think that Hawkes wouldn't take it from you."

"Maybe not in theory, but it's done in practice all the damn time."

"Then we're at an impasse."

"We're *not!* I'm dumping you!"

"You sound more and more like a real girlfriend all the time. I thought we had a lovely time last night."

"Not lovely enough to keep you from heading out to a strip club afterward!"

"That's different," he said.

"It's totally *not different.* Seriously, you *can't* do this anymore. If Hawkes finds out, I don't know what I'll tell her. It's time for you to get right with Jesus—"

"That's the second time you've mentioned Jesus in the last few minutes."

"If I thought a baptizing would reform you, I would hold your head under the water in a river myself."

"Luckily, I was baptized as an infant, so I won't be in

danger of drowning."

"*Ugh.* You Episcopalians are weird. Seriously, Arthur. *Never, ever again.* Got it?"

"Yes, I am chastised. I understand the ramifications." The sheets rustled again.

A terrible thought wormed into Gen's head. "You're at home, right?"

"Yes, I'm in my own bed."

Gen did not want to ask this one, either. "And *alone,* right?"

"I never bring women back to my apartment or to Spencer House. The fuss in the morning is distressing."

"Well, there's that, at least," she sighed.

"I'll see you this afternoon," Arthur said, "in court."

"You mean to polish me up, right? You didn't get arrested last night, did you?"

He chuckled, a low, dark sound. "No, I wasn't arrested last night. Yes, to polish you up."

THE DOM/SUB JUDGE

THAT afternoon in court, Gen was cross-examining a witness in what had to be the dullest court case, ever. Octavia was supposed to be lead litigator on this case and in all cases because Gen was only a pupil barrister, but Octavia was sitting up perfectly straight in her chair and wearing large sunglasses because she was asleep. She hadn't even dropped her pen, but the pen had left a black squiggle on the yellow legal pad as her arm had dropped a few inches.

Gen was making good progress on the court case, citing perfectly relevant cases in all her arguments and retorting to all the witnesses, when a paper sailed over her shoulder.

The note read, in Arthur's neat, block handwriting, THE JUDGE IS FUCKING THE BAILIFF, AND THE BAILIFF IS DECIDING HIS CASES. JUDGE IS THE SUB. BAILIFF IS THE DOM. BAILIFF WILL TELL THE JUDGE HOW TO RULE. DUMB IT DOWN. PLAY TO THE BAILIFF.

She glanced back at him and mouthed, *Are you kidding me?*

Arthur shook his head, the sunlight glinting on his black hair and hard cheekbones. No, he was not kidding.

Gen spent the rest of the case playing to common sense and emotions. The bailiff, a sturdy, tattooed man with a wide, leather belt, nodded when she scored those kinds of points.

Sure enough, when the judge retired to consider the case and write his verdict, the bailiff trotted into his chambers after him, already unbuckling his belt.

Arthur winked at Gen, and she won the case.

Later, over a quiet supper in a restaurant with snowy china and sparkling crystal wine glasses, she asked him, "How did you know?"

"Body language," Arthur said, laughing. "Every time the bailiff became bored with testimony or arguments, the judge started showing nervous tics, fiddling with pens and such, and watching the bailiff instead of listening to you and your learned opponent."

Learned opponent. Gen chuckled. Arthur had picked up the lawyer lingo fast.

He said, "I would lay odds that the bailiff punishes the judge for boredom in the courtroom and instructs the judge to rule against the more boring barrister."

"Would he do such a thing?"

"Unless the sub uses a safeword, some Doms can do just about anything. That's why subs have safewords because they have the ultimate power to stop. Otherwise, it's just abuse."

"Good Lord," Gen said, "and this was a motion to decide which court would hear a complaint by a bank against one of its investors for late-submitted documentation. I'll bet that judge has welts tonight."

Arthur smirked, "Chances are, he's loving every minute of it."

Chambers High Tea

THE sun shone in the long windows of the best conference room while Gen poured tea for the senior barristers of chambers. Steam curled from the fragile china cup as the tea spun into it.

James Knightly sidled up to her. "Have you heard that Nigel Hancock's girlfriend is in the family way?"

"Yes, James," Gen said, adding a lump of sugar into Octavia's piping hot tea and watching it dissolve. "Everyone has. From you. For days."

"I'm taking up a collection for a baby gift," he said.

She stirred the tea. "I'll just bet that you are."

"I was thinking a pram," James said, "for when they take *long morning walks* in the park with the new baby."

"Just quit harping on it," Gen said. "Anyone would think you have baby fever yourself."

A Stalker and Lebanese

A few hours later, when Gen was ready to leave chambers for the day, she texted Arthur so he could pick her up. She was waiting on the curb in the dark winter night when Pippa drove up in the Bentley.

As the car coasted to a stop, the back door opened while the car was still moving. Arthur stepped out, walking, from the moving car.

"Hey!" Gen called. "Hey, look. We should probably—"

Arthur walked right by her, his unbuttoned suit jacket fluttering as he strode by.

"I'm right here!" she called after him.

She was just turning around to go after him when Arthur grabbed a man three steps behind her by the lapels of the guy's coat and drove him back against a wall. Arthur snarled, "Who are you?"

The guy had his hands up by his shoulders. A gray-streaked beard covered his ruddy cheeks. "What the bloody hell are you doing?"

"You've been following her for two days."

"No, I have not!"

Arthur spoke quietly, quickly, "You drive a faded red banger, a Saab, about ten years old."

The guy stuttered and glared at Arthur. "How did you know that?"

"Because you are shit at surveillance. Who employs you?"

Arthur's low, intense voice was far scarier than if he had been screaming. Gen stood back and clutched her briefcase to her chest.

"None of your business!" The guy squirmed, trying to fight, but Arthur held him fast against the wall.

"It's Christopher, isn't it? Christopher Finch-Hatten is paying you."

The guy's arms flailed, slapping and punching at Arthur, but Arthur blocked the guy's arms and grabbed his wrists.

He said, "I asked who was paying you."

The guy's dark eyes widened, and he was nearly hyperventilating. "I do not know that name. I am not a private investigator."

"You're shit at lying, too. If I see you following her again, I'll ring the police for stalking and sort you out in the meantime."

Arthur shoved the man hard against the wall and let him go. He walked back to the car where Gen was standing, frozen.

He told her, "Get in the car."

Gen looked behind Arthur, but the guy was scurrying down the sidewalk toward a dirty red Saab.

She got into the car and asked Pippa, "Does he do that often?"

The driver shook her head. "Not to speak of."

"Oh, okay." That was a negative, right?

Arthur got in the other side of the car, and Pippa pulled the car into the thick, London traffic on the left side of the street.

Arthur turned to her. "About court today—"

"Who was that guy?" Gen demanded.

Arthur shrugged. "A private detective, I think, and terrible at his job. I imagine he was hoping for compromising photographs."

"Why did you *do* that?"

"So he would leave you alone."

"You can't run around and *threaten* people like that! What if he calls the police?"

Arthur smiled. "I'm sure it won't come to that. Now, about court today—"

Gen shook out her hands, trying to shake the crazy away. *"Fine.* Fine. You win. We won't talk about the guy you threatened with violence any more. In court, I was awful, right? I'm hopeless?"

Arthur's startled glance was a little reassuring. "No. None of those. What would you like for supper? Indian? Lebanese?"

"Sure. Anything. Whatever."

"Now, now," Arthur said. "You're my girlfriend. If we were actually dating, you could play the whatever-you-want card. But since we're in a long-term, committed relationship, we should be past the point of these little self-abnegating games. Tell me what you want for supper."

"Okay. Lebanese," Gen said.

"Lebanese, it is. Pippa?"

From the front seat, Pippa said, "Right-o, Lord Severn," and steered the car into a sharp left turn around a corner.

It still freaked Gen out, sometimes, that they were driving on the wrong side of the road, and the driver sat on the passenger side of the car. *Creepy.*

The restaurant was close to Lincoln's Inn, and the waiter who bustled up to them when they came in the door shooed them into a private room at the back of the restaurant. After they ordered—grilled chicken and salad for Gen and a falafel wrap for Arthur—they settled down to talk privately.

"So, what did I do in court that was terribly plebeian?" she asked.

Of course, that was the moment that her phone beeped with an incoming text from her boss. Octavia Hawkes was assigning her another case, a medical malpractice defense. Fifteen arch files would be delivered to Gen's office from the instructing solicitors the next morning. The trial would be in two weeks.

Seriously, why were all these other trials so dang speedy

but Arthur's had been dragging on for *years?*

Gen thumbed her screen, saying that she would be pleased to take the case and thanking Hawkes for her confidence.

Arthur rolled his wine glass stem between his hands. "I need to ask you a question, a personal one."

Gen swiped her finger across her phone, replying to another lawyer about another case.

The polish didn't quite meet the bottom of her nail as her finger glided over the glass. Time for a manicure. Octavia Hawkes would be horrified at how slovenly Gen's nails looked.

One dressed for the job one aspired to, Octavia had assured her on several occasions. Octavia wore a *silk* blouse on most days.

Gen kind of wanted to come to work dressed as Catwoman, just to throw her off.

Gen told Arthur, "I'm your lawyer. You don't need to be asking me personal questions."

Arthur's gentle voice was low in her ears. "Have you been sexually assaulted?"

A wave of grief and shame tumbled Gen, and she dropped her phone but caught the flipping screen as it hit her thighs. "That's none of your business."

Arthur's hands were folded in his lap under the table. "We're pretending to be a couple. We're spending time together. I don't want to do or say something that will make things worse."

Her hand was shaking so badly that she couldn't continue composing the email. "It's just none of your business."

"I'm sorry," he said. "I'm sorry that it happened to you."

"Do not make me cry where a waiter is going to see, you bastard."

"I shan't mention it again. Have you discussed it with a counselor?"

"No, and I don't want to."

"I've heard they can be quite helpful."

"I'm not the only person that it's happened to. It's not even special. When you get a group of women someplace private, in a secret internet group or in a bar late at night without any guys around, you hear it. The official statistic is one in three, but it's *wrong.* It's *everybody.* Everyone has a story, and everyone deals with it. Some people deal with it better. Some deal with it worse. But everyone deals with it. So I deal with it."

Arthur had been watching her, not smiling, not scowling. His silvery eyes took in her speech without comment, just listening. He said, "I'm sorry it happened to you."

"You already said that."

"I suggest a counselor," he said.

"I don't want to talk about it with *anyone.*"

He looked down and adjusted his tie. "You're in a profession where people will attempt to manipulate you. If they saw anything similar to what I saw last night or in the courtroom today, and if they knew what they were looking at, they would know how to use that in court to disrupt your case."

Gen's hand cramped around her phone. "That's a horrible thing to say."

"There are many manipulative bastards out there, Gen." He stared into his wine. "I'm acquainted with enough of them. You shouldn't let them manipulate you, but they will try."

"Yeah, barristers play evil games like that. I don't know what to do about it, though."

He shook his head. "I can ask people about counselors. I don't know what else to say."

"If anyone in chambers found out that I was in counseling for a personal problem, they would use it against me. They're all snipers in there, whispering about each other, using anything they can against each other to be seen as superior. James Knightly won the Lombardi case in two days. *Damn,* that looks good for him. And then Knightly found out that another pupil barrister in chambers, Nigel Hancock, knocked up his girlfriend, and she's having the baby. Knightly keeps leaving gifts of baby booties and onesies in his cubby where everyone can see them, and now all the senior barristers think that Hancock has lost focus. Can't have a baby and be a powerhouse in chambers, you know."

Arthur nodded. "It's the British way."

"Plus, I just don't want to talk to someone about it. I don't want to relive it and think about it. I feel best when I just forget about it."

Arthur glanced at his phone. "The symphony starts in an hour or so. There's an interesting piano concerto on the schedule."

Gen glanced down at her black pantsuit, one of several that she owned that were nearly, but not quite, identical. "I don't think I'm dressed for it."

"You're fine. People wear denim, these days. Let's go hear some music tonight."

Waffling Witnesses

THE next afternoon, Gen was in court again, arguing what should have been a simple drunk driving case except that the witness, Nathan Singh, was being weird. In his deposition for the solicitors, he had been far more precise about who was doing what, when.

Now, Nathan Singh was waffling.

Waffling witnesses lost cases.

Gen frowned.

Octavia had another case to defend, so she had left Gen all on her lonesome in court that day. In the folder, Gen had found a quote handwritten by her previous pupil master, Horace Lindsey: *Some rise by sin, and some by virtue fall (Measure for Measure).*

Dang Horace and his cryptic quotes, but it was comforting to see his flowing handwriting and know that he had touched the folder at some point.

Arthur was sitting in the back of the courtroom, watching Gen. He wore dark slacks and a white shirt, open at the throat, no tie, and was taking notes on a legal pad.

Great. *Notes.* He should have all kinds of points to cover over supper that night. She should be all polished up in no time.

Even though the logical part of her brain was chastising her for being so snippy about an excellent opportunity to smooth out some of her rough edges and to meet the right people, the rest of her was fit to be tied. She was fine the way she was.

Unfortunately, no matter how fine Gen thought she was, she was not fine with the right people. One of her instructing solicitors had informed her that morning that his client had asked to be transferred to a barrister who understood English courts better. Even though Gen protested that she knew them as well as anyone and had gained a first at Oxford and was top of her bar course, she could hear in the solicitor's voice that it was a lost cause.

She wasn't British enough.

So, she needed to let Arthur British her up a little.

But first, she needed to examine this witness, who was hemming and hawing.

The case was pretty simple, a drunk driving case where the defendant, Joe Popov, had driven his car into a tree. Three other people had been in his car, and no one had been hurt, thanks to the excellent airbags in his car and a metric ton of sheer, dumb luck.

That tree could have been a playground full of toddlers, if there had been kindergarteners playing at two o'clock in the morning.

But still.

Gen had to defend Joe Popov, who had been driving while smashed and endangered everyone around him, because of the cab rank rule. When a cab was empty, they had to take the next person in the line for cabs for any fare, lest they be accused of discrimination. When Gen was offered a case, excepting for very specific situations, she *had* to take it.

Joe Popov had absolutely no spots on his previous record, by all accounts was a model citizen who worked hard on a loading dock all day to provide for his growing family, took care of his kids at night so that his wife could take an extension course, and had gone out with the blokes for a pint on a Saturday night. He was facing jail time. At the very least, if she couldn't get him off, he would lose his driver's license, which would be a hardship for the family.

Thus, she was trying to poke holes in the testimony of a witness, but Nathan Singh was being weird.

Gen asked Nathan Singh, who was standing with his hands on the rail in the witness box, "You, the other passengers, and the defendant were in the pub that evening?"

Nathan spoke with a middle-class Londoner accent that Gen should probably try to copy. "Yes."

"How many drinks did the defendant have over the course of the evening?"

Nathan said, "Eight or nine."

That was what he had said in the deposition. "And then you, the other passengers, and the defendant walked out to the car."

The witness nodded. "Yes."

"And the bartender didn't try to stop you from driving?"

"No."

"And you gave your keys to the defendant and sat behind the driver's seat?"

"Basically, I actually gave my keys to Joe over there, and then I basically got in the car and actually sat there for a few minutes while Joe fumbled with the keys a bit."

"You saw this from inside the car?"

"Basically, when I was inside the car, I was watching, and it looked like Joe was actually fumbling with the keys, basically."

"And then the other two passengers got into the car, and Joe drove out of the parking lot."

"Basically, I was in the back of the car, and Joe was actually driving that night."

Gen walked back to the table with her notes and her laptop. Arthur was sitting back, looking away, his long arms lying across the back of the bench.

A piece of yellow paper was lying on her keyboard. Written in neat, block letters was the note: THE WITNESS IS BEING DECEPTIVE. HIS VERBAL MANNERISMS

CHANGED WHEN YOU ASKED HIM ABOUT WHO WAS DRIVING. ASK HIM THIS: HOW WOULD YOU EXPLAIN IT IF THE BARTENDER SAID THAT YOU WERE DRIVING THE CAR?

Yeah, Gen could probably ask that. The bartender's deposition said nothing of the sort, only that the bartender hadn't left the building and hadn't seen who got in the car or who was driving. She couldn't say that the bartender said this, but this wording was just skirting the edges of what she could say.

Okay, sure.

Gen laid the yellow page on her computer, looked sideways over at the witness fidgeting in the witness box beside the bored judge, and asked, "How would you explain it if the bartender said that you were driving the car?"

The judge raised one eyebrow at her question, and his black brow nearly met the white rolls of the wig on his forehead.

Manic tremors raced through Nathan Singh's arms as he waved them overhead. "I didn't even see him out there! How could he have known that I was driving? Where was he? Was it CCTV? Was he spying on us? His testimony can't be admissible in court if he was spying on us!"

Gen clicked her teeth shut to keep her jaw from dropping.

She glanced back at Arthur, who was still staring at the side wall, but a small smile curved his lips.

Gen turned and walked back toward the witness. "So you admit that you were driving that night? That my client was not driving, did not hit the tree, and did not endanger other people's lives?"

"I've been tagged for drunk driving before! If I was caught, I would have gone to jail! Joe's never done anything. You should have been able to get him off with nothing more than a slap on the arse."

Gen turned toward the judge. "Your honor, in light of the witness's testimony that he was driving the car that hit the tree and that my client was not driving that night—"

The judge was staring at the ceiling with his hands folded over his stomach. "Put your client on the stand and see what he has to say. Remind him of the penalties of perjury, even if it is to take the blame for a mate and keep him out of jail. Bailiff, arrest Mr. Singh."

Gen strode back to her notes while Nathan Singh was hustled off the witness stand and arrested and Joe Popov was released from the dock to testify.

Joe Popov confirmed that Nathan Singh had been driving the car, drunk, and had convinced them all to say that Joe was driving, instead. He stared at his hands in his lap while he testified in a choked voice.

The judge dismissed the charges, and Arthur met Gen at the courthouse door to drive her back to her office for a few minutes before they went out to supper.

"Good job," he told her as he held the door.

"How did you know?" she asked.

He shrugged. "Considering my lifestyle moving among the upper and noble classes, I encounter liars, cads, and thieves daily. It's useful to be able to determine when someone is being deceptive."

Debriefing

"Popov was lying to me," Gen said to Octavia. They were sitting in a corner at chambers high tea after the drunk driving case. Gen had finished serving, and Octavia had invited her over to chat about her triumph that day. "He was lying to me about being guilty. He actually didn't do it."

"That's an unusual case," Octavia said, settling back in her deep chair with the scalding cup of tea that Gen had prepared for her. "It's usually the other way around."

"I have more of those than I can count," Gen said. "Everyone says that they *didn't* do it."

"Of course, they do," Octavia said. "If they said otherwise, we would have to report it to the court."

"It makes me feel dirty to represent people who are obviously guilty and lying to me about it."

"Oh, come now. If we only represented the innocent ones whom we thought were telling the truth, we wouldn't have a job. We're not Atticus fucking Finch."

"It feels like it's misleading the court."

"But you had the perfect counterpoint to that today. About eighty percent of our criminal cases are guilty, but we don't know which eighty percent. We can't determine it even when they tell us that they are innocent or guilty. Every single one of them deserves the best defense possible because some of them are innocent of the crime they're accused of. That's our job."

Computer Lads

ARTHUR sat at his computer desk, the six screens glowing around him. Video-chat windows were open on two of the screens, a total of six windows. In the windows, four men and two women wearing headphone and microphone sets were talking to each other and to him.

Headphones pinched Arthur's ears, but it was the best and most secure way to hear what the others were saying. A microphone hovered near his chin, a black protrusion that distracted him.

Blocky text and punctuation filled two other computer monitors, meaningless to anyone who couldn't read computer code. Arthur was reading through it, editing, while he was chatting with the other people. They were all doing the same thing.

"Blackjack, man, what is this with wanting to meet IRL?" Luftwaffe asked Arthur.

"It's been a few weeks," Arthur said. "It's nice to see that you guys still exist and you're not some Russian simulacra."

"Oh, that Blackjack," Vlogger1 said, tying her long, blue hair back in a ponytail again. "He likes meatspace."

"I don't know," CallousBitch said. "I might have to put on pants. I hate putting on pants."

"We could meet in Rolle," Arthur said. "Switzerland is beautiful this time of year."

They all groaned. None of them had any nostalgia for Switzerland. They had all lived there too long at boarding school.

"I heard of a new dive bar in downtown Paris," Racehorse said. His chat window was almost entirely black because there were no lights in the room behind him. His ebony skin blended with the darkness. He believed that the dark reduced the chances of video surveillance recognition picking him up. He held a small controller in his huge hands and was tilting it and clicking like mad, obviously playing a computer game in his dark room rather than working. "I hear it's less than two euros for their stout."

"That sounds great," Arthur said. "I'll bring the thing that I've been working on. You guys are gonna love it."

"Hello! Blackjack's been working on a new thing!" Racehorse crowed. "Is this like the last thing you were working on? The one that threw that election in Slovenia just by manipulating what news was on top of people's newsfeeds?"

No one died in that operation, and that government had remained a free democracy.

Arthur smiled. "I think you'll like it. How's work, VLogger One?"

"Same old, same old," she said. "The NSA never sleeps, and they never let *me* goddamn sleep. I'm still working on cracking the Ukraine's satellite office. That sucker is practically encapsulated in black ice."

Arthur chuckled at the science fiction reference. "Don't stroke out."

"If I don't get off my butt and get some exercise, it's a real concern. Racehorse, how's it hanging?"

"Keeps whacking my knees, and work is fine, too." He lifted his gaming controller, holding it above his head, and in the light from the screen, his thumbs blurred. "Anybody know anything about the targeting systems the Russians are using in Syria?"

"I heard they were the standard ones," Arthur said.

"They're not. The encryption is different. Otherwise, we would just let Black Rock do it. Anyway, now we're involved."

Vlogger1 asked Racehorse, "You wanna liaise?"

"Yeah, we're going to have to."

Arthur would never admit in his report that the CIA and the NSA would liaise on the Russian-Syrian missile targeting systems, just as the other people in the chat windows would not divulge this in their reports to their own intelligence services. They were a small cadre who helped each other, all within friendly services, and they were all *anciens roséens,* alumni of Le Rosey boarding school. With each other, they were all at the tops of their fields.

Arthur looked at the clock on the top of his computer. "Damn. I have to meet a lady for lunch."

He was meeting Gen for lunch, so he was allowing an hour to clean up and make himself presentable. Maybe he would watch her in court again that afternoon. Maybe they would dance at the charity event tonight, and he could feel her lush body swaying in his arms again.

Touching her was exquisite torture because there was no chance of Arthur fucking her. Beyond the fact that she was his barrister and thus off-limits—which might not have stopped him in other situations—the fear in her eyes whenever a man neared her was painful to watch. He couldn't imagine a situation where he could steer her into bed.

Ah, forbidden fruit. He would just have to imagine her sweet, ripe flesh because he would never devour it.

Hoots emanated through Arthur's earphones.

"Ew," Luftwaffe said, his German accent rising in his voice. "Blackjack has a social life. Aren't we getting fancy? See you tomorrow, and we should plan to visit Racehorse's dive bar in Paris soon. Meatspace can be interesting, even if one does have to wear pants."

Trollop Card

Gen was sitting in her office, grinding through piles of evidence that had arrived by courier for a hearing in two days, when her boss, Octavia Hawkes, stuck her head through the doorway.

Octavia said, "I need you in court with me this afternoon." She looked up and down what she could see of Gen's torso. "Are your nails done?"

"Just had them done this morning," Gen said, confused.

"Excellent. Is that what you're wearing?"

Gen glanced at herself. The black pantsuit that she was wearing was one of her better ones, a designer set found secondhand at a thrift shop. "Um, yes?"

"I have something else for you to wear."

"But you're three sizes smaller than I am, and about six inches shorter. Anything of yours would be, well," Gen grimaced, "too tight and too short."

Octavia's grin widened and turned devious. "Exactly."

Gen followed Octavia back to her office, where Octavia indeed had a skirt suit laid out for her.

Guess it was lucky that Gen had shaved her legs last night and kept a pair of pantyhose in her desk drawer for emergencies. She ran back and grabbed them.

In her boss's office, Octavia tucked and stuffed Gen into the too-small skirt, muttering, "Good thing you're wasp-waisted. It barely buttons."

Gen didn't answer because she was holding her breath. The skirt's waistband was nearly cutting her in half like a thousand rubber bands around a watermelon. The shirt's buttonholes strained over her boobs, gaping a bit between the buttons.

She looked up in absolute horror. "I can't wear this to *court.*"

"Of course, you can," Octavia said. "It's for Judge Roberts. I'm not Atticus fucking Finch, here. We use what methods we have to ensure a win. 'Military tactics are like unto water; for water in its natural course runs away from high places and hastens downwards. Water shapes its course according to the nature of the ground over which it flows; the soldier works out his victory in relation to the foe whom he is facing. Therefore, just as water retains no constant shape, so in warfare there are no constant conditions. He who can modify his tactics in relation to his opponent and thereby succeed in winning, may be called a heaven-born captain.'"

"You memorized all that?" Gen asked.

"I have memorized Sun Tzu's *The Art of War* in its entirety. 'The art of war is of vital importance. It is a matter of life and death, a road either to safety or to ruin. Hence it is a subject of inquiry which can on no account be neglected.'"

Gen shrugged. "Okay, then."

Judge George Roberts was a notorious lech and ogled all the women lawyers, but women also generally won a disproportionate number of their cases, especially if they, ahem, *dressed for success.*

Gen clarified, "So we're playing the Trollop Card."

"Quite." Octavia adjusted the lapels of the too-small suit jacket and started pulling the pins out of Gen's hair.

Gen grabbed the heavy bun on the back of her head. "What are you doing?"

Octavia said, "Letting your hair down, at least in the literal sense. I suspect that you're a lost cause, metaphorically."

Gen's hair tumbled around her shoulders. "Are you sure this is ethical?"

"Of course not. That's why it works every damn time, and our client will thank us for it, later. Is that *really* the bra you're wearing?"

"Yes, it *really* is the bra I'm wearing," Gen said.

"It's just beige." Octavia scowled. "And blah. And unnoticeable."

"That was rather its appeal."

"It won't *appeal* to Judge Roberts, and then we'll lose this *appeal.*"

"I see what you did there," Gen said.

"A-peel that one off, and we'll see what I have in stock. I always have an extra Myla or two, just in case."

Gen crossed her arms over her chest and didn't take her shirt off. "He's not going to be able to see it, anyway. My court robes are going to cover my clothes down to my knees."

"Nope. It's just a civil case. We won't need to wear the robes and wigs."

Then the judge would be able to see everything.

Maybe *absolutely everything* unless the blouse's buttons were sewn on with steel thread.

Octavia rummaged in her file cabinet by the wall. "And are those the shoes you're wearing?"

"Must we go through this again?" Gen's shoes were sensible black pumps with short, chunky heels, excellent for trotting to see a client in the cells or standing to address the court for long periods of time.

"Don't you have some Christian Louboutins?"

Those hideously over-priced high heels with the scarlet soles? *No.* Just *no.* Even if Gen had found some secondhand in a thrift store, she did not wear slutty shoes to work or at all, ever. "Haven't gotten some yet."

"Too bad. Judge Roberts does love the fuck-me shoes." Octavia rummaged in the file cabinet drawer, dropping lingerie over the sides.

"Besides," Gen said, "I'd be six-feet-four in those things. And I doubt they even make them in my size."

"Oh, you can special-order anything, if you know whom to call. Here's something." Octavia turned around. A scrap of lace dangled from one finger. "Try this on under that blouse."

The sheer lace bra tied up with ribbons. "I'm a double-D cup, Octavia. That little thing would explode."

Octavia frowned. "That utilitarian rag that you're wearing just won't do. The evidence in this case is flimsy—"

"No, that bra is *flimsy,*" Gen muttered.

"—and yet I *need* to win it. Quite honestly, the client was not on his cell phone when he crashed the car. He hadn't been drinking. Another car's mirror glared at him when he hit that damned, overbred rosebush, but just try to tell that to the horticulturist. I can't believe that she is suing the poor sod for thousands of pounds because she *might* have won a prize with her roses. *Try on the bra.*"

A knock rattled Octavia's office door.

Octavia yelled, "Just a minute," while Gen called, "Come in," trying to get out of stuffing her boobs in that inadequate bit of chiffon.

Arthur leaned through the doorway. "Hope I'm not interrupting anything. I'm here to take my girlfriend to lunch." He glanced at the two of them, and then his pale eyes settled on Gen. "Good Lord. It's like the naughty librarian, come to life."

"Ah, yes," Octavia said. "Your 'girlfriend.' How is that working out for you two?"

"Splendidly," Arthur said.

Gen piped up, "I've been keeping an eye on him as best as I can."

Octavia glared at Arthur. "I hope you've been a gentleman."

"I am the very definition of a gentleman," he said.

Octavia's lips compressed until they were an angry, red dot on her face. "I don't mean it that way. I mean that Genevieve is taking quite a risk for you, even though I've let it be known around the upper levels of the office that this is a ploy."

So Octavia had kept her word, which was probably why Gen hadn't had any blowback from the senior barristers about ostensibly dating a client. The other pupils were giving her the side-eye quite a lot, but their opinion didn't matter.

Hawkes continued, "But you still owe her a great deal, Finch-Hatten. I was ready to scrap you, and I still am."

Wow. Gen had never heard Octavia talk that way to a client. She had dressed down James Knightly more than once, but she usually oozed politeness and sympathy for clients. The only people whom Hawkes buttered up more than the clients were the solicitors who sent them business.

"So," Hawkes said to Arthur, "have you been behaving yourself?"

"I am a model British citizen, steadfast and earnest," he said.

She sniffed. "You make yourself sound like a Victorian, and we all know how perverted they were. Now, if you'd like to repay Genevieve for this great kindness and favor that she's doing for you—" Octavia's blue eyes glittered, "—take her to lunch and then to Harrods. She needs Louboutins and Myla lingerie for the afternoon court session."

"Now, now," Arthur said. "I've heard barristers compared to hired guns, but it sounds like you're selling something entirely different."

"The judge is a lecher," Gen told him. "We're playing the Trollop Card."

"Ah," Arthur said. "I'm quite familiar with the concept of a honeypot. Come, Gen. We'll find you some shoes and," he paused, "other things."

He held the door for her as she walked out, mincing as

she took baby steps in the too-tight skirt. Damn, it was a good thing that she had shaved her legs last night.

When she looked back, Arthur was watching her butt, and when he looked up and saw that she had caught him, he smiled.

It wasn't a sheepish smile, either. He was a gray-eyed wolf in a man's clothing, and his steady gaze was that of a predator stalking prey.

She shot a quip at Arthur over her shoulder. "Where do you want to go for lunch?"

"My apartment." His voice sounded more like a growl than his usual, smooth cadence.

Gen turned, shocked, but Arthur had already recovered his normal, slightly amused expression.

He said, "We had Lebanese recently. Sushi? Fish and chips?"

"Whatever you want," Gen stammered.

The complete lack of panic in Gen's veins surprised her. Maybe it was because Arthur was several steps behind her, not right up next to her. Maybe it was because they had known each other for a bit now, and he had backed off and never made another inappropriate move.

Maybe it was because they were walking through Octavia's small waiting room, and Octavia's personal admin, Germaine, and the clerk Miriam were watching Gen and Arthur with green, glittering envy pasted all over their faces.

That was a new feeling, and it ignited a warm glow in Gen's evil little soul.

They breezed through the office, passing clerks and pupil barristers, who stared at them, and senior staff, who didn't.

Once they were outdoors in the park-like courtyard of Lincoln's Inn and walking through the noontime sunlight toward the stone arch and the street, Gen asked Arthur, "Don't you think that was overstating things a bit?"

"Not at all," he said. "We're supposed to be dating."

"But you're overdoing it. No one will believe you."

Arthur stopped and turned toward her. Winter sunlight slanted over the buildings' roofs, casting black shadows on the straw-colored grass at their bases. A cool breeze cut through Gen's blouse, and she crossed her arms over her chest.

His eyes looked more silvery when they were outside, and his dark hair fell across his forehead. "It wasn't overdoing it."

"Arthur, come on. Look, I know who and what I am. I'm a damn fine lawyer and pretty smart. I work hard, as hard as I can. I like to think that I'm loyal and kind, or at least I'm working on that, too. But I'm not pretty. I'm not skinny. On my very best days, I'm a four."

Arthur blinked, and his mouth opened. "Rating women like that is improper."

"All you guys do it."

"Not me. Not my friends. It's atrocious."

"It is what it is, and I'm a four. A three if my hair isn't behaving."

"And even if we did rate women in that fashion, you're wrong about yourself." He looked around as if gathering himself. "You have gorgeous bone structure and a lush, ripe figure. I would have called you an eight, but that was before I saw you in this outfit. This makes you a nine-plus."

"I'm chubby, and no one likes that, not even me."

"The first time I saw you, I asked you to go to Majorca with me for a weekend. Surely you concede that I meant it. You certainly thought that I meant it at the time. You tried to punch me."

"That wasn't the first time you'd seen me. You'd just never *noticed* me before because no one ever does."

"I must have been blind drunk."

"You didn't look like it."

He shrugged. "That means nothing."

They began walking toward the stone arch and the street

just beyond it.

Gen said, "You picked up some of the prettier girls for a week of drunken debauchery."

"Had I been to lunch with Horace beforehand?" Arthur mused.

"Yes." Horace had always scheduled a lunch meeting with Arthur to converse about his case, and Gen had watched them walk out together every time.

They arrived at the Bentley, waiting for them at the curb.

Arthur opened the rear door for her and shook his head. "That man could hold his liquor. He drank me under the table every time I came into that office. No wonder I put off legal appointments until absolutely necessary."

She asked, "Really?"

"After one of Horace's liquid lunches, I was wrecked for the rest of the day. Often, I sent the girl shopping with Pippa and went back to my apartment to sleep it off. Lunch first, or Harrods?"

She told him, "You don't have to buy me stuff. Hawkes wasn't serious."

"I was serious. Either way, let's go."

Gen got in the car.

Arthur shut the door behind her and ran around to climb in the other side. He tapped the back of the front seat, and Pippa swiveled on the driver's side to look at him. Her pearl-gray hair was a little shorter today, a little more straight on the sides.

He said to the driver, "To Harrods. But to my apartment, first, since it's so close."

His apartment?

Gen held onto the door handle, quietly freaking out inside.

Meet the Dog

Gen gripped the car door's handle with one hand and clenched the other into a fist while Pippa drove. The car glided through the London traffic toward the Knightsbridge section of town, where the rich people lived.

The *really* rich, *really* upper-class people.

People like His Lordship Arthur Finch-Hatten, the Earl of Severn.

Well, Arthur would remain the Earl of Severn for as long as he didn't lose that lawsuit brought by his brother.

And that was Gen's job.

Hyde Park sprawled over one side of the street, bare trees reaching toward the midday sun.

An Edwardian-era apartment building occupied the other side of the street. It was as beautiful as a Victorian building, but it had been built of creamy white stone and columns and was less fussy than a Vicky.

Pippa drove the Bentley down into the underground garage and parked directly beside the elevator.

Arthur hopped out but turned to peer inside the car at Gen. "Are you coming?"

No, no, no, no, no. Not up to Arthur's apartment, not alone with him nor alone with *anyone* in an apartment.

Gen tightened her grip on the door's handle.

Pippa turned around, bracing herself on the steering wheel to twist in her seat. "The cleaning staff should be working at this time of the morning."

Gen looked straight at her. "They will?"

"Not that there is anything to worry about at any time, day or night, but yes. A staff of ten should be in the apartment. The staff reduces to five in the evenings until ten o'clock, when the staff goes home."

"Oh." Gen released her grip on the door handle. "Thanks for letting me know their schedule."

"Of course." Pippa turned back to look out the front of the car.

Gen opened her door, slithered out as modestly as that skin-tight skirt would allow, and followed Arthur to the elevator. Inside, he inserted a keycard into a security slot, entered a code into the number pad, and pressed the six on the panel.

He waited until the heavy doors thunked closed before he asked, "What was all that about?"

"Nothing," Gen said.

The elevator rose six stories into the air, weighing on Gen's feet in her sensible shoes, and the doors slid open to a small hallway.

The floor under her feet was dark, polished hardwood, and rough plaster covered the walls. A small table was set with a lush profusion of yellow and white fresh flowers, roses and carnations. Above them, crystal encrusted a tailored chandelier that lit the small entry area. Doors at the end of the hallway were open, and sunlight poured in.

Such a small hallway, and Gen relaxed. She had just assumed that he lived in some gargantuan mansion of an apartment that spanned half of London, probably because he was an earl and all.

But he was being sued by his brother. He was probably wasting thousands if not millions on his defense. Maybe he had had to economize.

Apartments in central London, especially in the haughty area around Hyde Park, were tiny, even the most expensive ones.

How nice, that Arthur lived in a modest space. Gen

actually felt more comfortable.

He said, "I'm just going to check on my dog."

"You have a dog?" she asked, following him toward the open double doors.

"Just a small dog," he said. "He's such an ornery little thing that he often gets closed up in one of the bedrooms or closets, and no one notices for hours. Sometimes, they forget to let him out for too long."

"Out? Do they walk him over to Hyde Park to—" Gen stopped herself before she said something earthly and ranch-related, "—do his business?"

"Oh, no," Arthur said.

They turned the corner.

An enormous living room opened up in front of them.

Gen screeched to a stop.

The walls of the long, spacious room were dark, but several sets of white couches and chairs lightened the overall effect. Floor-to-ceiling windows opened the room to the terrace outside that wrapped around the whole building.

Beyond the glass, four patio sets were surrounded by small topiaries in white pots, all perfectly trimmed into spirals and balls on sticks. The balcony jutted out on one side, where there was a small grassy area.

Arthur said, "He has a yard for his, *ahem,* business."

A *yard.*

On the sixth floor.

How insanely extravagant.

Gen should have remembered that Arthur's apartment required a staff of ten to clean it every day. It was *huge.*

Because of course, it was. Arthur was a bloody *earl.*

Gen was just his little lawyer who should not gawk like a prairie hen. "Nice place," she said.

"Thanks." He walked over and opened one of the folding glass doors that closed off the outside, leaving it open about a foot. Cool air blew into the apartment.

"So this is home, huh?" she asked.

"Spencer House is home, but it was open for Christmas until just a few days ago and will be open for two more weekends. Sometimes I go back during the week, but mostly I stay here in town." He laughed. "It's the opposite of what my ancestors did. They retreated to their country houses to escape the heat and smell of the London summer and lived in town during the winter."

"Oh, yeah," Gen said, trying in vain to look sophisticated and like she had known that and understood the irony.

"I'll be right back. If you'd like something to drink, the staff should be around." He jogged to the other end of the room—*jogged* because the room was so enormous—and disappeared into another door.

Gen turned, surveying the living room. On the one long side, the living room opened to the balcony.

On the other side of the room, plants topped a half-wall. Beyond that, short stairs led down to a dining room with a long table set for eighteen people. Bookcases behind the dining table rose two stories into the air, stuffed with books and small pieces of art and pottery.

Somewhere far inside the apartment, barking echoed on the mirrored columns and glass walls.

Arthur came jogging back. A small Jack Russell Terrier was chasing Arthur's heels and nipping at his pants legs. The dog was mostly white, but brown stained its ears and face except for a white stripe that ran between its eyes and over its head. His ears were below Arthur's knees as they ran.

When Arthur was halfway through the room, the dog broke off its pursuit and streaked for the door that Arthur had left ajar. It sprinted outside to the grass area and skidded to lift its leg against the one dying topiary bush on a corner of the lawn.

Gen could see the relief on the dog's face as he peed for minutes.

"Got to him in time today," Arthur said. "I don't know

how he keeps getting locked up. I've spoken to the staff about it a number of times, but they don't know how he continues to get trapped in bedrooms and closets. He's just a naughty little dog."

"Yeah, dogs often resemble their owners," Gen said.

The dog shook off everything and bounded inside and over to them. From his exuberant body language—lolling tongue, perked ears, and wagging tail—Gen could see that he was more than friendly as he approached.

"What's his name?" Gen asked.

"Ruckus."

The dog skidded to a stop at her feet and then bounced in place, bounding as high as the middle of her chest with each hop. "Suits him."

Arthur said, "I think it became a self-fulfilling prophecy."

"He sure has a lot of energy."

"He's a young dog, scarcely more than a puppy. He might still have a bit of growing to do."

The dog bounded closer, pushing off Arthur's chest at the top of each bounce with his front paws.

Gen asked, "How long was he locked up?"

Arthur frowned. "I left a few hours ago. I had some business meetings this morning. Couldn't have been too long."

Ruckus bounced a few more times and settled, though his tail was whipping around so hard that his butt was wagging. His white coat shone in the sunlight, clean and healthy. From what Gen could see, his claws had been trimmed and perhaps painted with clear polish.

"He's cute," Gen said.

"I've only had him a few months."

Gen crouched down and scratched the dog's ears.

He jumped up on his rear legs and licked her face before she could move out of the way, taking a swipe of foundation and rouge on his slobbery tongue.

"Oh, good Lord!" Arthur started to reach for him.

Gen laughed because she had grown up around plenty of farm dogs.

"Now, now. Down!" She laid her fingers on Ruckus's nose and guided him downward to sit.

The dog flopped over on his back and squirmed, and she switched to rubbing his belly. His clean fur was silky under her palm.

Arthur retreated and watched her petting the dog. "A friend of mine, Maxence, found him in Africa, abandoned and starving, when he was just half-grown. Max cannot let a creature suffer, so he took him in and brought him to me just a few days later when he came to London for business. I think he's mostly Jack Russell Terrier, though I'm not sure what he was doing on the streets of Africa."

"Must have been quite a culture shock for him, going from starving in Africa to a—" Gen paused, but the word was precise, "—London penthouse."

"I cannot imagine what was going through Max's head. He should have taken the dog to a mutual friend of ours, Caz, who has an impending family and a large property outside of Los Angeles for a dog to run to his heart's content. Instead he brought the dog to a single man who travels constantly, lives a debauched lifestyle, is out until all hours of the night, and lives in a confined apartment in central London."

"Maybe Max thought that you needed him more." *Oops, had that slipped out?* She stopped petting the dog and stood.

Luckily, Arthur laughed. "I've always thought that Max might have a well-hidden sadistic streak. Perhaps he thought owning a dog would be 'good for me.' He *is* trying to save the world."

The dog flipped over and sat up, resting one of his paws on Arthur's shoe while he whined.

"Is he?" Gen was just making conversation sounds.

"Aren't we all?" Arthur reached down and ruffled the dog's ears, then brushed off his pants legs where the dog had been pawing him. "All right, now that I've rescued the dog from imprisonment once again, let's go see what they have at Harrods."

Ruckus followed them all the way to the door of the apartment, nipping at Arthur's heels in a desperate bid for attention, and Arthur gently nudged him back inside as the elevator doors slid closed.

Gen fidgeted, uneasy. That little dog needed exercise and not to be cooped up, even if that apartment was probably a dozen times larger in square footage than the parcel of land that her mother's terraced house stood on. Having grown up on a ranch in Texas, she had been around and understood all sorts of animals: cattle, horses, cats, and dogs. That little pooch needed more than what Arthur could give him.

She asked, "Did you have dogs growing up?"

"Oh, yes," Arthur said.

Okay, maybe he did understand dogs. Gen shrugged as the elevator descended, jiggling as it lowered them toward the car garage.

Arthur continued, "My father had a pack of beagles for hunting when I was a child, but they were given away after my parents died and Christopher and I were packed off for other parts."

Kind of like barn cats or a cattle herd, then.

"But those aren't pets," she said. "Didn't you have pets?"

"Pets weren't allowed in the dorms of Le Rosey. Max managed to keep a field mouse that came in for a few years, feeding it from what he managed to smuggle back from the cafeteria. It was very fat and slept in a shoe box. It lived a few years, a better-than-average lifespan and lifestyle for a wild mouse."

"But you've never had a dog before. Not one that you personally spent time with and were responsible for."

"By those criteria, I guess Ruckus is my first pet," Arthur said.

Well, it wasn't Gen's place to criticize Arthur's pet-owning skills. The dog was obviously healthy, groomed, and well-fed and wasn't cowering as if he had ever been abused.

Ruckus was acting as if he hadn't ever been disciplined, either, but that was a wholly different set of pet ownership skills.

Harrods and Triumph

GEN looked out the side window of the Bentley while Pippa maneuvered it through the streets of London, slipping sedately through traffic until they pulled up at the freaking castle that was the Harrods of London department store in Knightsbridge.

Like Selfridges, Harrods was a city block reaching six-plus stories into the air. The department store was mammoth, almost twice as large as Selfridges, with over a million square feet of space to sell stuff. Plate glass windows lined the ground floor, each showcasing a tableau of things you could buy in there and topped by a green clamshell awning.

Gen emerged from the car and followed Arthur down the sidewalk. The first window that she walked by held a display of a dining room table covered with a delicate lace tablecloth and a teak box stuffed with an exclusive line of tea bags. Around the wooden box, crystal jars of jams and jellies, biscuits and cookies, and sugars from three different sources and five different continents glittered in the spotlights inside.

If she had eaten any of that sugary stuff, she would not have been able to even look at the next window display: designer clothes from Paris painted onto deathly skinny mannequins. Seriously, they were all bald and frail and alabaster white, and they all looked like they were going to die of some horrible bleaching wasting disease to fit into those luxurious couture dresses.

Luckily, Gen was in no danger of either starving to death

or fitting into those luxurious couture dresses. Each one probably cost more than she would make her first year as a full-fledged barrister, anyway.

Wow, those mannequins were freaky. So *emaciated.* And *bald.* And bleached so blindingly *white.*

They walked in through Harrods main entrance into Ladurée, a perfect Parisian tea room restaurant where Gen and her mother used to come for high tea. The macaroon cookies were baked in every flavor and pastel tint under the sun. The cookie case looked like a pale, subdued sunset smeared into an oceanscape, and the room smelled like the roasted almonds that the cookies were made of.

Around them, the chandelier showered light on tiny, white-draped tables surrounded by red velvet-tufted chairs. Gen and her mother liked to sit away from the counters when they drank their tea out of the china cups.

She tried not to think about that. Her mascara wasn't the waterproof kind.

Gen followed Arthur, pushing between people trotting among the little restaurants and grocery shops within the huge department store, kind of like the whole place was a huge Harrods mall with all the little Harrods stores inside crammed up against each other.

From there, she followed Arthur through the cheese shop, the pastry shop, past the oyster bar and sushi bar, all of it packed with people hustling among the towering displays of cheeses and boxed pastries and chocolates and the crowded counters. Everyone bustled through and toted their green bags stamped with *Harrods* in gold.

Everything in Harrods glimmered with gold: the walls, the counters, the ceilings, and especially the sphinxes.

So many sphinxes crouched throughout the store—those Egyptian statues with their lion's paws and women's heads, gilded flesh or faux stone finish and striped headpieces—that Gen wasn't impressed so much as thinking that someone had a *thing* for sphinxes.

A really serious *thing.*

There had to be a word for that. Sphinxophilia? Sphinxosexual? Sphinxy-kinky?

She didn't need to go any further down that line of thought.

Gen followed Arthur from the restaurants section into the perfumery, and the aromas of cheese and chocolate and fish rushed away from the onslaught of roses, spices, and vanilla.

Her eyes stung and watered from the fumes.

She followed Arthur's broad back as he dodged through the people crowded between the counters, and they found the escalators going up.

They rode the escalators up just one floor and walked through racks and towers of panties and bras—my God, they must be in lingerie and this was where he was supposed to buy her expensive underwear that he was *never* going to see her in—to a small shop where all the shoes sported bright red soles.

They had arrived at the Christian Louboutin Shoe Boutique.

Arthur waved Gen forward into the store and lounged in a chair while a saleswoman measured Gen's ticklish feet and discussed her options. They stood before the display, a carousel of hideously expensive shoes, and Gen stole a glance back at Arthur.

He was holding his phone clutched in his hand, the glowing screen slightly turned toward her, but he was also checking out her backside again. His gaze traveled from her ample bum in that too-tight skirt, down her legs to her clunky schoolmarm shoes, and back up. He lingered on her hair, curled in waves from her usual tight bun before Octavia had pulled out the pins.

He caught her watching him, and he smiled at her with that wolfish, predatory grin before he returned to whatever was on his phone.

Maybe he liked Gen's legs. It wasn't inconceivable that

someone with odd, overstimulated taste might like her legs, even if it was just for their chubby novelty.

No, probably not. Her mother had often lamented Gen's "cankles." No one liked her legs.

Gen turned back to the shoes.

Astonishingly, the woman did have scarlet-soled Louboutins in Gen's overly large size. Several pairs, in fact.

Gen was trying on another pair, chatting with the woman who had turned out to be so nice and marveling at how the clerk had managed to find shoes that fit Gen's big, wide feet so perfectly, when she caught Arthur leering at her again.

Well, not leering, precisely. His steady observation of her legs and the shoes wasn't creepy. His steely eyes just showed that he seemed very interested in the way she turned her ankles while she was trying on the shoes.

Those red soles must be flashing at him.

Gen stood and turned around, feeling the leather cupping her feet and Arthur's gaze on her legs. The stiletto heels pushed her feet up farther than she was used to, but she managed.

When she turned back, Arthur was still casually slouched in the chair, his long legs crossed at his ankles, watching her.

He looked up her body, slowly raking her, until he looked into her eyes and said, almost off-handedly, "Those look good on you."

She shook her head. "They're too expensive."

"I said, they look good on you." He held a black credit card for the clerk but didn't look away from Gen's eyes. "She'll wear them out."

"I guess the court date is right after lunch," she said.

The clerk smiled. "I'll just put your old shoes in the box, honey. It'll be fine."

While they walked the few steps from the Louboutin store into the lingerie department, Gen said to Arthur, "I don't like that Octavia essentially blackmailed you into buying this stuff for me."

He shrugged. "I don't mind it. It's certainly a change of scenery for me, and you are keeping me out of trouble for the afternoon. That's the whole point of this relationship charade, isn't it?"

"Kind of looked like you were having fun," she said.

One side of his mouth tipped up. "You have no idea."

"Are you going to watch me try on the Myla bras, too?"

Oh, no.

"I'm sorry," she stammered. "I didn't mean to say that. I really didn't. That was awful and unprofessional, and I'm your *lawyer.*"

Arthur was laughing a deep, good-natured chuckle. "I wasn't aware that watching was an option."

"It's not. It's really not," she back-pedaled.

He laughed again and set the green Harrods bag containing the shoebox on an end table beside an upholstered chair. "Then I'll wait here on the perimeter."

"I really shouldn't let Hawkes pimp me out like this," Gen fretted. Dressing so slutty anywhere, but especially at work, gave her the icky shivers, and she felt like she constantly needed to be ready to fight.

"But it isn't for her titillation. It's to manipulate a judge."

"Does that make it better? Really?"

"Probably not."

Another clerk found Gen wandering around, confused, among the piles and racks and stacked boxes of lingerie and whisked her off to a changing room. She found several sets that fit Gen perfectly and provided enough support for her double-D's. However, she felt, ahem, *freer,* than she usually did in her more traditional bras. Her boobs jiggled more when she walked and swayed when she shrugged. Pale blue ribbons, not proper straps, went over her shoulders and were just visible through the too-tight white blouse.

If Arthur had been sitting on the chair in the corner of the dressing room, the one beside the mirror, when she put the lingerie on her naked skin, would he have smiled?

Would his silvery eyes have watched her, dipping to look at her body?

Probably not.

Well, Judge Roberts would probably appreciate her effort. She hoped that he appreciated it *enough.*

At the cash register, Gen was just pulling out her wallet to pay for the ridiculously expensive bra and matching panties, but the clerk waved her away. "The gentleman already took care of it."

"But I should—"

The clerk smiled at her. "I couldn't argue with him."

Arthur had probably smiled at the clerk and flirted with her, and the woman literally hadn't been able to say no. Or maybe he had just held out that magic, black credit card of his that salespeople and waiters liked so much. "Yeah. I guess not."

She went over to where Arthur was tapping on his phone, texting something. The little Harrods bag holding her old underwear swung from her fingers. "Ready for lunch?"

"Of course." He looked up.

His silvery eyes found her face first, and he smiled at her, but his gaze followed her hair flowing over her shoulders and wandered to her chest. His eyes traced the blue ribbons that showed through her blouse and dipped down to the generous swells of her breasts that were rounder, softer, than when she had been wearing her normal, restrictive bra.

His lips parted, just slightly, and the usual sharpness of his gaze became fuzzy.

Because Gen was standing so close to where he was sitting, when Arthur looked up at her, she saw the dark pupils in his silvery eyes expand.

When he spoke, his voice was lower, huskier. "Let's have lunch. I seem to have worked up quite an appetite." He stood.

In her new, very high Louboutin heels, Gen was just a fraction of an inch shorter than he was, but he was still taller. He looked straight into her eyes, back and forth between them, and smiled.

Gen said, "All right."

The store's air-conditioned atmosphere must have dried out her throat because her voice sounded choked, too.

After a quick lunch in one of the restaurants tucked away on an upper floor, Arthur mentioned, "Why don't you pick out a dress, while we're here? There is an event tomorrow night."

"I can wear that red dress again."

"From what little I understand about these things, no, you can't wear something twice. You'll have clients there. I can have Graham meet us here for a consultation, or you can pick something and he can alter it. He has your measurements, right?"

Gen picked out a long, black dress, with Arthur pretending not to watch her again. His gray eyes seemed to turn smoky when he looked at her in a few of the gowns, especially the more form-fitting ones. The black one that she decided on clung to her curves and pushed up her boobs far more than she would have worn otherwise, but she had always preferred sparkly tents and tarps, as her mother had called them, when she had been forced to go to a party.

After lunch, Arthur and Pippa drove Gen back to her office, where Octavia Hawkes approved of the shoes and lingerie.

Court went swimmingly.

Octavia Hawkes presented their case succinctly and jiggled when she giggled, twice. She had Gen cross-examine a witness, walking slowly in front of the judge's bench and turning while Judge Roberts leered down her blouse from his perched bench.

They won the case.

Because of course, they did.

To celebrate, after Gen had changed back into her pantsuit and they were roundly congratulated at chamber's high tea at four-thirty, Octavia Hawkes took Gen out for supper with several other senior barristers, all of whom smiled indulgently at her.

Octavia mentioned, seemingly in passing, "Gen here is doing splendidly with the Finch-Hatten case. She's been posing as Lord Severn's girlfriend, you remember, to keep an eye on him. He hasn't been in trouble for over a week."

That wasn't quite true, but it soon would be.

One of the senior barristers, David Trent, shifted his bulk toward her. "Yes, we heard that you were taking one for the proverbial team."

Gen laughed. "Only proverbially, I assure you. In the literal sense, I'm not taking one for this team or any other."

David laughed, his belly bouncing with mirth. "That would be above and beyond the call of duty, wouldn't it?"

"I should think so, especially when I can use my wily barrister skills to *talk* him into keeping out of trouble."

David's smile turned from mildly scandalized to thoroughly amused. "That's the type of skills we need at Serle's Court, keeping the clients in line but not crossing the line." He winked at her. "Your pupillage seems to be going well."

She smiled back at him. "I hope so."

"Yes, winning the Finch-Hatten case would look quite well for you when we discuss tenancy," David said, "and it would look quite well for Hawkes for her silk application. When is that decision coming down?"

Octavia smiled at Gen. "Applications open on February sixteenth, just about two weeks from now."

Winning Arthur's case was important for all of them.

Second Party

THE next evening, Gen was again sitting in the back seat of the car with Arthur while Pippa drove them to another party. The black dress had indeed been altered to perfection in the meantime so that it fit snugly over the cast iron underwear that Graham had bought for her. It flattered her curves so well that Gen was just fine with not being able to breathe. She hoped she didn't pass out from lack of oxygen.

Sitting beside her in the back seat, Arthur said, "Shall we polish you up before the party?"

"All right," Gen said as if she were not concerned at all about that.

"First," his voice was quiet and calm, "when someone says, 'How do you do,' you should reply with the same phrase and only that. It's merely a pleasantry and acknowledgment of the introduction."

"Seems kind of unfriendly not to talk," Gen said. "Seems like they're trying to start a conversation."

"It's British. It doesn't have to be friendly. It may lead to other conversations later, if both parties are so inclined."

"All right."

"Be pleasant and reserved. Be amused but not excitable. Don't try to be friendly, merely open to friendliness if the conversation turns that way."

Gen fretted. "A lot of things in the law chambers are starting to make sense."

He leaned in. "Look, you're a lovely person. Let them discover that. Don't give it away."

Gen set her fists on her wide hips, which was not easy to do around the seat belt strapping her in. "How would you know that I'm a lovely person? All I've done is hitched a ride on your coattails to fancy dress parties, spent your money on clothes for myself, and tried to repress your chosen lifestyle because it's convenient for my job."

Arthur laughed. "You told me to get a more experienced barrister though it risked your career—"

Gen snorted. "I was drunk that night."

"—and my dog likes you. He's an excellent judge of character. The one time my brother, Christopher, showed up at my apartment, Ruckus tried to chew his foot off at the ankle."

"Oh, no. What did you do?"

"Pulled him off and fed him pepperoni in the kitchen. It wasn't a deep bite. Hardly any blood."

"You didn't, really."

"Absolutely. It occurs to me that Ruckus would make an excellent watch dog, given half a chance."

"God, think of the liability if he actually hurt someone."

"Spoken like a true barrister."

"You can't let him bite people. You can't even let him snarl or growl, for that matter, or jump up on people or slobber all over them like he was doing."

"Indeed," Arthur said.

She should have known that he was egging her on. "He has to heel when you're walking, behave in public, sit down, and repress all those bouncy instincts of his."

"Yes," Arthur said, "exactly. When in public, one must sit down and be well-behaved. Don't growl or jump up and slobber all over people."

Gen lowered one of her eyebrows at him. "That was convenient."

"Just a happy accident, I assure you. So, while we're at the party, *heel.*"

"Fine," she said, pretending to be put out, but quite

honestly, it was an apt metaphor.

That night's party was at someone's apartment, and it was, as Arthur said, "A small gathering to celebrate someone-or-other's daughter's engagement, the fourth reception of its kind for the bride-to-be and a small one for people who might not attend something large and public."

Gen stood beside Arthur as they rode a glass elevator up to the top of another posh apartment building. She was wearing the Louboutin shoes again. Arthur must have noticed that she was taller than usual because when she stood beside him in the elevator and the city lights fell away below them, he straightened, measuring her with his eyes, and smiled. He still had a few inches on her, but she was north of six feet in those stiletto heels.

Two hundred-ish glittering, perfect people were milling about in an enormous penthouse on top of a building in one of London's fashionable districts. Not Arthur's apartment, though. This one belonged to Lord and Lady Somesuch of Somewhere, but Gen couldn't remember their names for more than a few minutes.

Arthur knew most of the people there, of course, and introduced her to everyone.

When Arthur smiled at her with his warm, affectionate smile after each introduction as his "close friend," she almost believed him. She should be careful not to believe too much.

Heck, she was a barrister. That was probably overall good advice.

They made the rounds of the party, shaking hands, and Gen answered, "How do you do?" to everyone who said it to her, which was most of them.

What shocked her the most was the way that most of the people whom she said it to seemed pleased and relieved at only that little statement, and they moved on to less personal topics of conversation like the weather or the drinks, rather than risk speaking of something so intimate as how someone was doing.

Okay. So now she got it.

Arthur was just getting her a drink at the bar when Gen spotted a familiar couple across the room. The woman's silver and gold hair was twisted up like a thick rope of jewelry.

"Oh, look," she said. "There are your friends Elizabeth and Bentley, again."

"Where?" Arthur asked, scanning the room.

"Over there, by the bar." Gen waved over the crowd to them. Elizabeth smiled and waved back, but then turned back to her conversation.

Arthur took her elbow and steered her toward the other room where the party had spilled into the dining room, which was a convenient place to set drinks while nibbling on shrimp.

Again, bowls of shrimp were laid out all over the place. Their little tails ringed the edge of the bowl like ruffles.

Gen bet that all these fancy-butt parties had those huge, glass bowls of shrimp on ice, but no one ever laid out a nice seven-layer dip. These upper-class people would probably go ape for some proper seven-layer dip.

Or Jell-O shots.

Arthur said, "There are some other people I want you to meet."

Other people were over in that other room, all right, and there were yet more people all over the place. Gen was dizzy with names and occupations and children's names and hobbies and events, but she smiled and said, "How do you do?" when prompted.

So many people.

At one point, she found a bathroom and made use of it, just to breathe for a few minutes, if nothing else.

When she came out, she saw Arthur walking across the room toward the bar, and there was a moment—she almost didn't believe she saw it because it was so quick—but Arthur clasped hands with Elizabeth, the older woman Gen had met, as he passed her. They didn't acknowledge each other, didn't look at each other's eyes, didn't speak. The instant of contact looked like a secret handshake or a magic trick.

Gen forced her way through the crowd, wedging herself between the men in suits and modern tuxedos and the women wearing black satin, gray lace, or navy blue silk. Everyone blocked her way as she tried to make her way over to him.

By the time she found Arthur, by the bar of course, he was standing with his hands in his pockets. "I ordered you some white wine."

Gen smiled at him. "Sounds great. Why didn't you say hi to Elizabeth?"

"Which Elizabeth? There are at least five, here. I know most of the people in attendance. Thanks to generations of inbreeding, I'm related to most of them, too."

"No, that woman that you introduced me to. Her husband's name is Bentley."

"I don't know what you mean."

"You touched her or something."

His gray eyes looked so confused, even though he was smiling. "I have no idea what you're talking about."

Arthur was so gorgeous when he smiled, his lips curving over his straight teeth, his laughing eyes twinkling like frost in the sunlight rimmed by midnight blue.

She said, "I'm sorry. It must have been nothing."

He took his hands out of his pockets and reached for the glass the bartender was offering him. "Here's your wine."

Hours later, Gen was glad to finally escape.

Pippa and Arthur drove her home.

On the way, Arthur tapped the back of the seat to get Pippa's attention and said, "Two. Maybe three."

Pippa nodded.

Gen asked, "What was that?"

He smiled at her. "Minutes that I'll be inside your house

to check your new locks."

"Thank you for those, but I really don't think they're necessary."

"Good locks are important, even if we're only pretending to be a couple."

At least she was getting new locks at her house and office out of this arrangement.

Pippa stopped the car in front of Gen's place, the ramshackle mouse-house propped between the other row houses.

Though Gen assured Arthur that the locks were more than adequate and properly installed, he bulled his way inside her small, terraced house. After seeing Arthur's penthouse apartment a few days before, her mother's little house had seemed so ragamuffin.

Arthur walked past her, despite her protestations, into the tiny space that he must have thought of as a closet with a couch. He inspected the new locks that he'd had installed on her windows and doors.

He poked at the locks on one of the windows on the rear of the house overlooking the small garden and frowned. "You need an electronic alarm system, one that will alert the police."

She told him, "This neighborhood is really safe. I caught heck from my neighbors the other day when I let you in here because they didn't know you. They're probably all watching from their windows to make sure that you leave at a Godly hour."

"I'm not worried about your neighbors," he said, peering up through the window at the houses across her small yard and the fence beyond.

"Then who are you worried about?"

He kept looking out of the window. "People who are not your neighbors."

Well, it made sense that Arthur was paranoid. He was worth billions. Doubtlessly, one of the reasons that he had been shuffled off to a boarding school in the remote Swiss Alps was the threat of kidnapping.

Gen bit her lip. That must have been a terrible way to grow up, locked away with all the other kids who were worth more as hostages than for their souls. "I'm sure I'll be fine, Arthur. There's no reason for anyone to care about me."

"You might be surprised." He tapped the window lock. "Have a good night, Gen."

Accident

On the way home from dropping off Gen, as a dark coldness filled the back seat of the car, Arthur leaned forward and said, "Pippa, find a place to pull over."

"Problem, sir?" Pippa's head, checking her mirrors as she looked at the streets and car parks that they passed.

"Yes. Two cars over, one back. The black sedan. Let it pass when you pull over."

"There's a green sedan, too," she said.

"Yes." Ah, Pippa has seen them, too. The cars had followed them from the party to Gen's house and onward. He had made sure that all three had followed him. None had peeled off at Gen's place.

He had been followed more and more, lately, by several cars, which meant a surveillance team. One time, he had been quite sure that four cars had been following him, a new record. Even Elizabeth didn't rate four cars.

Pippa pulled the Bentley into an alley and stopped it.

Arthur shoved his door open and leapt out, slamming it behind himself. As he reached for the driver's door, the door lock popped up and Pippa was already across the seat to the passenger side, her legs balled up as she scooted out of his way. Arthur slid into the driver's seat, jammed the car into reverse, and jumped into traffic as Pippa buckled her seatbelt on the passenger side.

Pippa may have been a professional chauffeur, but Arthur had more specialized training.

The black car tailing them had already passed them, but

the green car he had suspected was the second tail had pulled into a parallel parking space to wait. As he watched in the rearview mirror, it slid into the stream of traffic a few cars behind him, its headlights a little brighter than the other cars in the nighttime London traffic.

Cheeky of them to send someone into London to watch Arthur at home. When he was in Europe, he expected surveillance and took countermeasures, but being followed through the streets of Britain was new.

Arthur drove through the fluid London traffic, heavy for that late at night, drifting through lanes and turning quickly onto side streets. He doubled back once and became quite sure that a third car, a white economy sedan, was following them.

The car pinged because he hadn't put on his seat belt, and he gunned the engine. It roared down the dark street.

He sped, cutting between cars and taking quick turns. Pippa watched the passenger mirror and by turning around, informing him of the other cars' movements.

Elizabeth had passed a micro-USB stick to him at the party. When he'd had a moment of privacy, he'd examined it using his phone. Several files had been placed in a folder called "Examine and Report." A second folder, titled "Personal," contained a note that admonished him for his relationship with Gen. The note had clearly been written by Elizabeth herself. Arthur had seen too many examples of her Germanic-influenced grammar over the years to be fooled into thinking that it was from some other director. In the note, Elizabeth reminded Arthur that he was to "cultivate" Gen, to make sure that Gen was exceedingly invested in victory in his court case. Winning that court case and retaining his title and wealth was of utmost importance.

How the devil was Arthur supposed to cultivate Gen when Elizabeth so blatantly warned her off? Her comment in the ladies' room that Gen had relayed to Arthur still rankled him.

Such contradiction. One might get the impression that Elizabeth was personally conflicted in the matter, but Arthur knew better than that.

In the rear view mirror, Arthur saw bright headlights swerve through the night to follow them around a corner.

Damn it.

Those tails might be from several different agencies, or they might be following each other, following him.

They might be dispatched by the CIA or the Mossad, too.

The Egyptian Gihaz al-Mukhabarat al-Amma was pissed at him right now, with good reason.

So was the Russian FSB, for excellent reasons.

Arthur smiled and whisked the Bentley through the traffic, whipping around other cars and spinning the wheels down side streets.

The other cars were still there.

He sped up, tracking their headlights through the dense London traffic.

The seatbelt warning alarm chimed again.

He could lose them. He knew he could. If he could just get an opening around the next corner to dodge through the rabbit warren streets of Westminster, he knew that he could lose the tails. Damn it, he was better than this.

Pippa said, "Arthur, watch that—"

A blinding whiteness.

Pain flashed through him.

Darkness slammed his ears and eyes from both sides.

He reached through the darkness, trying to stay conscious.

Gen.

An Extreme Option

When Octavia Hawkes called Gen into her office the next day, Gen knew that it must be about Arthur even though she hadn't seen any new evidence against him that morning. Gen had been all over the gossip pages, clicking and searching on her phone while she was doing her make-up and getting dressed in her small bathroom, but *nothing* new had shown up.

Maybe Octavia had found the pictures from the Parisian strip club, but those had been out for almost a week. Gen had had trouble finding them again because they had dropped off the bottoms of the pages and into the archives.

Surely, he could not have gotten into trouble last night. He had dropped her off at home well after midnight.

What was wrong with Arthur that he would go carousing so late at night, and what could he have done that was so spectacular that he had ended up on the gossip websites once again?

Or, what was wrong with Gen that she was so exceptionally boring and tedious that she drove a man to do something so insanely stupid just from being in her presence for a couple of hours?

Really, that question was every bit as valid as the one about Arthur.

When Gen knocked on Octavia's imposing office door, Octavia was standing by her window, glaring at the rooftops around the buildings of Lincoln's Inn. When Octavia looked over at Gen, her mouth was the smallest, angriest red dot that Gen had ever seen. The filler in her cheekbones stood out, making Octavia's face look even more skull-like.

"Sit down, Gen." Octavia barely moved her lips.

Gen sat. She folded her hands in her lap and waited for her boss to speak.

Octavia asked, "Have you seen them?"

Them? Oh, God. There must be more than one picture out there. "No. How bad are they?"

"Bad." Octavia resumed staring out the window.

Gen checked her phone. No texts from Arthur. She typed to him, *When will you be here?*

The reply came in a moment. *As soon as I can.*

Where are you?

In the courtyard.

"He'll be up here in just a minute," Gen told Octavia. "He's outside."

"I'm surprised," Octavia muttered.

Gen didn't want to ask why.

Had Arthur been thrown in jail?

Had he managed to get himself all the way to Paris again? Was he in jail in Paris or in some stripper's bedroom?

Had the pictures shown him to be, ahem, *tied up* in a most literal way that would impede him being able to make an appearance in his lawyers' chambers? Yeah, that would elicit sarcasm like that from Octavia.

Gen sat with her ankles crossed and her knees locked together.

Octavia fumed in silence.

Five minutes later, Arthur limped into the room.

Limped.

A dark bruise ran up one side of his cheek, and his eyelid on that side was swollen. His stiff posture looked like his ribs were taped from being broken.

Gen jumped up. *"Arthur!"* She ran to him and touched his shoulder, afraid to grab him because she didn't know how far or how deeply those bruises went. "What on God's green

Earth happened to you? Did someone jump you?" She went ahead and grabbed his shirt over his shoulder. "Were you in a fight? Did someone try to kidnap you? *Is that why you've been having new locks put on my office and my house, because you're in danger?"*

The eyebrow over his unbruised eye rose. "Car accident."

"Oh my God, Arthur. Come sit down." She took his hand and led him over to the chairs in front of Octavia's desk. "Is anything broken? Is Pippa all right?"

"Nothing broken." Arthur smiled lopsidedly at Octavia. "If I'd've known that I would receive this treatment, I would have driven my car into a wall sooner."

"You didn't answer about Pippa. Is she all right?"

"Pippa is fine. Not a scratch on her. She got me out of the car before the police got there. I took the brunt of it."

Gen sat him down in the chair, and because she didn't want to touch his bruised face and hurt him, she gently smoothed back his hair. "You poor thing. You poor, poor thing."

Arthur watched her, mostly with his eye that wasn't nearly swollen shut. She almost thought she imagined it, but he might have tilted his head and leaned into her touch. He certainly closed his eyes.

Octavia butted in, "The accident management company called this morning with the details. He was sideswiped. The person who caused the accident fled the scene, and he barreled into a wall, missing several pedestrians on the sidewalk. Witnesses said that he was driving quickly but not dangerously. Oddly, his blood alcohol was under the limit, barely."

Gen whirled on Octavia. *"You knew about this?"*

Octavia was staring at Gen, still angry. "I thought you knew."

"No." She turned back to Arthur. "I will sue the *shit* out of the other guy. I'll take his house and his car and rip the shirt off his back. He'll be walking naked down the street when

I'm finished with him."

"Hit and run," Arthur said. He spoke like talking might be hurting him. Dark purples and red stained his skin up one side of his face.

"When the police find him, I'll make him wish he had crawled into a hole and never come out."

"The police won't find him," Arthur said.

"Why wouldn't they be able to find him?"

"Just a hunch."

Gen heard her voice becoming shrill but could not stop herself. She clutched his arm and stared into his battered face. "Was someone trying *to hurt you?"*

"Oh, no. Just a wrong place, wrong time thing, I'm sure." He brushed off any other implications with a wave of his hand.

"And yet," Octavia said, "there are newspaper items about your driving before the accident—erratic, high-speed driving, perhaps negligent—with pictures of the crashed and smoking car."

Gen felt stupid when she squeaked, *"The car caught on fire?"*

"Just a little bit," he assured her. "Practically not at all."

Gen turned to Octavia. "I don't know what to say."

Octavia's red lips were still pursed into an angry dot. "I would say that, despite the girlfriend charade, you're not keeping him out of trouble."

"He was in a car accident! It's not like he was caught in a compromising situation."

The black lines of Octavia's eyeliner and heavy mascara narrowed around her brown eyes. "No. That was last week in Paris, wasn't it?"

Oops.

Guess those pictures of Arthur with the three strippers weren't as buried as Gen had thought. "I'm sorry," she started.

"I only saw them this morning after his solicitors called. This is ridiculous," Octavia said. "Lord Arthur Finch-

Hatten, I am hereby withdrawing as your barrister, which means Gen is off your case, too. We don't fight hopeless causes like Atticus fucking Finch. Call your solicitors to find someone else to argue your case."

"No!" Gen stood up.

Octavia's lips were pressed into a hard line, and they barely moved when she spoke to Gen. "You can't keep him out of trouble. Every time he drops you off at your house, he runs off like a tomcat that scents a female in heat. Not one but *two sets* of scandalous photos *and* a car wreck with suggestions of reckless driving in a few weeks? *Two* incidents would have been enough, but three? *Impossible.* It is *impossible* for us to continue as his barristers if he insists on living his life in this irresponsible, indefensible manner."

"I could move in with him." Gen slapped her hand across her own mouth. *What was she saying?*

Arthur staggered to his feet. "I agree."

Gen looked at him. *My God, he was serious.*

"What!" Octavia's jaw dropped as far as the tucked skin on her face would allow.

Gen asked him, "Are you okay with this?"

"I am entirely in your hands," he said, bending from his trim waist in what looked like a courtly bow, a sore and stiff courtly bow.

Octavia said, "This is an outlandish scheme, entirely ill-advised."

Arthur said, "The problems are occurring when we return Genevieve to her house, so she can stay at my apartment or at Spencer House."

Octavia spoke to Gen. "No matter what I asked you to wear for Judge Roberts, I will not act as your literal pimp. This is insane."

Gen protested, "I'm *not* sleeping with him."

"Yes, and if you keep saying it *just* like that, the other barristers *might* continue to believe you. If you shack up with him, they will not."

"I'm not sleeping with him!"

Octavia eyed Arthur and asked Gen, "You're truly not?"

"No! That's not the point, anyway," Gen said. "The point is to keep him out of trouble."

Arthur said, "Even with the new locks that I have had installed at Gen's apartment and in chambers, her security is inadequate. She needs better security measures. She might as well stay with me for a few days or so until we can update her system."

Octavia rounded on Gen. "You can't install non-standard locks on your office door."

Gen said, "He was worried about his personal information being stolen."

"What if we needed a brief from your office?"

"I'm *always* here."

"What if you were sick? Injured and in hospital?"

Gen planted her fists on her hips. "I'd drag myself in, holding my intestines in my hands, and unlock the door."

"What if we needed it immediately?"

"That's enough," Arthur said, holding his hands up. "I furnished the Head Clerk a copy of the key."

Octavia frowned as best she could, but her lips couldn't turn down very far and her forehead didn't move at all. "I'll check with Celestia. I suppose that's sufficient."

"About Gen moving in with me," Arthur pressed.

Octavia stared up at him, her head tilted far back. "You could just behave like an adult without anyone babysitting you."

"Evidently, that's unlikely," he said.

"Why?" Octavia asked, glaring at him.

Gen said, "His trial isn't due to start for months, anyway. We keep postponing it."

"Why are we postponing it? Every time we do, *His Lordship—"* Octavia could make her words pour sarcasm when she wanted to "—does something *asinine* and gives them more evidence."

"It was Horace's strategy," Gen said. "His notes said that, because the losing outcome was so dire even if unlikely, forestalling the trial was preferable. Plus, we think that the claimant is paying his lawyer on a no-win, no-fee basis."

"That's odd," Octavia said. "Orval usually doesn't take cases on that basis." The law is a small world.

"But delaying is certainly a viable tactic."

Octavia frowned. "Indeed, but it runs up costs and delays the inevitable, tying up time and resources. Solicitors send over trial instructions for just this reason."

Arthur said, "About Gen moving in with me."

Gen looked up at him, watching the serious expression on his battered face and in his silvery eyes, or at least the eye that wasn't swollen nearly shut.

Octavia said, "You're rather intent on that, aren't you?"

"My places have better locks and security systems," Arthur assured her.

Places. Plural.

Disgustingly rich people were weird.

Octavia said, "But Gen isn't the one who looks as if they've been through a meat grinder. It seems that your protection is not particularly effective." She turned to Gen. "We should drop this case *today.*"

"No," both Arthur and Gen said. They looked at each other.

Gen said, "I can keep Arthur out of trouble. I'll move in with him to do it, and we'll win this case. No more stalling on it, either. We'll set a court date."

Octavia glared at both of them. "You had better be correct about this, Genevieve. We'll give it one more month, but I want to see a court date on the calendar or you could face other challenges. Sun Tzu said, 'When your weapons are dulled, your ardor dampened, your strength exhausted and your treasure spent, other chieftains will spring up to take advantage of your extremity.'"

"We promise," Gen said.

Octavia whipped around and glared straight at Arthur. *"And no touching."*

THREATS

AFTER Arthur arrived home from Gen's law office, he collapsed into his bed.

Ruckus, his little dog, was sleeping on the other side of the bed, miracle of miracles. The beast had bounced beside his bed for twenty minutes, begging for a walk, when Arthur had crawled into the bed, sore and thoroughly exhausted.

The emergency room physicians at the hospital had assured him that his ribs were not broken, just bruised, but he was quite sure that at least one was cracked. He had had broken ribs before, more than once. He knew what it felt like. It felt like this sharp pain cutting through his side when he breathed. Each inhale and exhale moved the broken bone.

The pain pills should take effect soon, he hoped. A bit of sleep before that supper tonight would be welcome.

His face throbbed. More bruises, he was assured. That, he believed. His skin felt swollen and scraped, but the bones underneath felt whole.

His phone chirped the normal tone, and he picked it up.

The screen read *Serle's Court Barristers.*

He swiped the dot, and the pain receded for a moment at the prospect of hearing Gen's voice. "Yes?"

A woman who was definitely not Gen Ward said in a lower, angry voice, "What are you up to, Arthur?"

Ah. The call was from Octavia Hawkes, Gen's pupil mistress, not Gen.

Disappointment rolled through him, flattening him to the

bed.

Arthur almost dropped the phone.

He would have to think about that, but later. "Yes, Octavia?"

"Arthur, we need to discuss your idea about Genevieve Ward moving in with you."

"It was actually her idea to move in."

"This had better not be some scam to get that girl into bed with you."

"It isn't," he protested. "I wouldn't."

"Oh, bullshit. Your usual *modus operandi* is to whisk a woman off to some overly warm locale, buy her a range of bikinis and lingerie, and throw money and alcohol around until she falls on her back."

"I do not." Arthur shouldn't have bothered wasting his breath with that denial. Those pain pills must be making his brain fuzzy.

"I swear to God, Arthur. To be frank, she's a nice girl. She's a hard worker and a sharp barrister, and I think she may be an excellent addition to Serle's Court if you don't fuck it up for her. If she's caught fucking a client, the best I can do is to get her a third six in some other chambers, where she *might* have a shot at obtaining tenancy, but that's if she isn't hauled before the Ethics Board or the Bar Council for ethics violations."

"Yes, Oct," he said.

"If you ruin her chances, I will drop your case, and no one else from Serle's Court will touch it. No one from *any* reputable barristers' chambers will touch it. You'll have some hack representing you, and you will lose your earldom, all the wealth associated with it, and your status. For all I know, you'll have no means of support. Do I make myself perfectly clear?"

"Yes, Oct."

Her tone softened. "Don't fuck her over. You've broken enough hearts in this office."

"Surely you don't mean yourself."

"I knew what you were, Arthur. I meant Lily, Celestia, Evelynne—"

Arthur cringed with each name Octavia Hawkes listed.

"—Lacey-Jade, Darcey, Zarah, Summer—"

"You forgot Maddison," he said.

Octavia's dry tone chastised him. "I was going to ask you whether I should go on because I was tiring of listing names."

"Oh. Please don't." He stretched. His bruised and battered muscles groaned inside him.

"They were all admins, clerks, or weren't associated with your case. Gen is different. I hate to use the term in this day and age, but you could *ruin* her."

"I'm aware of that, and I—" Dare he say it? "—I *like* her, Oct. She seems kind."

"You have no idea, Arth."

He laid his head down on the pillow, resting. The linen cooled his cheek. "Don't I?"

"Probably not, and it's not my place to discuss it with you. Now, don't fuck her and ruin her chances with us and with the Ethics Board, all right?"

"I won't, Oct."

"Good. You looked like crap this morning."

"You didn't. You looked sharp as always. You're formidable in court."

Her softer voice sounded pleased when she said, "Get some sleep, Arth."

After Octavia had hung up the phone, instead of getting some sleep, Arthur dialed a different number.

"Yes," a woman's voice said.

Arthur said, "I've had a problem, and I'm going to need some help."

Shacking Up

THAT evening after work, Gen was driven back to her place by Pippa to pack up a few things. The driver's shining gray hair was neatly combed in place, and her skin was smooth, unscratched, and unbruised. She hopped when she bustled out of the car to open Gen's door.

Dusk was settling over the narrow streets of London as the car, a shiny, black Rolls Royce Phantom, growled in the cooling air. Minuscule twinkling lights salted the car's ceiling like stars.

Jeez, who had a *Rolls* as their back-up car?

"Are you all right, after the accident?" Gen asked Pippa.

"Perfectly fine, but *I* was wearing my seatbelt," she said. "One bruised shoulder from the belt, and the airbag skinned my nose a bit."

Gen couldn't see the abrasion on Pippa's nose. "I'm glad to hear it. Where's Arthur?"

"Resting before supper tonight. There's another charity event to attend, I'm afraid."

"I can't believe he's taking me to all these things."

"I can't believe you're going with him. My God, they must be boring. I'd rather wait in the car with a book."

"You wait in the car? Oh, we can get a taxi."

"First of all, it's my job. I'm being paid quite well to read a book in a very comfortable car. Second, there are usually rooms where the other chauffeurs wait, but then I would have to talk to the other humans and pretend that I liked them."

Gen laughed. "All right, then."

"And Lord Severn has had a few dresses sent around for you. He says that if you would like to go shopping, you're to take his card and I'm to drive you. However, in the interest of time, dresses are already at his apartment. Graham picked them out."

"I'm sure they're lovely. Can you tell him thank you?"

"You'll see him in an hour or so, and I believe that he is sleeping now. The emergency room and X-rays took a while last night, and then he had some early business meetings." Pippa stopped the car in front of Gen's mother's house. "I'll be waiting right here when you come back with your things, reading my book. Don't rush."

Gen rushed.

She dashed around her bedroom on the third floor of the cozy house, a converted attic space that was still smaller than she imagined any of Arthur's closets to be. She tossed her several business suits into a garment bag and jammed handfuls of pantyhose, underwear, and bras in the bottom. Down the stairs to the second floor where her mother's bedroom and the full bathroom were, and she used her arm to scoop all the makeup on the counter into a shopping bag.

Done.

She raced out of the house and cranked the key in the three shiny new locks.

Pippa had reclined her seat and was reading a thick paperback. A sword and a crown were painted on the cover. "Back so soon? No one even died yet."

"No problem. I just needed a few things." She wrestled the overstuffed garment bag into the back seat ahead of herself as if it were a six-foot-tall drunk slug. "I'm sorry it took so long."

"Not too long at all," sighed Pippa, closing her book. "Off to Lord Severn's."

Pippa rode the elevator up with her, showed her how to use the security card, told her the code, and handed the card over to her.

Gen said, "Oh, I couldn't."

Pippa shook the card at her. "Of course, you must."

It was logical that she should have a key to the apartment if she were living there. Gen tucked the card in her wallet.

Pippa said, "And Lord Severn would like you to utilize one of his cars while you're here. You'll meet his other driver tonight."

"I wondered if you ever got a day off."

Pippa smiled at her. "Lord Severn treats us very well, as well he should. I could tell you such stories."

"Oh, please do," Gen said.

Pippa winked at her. "But he pays us too well." She ushered Gen from the entryway into the apartment. "The staff will bring up your things from the car."

Pippa went back into the elevator and was gone.

Gen was alone in the sprawling living room, and the emptiness went all the way to the unoccupied creamy sectional couch and the vacant veranda and out into the empty air and the green swells of the treetops of Hyde Park across the street.

Wow, this place was big. Even if you broke up that couch into all its pieces and fit them together like a Tetris puzzle, it still wouldn't have fit in the reception room at Gen's little house.

Frantic scratching skittered, and Gen turned in time to see Ruckus barreling into the room at her. "Oh, no! *Down boy!*"

Ruckus launched himself through the air and bounced off her boobs. He landed on his back on the couch.

Undeterred, he leapt right back at her and sprinted around her legs in circles, his wagging tail whipping the backs of her calves.

"Ruckus, honey. Sit! *Sit!*"

Behind her, a man said, "Ms. Ward, I presume?"

She stood up from trying to grab Ruckus's collar. "Yes,

sir?"

Behind the living room, a half-staircase led down into a long dining room. A man stood there, his jet black hair slicked back against his head from his sharp widow's peak. His suit was as tailored and shiny as his hair, and his eyes glittered like obsidian. "I'm Royston Fothergill, the head of staff for Lord Severn. Mr. Hollands, if you would?"

Another man in a black suit rushed in and dragged Ruckus away by his collar, muttering, "Bad dog. Bad dog. Down. *Ouch.* Bad dog. You need your claws trimmed."

Royston Fothergill said, "Madam."

"How do you do," Gen said. *Hey, she remembered.*

"How do you do," Royston Fothergill said. His voice was pitched low, an octave below where his voice might naturally be, and quiet but firm. She couldn't decide if he sounded more like an old-timey butler or a vampire. "Lord Severn is still resting. I am to show you to your room and help you settle in. This way, if you please."

Mr. Fothergill led her across the wide room and into a long hallway that meandered farther into the high-rise building. The kitchen was predictably enormous, probably because it was meant for catering parties. The black stone counters gleamed, reflecting the silver appliances that Gen supposed were stainless steel but might have been actual silver. The breakfast bar across the center island seated six.

The hallway ran back into the house, and Mr. Fothergill motioned down the corridor. "You may go anywhere in the house except the third bedroom, the door on the right. That is Lord Severn's private study."

Oh, yeah. *Private study.* The room must be either a Red Room of Kinky Stuff or a home theater dedicated to porn. Yeah, Arthur probably had a couple of kinks that probably needed a whole room to deal with. Or maybe it was *worse.* What could be worse? Maybe he had something in there that needed to be hosed down afterward.

Ew.

The butler showed Gen to the first bedroom, where two women wearing black dresses were hanging up her business suits from her garment bag.

"I can do that," Gen said.

Mr. Fothergill ignored her outburst. "Your bathroom is in here," he said, opening a door in the side wall. Behind him, an alabaster white bathroom sparkled, and again, this little guest bath was far larger than the only full bathroom that Gen and her mother had at home. There were two sinks in this one, plus a soaking tub that Gen might have drowned in, had she not learned to swim at the local YMCA and the shallow, warm Gulf of Mexico off the Texas coast.

The king-sized bed that stood against one wall was dressed in ecru and trimmed with subtle threads of gold glinting in the winter sunlight.

Nice, the bedroom was nice, but Gen kind of wished that she had grabbed the red and green Rose of Sharon quilt that her mother had made when Gen was a kid. The quilt was a little threadbare, but the cotton still smelled like sunlight.

The bedroom smelled slightly like fresh glue, like maybe the carpeting was new, but even more like the huge bowl of rose potpourri that stood between two vases packed full of fresh, white roses. The flowers reflected in the mirror of the dresser they stood on.

"Is the room all right?" she heard Arthur say.

Gen spun.

Arthur was leaning against the door frame, again dressed in the longest-legged denim jeans that Gen had ever seen. He had to have those custom made. No one made inseams that long.

The bruises on his face made her think of lemon juice seeping out of an eggplant.

"The room is beautiful. I can't believe it, it's so beautiful."

"I've never had a babysitter before."

Mr. Royston Fothergill and the two women looked at each

other and high-tailed it out of the room, excusing themselves to squeeze by Arthur. When they were gone, he walked over and sat on a chair, the chair beside the loveseat. The chair, loveseat, and coffee table filled some of the space in the huge bedroom.

When Arthur sat, he eased himself into the chair.

She said, "You were in a car accident last night. Don't you think you should beg off from the party tonight, take it easy?"

Arthur shrugged, his broad shoulders lifting carelessly, except that his left shoulder didn't drop as quickly as the other. He looked stiff, and he was still leaning over, his hands braced on his knees, breathing through his nose. "The benefit is for some earthquake, somewhere. If I don't go, others will be less inclined to do the right thing. Occasionally, I'm a good influence, no matter what people say."

He really shouldn't be running around the city all beat up like that.

Gen was standing in front of him, and she balled up her hands and set them on her hips. "Can't you just send them a check? We could stay in, maybe order some food from Mumbai Take-Away?"

Arthur looked up, his gaze climbing from her pantsuit knees all the way up to her eyes.

Looking down at him was a new experience. His cheekbones were even more pronounced, and his chin more triangular.

His head dipped as he swallowed. He didn't blink, and his silvery eyes were opened wide. The swelling was going down fast on the bruised one. His dark eyelashes were so thick that it almost looked like he was wearing eyeliner, except she was close enough to see that he wasn't.

He said, "Maybe we could do that, sometime. Maybe we could watch a movie."

"I'm not propositioning you. I'm not suggesting Netflix

and chill. You look like you've been run over by a truck, and maybe you shouldn't go out tonight."

"I was merely suggesting, some night that I don't have a scheduled engagement, perhaps we could watch a movie and get some take-away." His eyes were so silver-blue that they looked luminous. "Maybe we could make popcorn."

"Yeah," Gen said. Her breath was stuck in her chest like she couldn't quite inhale, and he hadn't looked away from her. "I'd like that."

"But we can't tonight," he said, sitting back in the chair and rubbing his hand over the shadow on his cheek. "We have an event, and I should shave before we go."

"You don't have to," Gen said. "You look fine."

"I should at least shave. I am thought to be thoroughly disreputable already."

"Those bruises look horrid, and a little bit of scruff on a man isn't a bad thing."

A slow smile started at the corners of his mouth. "It isn't?"

"No." *My God. What was she saying?* "I think it looks good on you."

He watched her for another moment, that smile spreading across his mouth. He said, "Then I'll just trim it up a bit around the edges. We are running late, and the sooner we make an appearance, the sooner we can leave tonight."

"Sounds good," she said.

Arthur grabbed the arms of the chair and pushed, levering himself to standing. He didn't wince, but one of his dark eyebrows twitched downward.

"Are you sure you're okay?" she asked. "That looked like it hurt."

"I'm fine." He straightened and sucked in a breath. "The A&E doctor prescribed some pills. I'll take some for tonight so that I don't embarrass myself."

What He Would Do

Christopher

Hours later, sometime near midnight, Gen held Arthur's warm, huge hand as he leaned against the wall of the elevator.

She asked him, "Are you sure you're okay?"

"I'm fine," he slurred. "A little buzzed. No problem."

Oliver, the driver who had relieved Pippa and driven the Rolls Royce to the hotel where the charity event had been held, was staring at Arthur. His dark eyes were huge on his face as he looked on with horror.

"He's never like this," Oliver said for the thousandth time.

"I think it was the pain pills," Gen whispered to Oliver. "And then his brother was there, and the two of them were matching shots in some sort of unspoken machismo drinking contest, but Christopher wasn't on Oxycontin for bruised ribs."

"My ribs are properly broken," Arthur said, "not bruised. I know what it bloody well feels like. Some thugs jumped me in Cairo a few years ago and broke my ribs. Got my wallet but not the flash drive they were after. Thugs. Assholes. *Thugs.*" He mumbled something else, maybe in some other language, but Gen couldn't make it out.

The elevator doors slid apart.

Gen said, "Come on, honey. Let's get you to bed."

"All right. If you insist."

From anyone else, that might have sounded leering and smarmy, but Arthur's monotone voice just sounded exhausted.

Gen led Arthur out of the elevator, and he walked under his own power, not stumbling, not falling all over things and slobbering, but he wove when he walked. He crowded up next to her, veering when he walked, and for a moment, her face was practically lying on his shoulder. Traces of the sweet spices and musk of his cologne clung to the warm skin on his neck, and a faint whiff of whiskey fell from his breath.

Oliver peered around Arthur at Gen. Oliver's Caribbean accent lilted when he asked, "Do you want me to stay? Help you get him to his room?"

It was after ten o'clock, so all the other staff had gone home. The dark apartment stretched across the building. The dim floor lights were glowing puffballs in the blackness.

Arthur told Oliver, "Thank you, but we're fine. Gen doesn't need to help me to bed at all. I am never *drunk.* And I'm certainly never hung over."

Several gossip websites had published photographic evidence to the contrary, but okay, whatever Arthur needed to believe to get him through the night.

He was thoroughly wasted at the moment. Every time he leaned against something, he fell asleep. His silvery eyes had dulled to gray-blue, and he hadn't opened them fully when she had led him from the car.

Oliver glanced at Gen. "What do you think, Miss? Are you all right?"

Arthur leaned against the wall and stared at his feet. "No one needs to help me to bed. I'm fine. Thank you both for your concern. Oliver, we won't need your services. Good night."

Oliver was still looking around Arthur's shoulder at Gen. His skin was browner but not much lighter than the arm of Arthur's tuxedo. "Miss?"

Gen had liked Oliver from the moment she'd met him, his easy formality and gentleness had made it easy to do so, and she didn't want to get him in trouble. "We'll be fine. I'm sure he'll be fine. I'll follow him to his bedroom and then leave him there."

Arthur left them standing in the foyer as he walked, carefully and in a mostly straight line, across the long, dark living room. Someone must have closed the thick, glass doors that ran across the room because the traffic outside was almost silent.

Gen told Oliver, "He isn't even swaying. I guess we'll be fine."

"All right." Oliver held out a white card for her between two stubby fingers. "I'll wait in the car downstairs for five minutes. Even after that, you can call me, and I'll come right back."

She smiled at him, "Thank you," but she took the card.

Oliver stepped into the elevator, and Gen chased Arthur through the living room. "Arthur? Honey? You okay?"

"I'm fine," he said, walking slowly. He reached out and touched the railing that divided the living room area from the step-down dining room but didn't falter.

"I know you're fine. I just want to make sure you get to bed all right."

"I'm fine." He trailed his fingers down the railing.

"I have never seen someone drink so much, and you fell asleep in the car on the way back."

"I hardly slept last night."

"It was really hard to wake you up."

"Ask the dorm mothers at Le Rosey how hard it was to wake me up for class. I sleep like the dead." He was still slurring his words.

"Just let me see you to your room." She caught up with him and took his hand.

Arthur pulled his hand away and stopped in the short hallway that led to his bedroom, which was far away from the guest bedroom where Gen was supposed to sleep. "Don't."

"Look, this might be just an arrangement, but that doesn't mean we can't be friends. A friend would pour you into bed and take your shoes off."

He was standing right in front of her in the dark, and the lights of London shone in through the glass wall and glinted in his eyes in the dark.

"And then what?" he asked. "And then you, also having had too much to drink—"

"I haven't had too much to drink." Maybe a few, but not too many.

"—would kiss my forehead good night, and I'd reach for you and pull you into bed with me."

"This isn't a stupid, shallow movie where the pretty people fall into bed for no good reason. I wouldn't do that."

"Maybe you couldn't resist me. Maybe I will cast my spell on you."

"Oh, good grief, Arthur. You make it sound like you're the ancient British god of sex."

"Maybe that's it. Maybe I'm the reincarnated Druidic Young God, and that's why every woman I meet hands me her panties and leaves with a smile on her face."

"Or maybe you're drunk and full of yourself, honey." Gen mused about it, there in the dark penthouse above London because she had had too much to drink. "Besides, sex is just poking and vague hip movements, maybe some moaning or squirming."

In the shadows, Arthur leaned on the railing, a dark figure in the darker room. "Are you a virgin?"

"Oh, God, no." Gen waved one hand.

He said, "You sound like you are."

"I assure you, I'm not. I just don't see what all the fuss is about."

He shrugged, the shoulders of his silhouette rising and falling. "The fuss is the best part."

"Everyone does the same fuss. It's all just more of the same."

"Oh, no, it's not."

"Your fuss can't be so different than everyone else's. What could you do to a woman that's so different?"

He stepped toward her.

Gen didn't step back, not this time. Maybe it was the dark, maybe it was the tequila punch, but the warm, spiced scent of his cologne drifted through the night to her, and something darker, more masculine, as his shadow loomed above her.

He ducked his head and whispered near her shoulder. "First, I'd turn her around so that she was facing this wall, here." He tapped the white plaster that separated the living room from the kitchen. "I'd press my body against her back as I kissed the nape of her neck and her shoulders that I had been looking at all night but couldn't touch."

"Oh, a wall. That's not so different." She couldn't seem to catch her breath, but she managed to say it.

He whispered, "I'd caress her ass and hips with my hands as I held her here, my mouth hot on her skin, and just as she was so sensitive that everything felt like pleasure, I would begin to bite. I would spin her around and kiss her mouth and touch her until she was begging for me to take her."

Arthur's breath brushed Gen's bare shoulder while he spoke, and she could feel the hard consonants on her skin, puffs of warmth when he said *spin* and *begging*.

His hand touched her hip.

He said, "Then, I'd shove her over the back of that sofa over there—"

They both glanced at the low couch, the creamy leather visible in the darkness.

His voice was lower, hoarser, as he whispered, "—with her hanging down the other side and all the blood rushing to her head, her dark hair draped over the couch, and with her legs off the floor and kicking and her gorgeous ass in the air. I'd bury my tongue between her legs and eat her pussy from behind until she screamed from a blinding orgasm like she had never felt before."

Gen said, "Um—" Her voice sounded more breathless, and her lips felt swollen even though he hadn't kissed her at all.

His hand warmed her hip through her dress.

"After that," he turned back to where his mouth was near her shoulder again, whispering, "I would spin her around, force her to her knees, and fuck her mouth and deep into her throat with my fist wrapped in her long, dark hair."

Gen swallowed, suddenly aware of her tongue in her mouth and her long, dark hair down her back.

"And then I would pick her up in my arms, kiss her hard, and take her over to that chair by the fireplace," Gen glanced over at the white chair that had looked so respectable until just then, "and I'd let her ride me until she came again, panting, and she collapsed against me."

Could he do all that? It seemed unbelievable that a man could be so extravagant, sexually.

Or, maybe it was beyond Gen's experience that a man *would* be so extravagant, sexually.

She asked, "And then?"

He growled near her ear, whispering, "And then I'd lay her lush, sumptuous body down on the floor, on that soft, thick rug over there in front of the fireplace. I'd take her slowly, gently, until she was quivering in my arms and her orgasm started deep inside her, spreading throughout her body, shaking her down into her very soul, devastating her. *Hours.* I'd stay with her for hours until that night was the most amazing in her life, the one that she would measure all others against."

Gen stared at the rug and at the cold fireplace—a dark square with mirrored tiles that reflected the London lights outside—where such a thing might happen. The room's warm air seemed stuck in her chest so that she could barely breathe.

Arthur stepped back, maybe half a step, leaving her

turned aside. She struggled to keep her wobbly knees from folding.

Good Lord, she would have slid right down the wall to the floor.

"That's not quite the same kind of fuss." She licked her lips, which felt unaccountably swollen under her tongue.

When Gen looked back at Arthur, he was standing back, but he was watching her. Darkness filled the room, gathering in the corners and shadows.

Arthur didn't move as he stood, still as a ghost. When she looked at the way that he was turned, she knew he must be watching her.

Gen entirely believed him. No wonder women reacted that way around him. It was like they could sense what he could do to them, what he *would* do to them.

She had a decision to make, right here. Her shaking legs and her leaden feet bound her to the floor, but she had to move.

Should she walk away or step toward him?

Back or forward?

Choose.

There in the shadows, Arthur was so tall that his shoulders blocked the white wall behind him. Once he grabbed her, she would be helpless. He could do anything to her. He could hurt her. He could hurt her *more.*

Gen slid her toe to the side. "I had better go to my room now."

He stepped farther away and opened his hand toward the hallway that led to her room, as gentlemanly as always, and nodded as she scurried away.

When she turned and looked back, he was standing with his hands in his pockets, watching her go.

Business Meeting

ARTHUR looked out the plate glass window. The city of London—glass, steel, and tarmac with occasional rivers of green or dormant-yellow grass—spread out fifteen stories below.

He sat on the one side of a long conference table with twelve other people, an even mix of men and women and a multi-cultural cross-section of upper-crust Britain. All wore business suits as tailored and expensive as his suit. All looked manicured, coiffed, and very wealthy.

Arthur was one of the younger people at the table, he estimated. Most of the other board members were in their forties and well beyond.

Where had Gen gone that morning?

Arthur had awakened at six o'clock in the godforsaken morning, still dressed in his stale tuxedo with his ribs and his face and his skull pounding in time with the flashing numbers on the clock beside the bed. God above, he was never wamble-cropped after a night of drinking—his liver was a glorious pinnacle of evolution—but that morning, he felt absolutely wretched.

Mixing Oxycontin with vodka was a terrible idea. He made a note of it.

By the time he had crawled out of the sheets and made himself presentable, Gen was already gone.

Pippa had been drinking coffee in the kitchen, she looked at him with knowingness in her brown eyes. She had crossed her arms and smirked at him. "Rough morning?"

Oliver must have narced to the rest of the staff. Arthur had long suspected that his staff collaborated on keeping tabs on him. They may even use some sort of phone app to facilitate it. He had caught them furtively checking their phones too many times.

"Where's Gen?" Arthur asked her, pouring himself a cup of coffee and praying that it was strong.

"Out," Pippa said.

He sipped. The stinging coffee was so bitter that his throat closed. *Excellent.* His staff knew how to take care of him. "Where did you take her?"

"She is perfectly safe and asked for it to be kept private."

"I'm your boss."

"You don't pay me that much." Pippa sipped her coffee and went back to reading her book.

An hour and a bit later, when he was mostly recovered from being as drunk as a lord, so to speak, Pippa drove him to a scheduled meeting while he watched for cars tailing them.

No amateurs out there today, but he found three cars discreetly following him instead of falling in with the flow of traffic. From their easy trade-offs, he could tell they were obviously professionals.

Hopefully, at least one of them had been sent by Elizabeth and her organization.

For an hour prior to leaving for the meeting, he had iced the side of his face and ribs, trying to reduce the swelling. He was certainly the only one in the board room who looked like he had been in a bare-knuckle fistfight.

The others were discussing how to advise the CEO of Britain's largest bank, considering some of the current political changes.

Arthur wanted to tell the CEO to harden his computer servers because they were exquisitely vulnerable to hacking, and that was certainly part of the current political climate.

But he didn't. Arthur behaved like a proper nobleman

board member and translated a few memos from one of their Russian associates for the board, which earned him approving nods from some of the other board members. Some of them were nodding to thank him. Some were confirming his translation was accurate.

Where had Gen gone that morning?

Arthur wasn't stalking her. Stalking was something else entirely, and she did live in his house. Surely, this interest in her whereabouts and her safety couldn't be considered stalking.

Wanting to make sure that she was safe was perfectly natural. *Friendly.* Like she had said last night, they were just friends. It was perfectly normal for friends to ensure each other's safety, to talk to each other about many things.

He also remembered, vaguely, the other things he had been telling her.

Things he had wanted to do to her for weeks now, ever since she had begun posing as his girlfriend.

It hadn't even been his idea that they should live together. Gen had proposed that she should move in with him. These thoughts could hardly be considered his fault. They were natural thoughts that any heterosexual male might have about a beautiful, voluptuous woman who was around him so very much.

They had lunch together several days of the week. He watched her in court often. He studied every move that she made, like when she bent over to check something on her computer and her round, curvy ass filled out her trousers so beautifully.

What man wouldn't have such thoughts? Arthur wasn't a saint. He had certainly never pretended to be a saint.

Quite the opposite.

The board of directors around the table was discussing cultural problems in the Middle East and a possible partnership, so he added a quick comment that the possible partner's electronic infrastructure was not as secure as it needed to be for this bank to do business with them. Some people took his advice. Others dismissed it and were more interested in the cultural problems that the bank would face.

He should be taking notes to include who said what about which in his report, but his hand was sore where his knuckles had bounced off the car's window.

And his broken ribs hurt.

Yet Arthur should remember his job and his duty, so he chastised himself to pay closer attention to the discussion.

The people around him talked about banking.

Arthur greatly hoped that he had not said anything off the night before. Afterward, his dreams had been all tangled up with what he had said to Gen, and he wasn't sure where the evening had ended and his drunken dreams had begun. He had dreamed all night of taking that pale blue dress off of her creamy skin, stroking the velvet of her flesh until she cried out his name, and burying himself in her until he could think of nothing but her softness and that flowery, delicious perfume she wore.

"Lord Severn," a woman's voice said.

"Yes." Arthur made it sound more like a reply than an admission that he hadn't been paying attention.

"Don't you think we should advise our European counterparts of this development?"

"Yes. Yes, of course." He had no idea what he'd agreed to.

He was due to meet Gen for an intimate lunch in a few hours and then watch her in court that afternoon.

Perhaps he could discern how much he had told her over lunch and apologize for whatever he had said. He hoped he hadn't mentioned some of the things that ran through his mind, things with ropes and leather ties and certain objects.

He'd been accused of many things, but being boring wasn't one of them.

But Jesus, if he had scared her off, he would kick himself.

He would especially hate himself because he knew that

something had happened to her, something that she would not discuss.

No matter what he had said, taking any of it back would be a lie.

Maybe he could plead drunkenness.

She might believe that.

She would absolutely believe that he was an idiot, so he might consider leading with that.

Around him, the discussion went on, and on, and Arthur gazed out the window, wondering where Gen had gone that morning.

Another Client Gone

After visiting her mother at the long-term care home for a few hours in the early morning, Gen was sitting at her small pupil desk in her closet-office. She interspersed typing briefs on her laptop with fielding emails from her friends Lee and Rose about where the Hell she had been lately and why she wasn't eating take-away curry with them every night.

Coffee, she wrote back to them. *I'll meet you in the library for a bit of pupilskive and coffee.*

Coffee in the library, because she was meeting Arthur for lunch and she couldn't work late that night. Arthur had added another charity supper to her calendar. Good God, he had charity events most nights of the week. Every different disaster and cause and problem had its own charity, and every single one of those had multiple events.

She wasn't sure why or *how* Arthur attended them *all*.

It did look good for his case when she listed the many, myriad causes that he personally supported.

Gen worked nonstop through the rest of the morning, reading depositions and devilling some briefs for Violet Devereux.

Devereux the Devil in the Devilhouse must be clocking at least four hundred billable hours a week, maybe five hundred. Her billing required two full-time clerks, whereas most of the other barristers in the firm shared a clerk with at least three other barristers. She was bringing in boatloads of money for herself and for the chambers, which received a percentage of her fees, so no one asked how she did it.

Really, no one had to ask. Everyone saw the little devils scurrying in and out of her office all day.

Gen was writing an opinion on a libel case, for which Violet Devereux would take credit and then pay Gen. Gen did a few of these briefs and opinions a week, sometimes one a day. Devilling paid for the things that her pittance of a stipend would not begin to cover, and Gen had no qualms about heading over to the Devilhouse to make some extra cash.

And yet, even when she was thoroughly engrossed in the law and ramifications of the libel suit, she could not stop thinking about what Arthur had said last night. Portions of it played in her mind behind the words on the brief.

It was all wholly inappropriate of course. Very NSFW.

Arthur should never have said it.

Gen should never have heard it.

And she certainly shouldn't have kept telling him to go on.

But she had.

And when he had breathed his warm, alcohol-scented breath on her shoulder and his hand had rested on her hip, she had almost—*almost*—turned and flung herself against him.

When she had fled to her room, she had locked the door behind herself, but her door had not rattled at all.

Arthur must have gone back to his bedroom.

Because of course, he had.

He probably had not even realized that he had been talking to Gen. He probably had thought, in his sloppy, drunken state, that he was talking to one of the models or actresses or strippers he dated. Or Peony Sweeting.

No one would talk that way to poor, plumpy-dumpy Genevieve Ward. Not considering her cankles, her fat butt, and her horsey face, and certainly never someone rich, ripped, and hot like Arthur Finch-Hatten. It was against the laws of nature, if not actually against the laws of Great

Britain.

Gen tucked her head down and got back to work.

At eleven, Rose and Lee showed up at her office door. Gen was ready to go for coffee in the library and met them at the door, holding her purse and her umbrella.

Rose Pennelegion pursed her full ruby-red lips—her lipstick perfectly applied as always—and patted her tightly coiffed hair.

Rose said, "What."

"The." Lee Fox looked over her over-sized sunglasses at Gen, her scarlet bangs almost touching the frames.

"Hell," Rose said.

"Are."

"You."

"Doing?" Lee finished.

They both glared at her.

Lee held out her phone, the screen aggressively facing out.

A picture of Gen with Arthur Finch-Hatten was on the screen. In the picture, Gen was wearing a dove gray gown covered with shimmering beads, and the cast iron underwear pushed up her boobs to nearly under her chin. Arthur's devious grin spoke volumes.

Gen said, "Yeah, about that—"

They bum-rushed Gen back into her office and slammed the door.

Rose started, "Gen, we are very concerned about your career and your well-being."

Lee said, "I don't know whether to stage an intervention or demand sex pictures."

"It's not what it looks like," Gen insisted, setting her purse on her closed laptop so she could hold up her hands to ward them off.

Rose said, "I should hope not."

"Oh, it's exactly what it looks like," Lee said, slapping her phone on Gen's little desk. "There are dozens of pictures all over the place. 'The Earl of Severn's New Girlfriend.' 'Britain's Favorite Playboy Settles for Barrister.' I found at least five different sets of pics this morning!"

"You did?" Gen grinned. *"Good."*

Rose and Lee looked at each other, having a whole conversation with mere flicks of their immaculately groomed eyebrows. Gen needed to learn to do that if she was going to pass for British someday.

Rose asked Gen, "And in what possible fashion could this be considered 'good?'"

"They're just pics of a boring couple, holding drinks, at a charity benefit. They're taking up real estate on the internet, and they're pushing down the scandalous ones," Gen said. "From those, you see that Arthur Finch-Hatten is dating a respectable, middle-class barrister and is supporting worthy causes. He hasn't been caught doing something stupid for over a week."

"But you're boinking a client," Lee said, her brown eyes huge and serious on her elfin face.

"I am not boinking him." Gen pointed to her forehead, from which her hair was pulled back rather severely in a ballet bun on the back of her head. "Is it tattooed on my forehead in diamonds?"

Lee frowned. "You would be better off keeping it on the down-low. You could be brought before the ethics committee for being involved with a client. No chambers would touch you."

"I'm not *really* dating him. It's an arrangement. He can't keep himself out of trouble, so I'm going places with him to be his conscience. He hasn't been caught in any compromising situations for over a week, and he certainly won't now that I've moved in with him."

They both reared back like they'd been slapped.

Lee yelled, *"You did wot?"* Her Cockney accent rose up, overwhelming the middle-class London accent that she adopted during the day.

"Oh, Genevieve," Rose said. "I can't believe that this is advisable."

Lee whipped her sunglasses off to stare at Gen. *"Are you a bleedin' idiot?"*

"Are you using that glasses trick in court, Lee?" Gen asked.

Lee studied her sunglasses. "Yeah, you like it? I think juries will like it. I got a pair of plain-glass specs so I can whip them off and stare at a witness."

"Yeah, no. It's kind of gimmicky," Gen said.

Rose sighed. "The glasses bit is a diversion, of course, to distract jurors so they won't focus on the problems with the testimony, *exactly like now.* Gen, did you move in with His Lordship Arthur Finch-Hatten?"

"Well, yes," Gen admitted. "Yesterday."

"So you are boinking him," Lee said. "You just haven't got the diamond tattoo yet. I hear they have a waiting period before you can get those things."

"I'm not bumping uglies with him."

Rose almost giggled. "Oh, your American aphorisms. How amusing."

"It's totally platonic. Completely and utterly platonic." It felt a whole lot less platonic after what he had whispered in her ear last night. "It's just for his image. Octavia knows about it, and she's assured all the senior barristers here that it's just an arrangement to keep him in line."

Rose and Lee had another twenty-minute conversation in the space of one glance.

"It's true!" Gen rolled her eyes at them.

Lee grumbled, "That explains some of the comments on these pics, then."

Uh, oh. "Like what?"

Lee said, "Like you guys are stiff around each other and don't *act* like a couple. No *chemistry.* Like it looks like an arranged marriage between Great Houses, except that you're a Middle-Class Mary. The gossip sites can't figure it out."

"Well, it seems to be working from my end."

"But do the senior barristers believe that it remains platonic?" Rose asked, musing to the ceiling.

Gen thought about it. "They seem to."

"What they say to you means nothing," Rose said. "You need to ask other people what they're saying."

"And more importantly," Lee said to her, "do you think that you can keep Lord Severn from making a farce of himself until his trial goes to court? M'learned friend, I submit that no one can perform this impossible task."

"It had better work," Gen said. "I lost another client this morning because I'm not British enough. I've had Octavia sit in client meetings with me, and she's as frustrated as I am. I've got all the right degrees. I say all the right things. I've got a pretty good track record of court wins at this point, much better than James Knightly or any of the other pupil barristers, but clients listen to me aping a British accent and run the other way. I can't make it work."

Rose and Lee glanced at each other again.

Lee said, "Yeah, I get it. If I spoke Cockney rhyming slang in client meetings, they wouldn't give me a chance, either. Rose, 'ere, is lucky, having grown up speaking the Queen's English at 'er posh boarding schools. Maybe you could take elocution lessons?"

"Maybe," Gen said. "Maybe Arthur could teach me how to speak correctly if I'm planning to stay in London."

Another quick glance between the two of them.

"Aren't you?" Rose asked.

Gen shrugged. "I will as long as my mother is alive. I promised her that I would keep her in Britain. She didn't like a lot of things about America, so I have to keep her here. She says that she can't understand people when they speak with that barbaric American accent."

"Yeah," Lee said. "I can see that."

More Threats

ARTHUR was leaning his head against the back of the car's seat, trying to rest, while Pippa drove him from the business meeting back to his apartment.

He should be writing down his notes and impressions.

He should be planning his abject apology to Gen.

Arthur listened to the traffic growl around the Rolls and drifted off, nearly sleeping.

His phone vibrated against his hip. When he glanced at the screen, the caller was tagged as unidentified, even on his rather over-powered phone.

He said, "Pippa, if you please."

His driver pulled into a car park between two buildings and grabbed her paperback as she stepped out of the car.

Arthur answered, "Yes."

"Are you *cultivating* the young barrister?" Elizabeth's voice asked him. She must be calling from inside the Vauxhall Cross building since his phone had not been able to identify her phone number.

He sighed. "Yes. As we agreed."

"It is of utmost importance—"

"It must be, if the matter warranted both a note on the micro-USB with so much identifying information *and* an unscheduled phone call."

Yes, he was sharp with her, but his whole body still hurt, especially since he would not take any more of those damned pain pills.

"I want to stress to you—" she said.

"I understand the situation."

"Your social position is paramount to your ability to gather the type of information we need."

"I understand the situation," he grated out.

"You must not lose the case, and you must *cultivate* the young barrister."

"I understand the situation," he said one last time. "I will do whatever is necessary to motivate the young barrister, just as I have always done all that is necessary, just as you trained me to. Good afternoon."

Arthur jabbed the phone's screen to hang up the call and rapped on the window to alert Pippa that he was ready to proceed.

Pain lanced through his hand.

Damn, he had forgotten about his knuckles. They were probably cracked, too.

Barrister-Client Negotiation

Gen ran down to the curb when Arthur texted her that he was coming up. He didn't need to come all the way up to her office to walk her down. The goals of their sham relationship were to keep an eye on the wayward earl and to plant gossip in the papers, not to foment gossip in her chambers.

"Lunch must be quick," she said as she stepped into the car. Arthur had opened the door for her, and she swung her legs inside. "I have court this afternoon, and the brief was *enormous.* It'll take all afternoon. It might have to be carried over."

Arthur stepped into the other side of the car. "We'll go to my club," he said. "They can be very efficient."

His "club" was a renovated house just a few blocks from Lincoln's Inn. They were whisked to a private room, and a waiter took their orders within minutes.

"But the whole point of these lunches is to be seen together," Gen told him. If people weren't buying them as a couple, these lunches might shore up their bona fides.

"I should like to apologize," Arthur said as he settled himself at the table. "I drank too much last night in addition to the pain pills, and I said some things that should not have been said."

Ah, yes. He had been drunk off his patoot and rambling lies. "It's okay, Arthur. I understand."

"I can't quite remember what I said," Arthur said. "After ten o'clock, everything becomes quite blurry."

"It's okay." Gen smiled at him, trying to set him at ease even though her heart seemed to have inexplicably sighed and was huddling, hurt, inside her chest. "You were matching shots with Christopher on top of the Oxycontin. If you'd've punched someone, I could have gotten you off on a temporary insanity defense."

One side of his mouth curved up, but he smiled more with his eyes. In the subdued light of the supper club, his shimmering eyes looked more blue. Maybe his eyes were picking up the color of the vivid blue tie that he was wearing with his dark blue suit. "I appreciate your kindness. I do apologize."

Gen waved her hand, slapping his apologies out of the air. Her eyes stung, which was weird. "Pshaw. You were practically hallucinating. You didn't know who I was. You probably thought that I was Peony Sweeting or one of those Parisian strippers."

Arthur leaned forward. "I knew who you were."

"Well, you were rambling, literally out of your mind. You might have said anything. You didn't mean any of it."

He was watching her, closely, his silvery eyes flicking as he looked from one of her eyes to the other. "I meant every word. I'm only wondering how much I said."

Gen leaned back and braced her arms on the table. "You didn't mean it."

"I've been attracted to you since we met. In the time that we've spent together, my interest hasn't diminished."

"You can't be serious."

"I'm absolutely serious. Getting to know you without having a sexual relationship is fascinating and unprecedented."

Ah. Gen opened her hands, letting any little bit of hope fly away. It didn't matter. "So it's just that you want what you can't have. I'm legally forbidden fruit. That's all."

"You put yourself down too much," Arthur said. "I hear it from you every day. It seems impolite to contradict you, but you're a beautiful woman. Your legs go on for days. You have a classically beautiful oval face. If I extol any more of your virtues, I'll have more to apologize for."

"You don't have to do this. I'm a grown woman. We have a business arrangement to keep you out of trouble so I can win your case. You don't have to schmooze me. Indeed, I'd rather you didn't."

"If the circumstances were any different, I assure you, I would absolutely take advantage of our arrangement to try my best to seduce you."

"Oh, you don't mean that."

"I've already told you that I mean every word of it. I am also aware that circumstances cannot be different. Octavia has warned me not to 'ruin' you in the eyes of your chambers. She says that you have a good shot at getting a tenancy offer—"

Gen straightened. "She said that?"

"Yes, and she said that you should not be caught in a relationship with me. After my case is over, I should like to take you out for a real date if you'd be amenable. I wouldn't destroy your career for a date."

"Yes," Gen said, breathless because she couldn't believe that she was saying it.

"Yes, what? That I shouldn't ruin your career?"

"That, too. But yes to the date. Yes, to going on a date," she stammered. "If we don't hate each other by the end of your case, then yes, we should go have coffee or something."

Arthur leaned in farther, and his strong fingers gripped the edge of the table. His intense eyes turned smoky in the dim light. "Coffee?"

"Yes, coffee. Just to talk. Just to see if there might be anything between us."

He smiled a slow, sexy smile. Not lascivious, but a promise. "I think so, too."

But they had to wait until the end of the case. They couldn't have a relationship or even a date before that.

It absolutely would ruin her career.

No matter how good she was at arguing points of law or whipping up a jury's righteous indignation in a courtroom, having a real relationship with a client was a visit to the Ethics Board and an exit from chambers. Straight-up lying about a relationship with a client would get her blackballed from every set of chambers in Britain.

So they had to wait.

Right?

Binding Authority

THAT afternoon, Gen was sitting at her table in court, listening.

The claimant's lawyer, who was of course her nemesis-in-chambers, the handsome James Knightly, went on and on and on and on about his client's case.

And on and on.

She was taking notes diligently, even though she had already answered all of his points in her brief, weak as it was. Indeed, she had a copy of her brief and was ticking off the points that she needed to hit in her rebuttal.

Well, some judges didn't read briefs, just like some barristers didn't read the solicitor's instructions before they walked into court.

So she had to nail that rebuttal.

This case was weak, so damn weak. She wasn't even sure why the solicitors had sent it around, except that perhaps the claimant wouldn't give up and would not accept any offer to settle at any price.

It was even a civil case for money, not a criminal case, but Gen always did her best for her client.

This was just a waste of everyone's time, anyway. She was going to lose and lose hard.

Her client was going to have to pony up a heck of a lot of cash that he didn't have.

The judge called for a quick break before Gen began her arguments, and Arthur leaned over the bar to motion to her.

She walked back and whispered, "What?" as she was

clutching her notepad.

Arthur leaned in and whispered, "Do exactly as I say. Stand up and say only this, 'The appeal is misconceived since it has failed to refer to the binding authority of Tambling-Goggin v. Pye.'"

Gen grabbed her phone, starting to search for that particular decision. "I can't believe that such a short response can answer James Knightly's skeleton argument. It's not complete."

"Look at the barristers who argued the case."

Gen swiped her fingers over the page, enlarging the text. "It says Williams, Gendry, and Marks for the claimant, who won the case. Wait, Marks? As in Judge Marks?" She looked up at the empty bench, where Judge Marks's nameplate shone in the overhead fluorescent lights.

"Quite," Arthur said.

"He argued a case almost exactly like mine and won with it?"

Arthur smiled, and the sly gleam in his eye was sexy as heck. "One of his finest hours."

"Oh, *Arthur.* This is *amazing.* I thought I was going to lose this case."

He leaned back. "Sometimes, if you know just whom to cite, you can work wonders. Make sure you look like a cat who's been in the cream when you stand up and say it. Marks will be ever so amused."

Oh, what the Hell. It was better than anything she had.

Back in the courtroom, when it came time for her response, she stood straight, looked straight at Judge Marks and grinned, and said exactly what Arthur had told her to say.

She glanced over at James Knightly, still grinning, and bit the corner of her lip.

Terror widened James Knightly's English blue eyes.

He slammed open his laptop and typed frantically, not even bothering to cover up his ignorance of the referenced case.

He scanned the page, his head vibrating side to side as he read.

At the end, he flopped back in his chair, the very image of what defeat feels like.

Gen tried not to gloat.

But she was unsuccessful.

Because it was awesome.

Later, as night was rolling through the streets of London and the streetlights were turning on to keep the darkness at bay, Gen trotted out of Lincoln's Inn and through the park-like courtyard.

Arthur was waiting for her beside the Rolls Royce, holding her door. She stepped into the car and dragged her purse into the back seat. Arthur shut the door behind her. In the evening, the stars sifted over the ceiling inside the car were even more diamond-like.

He got in the other side, asking, "How did it go?"

Gen exclaimed, "I did just what you said. As soon as the other lawyer figured out what that case was and that Judge Marks, *that very same judge,* had been the lawyer that had argued it, he accepted a pittance as a settlement from my client. I can't believe that we got away with that. My client probably paid ten percent of what he should have been liable for. I wonder if we should have fought it out. We might have gotten him off the hook entirely."

Arthur chuckled as Pippa drove the car away from the curb. "I would say not. That case was unwinnable. It was only luck that I was able to shore you up with that gambit."

Gen dropped her purse, and it tumbled to the floor of the car. "But, Judge Marks had fought a case *just like it* ten years ago and won. It was *precedent.*"

"Oh, no," Arthur said. "Judge Leopold Marks spoke about that very case, Tambling-Goggin v. Pye, at a political fund-raising supper a few months ago. He is disgusted with himself for having taken the case and called it one of the gravest miscarriages of justice that he had ever participated in. Marks said that if a like case ever came before him, he intended to right the grievous wrong."

So Judge Marks would have ruled against her no matter what if she had not settled, and she would have lost the case in a most spectacular fashion, had she fought it out.

But that wasn't the problem.

She said, "You manipulated me."

"I showed you a path to victory in a hopeless case. With Judge Marks presiding, there was no other way but to settle."

"But you didn't tell me everything."

He shrugged. "You essentially won the case. You certainly found the very best outcome."

"I can't believe you manipulated me like that, like a *pawn.*"

"To excel at being a barrister, you must rarely, if ever, say what you mean." He leaned toward her. "It's the British way. Play the game for yourself. Don't allow yourself to be a pawn. Be the king."

Barristers did play evil games in court and in chambers, and they did it *all the time.*

"You say that like you're a king instead of an earl," she tried to quip, even though her eyes were tearing up. *Damn it,* she should have known the precedent and known what it meant. *That's* what stung the most.

"Oh, I'm not the king," Arthur said. "At best, I'd say I'm a rook. In the Great Game, I wouldn't want to be the king. A rook is far more nimble."

Chambers High Tea with Sun Tzu

Gen shoved a whole cookie in her mouth. The shortbread smelled like butter and chocolate in her sinuses.

Across from her, sitting in an office chair and sipping a cup of steaming tea, Octavia raised her precisely sculpted eyebrows. "Rough day in court?"

Gen swallowed the cookie crumbs. "I lost, but I won. I settled a case for far less than my client should have been on the hook for. I practically robbed a very deserving claimant."

Octavia's devious smile curved her lips. "Bravo, Gen."

"To be honest—"

Octavia pursed her lips and shook her head.

Gen corrected herself, "To be frank," because barristers never admitted honesty, "I accidentally manipulated James Knightly into settling a case for far less than he should have. He's a chambermate."

"No, he's your competition for obtaining tenancy."

"It wasn't fair."

"Now, you're getting the hang of it."

"I used his ignorance of a precedent against him."

"Even better," Octavia purred. "You can't be Atticus fucking Finch."

Gen asked, "So what if we settle like that? Is that winning when you win with an unfair tactic?"

Octavia nibbled at her cookie, a rare indulgence. "It's the best kind of winning, actually. 'To fight and conquer in all your battles is not the supreme excellence; supreme excellence consists of breaking the enemies' resistance without fighting.' Sun Tzu knew his shit."

Hacking Her Phone

Arthur held the elevator doors for Gen and followed her into his apartment. A quick glance at the winter sunlight streaming through the windows of the living room assured him that they had a few hours before that night's soiree.

Gen was stabbing her phone with her index finger and frowning. That little line that he associated with her cute baby-tantrums had formed between her eyebrows. Watching her buy the plot was like watching a puffball kitten lay its ears back and attack one's foot in adorable fury.

She muttered, "Stupid thing."

"Is there a problem?" Arther asked her, refraining from craning his neck to spy on her screen.

Gen complained, "My phone is so dang slow. I tap an app to open it, and it pauses, so I tap it ten more times. When it finally opens up, it registers those ten taps as trying to do something in the app, and it goes all over the place and does something stupid. I think I just set my weather location to Abu Dhabi."

He laughed. "I might be able to optimize it, if you like."

"You? The Earl of Givesnofucks? You're a computer nerd?"

He touched his chest in mock horror. "Oh, of course not. However, all of us spendthrift nobles have our toys."

She frowned. "Oh. I guess so."

He held out his hand. "May I?"

She shrugged and handed it over.

Arthur asked, "Is there any place on it I shouldn't look?"

Gen laughed. "No naked pics or sex tapes, I promise. I'm not that interesting."

Oh, Arthur disagreed. He found her very interesting, absolutely fascinating, as a matter of fact. While he wouldn't have poked around her files for boudoir pictures of her, he would have happily perused if she had offered to show them to him.

Or if she had offered to take some especially for him.

God, what a thought. His dick grew heavy in his shorts at just the thought of Gen in lingerie, maybe looking over her shoulder at the camera, framed on her voluptuous ass and thighs—

Another train of thought was in order, lest he embarrass himself.

Arthur asked, "Which of these apps do you not use, ever?"

Gen sighed, her bosom heaving, and Arthur did his best not to look at her chest. "There's so many, but I can't figure out how to get them off my phone."

He concentrated on her phone, instead. "Many phones are pre-installed with bloatware, and you have to inspect the code of the operating system to uninstall them. Can I get this back to you in half an hour?"

She shrugged, and her body jiggled under the severe black suit that she wore. By the way her breasts floated under her top, Arthur was quite sure that she was wearing the Myla lingerie he had purchased for her, a captivating thought.

Self-torture wasn't his usual modus operandi, yet he could not seem to stop. He was at half-mast already. Just being around Gen was beginning to become physically painful.

Gen said, "Sure. I was just going to shower before the thing tonight."

And now he had that image in his head.

Perhaps smashing his face against the wall of his computer cave would relieve the pressure.

He said, "I'll have this right back to you."

Arthur took the phone to his computer cave, the room with several large towers and servers and many screens, and plugged it into his computer. He broke apart the phone's rudimentary security software in seconds and deleted all the bloatware. By looking at her data usage, he found quite a few apps that she had never opened nor registered in the eight months that she had had her phone, so he deleted those. Then, he installed a much better security program.

One never knew when some nefarious person would try to hack her phone.

He was pleased with himself, as he had resisted the urges to install an access program or to cruise her pictures.

Arthur was, after all, the very definition of a gentleman.

He tested the apps. They snapped open and ran flawlessly.

When he gave it back to Gen, she exclaimed over it, smiling and thanking him, and she touched his shoulder while she watched images flash over the screen.

Arthur smiled gently at her. "My absolute pleasure."

Days Turn Into Weeks

DAYS turned into weeks, and Gen lived with Arthur in his apartment.

Every night, Arthur had a scheduled charitable or political event. She wondered how he kept them all straight in his head until she saw that his head of staff, the inscrutable Mr. Royston Fothergill, programmed everything into a shared calendar that everyone received, including the drivers, Pippa and Oliver.

Every night, as they came home to a dark, empty apartment with no staff around to observe them, Arthur gave her a most ardent handshake in the kitchen when he told her good night.

The first couple nights that they had lived together had been kind of awkward, especially after his Oxycontin-and-alcohol-fueled—Confession? Diatribe? Promise?—and so on the third night, Gen had stuck out her hand to shake before they walked to their different hallways. Arthur had laughed at the absurdity of it, and now every night, they shook hands before retiring to their separate bedrooms.

His hand was always warm and soft around hers, a moment of careful contact that she came to look forward to.

Gen often visited her mother in the mornings and left before Arthur was up, but when she didn't go to the nursing home on Wednesdays, Arthur left the apartment about the same time that she left for the office.

There were business meetings for him to attend, business and charitable boards that he served on, work that had to be done on his country house, and some other sorts of meetings. He wore bespoke business suits on those days, all perfectly sharp and tailored like the upper-class gentleman that he most definitely was.

In the afternoons when Gen got home, Arthur usually emerged from that room farther back in the hallway from hers, the room that might be a Kinky Room of BDSM Pain or whatever. On the days when she was standing there when he shut the door behind himself, when he finished rubbing his eyes, he looked up, saw her, and smiled. Sometimes his smile was tired and careworn, but he smiled at her.

On those afternoons, he wore jeans or khakis and tee shirts over his broad chest.

One tee shirt was yellow with the word *Enigma* in an eye-shaped thing. She figured that it meant the Enigma machine, a Nazi mechanical code machine that the British had cracked during World War II, another reference to *the War.*

Another time, his blue shirt read, *There are only 10 kinds of people in the world. Those who can read binary, and those who can't.*

Gen had puzzled over that one.

Another day, his green shirt had two fish skeletons on it with the word *Twofish* below it.

Maybe it was a bar somewhere.

Ruckus still bounded around the apartment, but Gen began taking him for walks in Hyde Park.

The first few days, the pooch shot ahead, hit the end of the leash like running into a brick wall, and clawed his way down the path with his ears back, snarling as he dragged her through the park. It was a good thing that Ruckus was a little Jack Russell Terrier instead of a Labrador or Newfoundland. He might have wrenched Gen's arm from the socket.

On the third day, she tapped him on the nose with her finger and told him *no,* no pulling. His soulful gaze up at her almost made her laugh at how appalled he was.

Over the next week, he learned to trot at her side, and then he was a joy to take for walks. After all, as Gen had learned from her ranch days, a tired dog is a good dog.

That sentiment was true of many mammals, Gen decided.

Her mother's health remained the same as it had been for months. She couldn't move, couldn't speak, couldn't communicate. When Gen was there, her mother was less agitated, so Gen still went five times a week: four weekday mornings before work plus Sunday afternoons. Most of the time, Gen read aloud the mystery novels that her mother loved.

Her mother seemed to groan in the right places, during the pauses where she might have said something. The thought that her mother might still be in there was comforting and yet frightening as Hell. At least the television was on a lot of the time, in case her mother was alert and trapped inside an unresponsive body. Gen wasn't sure which way to hope for, so she just kept reading books to her.

A week later, she bought an MP3 player and loaded it with audio books. The nurses said that her mother was calmer, a lot calmer, all the time, so Gen kept refreshing that with new books. Her mother had never liked the telly.

During a few visits, briefs for a case that she was working on had come in overnight, so Gen read those out loud to her mother with the room's door shut. Even though Gen suspected that she was abusing her mother's good graces, her mother seemed to stay calm during that, too.

One day, Gen said, "Momma, there's a guy, and I'm not sure what to do."

Her mother's eyes tracked floating dust mites near the ceiling.

She said, "His name is Arthur Finch-Hatten, and I think I might like him. We spend a lot of time together because of work, and I think I might be liking him more and more.

The problem is that he's a client, so you know what that means. He said that after the court case he's involved in is over, that we should go out on a date. He did say it, and I said yes, so there's that. I'm just not sure what to do about it *now.*"

Her mother didn't move in the hospital bed, except that her right hand, the side that she could move a little, flinched and rolled.

Gen smoothed the quilt over her mother, a scrap double-wedding ring pattern that her mother had made when they lived in Texas. "I wish you could tell me what to do about him."

She looked up. The door to the bright hallway outside was closed.

Gen continued, "I'm still having problems from that night, even though it was three years ago. I don't know what to do about it, but I feel like I have to do something. It shouldn't be like this. *I* shouldn't be like this."

Her mother's hand, frail and bird-claw-like, rolled back and forth on the quilt, covering a blue section of quilt blocks and then revealing it, back and forth, on and off.

"I wish you could meet Arthur," Gen said to her mother. "I wish you could tell me what you think of him."

And then, as always, she kissed her mother on the cheek and left her in the home.

The money that Gen paid to "top up" the National Health subsidy, as substantial as it was, was worth it. Gen just had to figure out a way to keep paying for it.

Devilling for Violet Devereux at the Devilhouse wasn't quite paying all the bills.

Her mother's savings account balance dipped lower every month.

The math was easy: in two months, Gen must find a way to bring in substantially more money, or the system would move her mother back to the awful, unkempt, unethical nursing home outside of London that was too far for Gen to visit.

There must be more money.

Poker Tell

For her court case with Octavia that afternoon, Gen had read the brief that the instructing solicitor had sent over the day before.

Open and shut case.

Open and shut *losing* case.

Gen had visited the accused in the courthouse cells before the trial, juggling her cases overflowing with tranches of evidence from this case and his prior convictions. The solicitor had sent them all over to chambers, probably so Octavia Hawkes understood what she was getting into, which meant Octavia had understood very well and had thus passed the losing case on to Gen.

But Octavia also knew that Gen wanted to go into criminal law rather than civil, so Hawkes passed most petty offenses over to her and just sat at the table, looking as if she were informed about the case. This was straight in line with her previous actions.

And yet, Arthur's comment about Hawkes applying for silk rankled Gen. Being named a QC was hard, really hard, and whispers were that it was even harder for a woman.

But Hawkes would not throw Gen under the bus to further her career.

Probably not.

Gen shook her head. No matter. She had a case to fight today.

Grant Williams was a career pickpocket. He had been plying his trade in the Tube on a crowded train, directly beside a plain-clothes policewoman.

Just bad luck.

The bailiff twisted the keys in the heavy steel door and leaned back to open it. "'Ere ya are, miss."

"Thank you, sir." Gen crammed all her cases under her left arm, held out her right hand, and said, "Pleased to meet you, Mr. Williams. I'll be representing you today."

Her horsehair wig slipped on Gen's hair, and she righted it. With the flowing sleeve of her court robe, she slapped herself across the face. The chemical, flowery scent of dry cleaning solution shot up her nose and clung to the back of her tongue.

The accused man, Grant Williams, was almost six feet tall and had the dark hair and good looks of a movie actor. Perhaps his parents had realized he would grow up to look like Cary Grant when they had named him. Maybe he had been a failed actor before he turned to a life of crime.

Gen needed to get over such fanciful thoughts. *Fight the case.*

Mr. Williams stared at Gen's extended hand. "I should know better than to get nicked in the winter." His middle-class, London accent was a drawl to her American ears. "All the baby barristers come out to try their hand at playing with people's lives. Where's your pupil master?"

Gen dropped her hand. Barristers don't shake hands, and she had forgotten because Texans do.

She said, "I'm not inexperienced, Mr. Williams, and I will be representing you today. Your solicitor sent over your files yesterday. Is there anything else you should tell me? Any extenuating circumstances?"

He shrugged. "I have three small children to support."

"And you support yourself by?"

Grant Williams grinned. "Odd jobs."

Lovely. He was admitting a life of petty crime.

"And how are these children regularly supported?" she asked.

He blinked, a little dismayed. "Their mothers support them, but I chip in."

"Oh, splendid," Gen muttered. A deadbeat father with multiple baby mommas on top of it all. She peered at him, frowning.

He must have seen her disappointment because he insisted, "But I chip in as much as I can. My youngest needs school uniforms for next year, so I needed money. That's the only reason I took a few quid off that lady."

Gen wrote that down. "If you say so."

Grant smiled at her, a warm, sexy smile with straight, white teeth. "Don't you worry. Get me into the witness box, and I'll charm the pants off the jury."

Maybe she could use his looks to her advantage if there were women on the jury. Gen frowned and calculated the odds.

Hmmm. Usually, when Gen was confronted with a handsome man just a few years older than herself, she got giggly. Not this time. Her concentration wasn't perturbed in the slightest.

Maybe hanging around the insanely handsome Arthur had inoculated her against merely good-looking men trying to manipulate her.

Gen said, "Yes, well. Good luck with that."

"Let's hope the jury is made up of mostly women like it was the last five times."

So he was using his looks to get away with it. Just great.

At least he was merely a petty thief, not a murderer.

"I'll see you in court, Mr. Williams." She gathered up her cases of solicitor's instructions and swept out of the room.

She ate a sandwich out of her purse in a corner before the case and trotted into Court One with fifteen minutes to spare. Grant Williams was brought into the dock to observe the proceedings.

The evidence against Williams was quite damning, between the police officer who watched him do it and the

CCTV footage of him falling against the woman, jostling her, and taking an item out of her purse.

Extenuating circumstances would determine how long he was going away for.

Gen did her best to argue the sob story, that his youngest child of three, all of whom depended on him, needed money for school uniforms.

Octavia Hawkes sat beside her at the table, reading briefs for other cases. Occasionally, she looked at the court, nodded sagely, and went right back to working on something else.

After the other testimony, Grant Williams signaled to Gen that he wanted to testify.

Well, fine. She didn't think he could get into any worse trouble.

Grant Williams was called from the dock to the witness box, and Gen led him through his several children and his many money woes. She'd read all this in the brief. It was just a matter of getting him to repeat it while he was waxing rhapsodic about how wonderful his children were and how much he loved them.

Because Gen had seen the CCTV footage of the pickpocketing, which was about as non-violent as a crime could be and still be considered a crime, she asked him about that.

Grant Williams smiled some more. "She was a beautiful woman, well-dressed with expensive shoes. From what she was wearing and the easy way that she carried herself and her purse, I could see that she didn't need the money. Money was nothing to her. It wouldn't be right to take a bit of money off of someone who needed it, but this lady dropped a few coins after she bought a coffee and didn't bother to pick them up. One was a quid. She didn't take her receipt, either. Just unconcerned about the money."

So he was playing the Robin Hood card. Sometimes that worked.

Gen watched the jury, that notoriously erratic, twelve-headed hydra.

Some of the women tut-tutted.

One of the guys rolled his eyes, but he was laughing. Grant had caught his eye, and the two of them had a bromance-type rapport going.

A lad wouldn't convict a fellow lad, now would he?

Gen stood between the prosecution and defense tables and asked Grant, "And that was all? You just bobbled into her and took a bit of money? You didn't hurt her at all?"

"Not at all. I'd had a few pints that night—"

The jury guy snorted and nodded. He had done stupid things after a few, too, Gen just bet.

"—And so I just bumped into her and a bit of money that she didn't even need fell out of her purse," Grant explained. "I just scooped it up. It was practically cleaning up litter."

Jury guy nodded.

One of the other women was watching Grant intently. She probably had a thing for bad boys.

Grant caught the eye of his fellow lad on the jury again, and he continued, "And while I was at it, I grabbed a bit of a feel of her arse."

Panic zinged through Gen, professionally at the thought of her client admitting to sexual assault on the stand, and deep inside her stomach, a colder, more terrified shock.

"Thank you, Mr. Williams. That will be all. Thank you." Gen walked back toward the defense table while the prosecutor stood and advanced to methodically take Grant Williams apart.

Gen shook out her hands, trying to dispel the crazy spiders crawling up her spine.

Octavia glanced sideways at Gen but didn't say anything.

While Gen walked back to her table, Arthur was watching her from the gallery, his easy smile gone. His silvery eyes seemed as reflective as mirrors.

She shook her hands harder, but the thought of Grant Williams's hands reaching and grabbing, his fingers sinking into the woman's flesh, wouldn't leave Gen's mind.

Despite Gen fumbling and hemming her way through the closing argument, Grant Williams indeed walked out of court a free man that day to pick more pockets and, doubtlessly, charm more juries when he was caught the next time.

Car Conversation #2

Gen leapt into the back of the Rolls Royce—still a weird statement even inside her head—and Arthur slammed the door behind her. He strolled around to the other side of the car and folded his tall body into the back seat on the other side.

She was furiously digging in her bag, pulling her laptop out because she had downloaded a precedent she had to read that night. As her screen glowed and the file loaded, she asked, still watching the screen, "How was your day?"

Arthur crossed his legs toward her. "Fine. How did you think court went today?"

"Swimmingly." The precedent case was all loaded up and ready to read. She lifted the computer closer to her face to see it better.

Arthur leaned forward in his seat. "Pippa, could we have a moment?"

The driver found a parking lot within seconds—Gen was astonished at how she could do that in central London—and stepped out, holding a paperback book. Wintry air washed into the car.

"Do you think that court went well today?" Arthur mused.

"Look, I have a *thing* about that. I don't think I should accept sexual assault cases anymore. Octavia doesn't do rape."

"This wasn't rape," he said. "It was a case where a lad copped a feel when he shouldn't have."

"I defended him as well as anyone could have," Gen said. "He got off. I don't see what the problem is."

"Yes, as far as the logic and facts were concerned, you did as well as anyone could have, but the paper was rattling in your hands while you spoke."

"Yeah, well, I'll get better."

Arthur looked out of the side window. The small parking lot was behind some liquor stores and take-away restaurants. "You have a lot of 'tells,' like poker tells, and they make me worry about you."

"We've never played poker."

He shifted in the seat and crossed his legs away from hers. "Concerning your assault."

Gen felt her body curl inward, and she cringed into the corner of the car. "I don't want to talk to a counselor about it."

"I understand that, but I could teach you a few ways to conceal your reactions."

"Don't I do that now?"

"No. Anyone looking at you will know what you're thinking. I can teach you how to move so that your demeanor says something other than what you're thinking."

"You would teach me how to lie."

"You're a lawyer. You already know how to lie. I would teach you how not to get caught at it."

"And you could do that because—"

"I'm good at discerning when people are being deceptive."

"Like the way you knew that the doctor-for-hire was lying?"

The day before, Arthur had been watching her in court, and he had passed her a note that the doctor who was testifying that the claimant was completely disabled was lying. Gen asked the doctor a series of pointed questions, and she had admitted on the stand that she had only examined the claimant for two minutes in the lawyer's office and never received the X-ray films from the solicitor. Gen had won the case.

Arthur nodded. "Except I'll teach you to avoid detection."

"By your mystical means?"

"Desensitization, essentially."

"Oh, I get it. Look, I'm just your pretend girlfriend. You're not going to get any ass."

"I meant to avoid detection in court or social situations. At the charity events we attend, you draw yourself away from the men that you meet, but not the women. Upon observation, it doesn't seem cold so much as frightened."

"I don't look frightened," Gen argued, but she was just arguing for the sake of arguing. Sometimes, her back felt sprained from coiling herself into a spiral to get away from them.

"It draws a certain type of man like flies. You don't want to be the prey of that sort of man. Here, take my hand."

He held out his hand and laid it, palm-up, on the car seat between them.

Gen frowned at his open, grasping hand on the seat. "What am I supposed to do with that?"

"Take my hand." His voice lowered, not in anger, but what he said now sounded like a command that she wanted to obey.

Except that she didn't want to touch his hand.

But she did. She wanted very much to touch his hand. At the charity events during the evenings, she both looked forward to and dreaded the obligatory waltz.

And now his hand was sitting open, right there, on the car seat between them.

Gen tapped his palm with two fingers and pulled her hand right back, but his fingers didn't trap hers.

Arthur said, "Again. Longer this time."

She touched two fingers to his palm.

His hand stayed flat on the seat.

With his other hand, Arthur knocked on the window for Pippa to return to the car. Pippa snapped her paperback shut and walked around to her door.

"Keep doing it," Arthur told Gen as Pippa walked around the car. "Keep doing it all the way back to my apartment. Longer each time, and then hold it.

Gen poked his palm, then slapped at it with her whole hand.

With every time she batted at his hand like a nervous barn cat, the stupid panic retreated a little.

At first, Arthur watched the city slide by, and then he glanced at her hand.

Finally, when her hand was resting on his hand, her palm and fingers stretched out over his, he gently curled his fingers around hers.

He said, "Good, pet."

"What did you call me?"

"Oh, nothing, but that's good. Good job."

He held her hand the few blocks farther to his apartment. He smiled at her as the car tipped into the underground garage and they withdrew their hands.

She asked him, "So what are you going to make me do next?"

He shrugged. "I hadn't thought that far ahead."

TEA TIME

AFTER attending all those snobbish charity events with Lord Severn, Gen finally understood how the upper-class pupil barristers like James Knightly and Hayley Cheslyn must be put out by having to pour high tea for the senior barristers like groveling servants.

Gen didn't feel put out, of course. On her father's side, she came from a long tradition of bartenders and diner waitresses. It was probably why she was better at it than the pretentious upper-crusties.

Beside her, James Knightly was pouring a cuppa for his pupil master, Leonard Boxster. Two chocolate biscuits were already on the saucer. James whispered to Gen, "So I hear that you're putting in quite a few *billable hours* with your favorite client."

"Yep," Gen said, pouring tea for Octavia, who was across the room, sitting with her shapely legs crossed and gazing up at Leonard Boxster as if he were saying something interesting. Considering what Octavia said about Boxster behind his back, Gen doubted that was the case.

James blew vigorously across the cup of tea to cool it. "So many billable hours, so *late* into the night."

"Yep," Gen said. She wondered if James knew that he was spitting in his pupil master's tea, and then she wondered if that was the whole point.

David Trent wandered by and accepted a cup of tea from Gen, patting the bulk around his middle when Gen offered him a chocolate cookie.

James snarked to Gen, "You must be in *deep consultation* with His Lordship Arthur Finch-Hatten."

"Sod off, James," David Trent said. "You don't know a damn thing."

Nothing Less

Gen was sitting in her tiny office, squinting at her computer screen.

A headache was taking shape behind her eyes, a needling knife of pain.

No matter. Arthur had booked them to attend a small supper for a political candidate he supported that night. If this fundraising supper was anything like the last few, the room would be dimly lit, easy on the eyes, and she wouldn't need to squint at anything all evening long except Arthur, who was also easy on the eyes. She had to be careful that his puckish sense of humor and glimpses of his inverted-triangle silhouette, not to mention the fine contours of his butt, didn't make her too giggly.

Or maybe it was the wine he poured in her glass during these evenings that made her so giggly and blinky around him.

Whatever it was, she was getting a bit better at keeping her composure around him, or maybe her liver was just training up.

But she had to finish this brief before she could run back to his penthouse apartment and dress for the supper that night.

She'd been working on the Bloomer v. Limner brief for the last two hours, paring it down to a sleek dart of a document.

On the inside of the folder, sweet old Horace Lindsey had written, *Come, let's away to prison; We two alone will sing like birds i' the cage . . . and laugh At gilded butterflies, and hear poor rogues Talk of court news (Lear).*

Horace had been set to retire the next year and had talked to Gen often about a little place by the sea that he had wanted to buy to spend his remaining years in peace and quiet with Basil.

Horace hadn't realized that he didn't have time.

Corky Niles stuck her tousled head in Gen's door. "You busy?"

Gen and Corky had been casual friends at Oxford and during the bar course. Not close friends, but definitely more than nodding acquaintances. Corky was a sweet woman, a little precious, a little flighty, but nice. Gen had been glad that they had been picked up by the same chambers for their pupillages, hoping it meant that her pupillage would be a little more cooperative and bit less cutthroat.

Yes, Gen had been that naive. At least Corky didn't engage in the backstabbing.

"No, not busy at all," Gen lied. "Come right in."

Corky hopped in and sat in the other chair, fidgeting. "So I hear James Knightley is going around and telling everybody I'm pregnant."

"I hadn't heard that. To be honest, I don't listen to much that James Knightley says."

"It's not true. I don't have a bat in the cave." Corky grabbed a hunk of her hair and twirled it. "He's trying to sabotage me."

"He tries to sabotage everyone. I don't think the senior barristers listen to him. He's doing himself a disservice every time he opens his fool mouth."

Corky was holding a thick sheaf of paper in her hands.

Gen asked,"What have you got, there?"

Corky said, "Just a brief that I'm doing for my pupil mistress, Felicity Macdonald."

Gen tilted her head sideways to get a better look at the thick handful of paper. "That's all one brief?"

Corky said, "This one is only eighty-four pages."

Eighty-four pages? Had Corky lost her mind? Gen asked, "Are all your briefs this long?"

"Oh, no. Most of them are much longer."

Oh, Lord. Gen couldn't let Corky turn that in.

A small, evil voice in the back of Gen's head noted that a pupil barrister who wrote eighty-four page briefs wouldn't be offered tenancy, cutting the field from six candidates to five.

That was the part of her brain that was not Atticus fucking Finch.

Gen said, "Hand it over. Let's take a look at that and see what we can do to cut it down a little. Octavia says that judges generally don't like briefs that are over ten pages. And shorter is even better."

"Ten pages?" Corky squeaked. She handed Gen the heavy pile of paper.

Gen closed her laptop and spread the paper over her small desk. Even at a quick glance, she could see paragraphs and even pages that could be slashed down to just a sentence or two.

"This could take a while. I need to text someone." Gen swiped her phone to open it and texted Arthur, *I'm really sorry. I can't make it tonight. Caught at work. A friend needs help with a brief, and I can't let her turn it in as is. It would ruin her.*

Gen and Corky worked on the brief far into the night. When it was done, Gen was sure that Corky had a much better grasp on what to include, what to leave out, and how to say all of it as briefly as possible.

Corky thanked her and left Gen's office at about three in the morning.

Gen picked up her phone to call a cab.

Arthur had texted back, *I would expect nothing less. It's not an important event. I'll stay home, too. Call me when you need a ride.*

Nothing less?

Gen wasn't sure what to make of that.

She did call him for a ride, though.

A very sober Arthur picked her up at her office door, drove her back to his apartment, and shook her hand good-night in the kitchen, joking and laughing the whole time while she rubbed her eyes and giggled at him.

Another Lunch

GEN was sitting with Arthur, eating lunch in a health food bistro because she felt guilty for eating so much rich food at all the charity events that he took her to. In the evenings, every course had a sauce, and the sauces were thickened with butter or cream or both.

Red and pink construction paper hearts taped to the raw wooden beams decorated the small cafe because Valentine's Day was the next week.

"You seem to know everyone at those charity things," Gen said, just making conversation.

"I've lived in London for seven years, now. The usual suspects turn up at many of them."

"It does seem like we keep seeing the same people. At least you get to see your friends often."

Arthur stabbed his fork into his Buddha bowl of quinoa, tofu, and vegetables. "I wouldn't call them friends."

"What would you call them?"

"Acquaintances, perhaps."

"Do you have friends that you go out with, rather than to these black tie events where you just see acquaintances?"

"Yes, but I must be a good boy for the cameras."

"What, are all your friends strippers?"

He laughed. "No. Most are lads. A few birds. You wouldn't want to meet them."

"Maybe I would."

"They're a little rough around the edges," he admitted.

"Like, fight club friends? You don't sport enough black

eyes or split lips to be in a fight club. Although there was that one 'car accident—'" She used her fingers to make sarcastic quotation marks.

"Nothing so physical." He looked at her out of the corner of his eye. "Perhaps we'll have a pint with them one of these days if we can manage."

"Pints, huh? I thought you stuck to vodka tonics."

"Charity events require strong medicine. When I'm out with the lads, I drink stout or lager."

Fifteen Minutes

After yet another interminable charity event where Arthur dumped significant amounts of his ancestors' hard-won wealth, he and Gen walked into the darkened apartment across from Hyde Park. The clock read ten-thirty, an early night for them. They were usually out at least an hour later, sometimes much later.

The next day would be Thursday, which meant that Arthur would not see her until they met again that night. No intimate lunches for him, tomorrow. He had to run down to Vauxhall Cross tomorrow for a meeting with Elizabeth, and then the next day, he needed to go all the way out to Benhall in Gloucestershire for a meeting with his other masters. That would have been a five-hour drive each way if he didn't own a plane, which he did. The earldom's private plane was one of the few reasons that he was allowed to live in London rather than in the countryside. That, and because he had originally been recruited by Elizabeth before his true talents with the computers had become evident.

Also, if they hadn't accommodated both his lifestyle and his other responsibilities, he would have been useless to both his sets of masters.

But the fact remained that he had a few busy days scheduled, which meant his time spent with Gen would be minimal.

He wasn't quite ready to give her up yet for the evening.

Arthur asked her, "Watch some television?"

Gen startled and hopped away from him, just like she always did when he suggested anything.

His chest constricted a little. If Arthur ever found the asshole who had hurt her, Arthur would erase all evidence that the predator had ever existed on the Earth, and then he would kill him.

Arthur said, “Let’s just sit on the couch out here and watch the news or something. Maybe a comedy show.”

Gen glanced at the clock. “All right. I guess it’s not too late.”

“Just for a few minutes. Not a long-term commitment.”

She smiled at him, and his skin warmed. She said, “Well, no, it’s not a long-term commitment. That’s the benefit of being a barrister instead of a solicitor. We’re just hired guns.”

He laughed. “Come sit, and we’ll find something to watch.”

Arthur clicked a button on a control panel on the wall as he walked past.

A huge television rose out of a console by the far wall. The first time he had activated it, the sudden movement had started Gen, like everything did. When she saw what it was, she had laughed her bell-like laugh, and everything was fine again.

He wished that he could take the fear away from her. She was so vibrant, so lovely, so intelligent and sharp most of the time, except when something budged up against those memories.

It was probably best that she had never been specific about what had happened to her. He might have picked up salient details and ferreted out the guy, and then Arthur might have gone to jail. Killing a British citizen on British soil wouldn’t go away, no matter how much paperwork he did.

Paperwork. He shuddered at the thought. Several hours of each day were occupied by paperwork.

They flopped on opposite ends of the couch with about three feet of space between them.

Gen nudged those sexy, red-soled shoes off of her feet and stretched. A film of pantyhose covered her toes.

Arthur retrieved the remote control from the bowl beside the couch and spoke into it, finding a comedy news show for them to watch.

He couldn't watch the regular news anymore. He knew too much about what was happening and how it happened. The dumbed-down reporting of the facts with the implications that they had somehow *just happened* made him angry.

If the news were presented as comedy, however, he could laugh at it.

The first segment poked fun at politicians, always a plus.

They laughed at it for a while, looking over at each other to share the laughter. Gen's big, brown eyes glistened with laughing tears, and he felt like he could stare into them forever.

Her arm was lying on the back of the couch, and he touched her fingers while they were laughing. He didn't grab, just touched.

Just stroked.

Gen flinched, pulling her hand away.

Arthur muted the television. "Time for some more desensitization therapy."

Gen looked around the room, looking for an escape or help.

He said, "I won't hurt you. We've been alone dozens, if not hundreds, of times."

"Yeah," she said quietly, as much to herself as to him. "Yeah, that's right."

"You shy away from men like we are all made of scalding acid. You don't do it with women, just with men."

"I don't even notice I'm doing it."

"When men look at you, you rear back like they are

reaching out to grab you."

"I'm just putting some space between us. I like my personal space. That's not weird."

"You're doing it right now," Arthur said.

Gen frowned and looked at her lap.

"Like I said, for some men it's not the chase, it's the fear they like."

"That's not good," she said.

"Quite an understatement."

"Do you like the fear?" she asked.

"No. I don't like the fear at all. It makes me want to chase down the bloke who did it and see the fear in his eyes."

To see the fear in the bloke's eyes for a while, at least.

Then nothing.

Gen laughed. "Oh, you're joking."

He laughed with her. "Oh, I am." He wasn't. "So let's practice." Arthur turned himself on the couch so that he was facing her. "Look at me."

Gen struggled and managed to wrench herself around on the couch. "So now what do we do?"

He let his voice drop lower until deep bass tones resonated in his throat. "Come closer."

Yes, he knew what that voice was and what it meant, even though it could never mean that with Gen.

However, she responded to it very well.

That made him consider what else he might tell her to do.

On your knees, pet.

No, not with Gen. The chances of it going wrong were too high.

Lift your skirt, pet. Show me those luscious legs you hide from everyone.

Arthur blinked, trying to pull his mind back.

Gen was scooting closer to him on the couch, struggling with her long, red satin dress where it was binding her legs.

Take off the dress, pet. Sit on the floor, naked, at my feet.

Gen was almost over to the center cushion of the couch, and her skirt was riding up over her calves. She grabbed the material and dragged it up and over her knees.

The skin on her thighs looked so soft when it rubbed together. He could imagine burying his face between those thighs.

Don't cry out. Don't make a sound, or I'll stop.

"Arthur? Everything all right?" She was staring at him.

He drew a deep breath through his nose. "Certainly." He cleared his throat and let his voice drop again. He grappled with his phone and set the timer. "Now, look at me."

She stared at him, and her dark eyes were still dewy. "What do we do?"

"We just stay here. Look at me. Don't look away."

Both of them were bracing themselves on the back of the couch, their arms lying back there. Arthur's fingers stole over and touched her wrist.

Her hand flinched backward.

"Hold my hand," he said.

"I thought we were just staring at each other."

"You are fine with holding hands. We've done that exercise several times. No backsliding."

She nodded, and her fingers curled around his.

He stared into her eyes, and she stared into his.

"How long?" she asked.

"Fifteen minutes." He had pulled a number out of the air when he had set the timer on his phone.

"That's an awfully long time. In fifteen minutes, you could reconsider quite a few of your life choices."

"Every one of them brought us here. They must have been worth it." *Where did that come from?*

"I—" she blinked. "I guess so."

He looked into her deep, dark eyes, and she looked back.

In the beginning, this had seemed like an innocent exercise to accustom her to a man looking at her, even staring at her.

But now she was looking back at him, and her gaze was staring into his soul. Arthur felt like she was stripping all his defenses away from him.

He felt his eyes widening, and his lips opening.

He held onto her hand because he felt like he was falling.

She clutched his hand, too, and she was looking back and forth between his eyes.

Searching.

Finding.

And practically devouring him.

He couldn't look away.

He didn't want to.

Long minutes went by, and he drowned in her eyes. He could have sworn that she saw into the deepest parts of him, the parts that he kept hidden, the parts that must remain secret.

Ba-beep.

The timer on his phone chimed softly, and he pressed his thumb to the screen to turn it off.

Arthur sat back, leaning on the pillow behind him. He didn't let go of Gen's hand. Her fingers were so soft and small in his, and he desperately wanted to pull her into his arms.

Instead, he asked, "Are you all right?"

"Yeah," she said, but she was still staring at him. Her wide eyes didn't look like she was scared, not exactly. "You?"

"Of course," he lied.

His fingers firmed around her hand, testing. If he were to just tug on her hand, what would she do?

Gen broke the eye contact and looked at his hand. "I have an early day tomorrow," she said.

"Right."

"Early meetings."

"Of course."

"Really early."

"You always do on every day except Wednesdays."

"Yes." She bit her lip.

Arthur started to loosen his fingers.

She didn't.

So he clasped his hand around hers again.

He ought to shake her off and go to his room.

He wanted to pull her across the couch or leap on her himself, gather her body underneath his, and kiss her until she was whimpering for him to strip that red silk right off of her.

The torment was nearly unbearable.

He asked, "What's your early morning meeting about, tomorrow?"

"Just the usual," she said. "Just a commitment."

"Yeah?"

"Yeah." She bit her lip.

Arthur took three breaths before he said, "I'm glad you're going to these charity events with me."

"Yeah?"

"I like the company."

"Oh." She nodded, but it seemed like a disappointed nod.

He said, "I like *your* company."

She looked up at him. "I like your company, too."

Her fingers squeezed his.

He wasn't making a move. Because she was his barrister, she could be ousted from her chambers and disciplined by the Bar's ethics committee if she became involved with a client.

He didn't want that to happen to her, no matter how much his body strained to touch her, to press against her, and to move inside her.

Arthur opened his hand and dropped her fingers. His hand was instantly cold, and he had to stop himself from scrambling after her hand to pick it back up.

He said, "It's late."

"It's late," she echoed, and she held out her hand for their customary evening handshake.

He caught her fingers in his and drew her knuckles to his lips, kissing her hand.

"Arthur—"

He dropped her hand. "I'm drunk, and I can't help myself. It doesn't mean anything because I'm drunk."

They both knew he wasn't.

"Good night, Genevieve." He stood and straightened his jacket.

"Good night, Arthur."

She was looking up at him from where she was sitting on the couch, her dark hair framing her oval face and those huge, brown eyes, and she could not realize that she looked almost exactly as she would have if she were sitting, naked, at his feet.

The look in her dark eyes was not fear. The wide-open emotion looked like longing.

Someday.

The word pinged through his mind even though he knew it was unlikely.

Someday, she would sit naked at his feet, and then he would drive her mad, perhaps strip all this propriety and self-control away from her until she was a trembling thing, exhausted from ecstasy, ruined for other men.

After he was through with her, she wouldn't flinch from men's advances. She would just know that they wouldn't be good enough to make her scream the way that she had screamed his name.

Arthur walked away and got all the way to his bedroom before he realized that he hadn't been breathing. He closed the bedroom door behind himself and leaned on it.

He was sweating under his clothes. His arms and legs trembled.

This was lust. Gen was his barrister, and so he couldn't have her. That was all this was. *Lust.*

It just didn't feel like all the other times.

Arthur had not felt sexual frustration since high school, probably. He certainly hadn't felt any in college, not with women falling over themselves to be with the billionaire nobleman. Nor since.

That's all this was. He just wanted to get her into bed, and he couldn't.

Forbidden fruit.

Lust that made him not able to stop thinking about her, and worrying about her, and wondering if she was okay when he wasn't with her, and wondering if she was happy.

It was lust because it couldn't be anything else.

Arthur was thoroughly experienced with lust.

Anything else, not so much, so it couldn't be that.

His shirt was sticking to his back. He needed a shower.

On his way to his bathroom, he turned up the thermostat a few degrees. His bedroom had become chilly. That must be why he was shaking.

Maybe he was coming down with a cold or something.

It couldn't be anything else.

He liked her, yes.

He liked Gen's silly sense of humor when they joked around, he liked her kindness to his dog and his staff, he liked her industriousness at work, and he liked her lovely face and her masses of silky hair that he wanted to see spread over his pillows and clenched in his fist, and he liked her *legs.*

Gen had long, sexy, curvy legs that went on forever.

He wanted his hands on them. He wanted them wrapped around his back. He wanted to bury his face between them, and he wanted to see them tied up, spread, on his bed while he decided what he was going to do to her to make her beg for him.

Yes, he definitely needed a shower.

FIFTEEN MINUTES--GEN

GEN stood with her back to her door, resting against it, her heart racing.

Staring into Arthur's eyes for fifteen agonizing minutes had exhausted her. The intensity in his gaze had drained every cell in her body.

Leaving him had been even harder.

Those silvery eyes of his, tinged with blue, had always been sexy as hell, but she hadn't really *looked* before.

She hadn't *seen.*

Once he had looked into her eyes, his whole attention had riveted on her. She wasn't pinned back. She was drawn forward, toward him. He compelled her.

She hadn't wanted to look away.

She hadn't wanted to let go of his hand.

She hadn't wanted to leave him.

But their relationship was strictly defined. Yes, she could pretend to believe that no one would find out about them, but someone invariably would. James fucking Knightly would spread it all over chambers that she actually was fucking her client until even David Trent would believe him.

And what would she do if she did reach out to Arthur, if he touched her face and her hand and her neck and—

Gen stopped there, unable to go on even in her mind.

What if she freaked out like the stupid, scared idiot that she was? What if she screamed and cried and had a full-blown panic attack?

What if he saw that?

She shuddered, thinking about that horror.

Okay, even though she felt shredded inside and yet completely whole, she needed to sleep. She had an early morning the next day visiting her mother.

Gen changed into her jammies, dragged the comforter off the bed, and rolled up in it to sleep on the loveseat, cramming her long legs into the tiny half of a couch.

DEVILLING AT THE DEVILHOUSE

THE next week was a busy one for Gen as she worked through Arthur's files, trying to get ready for his case.

The balance in her mother's bank account sank lower with every passing week even though Gen worked her butt off to supplement her mother's care.

Gen started dropping by the Devilhouse twice a day, once in the morning and once after lunch, to pick up extra work from Violet Devereux. She wrote briefs on so many different subjects that her head spun. The bar course hadn't been nearly as varied as a week of devilling for Violet Devereux.

She managed it all, somehow, keeping up with her visits to her mother, devilling for Devereux, her pupillage work from Octavia, preparing for Arthur's case which loomed ever closer with each passing week, and her increasingly less-than-sham relationship with Arthur.

Indeed, she couldn't stop thinking about him.

A Devilhouse Discussion

GEN was sitting at a small cafe table with Arthur, waiting for their lunch.

Arthur was leaning back in his chair, his hands in his pockets, looking at something on his phone.

Below the table, Gen's ankle rested against Arthur's. They never did anything so gauche as to play footsie, but his leg warmed hers.

She hated to admit to herself that she liked it. Any touch of his flushed warmth through her body.

Ever since they had done that staring thing, nothing about Arthur scared her quite so much. When he touched her, it didn't feel like electric prickles and static shocks. His warmth soothed Gen, and she began seeking ways to feel that warmth like a cat searches out the heating grates.

A waiter placed their plates in front of them, grilled chicken and salad for Gen and some falafel kebabs for Arthur.

Gen mentioned, "I went over to the Devilhouse to earn some extra money today."

Arthur jumped in his chair. His silvery-blue eyes widened. *"I beg your pardon."*

She pierced the salad with her fork. "Yeah, I got several briefs."

He sat back in his chair and coughed hard, banging his chest with his fist. His black hair swung around his head.

"Jeez, are you all right?" She jumped up and ran around the table to pound him on the back.

"Fine. I'm fine. Gen, why would you go to the *Devilhouse,* of all places?"

"All the other pupil barristers are doing it."

"That doesn't mean that *you* should be doing it."

Gen made a face at him. "Why shouldn't I? Everyone devils."

He dropped his hands to his chest and clutched his shirt. "You've made it into a *verb?*"

"Devilling? It's been a verb for years." She flipped her napkin onto her lap.

"For *years?* I didn't even know there was a Devilhouse in London."

"Of course there is." His distressed tone perplexed her.

He said, "I must call a friend of mine. He could have saved me dozens of trips to the States. But *why?*"

Gen told him, "There are lots of them."

"What?"

Man, she might as well have told him that there were dozens of alien spaceships landing in London. "Of course. Seriously, *everybody* devils. Well, all the pupil barristers, of course. Can you imagine a QC doing that?"

Arthur combed his hair back with his fingers. "I knew that barristers often frequented places like the Devilhouse, but I didn't know that they *worked* there."

"There's a Devilhouse at pretty much every law firm, or at least a lot of little devils."

"At law firms?" Arthur froze and then squinted at her. "I think we may be talking about two very different things."

Gen frowned. "What are you talking about?"

Arthur settled his hands in front of him. "Oh, no. After you. I insist."

She explained, "The Devilhouse is Violet Devereux's office in chambers. She farms out brief-writing to pupil barristers for a cut of the hourly fee. It's called devilling."

"Ah." He mopped his forehead with a napkin. "Yes, we are speaking of different things."

"What were you talking about?" Gen asked.

"Oh, no," Arthur said. "Never mind. Truly, trust me on this one. Never mind at all."

Valentine's Day

Arthur waited in his apartment by the doors of the elevator, holding a small, red box and fidgeting like a schoolboy.

Maybe he should have gotten jewelry. Women loved diamonds. No one ever returned diamonds. Or rubies or something. Rubies seemed traditional. They were red.

He should have gotten her flowers. Probably roses. Not red roses. Red roses symbolized romantic love, and he shouldn't imply that, not when they both agreed aloud that this was a sham relationship for the cameras and to keep himself out of trouble. Maybe pink or yellow roses. Yellow symbolized friendship.

Yes, he should have gotten her some yellow roses, maybe three or four dozen.

Arthur kept wiping his clammy hands on his suit trousers. Why would his hands sweat? His hands never did this.

In addition, his heart thumped in his chest like he had been running.

For a moment, the symptoms caused him to worry about poison. Some intelligence agencies, such as the Russian FSB, poisoned people for no good reason at all.

That was paranoid. Arthur was not paranoid.

But he should have gotten her a few dozen yellow roses.

Or white. Or pink. Perhaps blue.

Maybe five dozen to fill her bedroom with sweetness.

Even though vibrant, red roses would pair so much better with her dark hair, lustrous eyes, and exuberant laugh.

Gen skidded around the corner, wearing a clinging, red cocktail dress and holding a blue box. "Arthur, I didn't know what—"

She saw the box in his hand and stopped talking.

Arthur waved the box in his hand a bit and shrugged. "I realize that our arrangement is not a relationship in the most common definition of the word, but it seemed particularly unfeeling to ignore such a tradition, so I, well, Happy Valentine's Day?"

Good God, who was that idiot speaking?

"You didn't have to," Gen said, walking closer and smiling.

He lifted it toward her. "It's just a token. It's nothing, really. I should have done more."

She held out the blue box toward him. "It's also nothing. Just a little bitty thing."

They exchanged boxes and opened them.

Arthur opened his box and found chocolates. The inside of the lid said they were vegan.

"I didn't know what to get—" she said.

"They're perfect," he said, smiling. She'd remembered his vegetarian inclinations, and his chest felt too small for his thumping heart. "Absolutely perfect. Do you like yours?"

Gen looked in the box, and her lips opened. "Chocolate-covered strawberries are my *very* favorite. I *love* them."

"I'm glad." He was.

They stood, eating chocolate and taking care not to drip it on their clothes while laughing, before they turned, entered the elevator, and went to that night's charity function where they would, once again, pretend to be in love.

More Weeks

THE weeks rolled down the calendar.

Arthur became an integral part of Gen's routine, as much as visiting her mother, work at Serle's Court Barristers, sneaking away for lunch or coffee with Rose and Lee, and the constant, subconscious panic over which of the six pupil barristers would be the one to obtain tenancy.

Oh, Lord. Even though the decision about who would be offered a spot as a tenant in chambers was *months* away, office politics felt like a free-for-all frenzy-fight among six yappy little dogs, and the stench coming out their farty little butts was the looming tenancy decision.

During the afternoons, Arthur often met Gen for lunch and came to observe her in court. If he had little notes, they were relevant and short.

When Gen got home from the office and on the mornings when she didn't visit her mother, she called for Ruckus's leash. The two of them had at least some sort of a walk in Hyde Park.

Within weeks, Ruckus was meeting her at the elevator with the lead in his mouth. Luckily, he understood that she needed to change her clothes and shoes and trotted beside her to her bedroom, drooling around the leather strap in his mouth the whole way.

Watching how Arthur lived was an education in itself.

After he returned from business meetings or emerged from that locked room down the hallway from Gen's bedroom, his evening was scripted for him.

Mr. Royston Fothergill had Arthur's clothes ready after he freshened up. His admins bought gifts for him to give to the hosts or supplied whatever else he needed.

Arthur walked through his life like a prize show horse, groomed and coddled and pranced about the arena to do his tricks.

No wonder he occasionally went off the reservation with a couple of women to blow off steam.

Gen was coming to enjoy the evenings out with him more and more. She had never been a party girl, but Arthur was there to smooth over all the social stuff. He whispered notes to her about her law firm's clients, who they were, what they did, who they were in litigation with, and what they were really like.

It wasn't just his warm breath on her bare shoulders or neck that she liked. She was genuinely grateful for his information and guidance.

And he really could remember *everything.* He should have been a barrister. That kind of memory is killer when memorizing precedent.

"Lloyd Payton." In the crowd by the bar, Arthur turned her so that she saw the man over Arthur's broad shoulder but the guy couldn't see Arthur's lips moving. "Daughter is Sofiah. Currently Octavia Hawkes's client for a case involving his mill's shoddy goods. He's defending it to the hilt, but that mill hasn't turned out anything of quality since before the War. Be complimentary. Be formal."

While they were dancing: "In the black dress with the overabundance of gold jewelry, Isla-Belle Hext. Your chamber-mate David Trent's client. Suing her divorce attorneys for malpractice."

Arthur adjusted her hand on his shoulder like he did pretty much every time they danced their one waltz. No matter how precisely Gen placed her hand, he always corrected her. She wasn't even sure what he was fixing.

He continued, "Quite likely she'll win. Certainly deserves

a settlement from someone. Don't mention it, but tilt your head to the side in commiseration. She should nod in acknowledgment."

Over supper, "Prentis Hightower, across the table in the green tie, client of Rupert Hancock, QC. His son Raglan was at university and was hit by a missile that had been fired out of another student's anus. Seeking compensation for damages and mental distress. Yes, Gen, for being hit by a buttock rocket. Evidently, the burns on his back required skin grafts. Show very subtle amounts of real horror when you ask, obliquely, about his son's well-being. The lad has suffered quite a bit."

Over the suppers, Arthur told Gen tidbits of his life, from boarding school through college and since.

Over steak for her and butternut squash ravioli for him: "It was easier to sneak out of the dorms at Rolle than from the winter campus in Gstaad. Once I kept a car off campus when I was sixteen, Caz, Max, and I could be at the garage in fifteen minutes. During the music festivals like Montreux and Paléo in the summer, we would skive off school for a week and indulge. I bribed the dorm attendants to forget that we existed. No, no one worried about us. We were three male teenagers with nearly unlimited funds, passports, and no oversight. What's the worst that could have happened? Well, yes, perhaps a Turkish prison, but it never came to that."

Over chicken divan for her and vegetarian lasagna for him: "One time when I was in Las Vegas with friends, we were caught counting cards at blackjack. They couldn't prove anything, of course. It's just watching what's played and keeping track in one's head so that you can adjust your wagers based on the changing odds. Yes, a lot of people think it's magic and you know what the next card played will be, but it's not. It's statistics. It's math. Since the casinos started using longer shoes and shuffling before the cards get close to the end, counting cards has become ineffective. I learned it at school. There was a floating poker game in the dorms that went on for years. I kept losing spectacularly to an older boy, Wulfram, and a younger boy, Alexandre. Wulf finally let on that they were counting cards and, out of pity, taught me how. I taught Caz and Max, and we went back and cleaned out the upperclassmen that weekend, though I suspect some of that was pity on Wulfram's part."

Over Vegetable Wellington, herbed vegetables wrapped in golden, flaky puff pastry that shattered between her teeth, Arthur whispered, "When we're in a crowd, you mustn't say excuse-me and pardon-me to get through. I think you said them twenty times in a row."

"But, that's polite," Gen said, confused. "Being polite is very British."

"Yes, but we don't say that when we squeeze through crowds," he whispered. He glanced around and dropped his voice further. "British children are taught that when one belches in public, one says 'Excuse me.' One says 'Pardon me' when one audibly trumps in public."

Gen felt faint. "Oh, my. So when I was getting through the crowd—"

"People were probably wondering what you had eaten to cause such gastric distress."

"Oh my God!" They all thought she had left a trail of burps and farts through the crowd like a gaseous river of napalm floating behind her.

Gen considered crawling under the table. She asked him, "So, what do I do when I need to get through a crowd?"

Arthur said, "One contorts oneself into a knotted rope to fit through any available space, apologizing afterward, of course. There's often a great deal of saying 'I'm sorry,' and sometimes a standoff of insisting, 'No, after you.'"

"And if a person doesn't see you and doesn't move?" Gen asked.

"Well, then, it's perfectly obvious that both of you must stand there until one of you is dead."

Sometimes at night or in stolen moments, but always when they were alone, Arthur's voice would deepen to those compelling, sexy tones that made the hair on the back of Gen's neck stand up.

He convinced her to let him touch her elbow and shoulder with his fingertips while they talked, to sit beside her on the couch with their thighs touching, or to sit opposite her at tiny cafe tables, their knees encroaching on each other's space, and talking quietly, almost nose-to-nose.

In those moments, sometimes she couldn't breathe with the warmth of his body washing over her skin, left half-bare by the strapless or backless evening gowns, or the subtle scent of his cologne, cinnamon and fresh-cut wood and musk.

And always, his *eyes*.

His silvery eyes glinted in the moonlight, shone in the daylight when he laughed, and turned to molten metal when he looked at her and thought she wasn't looking.

Gradually, Gen got stronger.

At the charity events, when she didn't shrink back from men as much, she got an approving nod from Arthur and sometimes a wink. When a client of Octavia's shook Gen's hand with both of his and then grabbed her elbow in his enthusiasm, Gen smiled at him, and then Arthur smiled at her.

She didn't feel so shaky inside. Even her voice strengthened when she spoke in court, and Arthur's glances from the gallery warmed her.

Expensive, designer dresses were filling her closet at Arthur's apartment, each more sparkling than the last. Room was running out.

Gen didn't bother to lock her bedroom door anymore. Arthur was a perfect gentleman in every respect.

Through it all, there was a very quiet, very subtle flirtation between them. Whenever she said the word "coffee," even in the car, even if they passed each other in the kitchen in the morning, he looked up and into her eyes, a reminder that after this was over, she had promised that they would go for *coffee* together.

And just every now and then, sometimes when he caught her eye, there was a moment, a connection, a reliving of those fifteen soul-baring minutes on the couch where *something* happened between them as they stared into each other's eyes.

Still, when she went shopping for new ball gowns for the never-ending society and charity events, he came along under guise of staying with her for she was his babysitter. When she showed him new dresses that the fussy and very strict Graham had stuffed her into, Arthur's eyes turned to shining, liquid silver.

One time, for an event somewhat less formal than most of the charity balls and receptions, Graham allowed her to be seen in a black dress that skimmed the tops of her knees. It was too tight, Graham fussed, too cinched in the waist for a voluptuous woman such as herself.

When Arthur had seen her in it at Harrods, his eyes had traveled from the tips of yet another pair of Christian Louboutin red-soled pumps, up her legs, lingering on her calves and thighs, and over her body. He had started to stand up from his armchair as if an instinct had seized him, but he settled back into the chair and smoothed his bright blue tie into his suit jacket.

That night, when she wore the too-short and too-tight dress with the fuck-me shoes, Arthur's hands had floated around her, not touching her, not being grabby and groping, but his fingertips *almost* skimmed her shoulder, her neck, and her bare knees. When they sat opposite each other, knees almost touching, he reached down to hover his hands near her shins a dozen times.

When she crossed her legs, he ran a finger over one pointed tip of her shoe.

Gen watched his fingertip stroke the leather and didn't

move.

Their eyes met, and Gen didn't look away for long minutes.

Neither did Arthur.

One Friday night, late, hours after they had come home from another soiree and had danced with Arthur whispering secrets into her hair about the other guests, her clients, and himself, hours after she had gone to bed, the long handle on her door rattled.

Gen sat up on the loveseat couch that she was sleeping on, her hair spilling around her shoulders and her tee shirt stretched tight over her breasts. She held up the blanket that she had wrestled off of the bed. "Arthur?"

The door creaked open in the dim light from the cityscape twinkling through the window behind her.

No one came in.

Something clinked and jingled near the floor, however.

Gen sat up farther and looked down.

Ruckus had trotted in, holding his leash in his mouth, and flopped on the floor beside the couch.

The next morning would be Saturday. Ruckus had figured out that Wednesdays and weekends were his long-walk days in Hyde Park, and the little dog was ready whenever she was.

Trust that pooch to figure out how to read the date, or maybe Ruckus also had access to Mr. Royston Fothergill's shared calendar.

She laid back down on the couch and went back to sleep for a few hours.

Gen thought that she and Arthur were getting along splendidly. If someone had asked her to wager, she would have bet that they were becoming fast friends and their affectionate relationship would be obvious to anyone who observed them. They always seemed to be laughing together, whether in public or even in stolen moments in the apartment.

And there was that naughty sparkle in his silvery eyes when he looked at her.

So when Gen's pupil mistress called them both into her office to give them a dressing down, Gen could barely sputter.

A Man and a Plan

Once again, Gen and Arthur sat in hard chairs in front of Octavia Hawkes's imposing desk, shame-faced.

Octavia Hawkes stood by the window, her back to them, not even deigning to look at them.

Arthur whispered to Gen, "I told you about the time that headmaster at Le Rosey caught me in that girl's closet, braced against the walls so that I was flat against the ceiling, yes?"

Gen snickered. "I don't think Octavia is going to make us shovel sidewalks during our free period for a week in punishment. What did you do this time?"

"I did nothing," he whispered. "I am as pure as the driven snow. It's what made me think of it."

Gen laughed out loud at that but caught herself before Octavia fired her butt.

Arthur mused, "I still hate snow. I always finagle to spend Christmas with Caz in California or Max in Monaco, or wherever he has ended up."

Octavia Hawkes stood by the window, her hands clasped behind her back, staring out as the late winter sunshine lit her smooth face. She said, "No one believes you."

Gen said, "He hasn't done anything wrong for months. I just checked. There are no new pictures, *nothing.*"

Octavia said, "No one believes you two are a couple."

Gen's jaw dropped open. "What—us? Why not?"

"Evidently, you are 'stiff' together. There is no 'chemistry' between you. You do not pass 'the sniff test.'" Her sarcasm emphasized the quotation marks.

Gen looked at Arthur, who shrugged. She defended them, "We dance together in public at least a couple times a week. He's draped all over me like kudzu."

Arthur straightened. "I do not hang all over you like a teenager—"

Octavia said, "The gossip pages are saying that you two have less chemistry than any rock musician turned actor."

Arthur frowned. "Surely that's not true."

"God, yes. It's absolutely true," Gen said. "Rock stars *really* can't act."

And they both snickered like schoolchildren.

"Enough!" Octavia shouted. "Now, Gen, I'm pleased to see that the quality of your work hasn't diminished, and you are getting enough done here at the office—"

Well, that was good. Gen tried to relax a little.

"—but I still believe that this little experiment is not working. The main point was to restore Finch-Hatten's image."

"The goal was to keep him out of even more trouble," Gen said. "The only pictures of him on those damn gossip sites anymore are with me in very non-compromising positions."

"Definitely not compromising enough," Octavia agreed. "This isn't working, and it's too risky for you. I believe that you should move out of Finch-Hatten's apartment and end this charade."

"But he's being good!" Gen said. "The case is all ready to go, and he hasn't been on the gossip websites for weeks!"

"This case will rise on its merits or sink on Finch-Hatten's previous behavior. You would be better served focusing on other cases before the senior barristers decide to whom they'll offer the tenancy."

"The tenancy decision is at the end of September. We won't even get to trial before that, so I can't lose it."

"There will still be pre-trial motions and judgments, and

the gossip is still out of hand. The gossip bloggers have lost the plot about Finch-Hatten and his many women, from strippers to socialites to hookers. He's their favorite flavor of candy, and they don't believe that you're anything but a beard."

"What if we make out?" Gen asked. She didn't slap her hand over her mouth this time, but it was a close call.

"Gen?" Arthur asked.

She bulled onward. "Those stupid websites are saying that they don't believe us because there's no PDA, so we'll slobber all over each other a couple of times." She turned to Arthur. "The hearing isn't until November. We have *months.* We should be boring for a bit, hold hands and pecks on the cheeks, and they'll move on to more scandalous pastures. We can get through this."

"You seem adamant," Octavia said, and she nearly snarled it. A whole world of accusations lived in that statement.

She turned to Arthur. "Are you okay with that?"

He smiled at her, a slow, secret smile. "In this, I am in your hands."

"Okay, then. Don't we have a *thing* tonight?"

He checked the calendar on his phone. "A charity supper and silent auction for pediatric cancer. It's the Hope Ball."

"It's an actual ball," she said. "Like Cinderella."

"Except that the money goes to charity instead of the royal coffers."

"I don't have a ball gown."

"Graham will make sure you do."

Gen shot a look at Octavia. "So we'll make out for the cameras tonight. It's just to repair his image," she said. "It's to control the message. In reality, we are as platonic as neutered house cats."

Arthur *really* frowned at that one.

"So if they want *snogging,*" Gen had heard Lee and Rose use that very British word, "we'll give them *snogging.*"

"Snogging?" Arthur asked. "Did you learn that from the Harry Potter books?"

Gen shot him a filthy look, and they both cracked up.

"Stop it, you two!" Octavia thumped her hand on her desk.

"We've just been doing our best," Gen told her, "and the fact that some asinine gossip websites don't believe us enough is *ridiculous.* So, we'll turn it up a notch. We'll play barrister games with these paparazzi-pseudo-journalists, and they'll lose. They'll never realize how they've been played. It's only a few more months—"

"Eight months," Octavia insisted.

"—and we're pretty much set to go into the hearing. And he's been squeaky clean—"

Arthur chuckled again.

"—for weeks."

He kept chuckling.

"Oh, my God, *stop it."* And yet Gen was pretty close to laughing with him.

"Fine." Octavia glared at them. "You may try that. It is only eight more months," she sighed. "What trouble could you two get up to in eight months?"

Yeah, that was as ominous a statement as Gen had ever heard.

First Kiss

STANDING in the entryway next to the elevator doors, Gen held a handful of her silver beaded skirt, sweeping it to the side to get it out of the way while she checked the hem behind herself. The back of the ball gown—not just an evening gown but a *ball gown*—dragged on the floor just a bit, maybe six inches, while the front allowed the tips of her high heels to peep out. She suspected that the back was a train. People were going to be stepping on it all night. Maybe she could find a couple of safety pins and fashion it into a bustle instead, but Graham might have a cow if he found out she had altered the lines of one of his picks.

Arthur walked in, his wrist turned out as he peered down his shirt sleeve cuff. "I've dropped my cufflink down my sleeve again."

"Come here." Gen cupped her hands. "Shake it out."

Arther held his arm up and jittered his hand, shaking loose the tiny bit of metal. Gen snatched the glittering thing before it hit the floor. Dark blue glittered amongst the gold. "Sapphires?"

"My grandfather was a judge in India for a time. Could you?" He held out his right hand, wrist up.

"Sure." She threaded the cufflink through his sleeve and snapped it closed. The faint scent of his cologne wafted from his sleeve: warm, apple-pie spices, clean wood, and musk. "There you go."

"Thank you." He checked it, testing the bar in back. "Yes, it's closed. I was having such trouble with it."

"You're so right-handed," she said. "Sometimes I'm surprised you can cut your food with a knife."

"This is a rather formal event," he started.

"Because the others weren't?" she laughed.

"This one, more so." He paused. "This is a bit embarrassing."

"Did I do something wrong?" Gen glanced at her dress, nerves jiggling because she didn't know if this dress was appropriate or underdressed or too garish. "Is this dress not right?"

"Oh, no. You look beautiful." He smiled, and his smile was a little sultry but mostly kind. "You're perfect. Your dress is lovely. It's not that. From what Graham tells me—"

"Oh, no. Did he say that my dresses cost extra because it takes too much material to cover my butt?"

"No!" Arthur laughed. "He said you needed jewelry."

"Oh." Gen didn't have any expensive jewelry, nothing like what the duchesses and models would be wearing. Her mother had a nice aquamarine pendant and earrings. They could stop at her home and grab that.

Arthur picked up a black velvet case that had been sitting on the entryway table. "I had some things retrieved from Spencer House. These belong to the estate, not to me, personally. If you like them, I can have replicas made."

He opened the case.

Nestled inside the black velvet, a galaxy center of fiery pinpricks glowed, thousands of them.

"Oh, Arthur," she breathed. "How beautiful."

"I can have one made for you that's just like it if you want."

She touched the swirls of diamonds on the necklace with just her fingertips. "No, no. I wouldn't dream of accepting such a thing as a gift. It would be amazing to wear it for just one night, though."

Arthur lifted out the necklace. "Turn around."

Gen pivoted. She didn't have to lift her heavy hair out of

his way because she had twisted and pinned the damp mass onto the back of her skull.

Arthur's hands came over her head and laid the necklace over her collarbone. So many diamonds decorated the collar that the weight was significant. Silvery wires and settings, probably platinum, held all the stones together.

She asked, "Where did you get such a thing?"

"Inherited it like everything else," he said.

"It must be old."

His fingers brushed her neck as he fiddled with the clasp. "Tudor era. Queen Anne gave this set to my several-greats grandmother. There. All done."

"She knew the queen?" For the thousandth time, rich people were weird. Gen turned around.

He held out his closed fist. "Oh, indeed. There are portraits of her at Spencer House."

Gen held her hand under his fingers, and he dropped two earrings that looked like mutant, crystal raspberries into her hand. She said, "I'd love to see the portraits someday."

"Would you?" His voice rose just a little, almost wistful. He got back into the jewelry case and came up with a bracelet and a ring.

"Sure. I mean, this is her stuff. It would be neat to see a picture of her and to see the whole house."

"It's in the country," Arthur said. "We would have to take a few days. A weekend. It's not open to the public until June, so we could go up one of these weekends. Here." He held out a thick string of diamonds between his fingers.

Gen laid her left arm on the bracelet. "You sound like you don't spend a lot of time there."

"Every moment I can," he said, clicking the bracelet clasp. "During the summer, it's open on weekends for viewing. I spend those weekends here, but in other months, I escape London for weeks at a time."

"It sounds like it's your private retreat."

He held out the ring, holding the circle in his long fingers.

"I'd love to show it to you if you can stand the drive and the countryside and the mud of the deer park. Most people don't care for it. They prefer the excitement of London."

He was still holding out that ring, a diamond ring, like he meant to put it on her finger.

Okay, there are very few instances in life when a man puts a ring on a woman's finger, and they are reserved for very specific occasions. Most guys would have dropped the ring into her hand like Arthur had the earrings, not held it out to put it on. Too much symbolism.

Arthur was still holding that circle out, and the look in his gray eyes here in the dim entryway could have been mistaken for seriousness.

Gen held out her right hand, fingers spread. "Oh, I could handle some peace and quiet. I miss the quiet of my dad's ranch in Texas. These events are fun, but staying in would be nice, too."

"Ah, yes," he said, slipping the ring over the proper finger of her *right* hand. "We're to watch a movie sometime, aren't we?"

She needed to lighten this up, right now. "That's right, buddy. You promised me a movie and take-away."

He chuckled, and then he glanced down the entryway. "We have a moment," he said.

"Pippa will be here in six minutes," Gen said, checking her phone. She let absolute certainty drop her voice because Pippa was always, *always* on time.

"Yes," Arthur said. "Six minutes." He bit one side of his lower lip, and he looked at her from the sides of his eyes.

They hadn't had even a moment to themselves after the meeting in Octavia's office that morning, the one where Gen had insisted that they suck face in public that night.

After work, Oliver had picked Gen up in the Rolls and driven her to the apartment, where she had barreled upstairs to shower. As she sprinted through, Mr. Royston Fothergill had informed Gen that Arthur was in his master suite, readying himself, and it appeared that he would be prompt.

Gen's hair was still damp underneath from where she had nearly finished blow-drying it, but she was standing by the elevators at the appointed time.

But now, this was indeed the first time that she had seen him, and Arthur was studying her like he wanted to say something, still biting one side of his lower lip with his straight, white teeth.

Finally, he said, "About what you told Octavia Hawkes this morning—"

"Not out here," Gen said. "Come on." She strode away into the apartment.

"Hey! Where are you—*Gen!*" Footfalls chased her into the apartment.

She couldn't go back to her guest bedroom. Housekeepers had rushed in as soon as Gen had walked out, armed with toilet scrubbers. She needed privacy to talk to him about making out in public tonight because she didn't want to be embarrassed to death in front of the people who took care of Arthur.

Behind her, Arthur said, *"Hey!* Pippa will arrive to collect us in just a minute. Where are you going?"

Gen gathered up the hem of her dress so that she wouldn't step on it and rip the gown down the front. Having to change her clothes would make them late. "We need to talk."

"Wait up!" He jogged a few steps and careened around her in the kitchen, his black dress shoes slipping on the tile. He grabbed the shining counter.

"There are housekeepers in my room," she said. "We need *privacy.*"

"Come on," he said. "My room is free."

Gen followed his broad back, dressed in one of his matte black tuxedoes, through the kitchen and toward the other corner of the apartment from hers.

To his bedroom.

He held one of the double doors open for her. "If you think we should speak *privately.*"

Gen stopped, her high heels skidding on the dark wooden floor.

It was just his bedroom. Arthur had been a perfect gentleman in many other situations where there was no one else around. If he wanted to hurt her, he'd had ample opportunity. This was no different.

It was just his *bedroom.*

Gen swallowed hard and forced herself to walk past him and over the threshold.

Okay. She had made it.

Inside, wide windows opened the room to the sunset sky, streaks of neon gold and amber slicing the sky with fire. French doors led out to yet more of the balcony that wrapped all the way around the building. Topiaries cut into green cones and spirals stood outside, planted in terra cotta pottery, and a thick, column-studded railing looked like a sturdy barrier.

Gen focused on the balcony and the breakfast table with four upholstered chairs outside.

Even though the bed was probably ten feet away from her to her left, Gen could *feel* it over there. The suffocating, white comforter and the malformed blobs of the pillows crouched.

Arthur shut the door behind her. The clicks of the knob and lock popped off the walls and brittle glass.

"We should talk." She stared at the thick moulding on the closed door that looked like walls within walls, an illustration of a prison.

Arthur repeated, "Pippa will be arriving for us very soon. The schedule—"

Sweat stung her forehead near her hairline. She blurted, "I think you should kiss me tonight."

Arthur didn't look excited. Indeed, he inhaled through his

nose, and he looked down and sideways at her, leery of what she had said.

"I told Octavia that we would make it look better," she said, "like we really are a couple." She flicked her hands, trying to shake the crazies out of her fingers.

"I'm concerned." Arthur's voice was pitched very low.

"I think we should—concerned?" Panic wrapped around her throat, and her voice squeaked.

"We're standing here in private. I'm two feet away from you." He canted his head to the side, inspecting her face and neck. "My hands are in my pockets. I'm not reaching for you. I'm not touching you, and yet I would say that you are about ten seconds away from a panic attack."

Gen slumped and let her butt rest against the wall behind her. Tremors ran through her legs and shook the floor under her. "I am not."

"Now you sound British, not saying what you mean, except that I don't believe a word you are saying. To be properly British, you have to make the other person believe it."

Frustration vibrated in her bones. "You Brits are all closed in yourselves, trapped in your little shells of propriety and in manipulating other people. You can't even move, you're so trapped. You can't even say what you mean."

"That might be so," he admitted. "But if I were to kiss you in public and you reacted badly, the websites would have all the confirmation they needed that our so-called relationship is a sham. If the press were to say that I am engaged in a public-relations facade, it would look worse at the trial."

Such an unemotional evaluation of their situation.

Arthur was more English than the heirs to the throne of England, and he was trapped in an English castle of his own making.

But so was Gen. She was trapped in a dungeon of stupid panic.

She *hated* it.

Gen pulled herself upright and, with two steps, closed the distance between them. His tuxedo touched the beads of her gown over her chest. Even though he was six foot-four or taller, with her super-high heels on, she stood almost as tall as he did.

She grabbed his tie near his collar. "So kiss me right now."

His silvery eyes widened, healed from the swelling and bruising from the car accident weeks ago. "I beg your pardon."

"Kiss me right now. Then we'll know whether or not I'll freak out tonight. Then we'll know whether this looks like a sham relationship or whether it looks real."

The reticence in his silvery eyes shamed her.

Oh.

Her heart crumpled in her chest.

It *was* a sham relationship, as he had called it. Arthur was acting the part of a devoted boyfriend for a few weeks so he could keep his noble title and billions of dollars.

He hadn't meant what he had said when they were out in public, and probably not when they had been in that restaurant, either, when he had asked her out on a date, and they had planned to have coffee and watch a movie at home, someday.

Because being British means not saying what you mean and yet making people believe you.

She had believed him.

A few weeks before, he had manipulated her into believing that she could win the Tambling-Goggin v. Pye case in front of Judge Marks so that James Knightly would see her confidence and settle it.

His suggestion to go on a date must have been exactly the same thing, a ploy to build up her confidence. She had needed to look confident because that was the best course of action.

Her fist around the dark silver silk of his tie loosened.

She said, "We don't have to go through with it if *you* don't want to. I understand. Hey, maybe I was just telling Octavia something to get her off our backs. Maybe I was being British, and I didn't say what I meant."

Arthur's hand touched her bare shoulder, near the strap that held up her dress. "Did you mean what you told Octavia? That we should try to make it appear more real for the cameras and the stupid websites?"

"I mean what I say. I told Octavia that we would snog in public."

The childish word made him close his eyes and chuckle. *Oh, the way that his dark lashes brushed his cheeks.*

"Yeah, *snog,*" she said. "I said we would *snog.*"

He shook his head, still laughing, and looked up. "Fine."

"Fine, what?" She couldn't breathe.

"Fine. We'll *snog.* But you kiss me."

"Wha-*at?*"

His hand touched her waist, and he pressed her spine just a little, guiding her a little closer to his chest. He lifted her other hand and wrapped her arm around his waist.

His voice was low in his throat, and their lips were only an inch apart. "You, kiss me. Now. *Here.*"

His body swayed, brushing hers through their clothes.

Oh, this was totally different.

Being kissed meant that she just had to survive it and not freak out. Having to initiate it felt a hundred times harder.

Arthur said, "Go ahead."

"It's probably a good idea," she whispered, looking at his lips and watching his gray eyes. His irises had quite a bit of dark blue around the edges of the pale gray. "Because we're supposed to be a couple. We should have been dating for a while. If we had been dating for a while, we would know where the noses go and stuff."

He murmured, "Right."

His warm, mint breath feathered over her lips.

Arthur wasn't just standing stiffly like a statue that she could bring to life with a kiss. His lips were parted, and his eyes fluttered half shut, not watching her but not mannequin-like.

She said, "Otherwise, we'll look awkward tonight. It'll be obvious. Everyone will know. The gossip sites will say that it was staged."

"Yes," he whispered.

His lips were almost touching hers. He was bending his neck so she could reach him.

All she had to do was *move.*

She wasn't a drunk, stupid, *helpless* college student.

Not anymore.

Gen pushed with her toes, rising slightly, and brushed her lips across his in the quickest butterfly kiss.

She pulled back, watching him.

He didn't snap. He didn't shove her up against a wall and pin her hands above her head or any of the other things that would have scared the shit out of her.

When her lips left his, he didn't move. He was unmoving like he was waiting for her.

"Again," he said.

His voice was so deep in his throat when he said that, so masculine, a gentle but undeniable command.

Gen rose on her toes and kissed him again.

This time, she touched her lips to his, and his lips parted under hers.

He was kissing her back, gently, and his other hand stole to her jaw.

His touch didn't feel like he was restraining her. His thumb brushed her cheekbone, and his fingers slipped into her hair.

Gen's heart swelled, and his tie slid from her fingers, catching on her writing callus. She touched his chest while he kissed her, feeling the hard flesh of him buried under the layers of silk and fine wool, and her hands rose. Muscle swelled under his clothes, and her fingers and palms found the round solidity of his shoulders.

Arthur lifted his head away from her, and she almost stumbled against him from the sudden lack of resistance. His breathing was high in his chest, the lightest bit of breathlessness. His hands still held her waistline and her jaw.

He whispered, "Are you all right?"

Gen nodded. She couldn't trust herself to speak. Her voice might squeak or crack, or she might say something stupid.

Something like, *Don't stop.*

He said, "Are you going to be all right tonight, in front of people?"

She nodded again, rubbing her chin and jaw on his palm. Her face tingled where his skin touched hers. His other hand warmed her waist.

"During the dancing," he said. "Not during the supper. Not during the auction. All right? Before the dancing, you should relax."

"Okay. I can do that. Okay."

A line formed between his eyes. "I've never felt like a wolf leading a lamb to slaughter before."

Gen drew herself up. "You're not. This was my idea."

The line didn't smooth away. "All right. Let's go."

He dropped his hands from her body and held the door for her.

Gen wandered out of his bedroom and somehow managed to find her way through his apartment and to the elevator, even though her brain was full of buzzing.

HOPE BALL

GEN was fine during supper and fine during the silent auction, but the dancing was coming soon.

And then Arthur was going to kiss her.

Yes, it was an actual ball and she was going to kiss Lord Severn around midnight at the ball.

That didn't sound ridiculous or anything.

At least he wasn't a handsome prince. That would have been completely ridiculous.

Gen swallowed hard, trying not to feel ridiculous.

The Hope Ball was held at the Royal Horseguards Hotel, a place that would have been too hoity-toity even for Gen's mother to be comfortable touring. The ballroom overlooked the glittering Embankment, the monstrous ferris wheel called the London Eye, and the river lights glistening on the River Thames. The hotel itself looked like a blue and white castle in a kids' fantasy movie. At the entrance, Gen almost expected pumpkin-like coaches pulled by horses with suspiciously mouse-like ears. Maybe with naked, snaky tails, too.

Inside the ballroom, the crowd was a swirling mix of men in black-tie tuxes and women in jewels and glittering ball gowns. Even a cowpuncher like Gen could tell that the intricately beaded dresses they wore were a step up from mere evening gowns. Some were crusted with thousands of beads that had been hand-sewn like Gen's. Some were detailed with delicate embroidery. All complimented the flashing diamond and other stone jewelry that the women wore around their necks, and on their wrists, and fingers, and in their hair. These dresses were *extravagant* in their refined elegance.

Gen tried to feel like Cinderella, but she felt more like a Texan Yankee in King Arthur's Court.

Heh, King Arthur.

She'd have to call him that. It might crack him up.

Man, she hoped that she didn't trip over her high heels and walk up the inside of her skirt, ripping the whole thing right off herself.

They sat at a round table near the stage with ten other people, and oversized Gen was careful to keep her elbows tucked in close to her sides. Arthur introduced her around because he knew everyone, of course. Gen was becoming comfortable with meeting all these people whose names were prefaced with The Right Honorable and Their Graces.

She asked, "How d'you do?" a dozen times at least, smiling the whole time, and heard exactly that back.

So weird.

A couple of David Trent's clients asked her advice on a minor matter. After the usual this-is-not-legal-advice and I-am-not-your-barrister disclaimers, she told them that David Trent indeed seemed to be following the best path and she hoped for the best for them. Their smiling nods to each other and Arthur's sly wink gave Gen some hope that she was getting better at this stuff.

Dessert was sugared strawberries again. Gen purred while she ate the decadent treat.

She caught Arthur watching her as she sucked a strawberry slice off her fork, his face impassive but for a small smile and his intense gaze as he watched her lips.

She and Arthur were milling around, looking at the lots for the silent auction. Arthur was at the next table, considering a yacht cruise, while Gen was looking at a basket of spa treatments.

Around them, the crowd surged, and people wove between them.

Gen looked around. "Arthur?"

He held up his empty glass. "I'm going for another vodka tonic. Wine?"

"Yes, please." She turned back to the spa basket, deciding what to write down. Arthur had told her that they needed to spend at least ten thousand pounds that night, to look like they were paying their way.

Spa basket. She could split it with Lee and Rose if she won it.

Beside her, Arthur's voice asked, "Enjoying yourself?"

"Thought you went for more drinks." She looked up, expecting to see Arthur's dark hair and silvery eyes.

Instead, the man wasn't quite as tall as Gen was, as she was standing there in her heels, and his eyes and hair were more pale than Arthur's. His face was rounder and softer, and he looked older.

She said, "Christopher."

The man nodded. "And you're with him again."

"Looks like," she said, shrugging. The antique diamond necklace was heavy on her collarbones. Wearing Arthur's diamonds in front of Christopher, who wanted Arthur's earldom, felt gauche.

Christopher leaned on the table with the spa basket. "You're his barrister, and it's every bit as unethical for a barrister to fuck a client as it is for a physician to fuck a patient. You need to recuse yourself from this case and get another barrister to try it, or I'll send around the photos that I have of the two of you."

"The gossip sites already have all those pictures and more. Why is that a threat?"

Christopher said, "I'll make sure you are thrown out of chambers, and no other chambers will touch you."

She couldn't argue that it was all a charade. Christopher would narc to his lawyer, and at the trial, they would tell the jury that it was all a sham relationship to make Arthur look like less of a lazy rich dude.

Instead, he would look like a scheming, lazy rich dude.

Gen said to Christopher, "You sound like a villain in a James Bond movie, cackling like that and telling me your evil plans. Have you even read the Evil Overlord List?"

Christopher frowned. "The what?"

"The things that stupid evil overlords do that screw them over in the end. Things like treating their army so badly that they rebel, killing their smartest general to show how powerful and ruthless they are, and *telling the good guy all their evil plans.*"

"I can tell you all my plans because you won't be his barrister any longer, not if you want to keep your job and keep your mother in that posh nursing home here in London."

Christopher Finch-Hatten was a doctor. Even though he was a plastic surgeon, the threat that he might do *something* to Gen's mother loomed large in her head.

"Besides," Christopher said, looking over the crowd around them, laser glints from the disco ball spangling his face, "you'll want to get as far away from Arthur as you can, professionally. If you think the pictures of him and the three girls were bad, you should see the ones my investigator has."

"Having someone follow your own brother to take blackmail photos is a shitty thing to do," she said.

Well, it was.

Christopher sneered, "He'll never recover from these new ones. They will *mortify* you. They will mortify *everyone* when I release them in October. By the way, I must thank you for setting a trial date. Now, I know just when to make sure that *everyone* who may be on the jury should see them."

"It sounds like you hate him. What did he ever do to you?"

"He's not even a real Englishman," Christopher said, his lip twisting. "He was raised in Switzerland and spent his vacations in the Netherlands, Monaco, or France. He didn't come home for *years,* sometimes. The earldom should go to someone who *loves* Britain, who has a family and will conserve the estate and revere it, not someone who is squandering it like pirate booty on liquor and European prostitutes."

"He doesn't do that," she said. "And this charity thing is to pay for digging wells so that kids in Africa won't die of dysentery. He's not *squandering* it."

"Yes, but the estate is still hemorrhaging money. It doesn't matter if it's for 'good' causes."

Gen could hear Christopher's angry sarcasm.

Christopher spat, "Taking the earldom away from Arthur would be an act of kindness. Without unlimited funds, he may not drink himself to death."

Asshole. "That's harsh, Christopher."

"Ah, but it's true. Here he comes. Think about it. You should get away from him, and if you do, I won't release those damning photos. Think about that."

"What's in the pictures, anyway?" she asked, but Christopher was already walking away.

Gen considered following him and grabbing him by his shiny black bow tie, but British people didn't make a scene. British people would mention it in passing to others who would sniff.

Arthur returned and handed her a glass of wine. "Thinking about the spa package?

Gen said, "Your brother just threatened me."

"Did he?" Arthur's mouth curved up as if he were slightly amused, but his knuckles whitened where he was holding his drink.

She stepped closer to him. "He said that if I don't drop your case, he'll release a stack of 'worse' photographs of you."

Arthur shrugged. "So?"

"I should get Octavia to put another high-powered

barrister on your case, someone like David Trent to sit second chair. I can't do it. I'm not good enough or experienced enough, anyway. If I quit, maybe he won't release them."

Arthur told her, "Whatever he said to you, it's a lie."

"He said that he had *worse* photos of you, worse than the one with the three women, and that one woman was a drug dealer. He's going to release them in October, just ahead of the trial, to poison the jury pool. What did you *do?*"

"You mustn't do what he told you to do. He's trying to leverage the photos by creating chaos on my defense team. Quite smart. Whatever he said, it's not a threat. It's a promise. He will certainly release any and all photographs if they will create havoc."

"What are we going to do, then?"

"I'll protect you. You won't get thrown out of chambers."

"You can't protect me."

"You might be surprised what I can do. Are you going to bid on this spa package?"

"I've lost my taste for this. We should go home."

"Home, huh?" he asked, his silvery eyes sparkling at her.

"I mean to your apartment. We should get out of here."

"Now, now. We aren't going to let Christopher run us off. Besides, we belong here. He doesn't."

"That sounds snooty."

"Quite. I am a sought-after philanthropist, which means that I can be counted on to drop bundles of cash for worthy causes. Christopher is trying to wheedle his way into these events in case he becomes the Earl of Severn. He will need the connections that one makes at events like this."

Gen wrinkled her nose. "That's awfully mercenary of him."

Arthur looked over the room. "It's how things are done. Bid a thousand pounds on this spa package."

She fretted, "It's worth five hundred at the most."

"It doesn't matter what it's worth. It matters how much

we drop on it. Children in Africa need their wells."

Gen bent over and wrote the sum and their names on the card. Her writing was spiky because her hand was still shaking so hard, and the spangles from the disco balls running across the card made what she wrote even more impossible to read. "If you just wrote a check rather than to go to this flashy party and buy these baskets, it would probably dig more wells."

"Yes, but three-quarters of these people wouldn't write a check at all, were it not for the flashy party. Plus, everyone is here and watching each other. Peer pressure will increase all their contributions. These events always net more money than a simple fundraising drive."

"Oh. Now I feel guilty that we're not going to two of these extravagant dress-up parties every night."

Arthur grinned. "That's the spirit."

A few drinks and astronomical bids on baskets of useless luxury goods and services later, the crowd moved into another ballroom, one that was set up with a Beatles cover band in the corner.

"Dancing," Arthur said. "Come on."

Rich people get even weirder when they get down and funky.

Gen looked around at the charity goers, all wiggling to the Beatles.

"I—wow. I thought most of these things were waltzes," she said, looking at the crush of people under the flashing stage lights, all banging into each other.

"We can keep to the edges," he said. "No reason to get in the middle of all of that." He bent to whisper near her ear, "We'll be more visible that way."

Because he was going to kiss her, here in public, for the cameras.

"Right," she said. "Edges."

Gen followed him over to a side of the dance floor, just where the parquet floor met the carpeting. They jostled their way into a gap, and Arthur was just reaching for her hand to dance when something knocked into her.

Falling.

She reached out as her knees buckled and she flipped forward, trying to catch herself before she smacked the floor.

Arthur's strong arms grabbed her, cinched around her waist and back, and he picked her up and set her back on her feet just as a flash blazed out of the crowd.

Gen was holding onto Arthur's arms. His biceps rounded and strained the fabric of his tuxedo jacket.

Arthur asked her, his voice pitched low and concerned, "Are you all right?"

She didn't let go of him. Her legs were trembling, and she might fall into a heap. "Yes. Fine. What was that?"

Arthur looked over her shoulder, and the expression on his face went blank. The line between his eyes smoothed, and he became as handsome as a cold statue. "Christopher, did you push her?"

"Oh, no, no. Just an accident, I'm sure. Ever so sorry, there," Christopher said to Gen, his pale eyes reflecting the purple and green stage lights revolving overhead.

Pushed? Christopher had *shoved* her and she had *fallen?* Snakes of memories slithered up her brain, crawling on her, and she shrank back from him.

Arthur slid one arm around her back, holding her closer, and his voice was so low that he sounded grim when he told Christopher, "If you touch her again, I will punch you in your fucking face."

Gen's eyes widened. Direct threats were very not-British, but anyone watching them would never have known from Arthur's placid expression that he was threatening Christopher.

Christopher looked at his phone, which he held beside his head. "I say, that picture almost looks like Arthur is grabbing you and you're fighting him off. Have a good night." He strode off into the crowd.

Gen leaned against Arthur's broad chest, letting him hold her up. "Let's go home."

Arthur said, "This is harassment. This must stop."

"We could counter-sue," Gen said, perking up. Arthur might have threatened Christopher with bodily harm, but she could slap that jerk with a lawsuit that would beat the crap out of him.

Arthur ran his hand along her spine between her waist and the top of her dress. "We'll see. We shouldn't leave immediately." He sighed. "People will talk."

The Beatles cover band finished a song and started playing "Yesterday."

"I like this song," she muttered.

"Me, too." He caught her other hand up in his. "One dance. Then we can leave in an orderly fashion."

The tremors running through her wouldn't stop. His body was far closer than he normally held her when they danced, cradling her. His arm around her waist and back buffered some of the terrified vibrations, absorbing the panic out of her body.

Gen leaned her head on his shoulder.

His swaying stuttered for a moment, and she felt his head turn as he looked down at her. His arm around her back pressed her closer, holding her. He moved her hand on his shoulder up, closer to his neck.

They shouldn't allow Christopher and his machinations to derail their plan. Damn it, if Christopher had gotten a bad-looking photo, they needed to counteract it with the one they had planned.

"Okay," she said. "Let's do it. Let's do it for the cameras."

"I beg your pardon?"

"Kiss me," Gen said. "Just do it."

"No." Arthur looked around, peering over the heads of the other dancers. "It's not the right time. The point of this exercise was to distract from the problem. If I kiss you now and it upsets you, it will add to the disturbance, especially after what Christopher did."

"I'm fine. I'll be fine."

His arms tightened around her waist, and she just barely felt the warmth and softness of his lips on her hair.

Gen melted against him, resting her cheek on his shoulder. Just for that moment, the place that she felt safest was in his arms.

Near her ear, he whispered, "It's not the right time."

Hacking His Phone

After dancing, as they pushed through the crowd on their way out of the Hope Ball, Arthur paused by the bar, looking around the packed ballroom. Between the band's electric guitars and over-amplified drum kit and the shouting crowd, he could hardly hear himself think.

Gen looked back at him and then toward the exit. The Duchess Sarah diamond set glittered around her neck and on her tiny ears as stage lights whirled through the darkness.

On the other side of the bar, Arthur's brother, Christopher, was drinking something dark in a glass and talking to Lindsey Norris, a high-ranking pencil-pusher in the National Health Service. Christopher was shaking his phone and showing Norris something on the screen. Arthur couldn't hear his voice over the hundreds of people around them, all shouting to be heard over the music and the other shouting.

"Just a moment," Arthur told Gen as he took his phone from his jacket pocket. "I need to check something."

Gen settled down with a bowl of cocktail peanuts and a very attentive bartender asking her what she would have. Arthur had tipped the woman heavily a few hours earlier, not out of any fiendish plan but just because guests at these charity events could be stingy, not tipping properly for the free drinks.

He enabled his phone's hotspot and named the free wifi that he created *Royal Horseguards Hotel Guest 2.7.*

The hotel's wifi was slow, as is the case where almost a

thousand people connect to a network, not that Arthur had allowed his phone to join it, of course.

Arthur's phone's hotspot was much faster.

Within seconds, guests' phones began automatically latching onto his wifi as they sought the fastest connection.

He had a bait screen already set up, a link on a white screen that asked the user to click the link to accept the terms and conditions.

The link downloaded a virus onto their phones.

Why would Arthur have a bait screen and virus ready to go on his phone?

Because sometimes, even for the best of men, the black hat needs to come out of the closet.

For the vast majority of the people in the room, the virus would self-destruct in a few minutes.

Arthur watched his phone's screen, waiting.

Out of the corner of his eye, he saw Christopher tap his phone.

Christopher's phone number, which Arthur had noted on the incessant court papers, appeared on the scrolling list.

He smiled.

He tapped Christopher's number and then sent everyone else's phones back to the public wifi with a swipe of his finger.

But now, Arthur had control of Christopher's phone.

Arthur wiped some of the pictures off of the phone's internal card, including the one that Christopher had taken when he had shoved Gen on the dance floor. Christopher didn't have a cloud account to back up his pictures. That was a shame for him.

Arthur didn't wipe the pictures of Christopher's daughters, his nieces. Several pictures of the kids at various functions, dance lessons and sports practices, occupied some space on the phone's memory card.

That was sweet.

Arthur sent a bit of code into one of them, an implant,

and hoped that Christopher backed up his pictures on his computer hard drive.

Then he deleted all the contacts from Christopher's phone, copied and deleted the texts, and scrubbed all the saved internet passwords.

He left a small back door so that he could hack Christopher's phone whenever he wanted to, and he uploaded a bit of code that would send copies of Christopher's texts, pictures, and internet activity to an account for Arthur to watch.

No compromising pictures of Arthur were on the phone, however. If such photographs did exist—and Arthur had no reason to believe that they didn't—then the private investigator probably still had them. Hacking Christopher's phone was an exercise in mere revenge, not in managing the situation.

Still felt brilliant, though.

Over on the other side of the bar, Christopher's gestures grew bigger, flailing wildly.

Arthur allowed himself a small smile. He probably wouldn't have hacked Christopher's phone under other circumstances, but he'd had quite a lot of those vodka tonics. Everything devious seemed like a jolly good idea at that moment.

Indeed, the warmth from Gen's body washed over his hand that was near her waist, and that dress clung to her curves like it had been painted on. Dancing with her in his arms had wound his body up until he was ready to grab her and pull her tight to his chest.

He wouldn't, but the image of her breasts pushing against his chest and the feeling of her arms around his neck from earlier when they had practiced kissing would not leave his mind.

He wanted more. He wanted her *now* or at least when they got home. When they walked into his dark, empty apartment, he wanted to lift her in his arms, carry her to his bed, and tear that gown off her.

He might leave the diamond set on her. The way the gems sparkled against her soft skin enticed him.

He might not want to take the time to get it off of her.

Must be the alcohol talking. Arthur knew better.

Maybe—and he paused, considering the advisability of it —maybe he would take her to Spencer House for the weekend.

The manor house felt like home to Arthur in a way that the apartment never did, and he wanted to see what she thought of it, whether she liked it, whether she might enjoy the deer park, the formal gardens, or the art collection.

Yes, Gen and Spencer House. The anger washed out of him at the very thought.

He asked Gen, "Ready to go home?"

"Sure." She said to the bartender, "Thanks, honey!"

"You're quite welcome." The bartender grinned at Gen.

Arthur slipped the bartender another twenty quid and earned himself a smile, too.

Desensitization Therapy

Gen paced in her room.

She'd had too much to drink, she knew. That last glass of wine she had chugged while Arthur had been fiddling with his phone had been one more of several too many.

Christopher was such an asshole, and just seeing him standing there, sneering after he had pushed her, had made her body lock up.

The alcohol had seemed to calm her down.

Now, everything was boiling in her head.

The court case, of course, was at the top of her mind. They hadn't managed to pull off the kiss in public like Gen had promised Octavia they would.

The hearing wasn't for months, and she kept combing through all the briefs and paperwork, searching for typos and tweaking the language.

But the alcohol was making her think crazier thoughts, too.

Things like, she and Arthur seemed to have a real friendship, a real connection. She didn't freak out when he touched her hand and when he held her close when they were dancing. All the crazy about men was calming down in her head.

She trusted Arthur.

She trusted him a lot.

And she wanted the crazy to go away forever.

Wine simmered in her veins, telling her that this was a very good idea.

Gen strode out of her bedroom, through the kitchen where she and Arthur had shared a firm handshake that evening, and to the short hallway to his bedroom.

Arthur's bedroom doorknob turned easily in Gen's hand. He didn't lock his bedroom door, either.

See? It was a sign.

The dark hallway stretched sideways to her right, toward the living room with the balcony beyond.

The door cracked open, the hinges silent as ghosts.

Gen pushed the door open.

Inside, the room was mostly darkened, except for a small light beside the door that shone on her face. She blinked as her eyes acclimated to the light, and she raised her hand to block the glare.

Arthur's voice came to her from the darkness around the edges of the room. "Gen?" he asked. "What are you doing?"

She squinted at the gloom again. "Um—"

Something heavy thumped on hollow wood like a small barbell dropped in a drawer.

On the far side of the room, wide windows cut into the wall nearly to the ceiling. Faint moonlight glowed in the panes. A silhouette of a man's form was a darker shadow in the gray. His broad shoulders tapered to his slim waist, and he stood with his hands braced on his trim hips.

His shoulders rose and fell as he sighed. "Come on. Let's get you back to your room."

"I'm not drunk," Gen insisted. *Not really.*

Okay, she totally was, but it didn't make a difference.

"I'm drunk, a bit." Arthur said, his voice right beside her in the dark. With the blinding nightlight near the door, she hadn't even seen him move in the blackened room. Slivers of silver from the night light traced the tops of his biceps below the dark tee shirt he wore. He said, "Come on. Time to go back to the guest bedroom."

In the beam from the nightlight, he held out his hand,

palm up.

Just like in the car and on the couch and all the times since.

All Gen had to do was reach out and take it—

—and Arthur would lead her back to her guest room like she was a naughty little girl, caught with her hand in the cookie jar.

Fuck it. This time, she was going to grab the cookies.

Arthur was as delicious as a big, chocolate, silver-eyed, crumbly cookie.

That analogy had gone south somewhere, but she was starving for him.

She grasped Arthur's hand and used the surprise to drag him forward a step toward herself. "I don't want to go back to my room."

His body hardened like he was straining against ropes. "Gen—"

"Call it desensitization therapy. Call it getting the hell over it. Call it whatever you want." She slid her hands up his chest, her fingers rounding over the heavy pectoral muscles on his chest and up over his shoulders. *Damn, seriously,* how much time did Arthur spend at the gym? "Make me forget."

His hands rested on her waist. "A month ago, you could barely touch my hand."

"But I got better. And now it's okay."

"When I kissed you earlier this evening, you nearly climbed the wall to get away."

"That was *before.*"

"Before what, a few bottles of wine?" His fingers squeezed her sides, just firm pressure. "You should have professional therapy, not one drunken night that might increase your distress."

"I don't want therapy." She leaned forward, pressing her breasts against the soft tee shirt that he wore. "I want you."

Arthur's deep inhale swelled his chest, pushing against

her. "You're making this very difficult."

"Then stop resisting," she said.

He untangled her hands from around his neck. "Your American boyfriends may have taken any opportunity to slake their lust, but I'm an Englishman. I can resist because it's best for both of us."

"Best for you? How is a case of blue balls best for you?"

He bent his head and brushed his lips across hers, the slightest of kisses, and he crowded her back against the wall behind her.

Trapping her.

Tremors crawled through Gen, shaking her body, rattling her bones against each other until she thought she would come apart, but Arthur had already retreated from her.

Near her ear, he whispered, "Because I won't do something that will harm you."

"I'll be okay. You can make me okay. We're friends, and maybe if I was with someone I trust, someone who knows what they're doing—"

"I am many things, but I'm not a sex therapist and I'm not a gigolo. I won't be used as such. And you might not be fine. If you are upset afterward, I wouldn't know what to do."

"I'm fine. Maybe if I had another drink—"

"And I certainly won't take advantage of you when we've both been drinking quite a lot. It was a long, upsetting evening."

"I'm sorry," Gen said. "I didn't mean to put you in a bad position. I should have known that I wasn't your type. I'm not anyone's type. I shouldn't have imposed."

"Oh, no." His breath warmed her shoulder through the chiffon of her evening gown. He'd stepped forward again in the dark. "On the contrary. It's a good thing that I am an Englishman and a paragon of self-control," he caught her hand and pressed her knuckles to his chest, "or else I certainly would have ravished you. Having a beautiful woman offer herself to me in my bedroom late at night is more than any man should have to resist." He chuckled. "I've had too much to drink. I'm thinking in French. It happens sometimes."

Under her fingers, his heart was racing like he had run miles.

She said, "I'm not your type, and it's okay. I know it. You don't have to say it."

"What should I not say?" he murmured.

"That I'm your type, when I'm not."

His lips brushed her knuckles, and his voice was low and husky. "You are my type. You're simply beautiful. Your hair is thick and lustrous, and I want to see it spread over my pillow and wrapped around my fists. Your body is lush and womanly, and I want to bury myself in you and forget everything. I would love to tie your arms and your long, *long* legs spread-eagled to those bedposts so I can look at every bit of you and play with you for an hour before I let you come. I wish I could strip this dress off you this very moment and have my way with you. If I'd had just one more vodka tonic, you would be in my arms tonight and probably in emergency therapy tomorrow. Let's discuss this in the light of day when we're both sober, shall we?"

She nodded because she couldn't think of a word to say. Everything he had said was spinning in her head.

"Come." He stepped back and, reaching over her head, opened his door wider. "Let's get you back to your bedroom."

He led her by the hand through the wide kitchen to her room. In the dim light of the kitchen, she could see his black tee shirt and pajama pants. The shirt had a triangle with an eye like the one that was on American money and some keys around it. The text around the symbol read: CRYPTOGRAPHY — IN MATH WE TRUST.

Huh. Weird. Gen would have bet that The Earl of Givesnofucks would have slept in a Jack Daniels or Red Bull tee shirt.

When they got to her bedroom, Arthur wheeled her inside and shut her in, closing the door firmly behind her.

Gen was just about to collapse in a weepy bundle of tears on the thick carpeting under her feet when a solid *thunk* vibrated the wall behind the door.

She peeked outside.

Arthur was walking away, down the hall, shaking his hand like he was trying to flick water droplets off of his fingers.

He growled, "Go inside. I don't have the fortitude to send you away again."

Tattoos

THE next morning was a Saturday.

When Gen visited her mother, she read a couple of chapters in the mystery novel they were working on—it looked like the main guy was a spy for the enemy!—but she sure as heck did *not* say a word about throwing herself at the hot earl and getting turned down.

If her mother had been able to speak, she would have said that Gen shouldn't have done it, that a man like Arthur was beyond her hopes.

Instead, her mother's frail body lay in the bed, covered by sheets and that double-wedding ring quilt. Blue circles looped over the snowy cotton.

Her mother, always slim, looked even thinner lately, but that was to be expected due to muscle atrophy, the nurses had told her. She was being fed sufficient calories through the tube up her nose.

Finally, Gen couldn't take it any more for that day and went back to Arthur's apartment.

She came inside the apartment to find Arthur standing in the kitchen, shirtless and sweaty. He was gulping a glass of water and wiping the back of his bare neck with a towel.

Running shorts clung to his muscular thighs.

It was the first time Gen had seen her client nearly naked.

Sweet baby Jesus.

Sweat trickled down the crevices between the rounds of his shoulder muscles and pecs and channeled down the deep crevice between the bricks of his abdominal muscles. His rough breathing expanded and contracted his torso, and those muscles glided over his ribs as he panted. Thick ropes and swells of muscle wrapped his whole body, and Gen couldn't stop staring at him. His smooth skin was pale golden all over, from his broad shoulders to his trim waist to the strong, lean muscles of his thighs.

Damn. He did not skip leg day at the gym.

Tattoos wound around his body.

One bright tattoo was etched into his skin on his forearm that held the glass of water to his mouth. On the thick cords of his right forearm, three shields were inked, surrounding some kind of triangular Celtic knot thing. The small tattoo was maybe three inches across on his pale bronze skin. A blue shield with three gold crowns pointed down at his wrist. The other two were a red and white diamond-patterned shield and an orange shield with a white cartoon lion on it.

His muscular back was decorated with a complex pattern of watercolor red and blue curving stripes. Tendrils of scarlet and azure ink crawled over his shoulders, twisted down his strong arms and his thighs below the hem of his shorts, and criss-crossed his broad body. Lots of his pale gold skin showed between the flowing color, but he looked like he had been draped and wrapped in red and blue ribbons.

Dang.

The matronly housekeeper standing next to him was holding a pitcher of ice water and averting her eyes.

Arthur noticed Gen and smiled at her. "Hi."

"Hi," Gen replied.

They both said, "Look, about last night—"

And stopped. And stared at each other.

The housekeepers stampeded out of the kitchen.

Arthur said, "After you."

"Nope. You, first," Gen said.

Arthur said, "Please, I insist."

"I'm fine. You talk. Go ahead." She didn't want to be the

one who set the tone for the conversation.

Arthur nodded. "It's Saturday. Let's go up to Spencer House for the weekend, if you want. We could come home tomorrow after breakfast."

"Okay." That was not what she thought he would say, and it sounded like they would be home in time for her Sunday afternoon visit to her mom. "I'd like to see Spencer House."

Arthur smiled at her, a slow smile. "I'm glad. If you have jeans and trainers with you, that might be a good idea."

For a manor house? "Okay."

While she threw a few things in an overnight bag, Gen dug under the long skirts in her closet to find her jeans and tennis shoes.

They packed and were in the car in under an hour. Arthur drove the Rolls Royce.

Ruckus sat in the back seat and, after some bouncing back and forth to look out the windows and hang over the back of the seat to pant warm dog breath on Gen's cheek, he settled down to sleep before they had driven out of London proper. He smelled clean-doggie damp like he had just had a bath.

Arthur said, "I'll probably switch this car out for something smaller while we're there."

Gen asked, "Where's Pippa?"

"I gave her the weekend off since we're going to the country house."

"That's nice."

"It feels good to drive. It's a problem to drive myself around in the city. Parking, you know."

"Plus, the last time you drove, you got loose and put the car into the wall," Gen mumbled.

Arthur laughed. "No one's chasing us this time. Or, they were, but I lost them already."

"You did?" She assumed he was joking.

"Probably the photographers my brother hired. One for

each of us."

Gen swiveled in her seat and looked out the rear window. The expressway rolled away behind them. "Really?"

"Those quick couple of turns lost them."

When they were outside of London, Arthur drove with one hand, and his other hand was turned upward on the console between them.

Gen hesitated, but then she slid her hand into his.

Arthur sighed. "I was worried."

She looked out the window beside her cheek. "I was worried, too."

Negotiation

Gen had seen pictures of Spencer House on a BBC program about the great manor houses, so she wasn't shocked to see the sprawling Tudor mansion appear as they drove up a lane arched with trees.

The house that grew, and grew, the closer they got.

It grew from a house into a mansion into a city block.

Bigger and bigger and *bigger.*

The TV show didn't do it justice.

Spencer House was a fortress, a small city within walls that rambled over the land and jutted into the sky.

They drove into the cobblestoned courtyard and turned the car around to drive past the other wings of the house to the garage area over on the side.

Ruckus looked out the back window, paws on the back of the seat, panting.

"This is your house?" Gen clarified.

Arthur said, "This is my home."

The dove gray and white exterior rose all around the car. A man met them when they parked in an outside parking spot.

The older man had a weather-worn face with tanned, thick skin. He wore jeans and a mud-splattered work shirt.

In the back seat, Ruckus went nuts, hopping and barking a long, happy conversation at the guy.

Arthur hopped out of the car and hugged the man, laughing.

The man clapped Arthur on the back and laughed

guffaws at him.

Arthur broke it off but kept his arm around the slightly shorter man's shoulders. The guy was still north of six feet tall. "Gen, meet Ifan Pryce, the gamekeeper of Spencer House."

"Pleased to meet you," Ifan said, extending his hand. The old man's eyes were bright blue, and he grinned a tobacco-stained smile. His accent was a little northern, maybe Welsh.

"So nice to meet you," she said and shook his hand.

Arthur said to him, "Gen and I are going out to the deer park for a few minutes."

"Ah, dark secrets, then," Ifan mused.

Arthur smiled at him. "We'll talk tomorrow morning, all right?"

"Ay-yep. Got a few things for you to look at on the accounts."

"Splendid. Could you see that our things are taken upstairs?"

"I'll get someone to look into it."

Gen got the feeling that Ifan Pryce could order Arthur around if he needed to.

Arthur let Ruckus out of the back seat and waited while the dog greeted Ifan.

Ifan ruffled the dog's ears and asked him, "You want to come run around with me, boy?"

Ruckus took a long look back at Gen with his big, brown eyes, and Ifan laughed, "Ho, ho!"

Arthur asked, "Gen, shall we?"

Gen followed Arthur, and when she looked back, Ruckus was trotting after Ifan.

The gravel in the parking lot area rolled under Gen's shoes. The three-story extension of the house flanked both sides of the parking area. Back in the olden days, the stables and workmen had their shops in this small town attached to the main building.

He led her out through a path around the side. "There are formal gardens in the front of the house," he said, "but I prefer the deer park. We have a herd of several hundred English fallow deer here, descended from the survivors of those hunted by King Charles and other royals on holiday."

"The hardy survivors," she quipped.

"Hardy, indeed."

Forest and grasslands surrounded the manor house, and Gen traipsed through the knee-high grass, hopping over stones and clumps of shrubbery while she chased after Arthur. The afternoon was warm for early March, just sweater weather, and the early spring air cooled Gen's face as she hiked.

"When I was a child, I used to visit my grandfather out here when I was on holiday from school," he told her, "and before that, my parents and Christopher and I came out here for the summer holidays and Christmas."

"I didn't know that you knew your grandfather. I mean, because you went to that boarding school in Switzerland."

"I knew my grandmother, too, although she died when I was around five. She used to insist that everyone eat *every* scrap of food on their plates *because of the War.* The previous earl was very gruff around children, very reserved. He was a product of his generation when children were seen and not heard, and fathers did not help raise children. I was always somewhat afraid of him as a young child, though he warmed to me later on. After my parents died, I was glad to return to school in Switzerland. I thought I might have to live here with him."

"That's awful." Gen hopped over a decaying log about the size of her leg. Mushrooms grew from the softening wood. "Why didn't you go live with your uncle?"

"My grandfather and my parents believed in boarding schools for children, especially for heirs. Christopher was only three, so my uncle took him until he was nine and sent up to Eton."

"I'm surprised that you didn't stay in the country. Switzerland is a long way away."

"It was for the best, I think. My grandfather did like me around for short times during holidays because I was a quiet child."

Impossible. "You? But you're so—"

He turned around and grinned, walking backward with his long legs covering the ground. His dark blue sweater reflected in the ice of his eyes like azure tints in glaciers. "I'm what?"

"You're everywhere. You're all over the place."

Arthur laughed. "I listened to my grandfather when he talked about our history here, and I liked to run about with Ifan and his grandson back then, too. Coming here made me feel connected to my family and Britain. Christopher was too young, toddling about. When he was little, he cried like little kids do. He hid behind my uncle even when he was older. My grandfather never took a liking to him."

"So that's why he didn't inherit much."

"No, that was planned before he was born. He was the spare, of course, in case something happened to me. Still, in case something happens to me."

"Are you going to do that with your children, leave everything to the oldest boy and not much to the others?"

"So far I don't have any children."

"That you know of," Gen chided him.

He laughed. "I'm sure I would be informed with a quick and thorough lawsuit, but I've been scrupulously careful. I imagine that I'll have to do the traditional primogeniture inheritance, though. It's the only way to care for these estates. They have to support themselves, and they can't do that if they're divvied up piecemeal over even one generation. Spencer House does not support itself now, even with rents and the National Trust. I kick in a lot from other sources to keep it running."

Gen bit her tongue about private jets streaking off to

Paris in the middle of the night and drunks pouring Cristal on strippers. "That must be tough."

"Oh, I could tell you stories."

"I'd like that."

He stopped walking, but he was still smiling. "I could show you the house tonight, if you wanted."

She touched his hand, just a quick tap near his wrist. "I'd like that a lot."

They hiked through knee-high, dry winter grass and new spring shoots for twenty minutes. Last year's grass crunched under Gen's tennis shoes, and the tender green growth smelled clean when crushed.

As they emerged from the tree line of the woods, a clearing spread open, and the herd of deer grazed on the grass and jumped over each other, gamboling. All the deer were about the same size, as March was too early for fawns. Their coats were all different colors: deep rust with black lines down their backs, tan with brown lines, almost black, and a few dark-eyed, white deer. Many of them had white or lighter spots. The hopping herd looked like an earth-toned quilt, flipping around from children playing under it.

Arthur stood with his hands shoved in his jeans pockets. "This is where I come when I need to discuss something that must not be overheard."

The afternoon sun warmed Gen's back, and her damp tee shirt under her sweater clung to her skin from walking out so far in the early afternoon. "Do you have a lot of secret conversations?"

"I mean with the deer. I talk to the deer. They're great listeners." He was grinning again, and she laughed at the way his silvery eyes turned merry.

"Do the deer answer back?" she asked.

"No."

"That's good. Jeez, you had me worried, there."

"About last night—"

"The deer don't know anything about that," Gen said.

"I'm serious."

So she stuck her hands in her own pockets. "I threw myself at you. I'm embarrassed about it, and I'm sorry that I put you in an awkward position."

"Don't be embarrassed. I'm honored. I'm humbled that you would trust me so. At the very least, it's a compliment that I won't forget, and I meant every word I said."

"At least all the words that you can remember," she joked.

"I remember," he said. "I remember every word and every moment and every brush of your skin, all night long, from kissing you before the ball to dancing with you in my arms. I remember that I was on the precipice of losing all self-control. I wanted to take you to bed and explore you for hours. Do you feel the same today, though?"

Gen blurted, *"Yes."*

Damn, she hadn't meant to say it like that. She should have been cagey and not said what she meant, led him a merry chase or something.

"Yes," Gen said again. "I feel exactly the same as last night. I want to get over it. You've already helped me with getting better around men."

"You'd have to trust me."

"I do. I do trust you. I don't trust anyone else."

"You haven't had a chance to trust anyone else," he said. "You're getting much better around men. Maybe a boyfriend, a relationship, would be a better choice."

"Like who? James Knightly? I'd rather never touch a man again."

"Who's James Knightly?" Arthur asked, his voice quiet, seemingly disinterested.

"A guy at work. He's such a gossip. He's backstabbing everyone, trying to get tenancy. I don't even know any men who interest me in the slightest."

"All right, so not James Knightly. You could see a therapist," Arthur said, but he sounded like he was reciting by rote, saying something that he was supposed to say rather than what he wanted to say.

"I don't want to see a therapist. Besides, counseling and things like that turn up during the selection process for the offers of tenancy. They would crucify me. There's so much gossip in the office, and all of it colors the senior barristers' decisions about tenancy. It all comes back to that."

"I could teach you how to cover your tracks, instead. You could attend counseling without anyone knowing."

"Someone would find out. Someone always does. Your brother has a detective following me as well as you."

Arthur puffed out his breath in something between laughter and derision. "It's easy enough to elude someone who's following you, especially someone who is so very bad at it." Sarcasm sharpened his voice.

"That doesn't matter."

"Unfortunately, for eight more months at least, I'm your client. That's the largest problem we have," he said.

Gen sucked in air and said, "I don't care."

"Good." Arthur stepped toward her and pulled his hands out of his pockets. His voice dropped. "I was hoping you'd say that."

"You were?" Her voice squeaked.

Arthur reached over and hooked one of his fingers around one of hers, the least possible skin-to-skin contact that still qualified as such. Her attention focused on his warm hand, one finger touching hers. "I have wanted you from the moment I saw you in that conference room. I have been waiting for months, sitting across small tables from you, feeling your legs against mine, riding in cars with you so close that I could feel the warmth of your skin, and dancing with you in my arms. I've been more patient than I have ever been in my life. I can hardly wait to feel your bare skin in my hands, to taste you, to make you scream my name."

Gen's throat closed so tightly that she had to force the words out. "I'll bet you say that to all the girls."

"I've never said anything like it before."

"You've never had to wait more than a few hours."

He chuckled. "That's probably true." His voice was so low, even gravelly. "Are you sure about this? If your chambers find out, you could get in trouble. The ethics board. Tenancy."

She forced her head to bob up and down, hoping that she didn't look too stupid or like she was lying. Those silver eyes of his seemed to see everything. Sometimes, it was unnerving, and he might be seeing even more than what he mentioned.

Gen said, "It's nobody's business but our own. I did hear of a case where it came out that a pupil barrister got into trouble for sleeping with his client, but that's because the client complained when it broke up her marriage. Plus, when the barrister denied that he had been involved with her, the client produced the barrister's underwear. He really shouldn't have let his mother sew labels into his underwear. I think that's what really sank him."

She needed to keep telling herself that. Otherwise, she might let something slip in the office.

He turned his hand around so that his large, warm hand wrapped around hers, more skin contact.

"I need to know some things about what happened to you," he said. "You didn't want to talk about it, before."

She nodded and tried to control her breathing. She still didn't want to talk about it.

"If you don't want to narrate the experience," he said, "you could tell me what things are hard limits for you."

Gen was stumped. "I don't know what 'hard limits' means."

"Sometimes, when one is engaging in certain lifestyles, you discuss soft and hard limits, things that you might be willing to do versus things that you absolutely will not do."

She frowned. "I don't get it."

"Restraints. Toys." With his other hand, he stroked her

shoulder over her tee shirt with his fingertips. "What I can do to your body or your mind."

Oh. He meant kinky stuff.

A tremor started in her chest. "I can't do that."

"Not *can't,*" he said, "but will not, or not yet. And that should be discussed and negotiated."

Gen tried not to let her hands shake. His fingers were still holding hers, gently but firmly. Letting go to shake the crazies away would be weird. "I would have to trust that you wouldn't cross those lines."

"I won't. I wouldn't." He was watching her face, his silvery eyes flicking as his gaze roamed from her eyes to her mouth. "And I have to trust that you will tell me where the lines are. I don't want to guess. I can't read your mind."

Considering how easily he sussed out when anyone around him was lying, she wasn't sure that last part was entirely true, but she saw the sense in the whole statement. "Okay."

"If you don't want to tell me what happened in the past, then you have to tell me what sort of things you aren't ready for in the near future."

"Okay." Gen sucked in a deep breath. Her hands quivered. She desperately wanted to shake the crazies out, but she needed to stop doing that. Her poker tell gave too much away. "Okay. Okay-*okay.*"

He waited, watching her, and his fingers trailed from her elbow to her upper arm.

She began, "No crowding me up against things like walls. No holding me down. No grabbing the back of my neck." The air in her lungs ran out, and she sucked in a desperate breath.

He nodded, his expression serious. "Continue."

"No tying me up or holding me so that I can't get away."

His smile was gentle. "I think you're metaphorically tying *my* hands."

Gen blurted, "No beds."

One of his eyebrows dipped. "No beds?"

"They give me the willies, a huge platform where someone can force you down and you can't get away. I can't touch a bed. I don't even like to look at them."

He peered at her, looking at her eyes. "Then where have you been sleeping?"

"On the couch," she admitted.

"The one in the guest bedroom?"

She nodded.

His eyes widened in horror. "On that *loveseat?* You've been *sleeping* on it?"

She nodded again, ashamed.

"A child couldn't sleep on that thing. Not to mention an adult, an adult like either one of *us.*"

Tall, and in her case, fat around the butt and hips. "I'm sorry. You don't think I ruined it?"

"Heavens, no. I'm mortified that we didn't know, that something wasn't done." His hand left her arm, and he ran his fingers through his thick, dark hair, holding it back. "We'll rectify that when we get back to London. As far as we are concerned, I never liked beds for anything but sleeping, anyway. Too commonplace."

Gen wasn't sure what to make of that at all. Maybe he did have a Red Room of Kinky Stuff in his apartment.

Arthur looked over at the deer, watching them leaping and running in the sunlight. He said, off-handedly, "You could tell me your assailant's name."

Gen looked over to watch the deer, too. "I don't want to."

"Do I know him?"

"I don't think so. I was a few years behind you at Oxford, so I don't think you would have overlapped with him. He wasn't in Trinity."

Arthur was still casually watching the deer, off in the deep grass. "Does he work in your chambers?"

"Oh, no. I would have chosen different chambers."

"Ah. Anything else you want to tell me about him?"

"No. Why?"

"Who his friends were? What his major was or what profession he is in now? Just so I won't say something wrong."

"It sounds more like you're fishing for information."

"Oh, no. I'm just an indolent earl, remember. I have no ulterior motives."

"Arthur, you aren't planning to look him up, are you?"

"Now, why would I do that? I will concentrate my efforts on you." He looked from the deer back down at her, his eyes smiling and kind. "I'm far more interested in helping you with your little dilemma."

"You're making fun of me."

"Not at all. I'm fascinated by you, and I have much to consider about our evenings, our experiences. Let me see if I've got it all: no shoving or crowding you up against walls or other things, no grabbing the back of your neck, no restraints, and no beds."

Gen was exhausted just listening to that litany of *thou shalt nots.* "You can't work around all that. No one can. I'm just going to have to find some other way to make sure no one finds out about it."

She let go of his grip and finally—*finally!*—shook the crazies out of her hands.

When she saw him watching her, she dropped her hands to her sides, ashamed again.

He said, "We'll start with those as your hard limits. As you trust me more, as you become more comfortable, we'll reevaluate what you want. We'll always discuss it first."

The air was still restless in Gen's lungs. "Okay."

"But here are my conditions," Arthur said.

"Oh?" Gen almost jumped backward. She hadn't known about this. "Like what?"

"You're mine, now," he said. "While we do this, you're mine. No other men."

"I haven't dated anyone in years and certainly not in the

last couple of months while we were supposed to be dating."

"Good. I can do with you what I will, as long as I observe your hard limits. You'll do what I say, when I say it, willingly, compliantly."

That was awfully weird. "What if I don't want to?"

"You'll do it even if you don't want to."

"What if it scares me? What if it's something that I didn't think to tell you or something that upsets me and I freak out?"

"You'll have safewords, words or other signals that will mean to slow down or to stop entirely. We both will."

"I don't know how that works."

"We'll discuss it. We'll practice. This is the important part: In reality, when we're working, you have all the power. You are the one in control because if you utter those words, I am honor-bound to stop."

"Okay," Gen said, breathing hard.

"Other than those words, when we're alone, you belong to me, body and soul."

"That's kind of scary," she said.

"You don't have to make any decisions other than whether it's too much and you want to slow down or stop. If it gets to that, quite honestly, I'm not paying close enough attention. It would mean that I've made a mistake."

"What do you mean, not make decisions? That sounds very retro."

"You don't have to think about it anymore."

"I do overthink things," she fretted.

"Give all your fear to me. You don't have to be afraid. You just have to feel, to experience, and to be mine."

"I don't know if I can do that."

"You have been," he said. "You've been doing it for months."

"No, I haven't."

He held out his hand, palm up. "Take my hand."

Gen laid her fingers in his and held on.

The smile that Arthur gave her was pleased, calmly pleased. "Good," he said.

She couldn't help but be just a little proud of herself at his praise.

"Just like that," he said. "You were afraid, but I told you what to do. You didn't think about it. You didn't agonize over it. You didn't think about your fear and your past. You just did what I told you to."

She had been doing it for months. "Just like that?"

"Just like that."

"I want to talk more about these safewords."

"Understandable."

"And we can't do that in court or when we're dealing with your lawsuit," Gen said.

"Of course. In that, I am yours."

She laughed. "Yeah, I guess you are."

"Shall we begin?" he asked, still holding her hand.

Okay, this might be the adventure of a lifetime. She might need therapy afterward, but she might be okay.

She needed therapy now, anyway. She probably wouldn't be worse off.

If she wanted evidence that this might work out, she could cite that she could touch him now, she was holding his hand, and she had kissed him. She hadn't been able to do those things with anyone just a couple months ago. Not at all. She would have had a panic attack just thinking about them.

And she liked Arthur.

They were friends, and they laughed together.

And . . . more.

Gen said, "Yes. Let's begin."

He tugged her hand, only enough to shift her balance so that she stepped toward him. Her fingers splayed on his shirt, and his rounded pectoral muscle beneath the soft cotton twitched under her hand.

"Good," he said.

Her face warmed at his words again.

Arthur positioned her hand on his shoulder, nearly reaching around his neck. He always adjusted her arms around him, every time they were close like this and every time they danced at the parties and balls.

He bent, lowering his face until his lips almost touched hers.

"Say you're mine, pet."

Gen braced herself and whispered, "I'm yours."

His voice was deeper and husky when he told her, "Kiss me."

The breeze freshened around her legs, cooling her skin, and the thick grass of the meadow stretched around them. Hills rose in the distance, past the deer that grazed so far away. Sunshine warmed her arms and back.

Arthur curled his arm up, his fingers turning in hers, and he positioned her other hand on his chest, too.

She was steadier on her feet, and it felt like he was holding her in his arms without holding her down. His other arm dangled at his side. His warm breath feathered on her lips.

The deer hooted and grunted on the other side of the field. The scent of sun-baked grass mixed with Arthur's cologne, cinnamon, dark wood, and a faint hint of musk.

It felt nothing like a small, dark, smelly room, late at night, after she'd had too much to drink and gone home with the wrong guy.

Gen rose up on her toes that last fraction of an inch and pressed her lips to his.

She didn't even feel the need to shake out her hands.

Green Light

Green light.

The dry grass brushed Arthur's jeans, scratching on the denim, and the sun was dropping in the sky.

Arthur held out his hand, palm up. "Take my hand."

Gen was watching him, her dark eyes wide, and she laid her fingers across his palm. The breeze blew her thick, dark hair around her head.

It was a good thing that Arthur was an English nobleman, a man who had been raised to be able to control every aspect of his demeanor and his emotions.

She had just given him the green light to seduce her.

The impulse seized him to grab her, tumble her to the mud and grass out here in the deer park, and have his way with her, but he wouldn't.

No, he had a very special seduction planned for Genevieve.

If she had merely been an innocent virgin, he would have ruined her, changed her into a wanton woman who appreciated sex in its most depraved forms.

But Gen was scared and broken.

Arthur wanted to build her into a new woman, one who was bold and strong, one who would go out into the world as an alpha female and fuck men until they begged for mercy.

Not Arthur, of course. He would be the one man who could match her, but that would be later.

That would be after she had become as strong and

beautiful as pristine marble, a Galatea to his Pygmalion. He would remake this broken woman into something sturdier, stronger, and a formidable, eternal paragon in a world of mere humans.

More defiant. More inviolable.

More British.

He would make sure that no one could ever break her again.

It wasn't just a seduction, though. It was much more like an intelligence operation, like turning a person into an asset that could be used. If he could convince someone to betray their country, their family, and everything they held to their heart, if Arthur could break a person into a compliant agent who would chew a cyanide pill rather than inform on him, he could rebuild Gen.

He was more than cultivating her. He was *turning* her.

In his job, if he screwed up turning an asset, he could blackmail them into silence at the very least.

He couldn't fail with Gen. He had to watch, to assess, to adjust his tactics until he found success with her.

He hated what had happened to her.

Finding that rapist was on his list of personal projects. If Gen would just slip a few times and give Arthur just a few tidbits of information or one really good one, Arthur would find that man and destroy him.

Gen's fingers held his hand.

"Come," Arthur said. "Come see Spencer House."

Games

After Gen and Arthur had walked back to the house through the golden fields of grass drying in the afternoon sunlight, Arthur told the staff that they would be dining out that night as he had not called ahead to arrange supper at Spencer House.

Gen saw several housekeepers sigh with relief.

A staff lady showed Gen to a bedroom, suggesting that she might freshen up before supper.

Blue fabric upholstered the walls and curtains, and the room was as soothing as a summer sky skimmed with clouds. Pale gold velvet covered the chairs around the breakfast table as well as the small divan at the footboard of the bed. The comforter on the bed was made out of cream silk, the same cream silk that lined the insides of the blue curtains that fell from the wooden canopy above the bed.

The effect was modern with an antique feel, as if the bed were saying, *This is reminiscent of how this room looked in Tudor times, but all this beautiful fabric is new for you.*

Gen glanced around the room, taking stock of the furniture. The little divan at the end of the bed was suitable to sit down on to put on shoes, but a statuesque woman such as herself couldn't lie down on it. Her head would flop over one of the rolled arms, and her knees would hang over the other. *Ridiculous.*

Maybe she could fold up the comforter and sleep on the floor. She nudged the carpet with her tennis shoe. The blue carpeting was pretty well padded underneath. Sleeping on the floor might be a good option.

The too-tight black dress that came just above her knees was laid out on her bed, and the Christian Louboutin pumps sat primly on the floor below the spread skirt.

Guess *someone* wanted her to wear that dress. Gen hadn't even packed it.

She flung a pair of black lace panties on top of the dress.

Those, she had brought in her bag. Just in case.

Gen showered and packed herself into the dress, struggling to zip it up. The zipper was one of those fragile little contraptions wedged under the dress's armpit, and Gen had been eating too well at all those charity suppers. No matter how much she walked Ruckus around Hyde Park, those sauces and desserts and drinks added up. She inhaled and wiggled the zipper up.

Luckily, the dress had good structure, and the whalebones made it look like she had gained those few pounds in her boobs.

Expensive clothes create optical illusions that the cheap ones don't. They were like the skinny mirrors that department stores have in their fitting rooms, but the dresses worked all the time.

She brushed her hair but left it down around her shoulders. For work, she twisted it up tightly in buns on the back of her head. Leaving it down felt good.

A shimmering two-seater was waiting for them as they descended the steps from the front doors of Spencer House. The blued steel car looked like a bullet with speed grooves.

She asked him, "An Aston Martin? Seriously?"

"Of course. They're fantastic cars," Arthur said, again dressed in a dark blue suit. He walked down the steps with her. "Simply beautiful."

Glowing light from the sunset played over the car's sleek curves. The headlights didn't look like the narrowed, angry eyes of a BMW. Instead, the slim lights and rounded bonnet appeared to look at the world with a cultured, very British side glance.

She asked, “Are you sure you’re not a spy?”

Arthur laughed, and his laugh rang off the gray tiles that shingled the house. “I’m an unemployed earl with far too much money and no responsibilities. MI6 would have to have lost their collective marbles to recruit me.”

She squinted at him, trying not to laugh. “That’s exactly what you’d say if you were a spy.”

He shrugged, but he was still smiling. “I guess you’ve got me there.”

When he looked at her, his eyes were the same color as the shining blue-gray car.

She wondered whether he did that by accident, or whether everything in the world that was beautiful was that same color as his silvery eyes.

Driving to the restaurant was alternately as thrilling as a roller coaster and as sedate as a pleasure cruise.

On long straightaways between rock walls and square-trimmed hedges, Arthur opened up the throttle on the Aston Martin DB11 to zoom through the countryside.

The G-force pressed Gen back in her seat. She laughed every time he did it.

As they coasted through towns and past houses, Arthur told Gen little stories.

One crofter’s house had post and rail fences around it. Arthur and George, Ifan’s youngest grandson, used to jump horses over the fences when they were children until Ifan caught them and chewed them out at the danger to the horses and themselves. Ifan taught him to jump horses properly and set up a steeplechase course with hedges and troughs to practice. Arthur’s grandfather had approved of the sport of steeplechase, since it was a proper sport for a gentleman, and so he had bought Arthur a properly trained steeplechase horse. He had gotten quite good when he had come home during the summers, to the point where he had ridden for the British national team in international competitions when he was in high school.

Another house farther away was owned by a lady who baked cookies, different ones all the time. During the summer, he and George used to ride the horses to her house every day for a cookie as if they were playing the lottery. "Some days, she made delicate chocolate zebra cookies like crisp croissants, and sometimes, she made oatmeal raisin rock cakes."

The restaurant was about twenty miles away in a mid-sized town. The parking lot held several sleek Rolls Royces and Bentleys.

Arthur explained, "This is one of the few overpriced places around here."

After a fawning hostess had seated them at a center table in the crowded main room, a waiter took their orders. The tables were spaced a bit apart, allowing the waiters to push carts between the tables. Classical music wafted over the quiet conversation.

Arthur leaned back in his chair as they waited for the soup course to arrive. He said, "You look smashing in that dress."

"Thanks," she said, pleased but also thanking the genius seamstress somewhere who had so expertly sewn the boning in it.

He asked, "What are you wearing under it?"

Gen glanced behind herself, but the waiter guy had already gone through the doors, thank goodness. Other guests were engrossed in their food or their conversations.

She said, "Underwear."

"Those weren't laid out for you."

"Did you have someone lay out the dress?"

"Of course, but panties were not laid out with it."

"How do you know that?" she whispered.

"Because I told her not to."

Gen was not going to be able to look any of his staff in their eyes. "Oh my God."

Arthur's voice was deep. "Take them off."

Gen looked around again. "I beg your pardon?"

"You heard me."

"But, someone might see."

"You should have about thirty seconds before the gentleman returns with the soup. You might want to hurry, pet."

He stared at her, smiling, his silvery eyes calm and confident.

He wanted to see her do it.

The people around them chattered and pinged their silverware on the china plates.

Arthur smiled a little more, maybe at her hesitation.

Did he think that she wouldn't do it?

Hey, she might have a psychological block about being touched right now, and she might be from the Texan backcountry, but that didn't mean that she wasn't up to *whatever* he could think of.

Actually, she wanted to watch the look on Arthur's face while she did it.

Gen smiled back at him.

She pinched the bit of lace on her hips through her skirt and tugged downward. The panties slid down, loosening around her legs and rubbing between them.

Arthur drew one side of his lower lip inside his mouth and bit down on it.

Geez, he was sexy when he did that.

She leaned forward to lift her butt off the chair a little and slid the panties down to her knees.

Gen hooked one finger in her underwear as they slid down her calves, and she stepped out of them, snagging the lace on the high, fuck-me heels of the red-soled shoes. She yanked and jiggled the panties free.

"Did it," she said.

Arthur leaned forward. The intensity of his gaze made his eyes look like molten silver. "Hand them to me under the table."

She stopped. *"Are you serious?* There are people around."

"No questioning," he said. His voice was still deep in his throat, but now it was more husky, rougher.

Fine. She could play his game.

Gen balled up the underwear and reached under the tablecloth, finding his fingers. She opened her hand above his. "Got them?"

"Oops. Dropped them," he said.

"What!" she whispered, imagining her black lace underwear lying on the floor, where she had the option of either letting someone find them later or crawling around under the tablecloth to retrieve them.

Arthur smiled. "I'm kidding."

He leaned back and stuffed something in the interior breast pocket of his suit jacket. Gen caught a peek of something black and frothy.

Okay, he had probably been kidding about dropping them.

The waiter appeared at the table, pushing a cart holding two bowls of soup and a champagne bottle in an ice bucket, just as the lace disappeared into Arthur's pocket.

Gen ate the supper acutely aware that, under the floaty skirt, she was naked from the waist down except for her high-heeled shoes. Every time she thought about it, the skin between her legs grew more sensitive.

She crossed her legs, squeezing herself.

Arthur watched her shift, and he stopped talking in the middle of his sentence, cleared his throat, and then continued.

They made small talk about people, Ruckus's improving behavior, and some books they had read, and they joked around.

It felt just like always between them.

Except that she wasn't wearing panties.

And he might tell her to do something else.

And she just might do it.

And occasionally, she caught Arthur with a small, secret smile.

They shared a creme brûlée with crackling sugar over the top. Gen let Arthur eat most of it because she wasn't sure how much more strain that zipper on her side could take. Plus, the steak with peppercorn sauce had filled her up. And the champagne. Bottles of it. But she took a few good bites.

In the car, before they left the parking lot, Arthur leaned over the center console of the Aston Martin—which again looked like something out of a rocketship—and ran one fingertip down the side of her neck and around to her collarbone.

"You were a good girl in there," he said, his voice low and sexy.

"Yeah?" she asked. His finger on the side of her neck and shoulder made her skin tingle.

"Oh, yes." He leaned over, nearly close enough to kiss her, and his warm breath smelled like sugar.

Gen didn't shift, didn't move, but she wanted to.

"What do you want me to do?" he asked, his breath feathering over her jaw.

"Kiss me," she whispered, scared again, but she had said it.

His lips brushed her jaw, and he backed off. "You'll have to be a *better* girl for that."

"I—*what?*"

"Do what I say, when I say it. No arguing. No excuses."

She sat straight up in her seat. *"Are you serious?"*

His voice dropped lower. "I'm always serious about this."

He leaned back and buckled his seat belt.

A very small part of Gen's mind warned her, *He's playing you,* but she told that part of her brain to shut up.

Okay, if he wanted to play games, lawyers could *play games.*

The History of Spencer House

GEN tried to make sense of *that* while Arthur drove them through the dark countryside back to Spencer House. He gave the car to a guy in the garage to put up for the night.

When Arthur held the car door for Gen, a breeze whipped at her skirt and she grabbed it, holding the material to her legs before the guy got a peek at her bare bottom. She almost dropped her clutch purse, trying to grab the material whirling around her legs.

Her head spun just a little from the succession of champagne bottles they had put away. Gen was a big girl and worked in a profession where many meetings were held over a liquid lunch, not to mention months of charity soirees with open bars, so she could hold her liquor pretty well.

Yet, *champagne.* What was it about champagne?

Under her foot, one sky-high heel of her fuck-me pumps skittered on gravel. She stumbled, reaching for the side of the car.

Arthur was already there beside her and grabbed her elbow, steadying her. Between his firm grip and the cool metal of the car, she was fine, and she laughed. Arthur was already smiling at her.

She could hold her liquor, though. She wasn't wasted.

Really.

They walked in a side door. Arthur said to Gen. "Come with me."

Gen followed him through the hallways of Spencer

House to a library.

Oh, and what a *library* it was.

Gen sighed when she looked at it.

Books-books-books-books-books.

White bookcases stretched to the ceiling that seemed to be at least twenty feet above her head. A lot of the books seemed to be sets, leather-bound editions that were covered in the same color with gilded stripes running down the spines of the whole set. Other shelves held dozens of hardbacks and paperbacks.

She trailed her fingers over the books. "You like to read?"

"Oh, yes," he said. "Summer holidays with my grandfather were often uneventful, especially in the evenings. During the day, I ran about with George, but I came in for dinner. The earl insisted that I dine with him and spend the evenings in the library. I learned to like reading."

"I thought you didn't come back to England much, that you spent your school vacations with those other guys, your friends."

"Caz and Max. After my grandfather died, I spent the Christmas holidays with their families to be around friends, but I spent many of my summers here. Sometimes I visited Caz and Max for a few weeks, but Spencer House is my home."

Gen practically dropped her tiny purse. "We need to document that. Part of Christopher's case is that you didn't return to Britain for years at a time."

"Utter rubbish. Copies of my passport from that time are in the files. I set foot on British soil at least twice a year, often for months. I just made little effort to see him or my uncle. They didn't particularly welcome me, the boy who would inherit what they thought Christopher should be entitled to. Most of the time, I came home."

Gen gazed at the high ceilings, several stories above her, and the bookcases and delicately carved furniture pieces that must have been antiques and worth a fortune. "It's hard to believe that this enormous mansion is a *home.*"

"Would you like a tour?"

A tour of a manor house that had been on a BBC show and that her mother would have fought tooth and nail to get into? "Yes, please."

Even though she still wasn't wearing panties.

But dang it. *Spencer House.*

Arthur's smile was a little shy, and he looked out of the corners of his eyes at her. "Maybe we can do part of it tonight. We could start here."

"That sounds good," she said quickly and dropped her clutch purse on a small couch.

He gestured to the tall bookcases around them. "This is the single surviving library in the house. There used to be eight or nine libraries, but many of the volumes were donated to make way for other art or sold when the estate was in dire straits."

"Oh," Gen said, a sad, descending sound.

"I think it's a shame, too. The art is wonderful, but at one time, we had three First Folios of Shakespeare, forty-three thousand first editions of other works, and fifty-seven Gutenberg Bibles. Most are gone."

"*Wow.* Really?" Gen tried to stop her mind from chanting *Books-books-books-books-books,* but dang, how amazing was all that?

"Yes, indeed. We still have some rare volumes collected here, but the majority of the Finch-Hatten collection is now art and furniture. And jewelry. Plus some sculpture. And a few tapestries. Some of the remaining books here go back centuries."

"That's amazing," Gen said, slowly spinning around to look.

He motioned to the ceiling. "This house was built in 1505 by Lord Charles Spencer, so it has stood since the Tudor dynasty."

"The Tudors. Queen Elizabeth the First and Henry the Eighth."

"Those were the Tudors. My family held dukedoms and other noble titles before they built the house, of course. Nineteen generations of Spencers and Finch-Hattens have lived here."

Gen was staring at the books, aware that some of these volumes were older than the United States of America. Far older. "How come you're only an earl then, if your ancestors were dukes?"

Arthur grabbed his chest. "Oh, you wound me."

"Oops. Sorry. Guess that's not a polite thing to mention."

He dropped his hand, grinning. "As a family goes in and out of favor with the monarch, one goes up and down the ladder of noble titles. For the last two centuries, we've held the Earldom of Severn. My many-greats grandmother, Margaret Spencer, the Duchess of Somerset, is the source of much of the family's fortune, though that has varied with time and the monarchs' favor, too. She took our family from minor nobility and some lands and raised them to be the most wealthy family in England for a time. Her portrait is in the next room."

"I'd love to see it."

He waved one hand. "You don't have to. Seeing musty old portraits and antique chairs can be taxing."

Gen turned to him. "I *want* to see it."

He bit one side of his lip, *sexy again,* and smiled at her. "If you'd like."

Arthur led Gen through tall, double doors to the next room over. Dark wood wainscoting and crown molding trimmed the red-upholstered walls and the wide fireplace. Silver platters adorned the walls, leaning on the top of the dark wood rail above her head's height. The enormous soot-stained fireplace looked large enough to roast a haunch of one of the deer they'd seen in the deer park, or maybe even a roast elk.

Gen said, *"Wow,"* yet again.

"This room has been preserved almost entirely as it was in Tudor times, except for modern wiring and such. Pitch torches are quite the fire hazard. Duchess Margaret was a special friend of Queen Elizabeth the first. She was Mistress of the Robes, the Groom of the Stole, Keeper of the Privy Purse, and Ranger of the Great Park."

"When you say they were special friends—" Gen began.

"I mean they were political allies, which was exceedingly important during Tudor times, far more so than anything else. You're interested in these trivia?" Arthur asked.

"Oh, yes," Gen assured him. She had always liked English history. Her mother had gone on and on about it, and it felt like Gen was seeing what she had only been told about. "Go on."

"All right, if you're interested. You can stop me whenever you want. I can ramble on about the house and the history of England for hours if you don't stop me. We can save some for future trips."

Would there be future trips to Spencer House?

Well, maybe. Depended on how *coffee* went in a few months or so.

And other *things* in the meantime. They might find out that they were totally incompatible in *other ways.*

She said to Arthur, "So tell me about Great-Grandmomma Margaret the Duchess."

"Here she is." Arthur gestured to a large painting, probably ten feet high and six feet across in a carved, dark frame. A woman stared haughtily out of the canvas, holding a staff, robes over her other arm, and golden keys attached to a chain at her waist. Her dark red gown matched the wallpaper. She looked down her nose at the viewer with deep brown eyes.

"She looks," Gen searched for a polite word, "imposing."

"Oh, she was," he said. "She ran Queen Elizabeth's government in many ways and was a fantastically wealthy woman. When Elizabeth's government nearly fell, several times, often when she refused to name an heir, Margaret called in personal favors to make sure that the right people supported the Queen."

"So she was a kingmaker," Gen mused. "Or a queenmaker, actually."

Arthur stared at the portrait as if he were reliving the past. "If Elizabeth's government had fallen, the War of the Roses would have reignited, and England would have been mired in another bloody civil war, perhaps for another century. It's not too much to say that she saved thousands of British lives with a few words in the right ears, essentially fighting bloodless wars. Bloodless wars are the best kind of wars. If you do them correctly, no one even knows they happened."

"She sounds like quite a woman," Gen said, watching him. His intent stare seemed like he was trying to speak to his ancestor across the centuries.

The smile had dropped away from Arthur's mouth, and his eyes glittered with a metallic sheen as he stared at the portrait. When he spoke, he sounded as if he were reading something that was written deep within him, something imperative that Gen should hear and understand.

He said, "Margaret lent money to the government, at interest, to pay for the war to defeat the Spanish Armada. She saved England with a few strokes of her pen or a little bribe or a bit of blackmail so many times. She could have been called a spymaster with all her manipulations and machinations that no one discovered until I read her letters, which are in the archives here at Spencer House, but she was far more important than that. Queen Elizabeth knew it, though. By the time Elizabeth died, Margaret owned twenty-seven landed estates, more than the Queen, and she left it all to one grandson, Arthur Finch-Hatten."

"You're remarkably well-preserved," Gen said, doing her best arch British accent. She still sounded dang Texan.

He laughed and shook his head, glancing at her with those silvery eyes so full of mischief. "Family names are reused as often as the family silver. My grandfather and my father were both named Charles."

"And you've all lived here."

"Since 1505, in this house. It has ninety-three rooms, thirty-one bedrooms, eighty-six fireplaces, and over seven hundred paintings." He winked. "I used to give summer tours when I was a teenager under an assumed name. A few people figured me out."

Interesting that he remembered the numbers. "It's a wonder you have enough walls for all those paintings."

Arthur laughed again, his somber mood thoroughly gone. He seemed so much like his jovial, devil-may-care self that it seemed incongruous that he had been so intense while looking at that portrait of his great-whatever grandmother.

He said, "Come on. Let's look at the gallery, where we have many more walls for paintings."

Arthur led her out of the Tudor Room and into a hallway, which converged to the main hallway in the middle of the house. The ceiling was at least four stories high there, maybe five, and paintings tiled the huge room. A wide staircase led up from where they were to the second floor, and a walkway ran around the edges of the gallery. Hallways led from it to the other wings of the house.

"That's Charles the First, over there. We put him on the throne."

"King Charles the First," she said, just to clarify that point. Because, you know, he was *the king.*

"That's the one. He sat for that portrait in one of the music rooms while he was at Spencer House to hunt deer. The art collection is one of the finest privately held collections in the world. Luckily, my ancestors had decent enough taste in art, and they managed to hold onto the collections through rough economic times."

A small herd of housekeepers, all in matching black

dresses, trotted past Gen and Arthur, hurrying off to clean something else in the enormous building. They all turned toward Arthur and nodded to him like a flock of curtseying geese.

Gen watched the servants scurry off. "Doesn't look like times were ever that rough around here."

Arthur shrugged. "In the 1930's and 1940's, times were rough all over England and the world. Owning art doesn't pay the bills. The art might have been worth a great deal, but the farmers weren't able to pay their rents. A house that is five centuries old requires maintenance, a lot of it. During those years, my great-grandfather, Earl John Finch-Hatten, let go all but the most essential staff. Five people, I've heard, for the entire estate, including the gamekeeper. They used to find Lord John sitting in the dining room in the evenings, polishing the silver. We tried to give the house to the National Trust at that point, but when the committee members visited, it was raining. Water was pouring into the Great Hall, right here," Arthur motioned at the carved wooden ceiling, now painted white, "right through the roof. It was pouring like a waterfall, buckets and buckets of water. They took one look and walked out. We nearly had to abandon it."

Spencer House might have been torn down or just fallen into a destitute husk, a horrifying thought. "Oh, *no.*"

"Thus we were stuck with it, all through the War."

"You mean World War Two," she clarified.

Arthur scoffed, "Of course I mean World War Two. I'm British. Before the War, we had a house in London, too, but it was destroyed in the Blitz. We had evacuated everyone, all the family and the staff, to Spencer House because bombs fell only rarely this far from London. We stripped Finch-Hatten House in London down to the plaster, all the books, the art, the furniture, even the linens in the closets. It was empty when the German bomb destroyed it. We saved everything we could from Finch-Hatten House, everything except the architecture."

She turned to him. "That's so sad."

"I've seen pictures. It was beautiful, though not as beautiful as Spencer House. This is the gem."

"It really is gorgeous," Gen said, still turning and looking at all the portraits of long-dead people, staring down at her across the centuries.

Arthur said, "This house was built to display art. It's a trophy house, so to speak. It's meant to show off our connections to royalty and our power in the kingdom. It was meant to awe and intimidate."

Gen looked around at the cavernous hall that held hundreds of priceless paintings and stood taller than the highest ladder she had ever been on. "It's working."

"Oh, come now," he said. "It's just a house."

She turned and looked at him, standing with his feet spread. "But it's not just a house, is it?"

Arthur looked at her a long time, his pale, silvery eyes taking on that somber tint again, before he said, quietly, "No, it's not just a house. My family has cared for this house, for this estate, and for Britain all our lives. It's always been something larger than ourselves or any particular building. It's the realm. It's the idea of Britain and freedom. We sided with the Tudors when Henry Tudor took the throne from the Lancasters in the War of the Roses. We supported the Hanover dynasty when Queen Anne died in 1714, and then we shored up Queen Victoria's claim in the eighteen hundreds. We've always been for England, and for the rest of Britain now, of course. We've been here for well over a thousand years, working to make England the best that she could be, the most free and the most stable, trying to save lives, and trying to keep the best parts of it alive."

That was amazing to hear from Arthur, the lazy, money-squandering earl.

"But your family never got the throne," she said.

He laughed, his seriousness broken again. "God forbid,

no. I don't think any of my family had royal ambitions, and I certainly would never have wanted it. No privacy. No choice in your life's work. These days, it's more like being the head show pony, and one's influence must be wielded carefully and without politics. They can't choose a side, even when the right choice is obvious. No, we Finch-Hattens have always been one of the silent powers behind the throne, the people who worked for good and freedom and change, and for our own power and fortune, of course. Can't forget that."

"Of course not."

There was a disconnect, somewhere. Arthur had been a child born into this illustrious, influential family, who had worked so hard to excel at steeplechase that he had ridden for the UK in big competitions and who had gained a first-class degree at Oxford in languages.

Now, he was a man who was frittering away his family's fortune, a ne'er-do-well, a cad, a drunk, and a rake, to use the old words. Somehow, he had turned into a guy with too much money and too much time, and he was being stupid about killing himself with it and destroying the fortune in the process.

What had happened to Arthur?

Maybe being orphaned at nine years old and sent packing to boarding school would do that to a guy.

He said, "At times, the Finch-Hattens were richer than the king or queen, and more powerful than the monarch, too."

"That's really interesting." How did one go from being the heir of one of the most powerful families in England to the Earl of Givesnofucks?

He said, "Yes, well, all ancient history, now. Can't do those things in today's world."

Ah, there it was.

He stepped toward her and ran one finger down the outside of her arm. "Shall we watch some television tonight?"

Her skin shivered because, even though he might have been a decadent nobleman, he was still a hot, ripped, well-dressed, well-spoken, sexy man who was standing right in front of her.

And she still wasn't wearing panties.

"Sure," she said, her mouth suddenly wet. "Let's watch some television."

He held out his hand, palm up.

Gen reached out and clasped his hand, holding on.

Forget Quirky Love

GEN followed Arthur back to the library, still holding his hand, where he locked the doors behind them with a quick flip of his wrist.

Yes, Arthur *locked* the doors.

She sucked in a deep breath and looked around herself at the books, the couches, and the coffee tables.

That furniture was okay. There were no beds. Couches and chairs did not scare her.

Really, she was fine.

She sucked in a deep breath and held on tight to her panic, stomping it down.

Arthur towed her by her hand through the library, past sky-high bookcases and conversation groupings of couches, and clicked a button on a remote control to make a television rise out of another piece of innocent-looking furniture, just like at his apartment.

Yet another silver ice bucket holding yet another champagne bottle sticking out of the ice stood on an end table. Two slim champagne flutes and a dish of sugared strawberries stood beside the bucket.

Okay, more booze.

Not that she needed it.

Her liver was in fine form lately. All those charity events with open bars had exercised it until it was almost as efficient as when she had been in college.

She was pretty relaxed from the champagne, though.

Relaxed was good.

Arthur took off his suit jacket, laying it over the arm of the couch.

A lot of the furniture in the library looked antique, made of delicately carved wood and tufted ivory moire or silk.

This medium blue couch, however, back in this little nook between the bookcases, looked more mid-century modern, upholstered in soft canvas-like fabric over its boxy frame.

He touched her arm, stroking her skin from her biceps to her wrist with one fingertip, and asked her, "Movie or show?"

The grandfather clock in the corner said that it just barely nine o'clock. They had been staying up until the small hours of the morning every night for those charity events. She said, "Movie."

He smiled. "What kind?"

"Oh, whatever you want to watch." She flipped her hands in the air, indicating that she didn't care at all. "I tend to end up watching girlie things, Hallmark movies and rom coms."

"That sounds good."

"Oh, come on. You probably want to watch some science fiction special effects thing, or maybe Shakespeare or some classical music concert."

"No," he said, chuckling. "I like to watch some of that, but I go to enough theater and charity events. I like comedy the most."

"Yeah?" she asked, almost as normally as when she was wearing underwear. She felt a little sexy, a little naughty, wearing a skirt that fell just above her knees, high heels on her feet, and no panties on her ass.

Yet, they were negotiating which movie to watch.

Just a movie.

The hottie standing in his magnificent library who had just taken her out to an expensive meal and plied her with bottle after bottle of champagne wanted to talk about movies and watching TV.

Fine.

He said, "I haven't seen the one that came out a year or so ago, *Forget Quirky Love.* It looked funny."

"Okay. Fine by me." Maybe, if they got to watching the movie, maybe he would stop talking and she could *suggest* to him, somehow, that *more* might be in order.

The champagne must be bubbling thoughts into her head.

He sat on the couch and picked up the remote, clicking on the television and fiddling with it. The champagne and sugared strawberries rested on the end table beside his elbow.

Okay, fine. She flopped on the couch beside him.

He glanced at her out of the corner of his eyes, the silver of his eyes becoming glittery with mischief again. "On the floor, pet."

Gen frowned. "What?"

"On the floor, at my feet, *pet.*" That time, his emphasis on *pet* was unmistakable. "You aren't arguing, are you?"

Oh, they were back to playing games again.

She said, "Um, no? You want me to sit on the floor, by your feet?"

"Yes, pet." His voice had dropped into that low, sexy register again.

"Okay." She slid off the couch and sat on the floor at his feet, folding her long legs to the side. "Like this?"

He smiled, his lips opening over his even, white teeth. "Good girl."

From where he was sitting above her, he could pretty much look down her cleavage, bared in the low-cut dress.

In front of her, the television that had climbed out of the coffee table flickered to life, and boxes scrolled as Arthur worked the remote control to find the movie.

The highlighted box stopped on *Forget Quirky Love* and flashed. The producer credits scrolled over an opening shot of a meadow covered with pink wildflowers.

Beside her, Arthur's legs shifted. She peeked up at him. He was leaning over to the champagne bucket, popped the cork with his thumbs, and poured the wine into the two glasses. He handed one down to her, and she sipped the sweet, fizzy wine.

So much champagne. Were they celebrating something?

Well, maybe they would be.

Gen had braced herself on her arm, but her elbow was already twinging. She was, after all, a big girl.

On the television, boy met girl, and they made jokes.

Arthur's legs were right beside Gen, so sturdy-looking in his dark suit slacks. He probably wouldn't mind if she just steadied herself by resting against his legs.

Not much. Just a little.

She shifted her weight and leaned against his legs.

Warmth touched her head, stroking down her loose hair.

From behind her, she heard Arthur murmur, "Good girl."

So this was okay. *Cool.*

During the movie, Arthur touched her hair, tenderly stroked her head, and ran his fingers down the side of her neck and over her bare shoulder.

Every caress sapped nervous energy from Gen until she was practically draped over his legs as he touched her, her head resting on his knees like a tired cat.

She didn't even notice that she was doing it, but as Arthur pet her head, her fingers stole up his leg, caressing his calf and then the back of his knee.

Again, Arthur whispered, "Good girl."

She peeked at his socks, emerald green and steel blue argyle. Again, she wondered what mood a nobleman had to be in to wear socks like that.

Eventually, as the hero and heroine on the television joked and misunderstood each other and joked some more, Gen trailed her hand up his other leg, the fine cloth of his suit slacks dragging under her fingertips. Thick muscle bulged on the backs of his legs, too. He must have a trainer.

That kind of muscle wasn't an accident.

Arthur squeezed her shoulder and then stroked her hair again.

Damn, that felt good. Her eyes felt dry, and her blinks got longer and longer.

Her arm looped behind his knees, and she caressed farther up Arthur's leg on the outside of his thigh.

On the television, the hero and heroine had their faces very close together, and they kept looking from each other's eyes to their lips. Lens flare striped across the screen, indicating *love.*

She finished the glass of champagne and passed her glass to Arthur, who poured her another half of a glass of liquid courage.

He asked her, "Are you getting drunk?"

"No. I'm tipsy. I might be giggly. But I'm not drunk."

"Good," he said. "I don't like drunk women."

"Really? Some of those pictures in the tabloids suggest otherwise."

He chuckled. "Things aren't always as they seem."

"But you went ahead and porked them anyway, right?"

"Not if they were inebriated." A shudder made it all the way down his leg under her cheek. "I don't sleep with drunk women."

"That still leaves a whole lot of women."

"That's true."

"Oh, you sound like that's such a problem for you. Poor baby."

"It is. Sometimes I don't particularly feel like it, but I can't weasel out."

"Oh, come on. You're not obligated to sleep with a woman, just like she's not obligated to sleep with you."

"It's not that simple. When you spend a few thousand dollars on an evening, the woman expects something spectacular, a scene. I often can't get out of it."

Actually, Gen could see that. That evening was kind of

disappointing so far. Considering the fancy dinner and her lack of underwear, she'd assumed that she would be on her back with her legs in the air by now.

A few willies at that idea seeped through the champagne.

She turned her head against his leg to look up at him. His hand moved with her hair. She said, "That must get old, planning a 'scene' instead of making love, being so in charge and responsible for everything."

"No." He was still staring straight ahead at the television, but he was smiling.

"Oh, come on. It must get boring after so many. No spontaneity. No emotional spark."

"No."

"Really?"

"Not at all." He shook his head, still smiling. "You're missing the movie."

"Yeah, but—"

"Watch the movie."

"Okay." She rolled her head back. The couple on the screen were kissing open-mouthed and hard.

Gen wondered if Arthur ever kissed like that, so passionate, so desperate. He'd always been gentle with her, but she suspected that he was holding back.

Above her head, Arthur said, "And pull your skirt up."

And there was the kinky part.

Gen reached down to her skirt by her knee and dragged the fabric up her leg. When the hem was in the middle of her thigh, she stopped.

"More," he said.

She slid the gauzy fabric over her upper thigh, baring her whole leg to him, a thick ham on the bone, as her mother would have said. The dress's hem clung to the very top of her leg, up near where her underwear would be, if she were wearing any.

She paused, looking up at him.

"More in back," he said.

Gen slipped the fabric up so that the curve of her bare butt showed.

"Good," Arthur said.

Gen turned back to the movie, her head resting on his thigh and knee, stroking his leg, and his hand caressing her hair and shoulder.

After a few more minutes, Gen felt his large hand tangle in her hair.

Okay, this was new.

Holding onto a thick fistful of her hair as a handle, Arthur gently turned her head toward him.

When she looked up to where he was sitting above her, he was holding a slice of sugared strawberry in his fingers.

Gen lifted her hand, reaching for it.

Arthur's smile turned more devilish, and he shook his head.

Oh, he meant to feed them to her.

Gen opened her mouth and waited.

Still holding her hair in his other fist, Arthur lowered the slice of red berry toward her lips and pushed it inside her mouth, rubbing his thumb over her upper lip as she closed them on the sweet.

His caress felt sort of like he was kissing her, but even more sexy.

He fed her another strawberry slice, a burst of sugar and bright flavor on her tongue, and he slid his thumb over her lower lip this time.

After a few more, with a few more rubs of his thumb over her lips, Gen moved her lips on his thumb, kissing it.

He said, "Good girl," and he fed her another strawberry.

This time, as he pushed the sweet fruit between her lips, Gen kept her lips open on the pad of his thumb. Sugar clung to his skin, and she sucked it off. He didn't look away from her, his silvery eyes intensely watching her.

She closed her lips and chewed the strawberry in her mouth.

Only a few berries were left on the plate.

Without looking away from her eyes and still holding her hair crushed in his other hand, Arthur reached behind himself and picked up another strawberry. He reached forward, feeding it to her with no hesitation as she opened her mouth for him and closed her eyes.

This time, she opened her mouth wider and sucked his thumb in up to his knuckle. She licked the strawberry juice off his skin, sucking and swirling her tongue.

Yes, she knew that this was essentially a preview for oral sex if he shoved his cock in her mouth, and she wanted to make it good. She'd had a bad experience—a really bad one—but that didn't mean that she was a prude or a dead lay.

Arthur pulled his thumb from her mouth and picked up the last strawberry from the plate, still bending to look at her from where he sat on the couch above her.

On the back of her head, his strong hand grasped a thick handful of her hair more tightly, holding her head.

He held the strawberry in his fingers, but he used the last knuckle on his hand to push down on her chin, opening her mouth wide for him. His silvery eyes glittered, watching her, becoming hotter as he smiled. His lips parted.

Gen watched him from under her eyelashes, her mouth wide open.

Arthur pushed the strawberry slice into her mouth and thrust his thumb in after it.

She closed her lips on his skin, sucking.

He gripped a handful of her hair, rocking her head, and watched her as he rubbed his thumb down her tongue, nearly to her throat. He pushed it in several times, splaying his other fingers up the side of her face over her cheekbone and angling her head where he grabbed her hair. His dark pupils widened in his silvery eyes, and he was breathing shallowly in the top of his chest.

Still, he watched her, his eyes so intent on her face and her mouth, watching his thumb plunge between her lips.

Gen sucked on his thumb, curling her tongue around his skin.

He pushed his thumb deeply into her mouth one more time before he pulled it free.

She leaned back and chewed the strawberry in her mouth. Her lips felt swollen from where she had been sucking on him, and sugar and the taste of his skin coated her tongue.

Under her skirt, the skin between her legs felt just as swollen as her mouth, like he had been rubbing her down there, too.

Arthur breathed, "Good girl," in a deep, dark voice. He smoothed her hair where he had been grasping it and leaned back to watch the movie.

Gen swallowed the sweet strawberry and turned back to the television, where the guy had his arms spread and was emoting wildly, probably expounding on his love for the girl.

Arthur stroked her hair, trailing his warm fingers down the side of her neck and shoulder as he arranged it down her back.

He glanced down. "Pull your skirt up."

Gen looked at her leg. Her black skirt had fallen back almost to her knee when she had sat up to suck on Arthur's thumb and eat the strawberries.

She slid the black gauze back up her leg. The smooth material coasted over her skin.

This time, she felt sexier as she revealed her leg while he was watching her.

"More," he said.

She pulled up the skirt, letting it drape down her ass in back.

"Good girl."

Gen was beginning to feel like Arthur's toy, a sexual plaything, subject to his whims and his use.

It didn't bother her nearly as much as it should have.

As a litigating lawyer, Gen was responsible, all day and

every day, for so many people's court cases and defenses that might send them to jail or might restore their lives, plus she worried every waking minute about affording her mother's care at the nursing home and her treatment there.

Arthur's inclination to take complete control over this section of her life sent desire coursing through her, followed by a serious flush of heat to her pussy.

Letting him have her body and decide what would happen to her was a relief.

Gen's eyes widened.

Arthur played some pretty serious games, and she was falling right into them.

FOR the rest of the movie, about fifteen minutes, Gen leaned against Arthur's legs while he stroked her hair and shoulders, his fingers skimming down her arms and over her shoulder blades as he smoothed the curls of her hair. A few times, just enough to keep her full attention, his fingers stole down her chest to brush the top rim of the cups of her dress over her breasts.

She leaned on his legs, rubbing his calves and thighs, daring to sneak her fingers up to trace the shape of his hip. When her hand stole toward his inner thighs, he crossed his legs, denying her.

By the time the credits rolled on the television screen, she was fidgeting, the naked skin between her legs sensitive and warm. Every time she squeezed her thighs together, her clit zinged a pang of longing up her body.

The television screen went dark.

If Arthur stood up and held out his hand for a firm handshake, Gen was going to tackle him and rip his clothes off.

And then she would feast on what was under those clothes, the triple-shield tattoo on his forearm and the blue and red ribbons that striped his back and down his arms and thighs, the thick muscle that wrapped his arms and chest, and the ripples of his abdominal muscles.

Her mouth had been around his thumb, and she was hungry for the rest of him.

Arthur held out his hand to her, palm up. "Take my

hand."

Gen slapped her hand into his, and he pulled her to her feet. Her dress fell down her thighs again. His hand steadied her until she balanced on her high heels.

He reclined on the couch, his lean body lying back on the wide cushions, and he patted his thighs. "Sit."

Gen started to turn and tucked her dress under her butt, preparing to back up and sit on his legs.

"No," he said.

Gen turned back. "Then how?"

"Over me," Arthur said. "Astride."

She would have her legs on either side of his, and her pussy would rest directly over his cock, right on the fine cloth of his suit pants.

She might leave a damp spot.

"But—" she said.

"Surely you aren't arguing with me," he said.

"*No.* Not arguing. It's just that—" Gen fidgeted, drawing her legs together and accidentally squeezing her clit again. Wanting leapt through her. She gasped a little.

"Yes?"

Her hands fluttered in the air. "I'm still not wearing panties."

"I should hope not." The glint is his silver eyes was pure mischief.

"You see, I might—"

"Is there a problem?"

"Well, I'm kind of—"

His voice was low, commanding. "Say it."

"Wet," she admitted.

His sexy smile widened. "Good girl. Sit here."

He clapped his palms on his thighs.

"Okay, then." She grabbed handfuls of the gauzy material of her skirt, lifting the hem while she saddled up on his lap.

His gaze drifted to where her rising skirt bared her legs.

Her knees rested on the couch on either side of his hips. "Are you sure?"

Arthur brought his hands around, touching her knees and then rubbing his hands down her calves. "Absolutely."

She settled back so that she was sitting with her thighs on his, probably not leaving a wet imprint of her naked pussy on his pants.

Probably not.

Under her bare thighs, the thin fabric of his slacks was soft on her skin.

His hands caressed her calves, running his palms over the muscles on the backs of her legs. He had tilted his head to watch his hands on her legs.

"Is this okay?" she asked.

"Splendid," Arthur growled. His hands rose, rubbing over the tops of her thighs under her skirt. The thin fabric caught on the cuffs of his shirt and the titanium watch he wore, and he pushed the hem of her skirt up to the tops of her thighs.

Gen settled her hands on his shoulders, steadying herself.

He looked up at her, his silver eyes molten. His shoulders rose and fell like he was struggling to breathe. He pressed one of her hands closer to his neck, where the warmth of his skin leaked out of his shirt collar.

His voice was deep in his throat. "Let us discuss your safe words."

Gen ran her fingers through his short, dark hair. He closed his eyes and leaned into her touch. She said, "I don't know what that means."

"Safe words are the ultimate power. You will always have the power to stop anything that is beyond your limits. If you say one, I will pause or stop entirely, depending on what you say."

"What if you don't?"

"Then I have breached your trust, and you should walk away from me and not look back. I will always honor your safe words. I will always stop."

She nodded.

"I remember your hard limits, what you said when we were out in the deer park. No shoving or crowding you up against walls or other enclosed spaces, no grabbing the back of your neck, no restraints, and no beds. But safe words. You need safe words to tell me if it's getting too intense for you, if *I'm* getting too intense for you. For now, let's use 'red' and 'amber.'"

"Amber? Oh, that's right. You Brits have 'amber' stoplights instead of yellow ones."

"They're traditional, if somewhat boring. We'll pick more personal ones later."

Her breath was blowing through her lungs and her throat. "So I say—"

His fingers grasped her thighs, gripping and releasing her skin. "If you want me to slow down or to pause, say 'amber.'"

Maybe she should have had more wine with dinner. A *lot* more wine.

His silky hair slipped through her fingers. "Okay."

He growled, "If you want to stop entirely, to halt everything, you should say 'red.'"

She curled her hands around the back of his neck. "Red. All right."

He was staring at her bare thighs, his fingers pulsing her flesh. "Say each of them."

"Amber," she said. Her voice was breathless and weak. "Red."

"Good." He slipped his hands farther up her thighs. "Good girl."

Her lips parted, watching his hands.

He looked up, saw her reaction, and smiled. "Now kiss me."

Gen lowered her head to his, brushing her lips across his mouth, but he caught her hair at the back of her head in his fist again and pushed her down to him. His mouth opened under hers, sucking at her lips, and Gen kissed him back, harder.

Arthur's other hand was still on her leg, under her skirt, stroking her thigh.

Gen's head was pulled back by her hair, stretching her throat. She was looking up at the high shelves of the bookcases when the heat of his mouth misted her neck. He touched her with his breath first, still sweet and sugary from dessert and with a whiff of wine from the champagne.

She held on, her arms wrapped around his strong shoulders.

He kissed her neck gently at first, his lips dragging on her skin. She gasped at his touch. Her arms tightened around his neck, pulling him to her.

She felt his hand tighten in her hair, pulling. He stretched her neck farther back and sucked at her skin, nipping her with his teeth.

Her core tightened, the muscles in her abdomen and back flexing.

She couldn't help herself. She leaned into him, arching her back.

Arthur's hand on her thigh moved backward over her bare hip, reaching around behind her, and he grabbed her ass with his strong fingers.

Arthur groaned against her neck. He growled, "What is that perfume?"

Wanting fuzzed her brain. "I don't know. Roses, vanilla. It's in a round thing."

He bit her neck near her ear, where she had stroked a bit of the scent. "Wear it all the time."

"I will," she gasped.

He grabbed the cheek of her ass harder, kneading it. "My God, you feel good. So *soft.* Better than I had thought."

Gen bowed her head over his. Shame washed up through the lust that swept through her. "I'm just fat."

"You're beautiful," he whispered into her neck. "I've been dreaming about you. I've wanted to get my hands on that ass of yours for months. Every time you sat down next to me and crossed your legs, I've struggled not to stare at your thighs."

"Nuh-uh," she said.

His low voice shivered on her skin, and his fingers tightened where he was holding her hair and her ass. "One time when I came into your office to pick you up for lunch, you were bending over a file cabinet. Your suit skirt was stretched tight over your ass. I had to hold onto the door frame not to run my hand under your skirt to see what you felt like."

He flexed his hand, grabbing her ass again, and he kneaded her flesh.

"You did not," she whispered, but she remembered several times that she had caught him staring at her with heat in his eyes.

"I could stay here all night," he whispered, "breathing in your perfume, your hair in my fingers and grabbing your ass, but I have a better idea."

Gen's nerves still trembled. "Wh-what?"

He let go of her hair and stroked down her shoulder. "Do you want to use a safe word?" he whispered.

"No," she said. "No safe words. Don't stop. I'm dying."

His low voice washed warmth over her neck. "Good girl."

He brought his hand around and under her arm, stroking her side where the zipper strained, and brought his hand up and under her boob.

Gen arched her back, pushing her breast into his hand, practically offering herself.

Dammit, she should be more restrained. She shouldn't be so needy.

He held her heavy breast in his hand and kissed downward over her collarbone to where she swelled above the top of the dress. His thumb grazed over her nipple through the black fabric.

Desperation shot through her, a jumping spark that raced along her body from her breast to her mouth and downward, making her ache between her legs.

Gen gasped and held his shoulders again, which evidently Arthur took as provocation. He grabbed her ass harder, jerking her toward his body, and his thumb rubbed her nipple while he mouthed her skin.

Her legs were still spread over his, and she hadn't realized quite how much her folds were stretched open. When he pulled her forward, the soft fabric of his pants rubbed over her aching clit.

Need erupted in her body, and she clawed at him, arching her back to push her breast into his hand and try to feel his pants against her clit again.

Arthur slid his hand inside the top of her dress, popping her breast free, and latched onto her nipple with his hot mouth.

Gen dug her fingers into his shoulders and let her head drop back, whimpering. She keened, "Arthur, please. *Please.*"

He licked her nipple inside his mouth and sucked deeply with his lips, and it felt like he was pulling her whole body into him.

His other hand slid around her hip to the front, his palm stroking her skin, and he rubbed down to her knee and then up the inside of her thigh.

Gen stopped breathing and held onto his neck, gasping against his skin, waiting for his hand to reach her. The warm scent of his cologne and a faint, masculine musk wafted out of his shirt collar. She pressed her face to his shoulder.

His fingers stroked the outside of her pussy with gentle, soft strokes. Her skin was so swollen that it should have tickled, but his delicate touch made her shiver and drove her closer to the edge.

Her voice caught in her throat as she whispered, *"Arthur,"* and pushed her hips forward on his hand.

The heel of his hand pressed her clit, and the tips of his fingers slipped inside her. Gen rocked back, driving his fingers deeper inside, rubbing, and his palm massaged every clenching nerve in her pussy as she ground down on him until a bright spark snapped through her, throbbing from her core up her spine.

Blinding white light filled her, and she fell against him, panting.

Dear Lord, it had been *years* since desire had driven her like that. Sure, she had occasionally relieved the shameful tension by furtively fingering herself, but that physical spasm was nothing, *nothing*, like when Arthur touched her.

She lay against him, drained and quivering, and blinked back tears. Emotions overwhelmed her, and she couldn't even name half of them.

His arms curled around her, holding her against his chest, and his hand reached into her hair again to press her cheek to his heavy shoulder.

Arthur whispered, "Good girl," near her ear.

Gen tightened her arms around his neck, recovering from the quick, blinding orgasm, and was now totally unsure how to act. She tucked her boob back into her dress, embarrassed by so much flesh.

He stroked her back. Occasionally, his hand drifted down to cup the cheek of her ass, his fingers gripping her flesh for just a minute before he caressed and soothed her again.

Good Lord, Arthur probably had blue balls. He'd taken care of her, but she hadn't done a thing for him.

Gen sat up, still straddling his lap, and pulled her hair over to the side.

Arthur's silver eyes were shining in the lights embedded in the carved ceiling overhead. He said, "You are so beautiful."

She reached down to his belt and picked at the leather strap threaded through the buckle.

"No." He pushed her hands away.

"But—" She touched his belt again, trying to pull the soft leather.

Arthur's voice lowered. "I said, stop."

"But you— I should—"

He grinned at her, even though his grin looked a little haggard. "You were a good girl, but not that good. You need to be better to earn that."

"That makes no sense."

"Think about it a little more."

The lawyer in Gen's brain woke up before her common sense. "To be clear, if I'm just a little good, you'll give me orgasms, but if I'm not any better than that, I don't have to reciprocate?"

"If you aren't a very good girl, yes, you will stall out at this, and that will get boring after a while, don't you think?"

"I think I could handle you doing that to me twice a day forever."

"Forever?" Arthur asked, humor glinting in his eyes.

"I didn't mean to say that," she blurted. *Oh, man.* She had been the first one to say something about a long-term arrangement, and that was pressuring him. She hadn't meant it and wasn't sure she would even want it. After all, Arthur really was the Earl of Givesnofucks, and she was a chubby, horsey-faced lawyer with a Texas accent. "Let's forget I said it, okay?"

That was weird. He was still smiling. "I won't forget."

"Oh, great. Now you've got something else to tease me about."

That devilish glint lightened his eyes again. "Indeed, I do. I must also mention, while you're considering your strategy, that if you don't progress in your training, you'll never find out what other talents I have."

"Training?" Gen was not okay with that word.

"That's the customary term for it," Arthur said. "We can call it anything you want. Submissive therapy, if you like."

"I am *not* submissive. I'm an assertive, modern,

professional woman."

His eyes hardened to a shiny silver, and his voice dropped. "Down on your knees."

Gen slid off his knees to the floor.

Arthur stood in front of her and unbuckled his belt. "Open your mouth."

If he undid his belt, he might take off his shirt so she could see *him* again, those corrugated steel abs, broad chest, and the tattoos of the tattered blue and red ribbons across his back and down his arms. She might see them *up close.*

No matter what, she was certainly going to experience at least *part* of him up close.

She opened her lips and watched his fingers slide his belt through the buckle.

It was going to be just like when she had been sucking on his thumb, rough, with her hair in his fist.

Her mouth watered, waiting for him.

Arthur left his belt dangling, and he used one finger under her chin to raise her face to him. "You can call yourself anything you like, pet, but you're a sub."

She closed her mouth. "A—A what?"

"A sexual submissive. You've heard of this, right?"

Gen stared at him, many things clearing up in her head. "And that makes you—"

"A Dom," he said. "It stands for Dominant."

"Why?" The word escaped her mouth before she could stop it.

"Because I like it, of course. I like it a lot."

"No, why are you doing this to *me?* Are you *training* me to be your *sub?*"

"No, no. I'm saying that you already *are* a sub. It's your nature."

Gen spread her hands over her knees on the floor. "Then why are you doing *this?* What's the expected outcome for *this?*"

"The endgame for you is to be able to engage in a

normal relationship, not a Dominant and submissive relationship. That's what you asked me for."

"Then *why?*"

"You couldn't stand to touch my hand a few months ago. You could barely dance a waltz in my arms for a few minutes. When I took the choices away from you, you were able to do it. Look at how far you've come. You're doing brilliantly."

She asked, "So, after some more time, after this Dom therapy is done, after you finally screw me, what then? Am I going to be all messed up?"

"No. If I were training you as a submissive, I would push all your boundaries until I could do anything to you, and you would submit. Your submission would be beautiful, graceful, and I would be proud to earn your trust. But you don't want me to do that, do you?"

"No." Her voice quavered and didn't sound sure at all.

He lifted her chin and looked at her, holding her chin between his thumb and the knuckle of his first finger. His silver eyes flashed as he watched her face very closely. He asked more softly, with a lilt of wonder in his deep voice, "Do you?"

Gen bit her lip and fidgeted with her hands. "I don't think so."

Arthur's dark eyebrows rose, and he hesitated before he said, "All right."

Gen pressed her hands to her knees. The right words had come out of her mouth, *right?* She had said no, hadn't she? At least kind of?

She wasn't sure that she had said no. As a lawyer, she would have cross-examined the heck out of any witness who had waffled like that.

"Are you going to do it anyway?" she asked him.

"Do what?"

"Make me into a submissive? Break my boundaries until you can do anything you want to me?" Her voice had an edge of eagerness that she hadn't meant.

"No." He was speaking with that deep voice of authority again, and it sounded as final in her ears as a verdict. "If you want to change the parameters of our agreement, if you want me to do that, you must ask. You must ask when we're both sober and not engaged in play. All decisions in a Dom and sub relationship must be made that way, not in the heat of the moment, not while under the influence of anything. You can't blame alcohol or passion later. You would have to make a real decision and ask me. Do you understand?"

Gen nodded. Disappointment threaded through her.

It would be embarrassing to ask, embarrassing to admit that she wanted such a thing, if she did.

She didn't.

She thought she didn't.

She wasn't sure that she didn't.

Arthur sat down on the couch and patted his lap again. "Come here."

She started to sit astride him again, but he swung her legs around so that she sat across his lap, cradled in his arms.

She whispered, "When I'm all done, once you screw me, is that it? Are you going to walk away?"

"Never."

"It sounds like you're going to."

He stroked her hair. "You'll still be my lawyer. We have to keep up the charade until the court date, no matter what. And as you have said, as I've said, we're friends. We've become friends. I won't walk away from you."

"We have quite a few more months until the court date in November."

"Months and months," he said.

"Are you going to throw me away after that?"

"No," Arthur said, pressing her closer to his chest. "I won't throw you away. You'll leave me, happier and healthier, but you will leave. Like all women, you'll get tired of the drunken debauchery and my wasted life as a nobleman and nothing else, and you'll leave."

She didn't argue because he sounded so sure that it would happen.

The First Chaise Lounge

AFTER an hour of being cradled in Arthur's arms and hearing that their tryst had a definite time limit, Gen untangled herself from him, begging off that it was late and that they had to drive back to London the next day.

He kept touching her hair, her shoulders, and when she stuck out her hand for an ardent handshake outside the door to her guest bedroom, Arthur caught her hand up in his and kissed her knuckles before he quietly said good night.

Inside Gen's guest bedroom, the small divan at the end of her bed had been replaced by a sumptuous chaise lounge.

The curved couch was upholstered in deep blue velvet, and the cushioning sank when Gen sat on it. Blankets and pillows were piled up on the end.

Tears stung Gen's eyes, and she flipped blankets onto the chaise before she went off to brush her teeth before bed.

She wasn't used to being taken care of.

Followed

THE next morning, Gen sat in the passenger seat of the Mercedes as Arthur drove them back into London, his palm resting on her thigh the whole way. Ruckus had been alternately hanging over the back of the seat and sleeping in the back while Arthur drove yet another car, a four-door Mercedes.

Seriously, she was beginning to think that Arthur had a car *thing*.

She had been a little shy with him that morning, not quite able to look him in his startling silver-blue eyes, but he had whirled her around in the Spencer House garage before they left, pressing his own back against a Tudor-era wall with his arm clamped around her waist, and kissed her. He'd thrust one knee between her legs, rubbing her as they kissed, until she sprawled against him, quivering.

Just when she had been ready to climb up him and pull his hair, he had whispered in her ear, "Tonight."

He had been driving for about twenty minutes, still on the outskirts of the city and many miles from the penthouse apartment overlooking Hyde Park, when Arthur muttered, *"Shit,"* under his breath.

Gen looked around. Ruckus was sound asleep on the back seat, and traffic was flowing normally. "What's wrong?"

He scowled at the rear view mirror. "Someone's following us."

She wrenched herself around in her seat, looking at the

flood of cars and trucks back there. The air from the vents chilled the back of her neck. "How can you tell?"

"Three cars back in the left lane, behind the lorry. Black Peugeot."

The traffic swirled and jumped around so much that Gen could barely see it back there. "Are you sure?"

"It's been following us since we entered the motorway and probably for some time before that. It changed lanes quickly at the flyover to stay with us."

Flyover? Oh, yeah. Gen would have said *overpass.* "There are a thousand cars on this freeway. You can't pick that one out."

"The Peugeot isn't driving like the rest of them. He's breaking the patterns. There are a blue Ford and a green Land Rover that I suspect, too, but that black Peugeot is definitely following us."

"Where?"

"They're farther back. When the Peugeot drops back in a minute or two, one of them will take its place."

Gen remained twisted in the seat, watching.

Two more exits down the freeway, the black Peugeot veered sideways and decelerated.

A green Land Rover slid into its empty slot.

"Jesus Christ, Arthur!"

"I suspected as much. We'll need to lose them. Hang on."

The car jolted under Gen, and she clung to the seat and the door handle so she wouldn't fall over.

Arthur whipped the car through lanes and took another expressway.

The green Land Rover didn't try to follow them, but the black Peugeot *and a blue Ford* got over in time to take the exit, still solidly behind them.

Gen told him.

Arthur nodded. "Keep an eye on them."

He whipped through the traffic again, taking an exit and turning quickly onto side streets. At one point, he pulled into a small parking lot behind a store and parked.

A blue Ford drove by, but it didn't turn in.

She asked him, "Who were they?"

He frowned. "Probably more private investigators hired by Christopher to keep tabs on us."

"You sure?" Gen asked.

Arthur frowned harder. "No, but I don't know any more than that."

The Second Chaise Lounge

After they returned to Arthur's penthouse apartment in downtown London that Sunday afternoon, after the excitement on the highway, Gen dumped her bag in her bedroom and hailed a cab to her mother's nursing home.

She ran into her mother's bedroom and slid into the chair beside the bed, holding the mystery novel they were reading.

Her mother's vacant eyes didn't track Gen as she rushed in, as usual. She always watched, though, hoping.

Gen read for a few hours, blinking back tears.

Afterward, she made her way back to Arthur's apartment and was unpacking her few toiletries from her overnight bag when someone knocked at her bedroom door.

Apprehension crawled through her.

Arthur might have some new demands. The worry turned to excitement in her stomach.

She cleared her throat. "Come on in."

Mr. Royston Fothergill, the head of staff, leaned into her doorway. "Madam, if we may disturb you for a moment?"

Dangit. "Um, sure?"

He led a team of stout men who strode in, walking with purpose toward her small conversation grouping, the chair and loveseat. Mr. Royston Fothergill wore khakis, a blue dress shirt, and loafers instead of his usual suit. The pants sported a knife-edge crease down the fronts of his legs.

She asked him, "What's going on?"

Mr. Fothergill drawled, "We're redecorating."

"On a Sunday afternoon?"

"Necessity dictates."

The stout men picked up the chair and loveseat, lifting with their legs like professionals.

Gen scooted out of their way as they carried the furniture toward the door. "Is there anything I can do to help?"

"Tell us if you like the changes."

"But what are you—"

After her furniture had been carried out, other burly-looking men walked in, carrying new furniture. The blue upholstery looked soft and somewhat overstuffed.

Gen asked, "But what is this—"

The men arranged the furniture into a sectional, a couch on one side, and a long, wide chaise lounge jutting out from it.

Housekeepers followed them in and dropped sheets, blankets, and comforters on one end of the couch.

It was a bed, but not a bed. It was definitely a couch, but it looked far more comfortable than the loveseat. "Oh."

Mr. Royston Fothergill said, "In the future, Ms. Ward, please inform the staff of anything that would make you more comfortable. We are at your disposal. You needn't involve Lord Severn in the matter. He has enough on his mind, and we are here to ensure that you are entirely comfortable."

Gen asked him, "Was he upset? He didn't yell at you, right?"

"Lord Severn has always been a most considerate employer, but he was dismayed that your needs were not met. It is our job to make sure that you are well taken care of. You must tell us."

So she hadn't been being undemanding. She was making their jobs harder by making them guess what she needed. "I will."

His dry tone acknowledged her agreement. "I'll inform the staff."

The Back Door

Arthur was in his computer den, working through some code and conferring with Vlogger1 and Racehorse about what governments were behind the events that they had all seen on the telly that night. What was shown on the telly was only the surface, of course. The commentators couldn't say what was obviously going on because no one in any government would confirm it.

So the real story was never told, was it?

Arthur's phone farted.

Yes, the alert sounded like a wet, nasty one.

Arthur used that ringtone for everything relating to his brother, Christopher: texts, phone calls, emails from him, and a news alert.

Yes, it was juvenile, but sometimes one must indulge in the juvenile.

He turned his phone over, saw what was written on the screen, and started backing out of the code that had been open on the computer monitor.

"Got to go, lads," Arthur said, typing fast. "I'll see you soon. I should be in Paris for Pierre Grimaldi's wedding next weekend."

"Have fun." Racehorse's video call window was almost entirely dark. A thin line of light crested off his nose and one cheekbone.

"Will you be there?" Arthur asked.

"Too much surveillance," Racehorse said. "I can meet you for a drink at that dive afterward."

"Excellent plan. Vlogger1? You going?"

"Oh, hell, yeah," Vlogger1 said. "I wouldn't miss this one. Friederike's getting married." She meant Pierre's fiancée. "You know that bash is going to be *epic.*"

"I'm not sure who she's getting to do the music at the reception, though," Racehorse said. "There're so many rumors."

"I heard she's flying over the whole London Philharmonic," Vlogger1 said. "You know Friederike, always right up in everyone's business. That woman could launch a coup."

Arthur shrugged. Most coups these days were orchestrated by computers and were imperceptible. A few decades or centuries ago, though, Friederike would have been a formidable political force as she rallied aristocrats to one cause or another.

He said, "I've got to jet. See you guys."

Arthur snapped the video chat windows closed and flipped his phone onto its screen. He didn't want to be disturbed.

When Arthur had hacked his brother's phone at the Hope Ball, he had tagged several pictures of Christopher's girls with a bit of his favorite malware.

Evidently, that morning, Christopher had downloaded those pictures onto his computer, and so now Arthur had a back door into Christopher's computer and all his files.

He turned on the computer's webcam. A desk chair stood in front of bookshelves crammed with medical journals and stacks of paper. This computer was probably in Christopher's home office.

As Arthur roamed around Christopher's computer, he discovered that the desktop controlled the house's local area network. Quite a few devices were hooked up to that LAN.

The thermostat.

The security system, including the cameras.

Baby monitors.

Christopher's wife's computer.

The curtains.

Electronic personal assistants.

Everything.

Arthur roamed Christopher's house for a few moments, a ghost in the ethernet, his long, electronic fingers stroking the devices that were now entirely his. He left malware in all of them. If Christopher found Arthur's malware in his computer, Arthur could jump back in through any of those internet-connected devices and reinstall his control on the computer in minutes.

After just a few moments of surfing the wires, Arthur dove deeply into Christopher's computer, looking for the pictures that Christopher had assured Gen would *mortify* her.

The file was called *October Surprise Blackmail.*

Arthur sighed. Christopher was smart enough to get through medical school, but he would have been crushed in the Great Game. It took a healthy dose of paranoia and a touch of psychopathy to survive in that.

Inside the folder, the metadata in the pictures told Arthur that the ones he had found were copies, and the originals were on other computers at other ISPs, elsewhere. Deleting these would do nothing. Christopher's PI would merely email him fresh files.

A spreadsheet of ads purchased in London and national newspapers, spread over the entire month of October, was a bit of a shock. Christopher wasn't taking chances with merely giving his pictures to reporters and hoping they wrote a story. He planned to run large ads in the papers and online. Christopher must have spent millions of pounds on those ads to ruin Arthur, his brother.

Jesus, what kind of a sick bastard did that?

One who was trying to poison the entire jury pool, of course. It was the desperate double-down of a man who had racked up millions in legal fees on a foolish case.

The pictures on Christopher's computer did mortify

Arthur. Heat flushed his face and his chest, and he sat back in his chair in a cold sweat, swearing.

Those pictures could never be released.

If they were, Arthur would probably be dead within twenty-four hours.

Gen would probably be collateral damage because she was around him.

Certainly, though, if Christopher released those photos, people would come after Christopher, his wife, and his girls. Christopher's whole family would die, too.

Arthur leaned forward, bracing his elbows on his desk and rubbing his face.

He had to figure out a way to stop this.

Damn it. Why couldn't it have been hookers and blow?

Tonight

THAT morning, when Arthur had spun her around in the garage, kissed her, and driven her into a frenzy, he had promised her "Tonight," so she had backed off and suffered through the car ride with his hand on her thigh and the whole rest of the day.

Well, now it was *tonight.*

They had a small function to attend, Arthur had texted her.

Gen dressed in yet another new dress because Arthur absolutely would not allow her to attend an event in a dress that had already been seen. Her closet was stuffed with formal dresses. To get new ones in, she had to slide her hands in and mash the old ones aside. It was stupid, how much money Arthur was spending on clothes for her.

The dress was the second-sluttiest thing that Graham had allowed her to buy, a dark red cocktail dress that reached just past her knees with a flaring skirt.

And no panties.

She had attended Oxford and a strenuous bar course. She knew how to take the initiative.

Gen was waiting by the elevator at eight o'clock, just like usual. The staff trickled out until only Pippa was in the kitchen, and then she had gone downstairs to prep the car, as usual.

Arthur sauntered around the corner from his end of the flat. His dark hair was plastered to his head and flopping all over.

"Arthur, honey?" Gen tilted her head at him. "Did you forget to comb your hair after you showered?"

Arthur looked up as if he could see his own hair and touched his head. "I suppose I did."

He ran his hand through his hair like he was trying to finger-comb it.

Now, his hair stuck up in places and looked like black, snarled weeds.

"Sugar, let me help." Maternal instincts strengthened her Texas accent. "You're making it worse."

He bent his head, which she didn't really need because she was wearing Louboutin fuck-me shoes, because hell-yeah she was. She was giving off every do-me signal short of painting her arse red like a macaque in heat, hoping it inspired Arthur to do something to her like he'd done last night.

Actually, given that she was wearing a dark red dress over her butt, she kind of had painted her arse red like a macaque in heat.

Well, whatever worked.

She flicked his hair with her fingers, trying to get the soggy strands to lay right. Water dripped off the ends. "Did you even towel your hair?"

"I don't know." His low voice was flat like something was crushing it.

She led him to the kitchen and grabbed a clean towel out of a drawer. "How can you not know if you dried your hair?"

"I don't remember." He sounded distracted, and his head was turned away from her.

"You? Not remember?" Gen roughed up his hair with the towel, taking a lot of water out of the dark strands, and managed to drag his hair into a fair semblance of its usual style with her fingers. "That's not like you."

He straightened. "I have a lot on my mind."

She tossed the towel into the bin beside a pantry. "More

on your mind than when we left your huge earldom estate this morning and drove your fantastically expensive car to your penthouse apartment and its staff before your chauffeur takes us around tonight?"

Arthur looked away from her, frowning. "Well, when you put it that way—"

Gen stared at him. He sounded like he was trying to joke, but she was entirely unconvinced. "Arthur?"

"Hmmm?" he hummed, still turned away from her, toward the end of the kitchen and the windows that looked over London.

"What's wrong?"

"Nothing," he assured her. His tone sounded a little more jovial, but a line creased the skin between his eyebrows. "Nothing at all. Let's have a good time tonight, shall we?"

His hand touched her back at her waist over the thin silk of the dress, and his body went still.

Gen didn't move, either.

Arthur's hand trailed downward a few inches, caressing the small of her back over her tailbone.

He was feeling for a waistband.

And she wasn't wearing one.

Gen waited while his fingers moved lower, over her hip and down the curve of her ass.

Beside her, she heard Arthur's breathing deepen.

He flipped the hem of her skirt over his hand and reached under it, grabbing the bare flesh of her ass.

He growled deep in his throat.

Damn, that was sexy.

She said, "I wasn't sure whether I—"

He palmed the heavy flesh of her ass, kneading it. "Don't speak."

Gen closed her lips.

He moved behind her, holding her waist with one hand and her ass in the other.

"Did you do this to please me?" he asked her, his fingers

tight on her butt.

Okay, no talking, he had said. She nodded.

His hand on her waist slid up her ribs, and his fingers closed on her nipple.

Gen's breath caught. She arched her back, pushing against both his hands.

Arthur whispered near her ear. "Did you think this would excite me?"

She nodded again, biting her lip.

His teeth raked the skin on her neck. He growled, "Good girl."

Gen grabbed the counter for balance. She suspected she would need to hang on.

Arthur crowded up against her from behind and pressed her between her shoulder blades, bending her down. The granite countertop chilled her, and her nipples hardened fast.

Behind her, the soft fabric of his suit rubbed her bare butt, and his hard-on pressed between the cheeks of her ass.

She wasn't sure what he was going to do to her, but she sure as hell wanted to find out.

He flipped her skirt up to her waist, and the air in the kitchen cooled the skin on her butt and thighs, but he still pushed against her. He held her down on the counter, her cheek pressed to the stone, and massaged her ass and thighs. His hand was so big that he grabbed handfuls of her flesh, stroking and kneading her.

His whisper, *"Glorious,"* was so soft that he might have been talking to himself.

Gen twisted a little, trying to see his face.

Arthur was looking down at her butt, smiling, taking a minute like he was enjoying the view. He must have felt her twisting under the hand on her back, still pushing her down on the counter, because he looked up.

He took a step back, and his hand left her back. "Turn around."

Gen had learned better than to ask what he meant. She straightened, balancing on her high heels, and held onto the counter as she swiveled and leaned back.

He stepped forward again, almost crowding her but not quite because there was nothing behind her back. No wall. Plenty of escape. She took a deep breath.

His hands circled her waist, and he lifted her, easily, and sat her on the cold counter. Her bare butt chilled, and the cold even touched the lips of her pussy under her. Her legs hung down, and she was barely sitting on the very edge.

"Remember," he said. "Amber, and red. If you say one of those, I'll stop. I'll stop everything because you're in control."

"Amber and red," she agreed, her voice hoarse and almost silent in her throat.

She shifted, trying to get away from the cold stone pressing against her and chilling her clit, but Arthur placed his palm on her sternum right below her throat and pressed.

Gen reclined back to her elbows, the chilly stone walking cold up her spine.

"All the way," he said.

She lay back, her shoulders and arms pressed against the granite slab.

He said, "Reach above your head and hold onto the other side."

Her fingers stretched upward, and she found the other edge of the counter with her fingertips.

"Good girl," he said. "Don't let go."

She wouldn't. She might fall off the counter and crush Arthur.

Gen rolled her head up to see what he was doing.

He lifted her legs, laying her knees over his shoulders, and kissed the inside of her calf.

When he looked up at her, looking first directly between her legs and then over her stomach and boobs to where she was peering at him, his grin turned absolutely devilish. He nipped the inside of her knee with his teeth, almost hurting her, but not quite.

Gen laid her head back and closed her eyes. She had gone commando on purpose. Cause, effect.

The heat from Arthur's mouth moved up the inside of her leg, a hot trail of his lips sucking at her skin. His cheek felt like satin on her thigh.

Damn, he was moving so *slowly.*

The anticipation was cruel to the point that she wanted to cry. His tongue was so hot, and the inside of his mouth so wet, that she squirmed, trying to scoot down to him, but she couldn't. Her arms were extended as far as they could go over her head to the other side of the counter, and she didn't want to slither off and be a sex-stunned heap on the floor.

Past her knee, far up the inside of her thigh where her leg bulged out a little, he paused, sucking, until pain snaked into her skin.

Oh, man. He'd left a bruise on her, a hickey on the inside of her thigh.

The thought of him marking her with his mouth turned her on more, and Gen moaned.

His cool fingers touched her folds, parting her, and he ran his tongue across her pussy, side to side.

Pleasure slid through her body.

He did it again, and again, each easy brush a glide of bliss that melted her.

Her fingertips loosened on the edge of the countertop above her, but she held on, just enough.

He licked her slower, more deeply, sucking on her quivering skin until she was panting, waiting for every new sensation.

And it was new. It was all so new.

His tongue worked inside her as he sucked on her clit, a slowly rising storm of sensation that overtook Gen, engulfed her, and swallowed her in darkness and pleasure.

Elevator

THEY got into the elevator, and both of them turned and faced the doors, parallel, not looking at each other. Very British.

In the elevator, Gen fidgeted for a moment, her thighs still damp from Arthur's mouth, and she finally asked him, "What would you have done if you were training me to be a real submissive?"

The elevator whirred around them and began to drop.

"Depends on where we were in training," Arthur said, also looking at the elevator doors. "If it were the first few weeks, probably the same."

"Oh." Gen stared at the numbers flickering above the doors as the elevator descended. "What if it wasn't the first few weeks?"

His voice deepened. "If it were still the first few months, I would have found something that vibrates and pressed it into you until you came. One has to improvise, you know."

"Oh. Sure. Improvise." Her body was becoming sensitive again, just thinking about him shoving something buzzing against her clit. She pressed her legs together. "And if we were further into the training than that?"

Arthur turned toward her and clamped one arm around her waist, dragging her against his body. The cinnamon and cloves of his cologne drifted from his suit, and Gen inhaled his scent.

He whispered, "Sometimes, exactly one of those two things. Other times, if I were in other moods, I would have found the kitchen twine and bound your hands behind your back. Then, I would have searched the cabinets for olive oil, bent you over the counter, and pounded your ass, pulling back on your wrists where I had tied you and rubbing your clit until you came so hard that people walking dogs in Hyde Park would have heard you scream my name."

Okay, that was a lot to think about.

A whole lot to think about.

Gen swallowed hard. "When you say my *ass*—"

"Anal," he growled, his breath hot on her neck. "I'd shove my cock in your tight, luscious ass and pound you until you came. Any guy can lick a woman to an orgasm. That's practically cheating."

It hadn't felt like he was cheating.

Arthur's eyes were blue-hot steel when he said, "But anal is a rare skill. Shocking a woman with how hard she can come with my dick in her ass, how much she'll scream, how she will lose control and beg for more, is simply *fantastic.*"

Gen's words swelled in her throat, and she wasn't sure what to say. She sputtered, "Um, okay."

His intense gaze pinned her as hard as his arm around her waist. "Why do you ask?"

She was sober, and this was not in the heat of the moment. What she said now *counted.*

Fear rose up. Terror choked her. Memories assailed her and spun her down a black hole.

Gen took a deep breath. She grabbed the lapels of his suit in her fists and said, "I want to know. I want to know what I *might* be getting myself into."

Arthur growled deeper in his throat, the words "Good girl," just barely recognizable in his gravelly voice. His arm around her waist tightened, pinning her body against his. His lips found hers, and he kissed her hard, shoving his tongue between her lips.

He slapped a button on the control panel.

The elevator bobbed to a stop under her feet, and she

staggered in her high heels. It rose toward his apartment.

Arthur leaned back against the wall of the elevator, dragging her along with him and pulling her arms up around his neck, and he swung his hand under her skirt again.

Gen looked down as the lump of his hand ran over her hip and around to the front, dipping into her cleft. He found every sensitive part of her, his fingers inside her, rubbing the stripe of sensation in there. His thumb pressed on her clit where she was already swollen from just listening to him describe what he might do to her and raw from his tongue minutes ago. A few thrusts of his long fingers up into her and his rough thumb pushing on her clit made her clench so fast that she gasped.

A few more, and she was whimpering, her core tightening into a knot that wouldn't release.

It was too soon. She couldn't come again.

She thought she couldn't.

Something nudged her asshole.

"Say yes," Arthur commanded her.

Gen held onto the lapels of his suit, almost crying with the tension. *"Yes."*

A deep burn crept inside her ass as he slid a finger in there, too. He was stroking against more nerves, penetrating her more deeply, more completely than she had thought possible. He ground into her, his fingers rubbing hard, driving her until she couldn't bear it and couldn't stop it if she had tried.

Gen cried out and fell against him, holding onto his suit with her eyes closed. The inescapable pressure drove her over the edge, rippling waves down to her knees and up to her head.

Her legs gave out, and she fell, driving his fingers farther into her and sending deeper waves running through her body. Her body throbbed with her release, tightening around his hand and pulsing on his thick fingers.

She bit back the cry, trying not to scream. *"Arthur!"*

In her ear, he whispered, "Like that, only louder."

PARTY

IN yet another elevator, riding up to the party after the car ride, Gen's thighs were damp from Arthur's mouth and her reaction. The hickey on the inside of her leg stung, and she swallowed hard, trying not to look thoroughly turned on by it.

She fretted, "I must look freshly fucked."

"No," Arthur replied, looking straight ahead. His voice dropped to that deep, sexy register, "But that can be arranged."

Gen was snickering as the doors opened to another genteel, perfectly appointed little hallway, where a huge vase stuffed with fresh flowers stood on a marble end table.

Time to be British.

Gen schooled her expression and held onto Arthur's elbow as they walked into the small party, a gathering of a few dozen people at yet another penthouse overlooking yet another park.

Seriously, the rich people sucked up all the best real estate. Gen's garden had a view of her neighbor's weedy patch and rusted-out window air conditioner.

Arthur raised his hand as he walked into the thick of the party. "Raleigh! It's been simply eons!"

Gen followed Arthur over to a distinguished-looking mature gentleman, meaning that he had more gray hair than wrinkles and was still whip-lean. She readied her *How-do-you-do's.*

The man brightened when he saw Arthur and then

beckoned him over. "Lord Severn, we must speak."

Arthur shook the man's hand.

Good thing he'd gone back into his penthouse apartment and washed his hands.

"First, may I introduce my very good friend," Arthur said with warm overtones that indicated so much more, "Genevieve Ward. Gen, this is Lord Raleigh Gage, Baron Sandys, of Ombersley in the County of Worcester. He's also a High Court Judge."

All of Arthur's polishing up lessons dove right out the penthouse windows. "I—A pleasure to meet you, my lord."

"How do you do," the Right Honorable and Learned Judge, Lord Gage the Baron and what-all else, said to Gen. He turned to Arthur. "I was dearly hoping we would happen to meet tonight."

"You could have called if it was urgent," Arthur said.

"It is better if it were discussed in passing," the judge said.

Even Gen knew that meant that the Judge shouldn't be saying this at all, but the upper classes talk amongst themselves at parties. Can't be helped.

The Judge glanced at Gen and said to Arthur, "Perhaps there is some place more private where we can talk."

"It's quite all right," Arthur told him, sliding his arm around Gen's waist. She leaned against his side. "Gen is my barrister for the case."

"I was wondering who you'd get after poor old Horace Lindsey died." He bobbled as if he was riding over a rough road. His expression clenched to a dismayed frown. "Your barrister is *here* with you?"

Arthur said, "Mention it to Octavia Hawkes. She'll explain."

"But m'learned friend is right here. We can't speak."

"Go ahead," Arthur said. "She's not a problem."

Gen shrugged and told them both, "I won't say anything."

"All right, if you insist." He shook off his discomforting thought and leaned in to tell Arthur, "Judge Howard has had to recuse herself from your case due to conflicts of interest."

Arthur grinned far too innocently. "Oh, that's too bad. Lady Howard was most friendly to our case."

Oh, God. Arthur had slept with the judge.

"Gossip of your *friendliness* with Judge Howard did make the rounds rather speedily," Lord Gage said, his tone as dry as a *brut zéro* champagne made without the pinch of sugar.

Where had Gen picked up snotty references like that? She would just assume that it was osmosis from Arthur, somehow.

The judge leaned in, his thin form bent in a sharp angle. *"Judge Sackville* was assigned to your case this evening."

Gen had no idea who that was, so she plastered an amused smile on her face and prepared to wait it out.

Beside Gen, Arthur stepped back as if shoved. *"Knox* Sackville?"

"Yes."

Arthur touched the side of his face at his temple like a migraine was forming there. "Are you certain?"

"Positive," the judge grated out.

Gen dipped her eyebrows and frowned at whatever it was that she didn't know.

Arthur muttered, "Fuck it all," and he straightened. "Thank you, Raleigh. We'll manage."

Gen held his elbow as Arthur walked her over to the open bar. Inside his sleeve, Arthur's bicep jumped.

He asked, "White wine?" with a lightness that Gen recognized as completely fake.

"Tell me who Knox Sackville is," she told him.

Arthur ducked his head and whispered near her shoulder, his warm breath brushing her collarbone, "Sackville is virulently anti-monarchist and anti-nobility. He works with an association that seeks to abolish the monarchy and strip nobles of their inherited lands and estates."

"That hardly seems fair." Gen tried to sound convincing on that one.

"He will be particularly amenable to Christopher's argument that Christopher is a middle-class Englishman, salt of the earth, who deserves the earldom instead of an upper-class, Swiss-educated, Eurotrash twat such as myself."

"Arthur!"

"Sackville will be more than happy to set precedent."

"Yeah, okay. That's bad."

"Yes, that's bad. That's very bad." Arthur sounded like he was on the verge of sarcasm or despair. Gen couldn't tell which. "Christopher doesn't know what he is playing with, here. He doesn't know how much he could lose."

"How much *he* could lose? Do you mean if the judge assigns costs because it's a frivolous lawsuit?" Except that it sounded like Sackville wouldn't do that.

"Gen, this lawsuit can't see court. We should settle. We should settle this in any way possible, no matter how much it costs."

She ducked her head to talk to him. "We tried. Horace tried settling for up to a third of the estate. Any more than that and, like you said, the estate won't have enough income to support itself."

"The estate doesn't support itself *now,* and it's too dangerous to let this go to trial."

"For the other nobility? For the monarchy?"

"No, not exactly."

Gen tilted her head to look at him. "What aren't you telling me?"

Arthur accepted his drink from the bartender. Gen presumed that the clear liquid was vodka and tonic again. He drank, rattled the ice, and sipped some more.

Arthur was delaying a long time.

A long, long time.

Way more than the five-second rule that indicated

deception. Was her client preparing to lie to her?

Arthur finally said, "You're the one who has files and files on this case. How would I know something that you don't?"

Oh, she could see this one a mile away. "You just answered a question with a question and didn't really answer, and you took far over five seconds to do it. That's evasive. You taught me that such an answer is a sign of deception."

His dark mutter shocked her. "So I did."

"What aren't you telling me?"

"If this goes to trial, no matter who wins, we will all lose."

"You know something. What is it?"

"I don't."

"I call bullshit."

"I beg your pardon."

"You aren't telling me something. Tell me, now."

"Gen, I *can't.*"

"I'm your lawyer. Privilege. Unless you've committed a crime, you can tell me absolutely anything, and I can't tell another living soul about it. Now, what is it?"

Arthur shook his head. "I don't want to discuss it."

Gen looked around the living room. Hallways led to doorways off the large living room. "Come on."

"What are you—Gen? *Gen,* come back here."

She strode off through the crowd.

"Gen!"

She busted her way through the be-sparkled and be-dazzled gowns and matte black tuxedoes to the back hallway.

Arthur's fingers plucked at her sleeve near her shoulder, but she kept going, right out of the crowd, through the kitchen, and back to an unlocked door.

The door opened to a bedroom with a big, stupid bed squatting in the center of the room.

Dang it. She had been hoping for a nice, clean bathroom. No matter.

Behind her, she heard, "Gen, where are you—"

Gen was a big girl who'd had a lot of martial arts training the last few years.

As Arthur stepped into the room, she grabbed him by his coat lapels, whirled him around, put his back to the wall, and kicked the door shut. A quick flick locked the knob.

"All right," she whispered, her arm across his chest and holding him against the wall. "You and Lord Gage were talking about the judge, and then you totally freaked. You were freaked out of your lordly mind before we left your apartment an hour ago, too. Tell me what is up with you."

"It's just the court case," he said, looking at the gauze curtains across the window. "It has caused some stress."

"Bullshit." She dropped to her knees in front of him, hoping to shock him. "I don't buy that for a minute, my lord."

Arthur lifted one eyebrow, and he smiled.

Gen grabbed his belt and yanked the leather strap through the buckle.

Rose Petals

A charge zinged through Arthur's chest to his groin at the sight of the lovely Genevieve on her knees in front of him.

He'd been planning on seeing this, eventually, but he'd been planning it for a moment when she was vulnerable. In such a case, fucking her mouth would cement his dominance.

Gen pried his waistband button open and unzipped his fly.

Arthur's dick grew hard, and his balls hung in his shorts.

He could still do the other thing later.

She reached in with her sure fingers and pulled his cock out, letting the massive thing hang in the air between them.

Arthur was aware of what he had. There was no use denying it.

Gen looked up at him, her pretty eyes wide. "Is that thing real?"

His dick bobbed in response.

"Are you *serious?*" She wrapped her hand around him near the base. Gen is a tall girl, a strapping Amazon of a woman, which attracted and fascinated Arthur no end. After all, dominating a woman is only an accomplishment if it's a fair fight. Her long fingers wrapped only part of the way around his shaft, and her wide palm didn't cover the length halfway. Not even close.

Gen said, "Oh, my Lord. I need to rethink some things."

"I like it when you call me 'my lord,'" Arthur said, pitching his voice low, commanding. "It is my title. Use that."

Gen looked away, nervous. "I don't know whether I can —"

"Open your mouth."

He stared down at her from his great height and didn't blink.

Gen blinked. She blinked her long eyelashes over her eyes twice.

Arthur said, "You say, 'Yes, my lord,' or you just open your mouth."

A hint of a smile curved her mouth. "Yes, my lord."

Lust and power rushed through him. "Oh, I like that a lot. Safewords won't work here, so you raise both hands and touch your ears if it's too intense for you. Understand?"

She nodded again.

"Now open your mouth."

Gen parted her lush lips and opened that pretty little mouth of hers.

Arthur reached around behind her and grabbed a handful of her hair, holding her head steady while he set his cock first on her lips, letting her taste him.

She sucked on the head of his cock, flicking her tongue around it.

It had been *months* since he'd had release, *months,* and he had been thinking about Gen that whole time.

He held her by the back of her head and pushed his cock in farther, cramming the head in and popping it free.

Her soft lips and wet little tongue on his hard cock were like fucking rose petals.

And you know how fragile rose petals are.

He pushed harder, angling his dick with his other hand, shoving it in and backing off so she could breathe before he shoved her head down on him again. Arthur didn't cram it all the way in. He didn't want to hurt her, and he knew how to hold back.

Her hands rested on her knees, braced for balance. She

didn't raise them to touch her ears, so he got rougher.

Using her hair clenched in his fist, he crammed his cock down her throat and pumped, fucking her mouth hard. Her lipstick smeared on his cock, bronze-red stripes that looked like a tattered banner on his darkening skin.

Oh, Lord. Her hot mouth was tight on him, and her tongue curled around his cock.

He wanted to fuck every part of this woman, to mark her with his mouth and his teeth and his hands and his come.

Greed for her skin and her body overtook him.

Her lips plumped around his cock, swollen.

He thrust harder into her.

Her hands stayed on her thighs.

So he kept going.

Going harder and stronger, shoving himself into her mouth and her throat.

His balls tightened, and the string of firecracker pops shot up his spine.

His mind shattered, and he floated in blankness and light.

He held her tightly over him, pumping his come into her wet mouth and down her throat.

Oh, Lord.

Honeypot

Gen sat back on her heels as Arthur slid down the wall, his knees collapsing. He was staring at the ceiling, stunned.

Damn straight, he was stunned.

He may have thought that he was fucking her face, but Gen knew that her oral skills were pretty good. It wasn't difficult, really, just an attention to detail and a nimble tongue. And pretty good control of her gag reflex. And strong throat muscles that could apply some pretty impressive suction.

Arthur still couldn't talk. He swallowed a few times, licking his lips and staring at the ceiling.

A terrible thought arose, that she might have sucked him into an aneurysm. "You okay?"

He cleared his throat and blinked. Intelligence returned to his blue-gray eyes, gradually. He whispered, his voice hoarse, "That was spectacular."

"Yes, I know." Gen put her fiendish plan into motion. "Now, what was it that you wanted to tell me?"

Arthur chuckled, still staring at the light fixture in the ceiling, and then laughed. He was still panting. "Oh, a honeypot. Smashing."

"What's a honeypot?"

He laid his head back against the wall. "It's when spies use a beautiful woman as bait to either lure a person to a place where they can be kidnapped, or to elicit information, or influence him. Sort of like what you and Oct were doing with the Myla underwear and Louboutin shoes with Judge

Letcher."

"Roberts," Gen corrected. "Judge Roberts."

"Whatever."

"And it's not a honeypot."

"You tried to use sexual favors to get information," Arthur said.

"Well, yes. But I need to know."

"That's a honeypot." He staggered to his feet, buttoning his fly and reaching for his flapping belt. "*You* are a honeypot, pet, and I am thoroughly trapped."

"Then tell me what's going on!"

He laughed, even though his laugh was a little ragged. "Oh, Lord. I needed a good laugh, too." He held his hand out for her. "Come, pet. We need to get back to the party."

Gen pushed herself back up to her feet. "Well, that was a wasted effort."

"But a fantastic one. Truly, a fantastic effort," he assured her.

"'Kay." Gen was less than thrilled with the outcome.

Arthur said, "I need to speak to Raleigh a bit more—"

Gen recited, "*Lord* Raleigh Gage, Baron Sandys, of Ombersley in the County of Worcester. That's a mighty mouthful."

"And you remembered it all. Yes, I need to speak to Lord Gage."

"Fine. Let's go." Gen followed Arthur back to the party.

As soon as they opened the bedroom door, the chattering conversation whirled around them, getting louder as he led her into the main room.

Arthur looked over the crowd.

That was easy for Arthur because he was so tall, and Gen was right there with him in her high heels. They both stuck up like wildebeests looking over the tall grass of the savannah.

Arthur pointed over at a corner and waved. "Lord Gage, may I have a word—"

"Lord this, Lord that," Gen muttered, just so Arthur could hear her. "Lords everywhere at these things. These parties are pretty much the House of Lords."

He dropped his arm and stared. "The House of Lords."

Gen craned her neck to see him. Had that post-blow-job aneurysm finally exploded? "You okay?"

"The House of Lords!" He grabbed her shoulders. "Gen, you're brilliant!"

"Well, of course, I am. International Baccalaureate high school diploma, gained a first at Oxford, and head of my class at the bar course, you know. Plus even being offered a pupillage. But what exactly are we talking about here?"

"The House of Lords! We'll pull my case out of the courts and throw it to the House of Lords!"

He hugged Gen in public and *everything*.

Then he wrapped his arms around her whole body and picked her up to spin her around.

"Arthur! Put me down!" He was *not* acting very British. Her long legs flew out and she nearly back-roundhoused an elderly lady. "Oh my God, I'm so sorry," she called to the woman as Arthur flung her around.

"That's it!" Arthur set her on her feet, tugged his cell phone out of his jacket breast pocket, and tapped the screen.

"You can't throw it to the House of Lords! It's not *done.* It hasn't been done for *decades!* For almost a *century!"*

He waggled his phone at her. "Just need to know who to call."

"No one can do that."

"One person can."

"Well, the House of Lords won't take it. And the court will insist that they have jurisdiction or something."

He grinned while looking at his phone. "I don't think they'll have the authority to argue."

"They will. The courts *always* have jurisdiction."

"Not always." His grin turned manic.

"The only person in the entire United Kingdom who could throw it to the House of Lords is—"

Arthur turned his insane grin toward her, and his silvery eyes were jumping with devilish sparks.

Comprehension dawned on Gen. *"No way.* Even if you could get it rerouted, Octavia will dump your butt, and I'm not experienced enough to argue *anything* before the House of Lords!" she whisper-shrieked.

"It's our only chance," he told her, holding his phone to his ear. "And they'll be able to settle the matter within weeks, probably before summer, before Christopher has a chance to publicize those pictures in October." He reared back. "Hello! Harry! Yes, it's Arthur. Yes, I'm sober."

Arthur trotted away from the party, holding his hand over his other ear and talking on his phone.

Gen was pulling on his elbow, saying, "Arthur, you can't do this. It's not going to work."

Arthur spoke into the phone. "Say, I've got a favor to ask of you and your grandmother. It's really important. Yes, I know what time it is. Sorry about waking the heir to the realm. And his heir, too. Especially sorry about that."

He swiveled the phone away from his mouth to tell Gen, "Babysitting."

And back to the phone call. Arthur said, "But seriously, there's something that I need, old cousin, and I need it *right now.*"

Gen stood next to him, staring, until she realized that other people were watching him out of the corners of their eyes and eavesdropping.

She hissed to him, "The middle of a party is no place for such a phone call," and led him to the kitchen, where waitstaff were loading up their gleaming trays with glasses of champagne and little bowls of iced shrimp.

The waitstaff were watching Arthur, too.

Dagnabbit.

Arthur was talking fast. "The monarch has the authority

to throw it to the House of Lords. It's the only way. Yes, under the old rules. They didn't change the rules on peer privilege because everyone assumed that it would just be for ethics censorship, not for anything of importance. However, we can utilize this oversight."

Gen tugged his arm, and he stumbled after her, back to the bedroom where she had blown him.

Arthur looked around, grinned, and said into the phone, "Now, Harry, we Finch-Hattens placed your ancestors on that pretty throne of yours, and we can throw you off any damned time we choose." He was laughing. "I don't know who would want the damned thing, but we could."

Arthur dipped one devilish eyebrow at Gen.

She was just totally aghast. "I can't *believe—*"

He asked the person on the phone, "Will you be at Pierre Grimaldi's wedding next weekend? We could go carousing for old times' sake. No? Just Wills and Kate, then. Well, I'm sure they'll be up to something eminently boring. I'll have to look elsewhere for a bit of fun."

Arthur listened for a moment.

Gen leaned her butt against the wall, staring at him.

"So you'll talk to her? Tomorrow? Tomorrow *morning?*" He winked at Gen. "*Smashing.* Thanks, Harry. We'll keep your family on the throne for another generation or so. Give my love to Kate. No, just Kate."

Gen snapped her jaw shut. The only person in the United Kingdom who could change the venue of Arthur's trial from the courts to the House of Lords was the monarch, the Queen herself.

But the Queen could do it.

Arthur tapped his phone and hung up. "It should be done by noon. Call Octavia and warn her. I must speak to Lord Gage over there about the House of Lords Committee for Privileges and Conduct."

"I can't believe you did that!" Gen exclaimed, flapping her hands. "I can't believe that you called *Prince Harry* to have *the Queen* throw it to the House of Lords and settled it all in two minutes flat!"

Arthur shrugged. "I guess I do have a bit of Great-Grandmother Duchess Margaret in me after all, at least when it comes to saving my own degenerate hide."

A Most Excellent Proposition

GEN made sure they escaped the party as early as was feasible, which meant the wee hours of the morning. They staggered in the door to Arthur's apartment with Gen setting her phone for an early wake-up call.

Upon receiving Gen's frantic text that Arthur's case was going to the House of Lords instead of court and would be heard *soon,* Octavia Hawkes had predictably and immediately scheduled a seven-thirty meeting for the next morning.

Seven-*frickin'*-thirty. Gen was often in the office by that time, but she wasn't usually conscious yet.

When they parted in the kitchen for the night, Arthur held out his hand for their ardent handshake, as usual. She grabbed his hand to shake on it, but he paused, the slightly drunken merriness leaving his silver eyes.

While he held Gen's hand, he tugged her and enclosed her in his arms.

Her bones locked up, but his arms and body wrapped her snugly in a warm cocoon. He smoothed her arms around him.

Gen grabbed Arthur around his muscular waist and hung on. Yeah, being so tightly pinned against him freaked her out a little, but it was *Arthur,* not just some guy. *Arthur* wouldn't hurt her.

Well, not unless they had talked about it ahead of time and she was into it, evidently.

She almost giggled. It came out as a hiccup.

Near her ear, Arthur whispered, "If you ever want to sleep in a bed, sleep in mine."

His voice was tight, practically strangled in his throat.

"Arthur?" she asked, leaning back to look at him.

His silvery-blue eyes had turned steely, so serious. "I don't want to let you go tonight, but what are we going to do, sleep here on the kitchen counter?"

"Yeah, no. That granite gets pretty cold on the bare tushie," she said.

Hey, it was true.

He chuckled, but he stroked her cheek with his knuckles. "I'm serious, though. If you can, *when* you can, just walk in. I'll be waiting."

She nodded. "Okay."

Arthur cradled her head in his hand. "This is difficult for me because I'm British. We don't discuss such things."

"Yeah, y'all have really pretty, shiny boxes around your hearts," Gen said. She snuggled more deeply into his arms "I don't know how y'all ever have children."

Arthur said, "But I think we've gotten to be friends, good friends. Haven't we, Gen?"

Her head ducked. Evidently, she'd gotten British enough to feel the weirdness creeping up. "Um, yeah? I think so?"

He stroked her arm, his large palm warming her shoulder and down to her elbow. "And now we're more than friends."

"Friends with benefits, I guess."

He was still stroking her arm. "Yes, I suppose you could call us that."

Us.

The word shook Gen.

The casual way that he had used it suggested so much. He had been thinking about the two of them as an *us.* There was an *us* to think about.

Us meant more than friends.

She asked, "What would you call—what *we* are?"

He adjusted his arms around her, holding her more

tightly to his chest. "I would call us—"

Gen waited. He was staring at the ceiling, his eyes open.

"—I would introduce you as 'my very close friend.'"

She tightened her arms around his neck. To the British, that essentially meant that she was invited to Christmas supper.

"Would you be all right with that?" he asked.

"You're already introducing me like that," Gen said, forcing the words through her clenching throat, "because I'm posing as your girlfriend."

"Yes, but what if I meant it?"

Gen found his hand and twined her fingers in his. Holding his hand this way, palm to palm, felt more intimate than just his arms around her. She said, "Then I'd say it and mean it, too."

He tilted her chin up and kissed her, a long, slow kiss that melted her all the way down to her toes.

His arms loosened around her. "Good night, pet."

"Good night." She paused. "Okay, I did some reading. You call me *pet,* but I'm supposed to call you something, right?"

Arthur shrugged. "Since it's not a true Dom and sub relationship, we don't have to go that far."

"But most people do, right?"

He raised one dark eyebrow. "Some people use Sir. Or Master."

She looked away. Those were both so staid and had weird historical overtones for an American. "Yeah?"

He tilted his head. "I liked it when you called me 'my lord.'"

"Yeah, you would," she snarked.

"If we lose the case, you'll be the only person who calls me that ever again."

She laughed. "You'd better be careful. You're going to give me an incentive to lose the case."

"If you asked to be my sub, it would be worth it."

She rolled her eyes. "Might be worth losing your earldom, your private plane, and Spencer House?"

He grabbed her hand and kissed her knuckles. "I suppose you wouldn't be interested in me without all those things, anyway."

She couldn't let *that* go unanswered. "Arthur, I'm your friend. We are friends. *Very close friends.* After this case is over, no matter how it ends, no matter what we do, I'll still be your friend. Never doubt that."

He nodded. "I didn't mean it that way. No one would be interested in me if I lose everything. None of these charities would reserve tickets for me if I were not able to afford to drop tens of thousands of pounds for an evening's amusements. Certain friends would doubtlessly find me no longer useful."

"That's sad, Arthur. You shouldn't hang around fake people like that." She held his upper arms. "You shouldn't let people like that use you."

"I am of use to them for my connections. I can call certain people on the phone—"

Like a freaking prince.

"—or see them at events—"

Like High Court judges whom he called by their first names or any of the countless Lords and Duchesses and Baronets and Ladies that Arthur had introduced her to at the charity balls.

"—and it's the right thing to do. It's important to me, Gen."

"Schmoozing?"

"Not a particularly charitable description of what I do, but yes."

She stroked his arm. "Then we have to make sure that you can keep doing that. We have an early meeting with Octavia tomorrow morning to ensure it, and then we have to plan how to schmooze all those people on the House of Lords committee to make sure they vote the right way."

"It will be quite the strategic operation," he agreed.

"Let's get some shut-eye so that we're as fresh as rattlesnakes tomorrow."

He chuckled. "A most excellent proposition."

"Nah," Gen said. "A *most* excellent proposition would mean that you wouldn't get any sleep tonight."

She left him in the kitchen, grinning and shaking his head.

Needed

Arthur was just turning in for the night, alone in his big bed except for Ruckus, who lay balls-up near the footboard and was already snoring.

He glanced at the pillow on the other side and considered what it would be like if Gen were sleeping there, her dark hair spread across his pillow.

Of course, he imagined her soft skin naked in his bed, the sheets molding to her curves as she rolled over, warm and sleepy, next to him.

If he were going to imagine it, he might as well make it a good fantasy.

His phone buzzed on his nightstand, and the screen said that the number was unidentified.

He sighed and picked up the phone. "Yes?"

Elizabeth's rough voice said, "You're needed."

Damn. "Where?"

"Geneva."

He groaned. "Don't make the dead drop on a stripper's ass this time. It's not funny anymore."

"You'll be informed where to go when you get there. Call the usual number." The phone clicked as she hung up.

Arthur sighed and considered whether he should punch the wall or his phone.

He called Pippa. "Sorry. Late-night jaunt to the airport. I'll be ready in fifteen minutes." He hung up.

Yes, it was better that Gen had a separate bedroom so Arthur didn't have to explain where he jetted off to at a moment's notice in the middle of the night.

Ah, there it was, the secrecy that poisoned all his relationships.

It was better they didn't know. It truly was. After the inevitable breakup, there were no problems with retribution in the form of exposure.

And the break-up was inevitable, even with Gen.

His other life, the secrecy and walls, would eventually drive her away. He'd already warned her.

Arthur swung his feet off the side of the bed.

Time to save England.

~~~~~~~~~~~~

Arthur's not done yet.

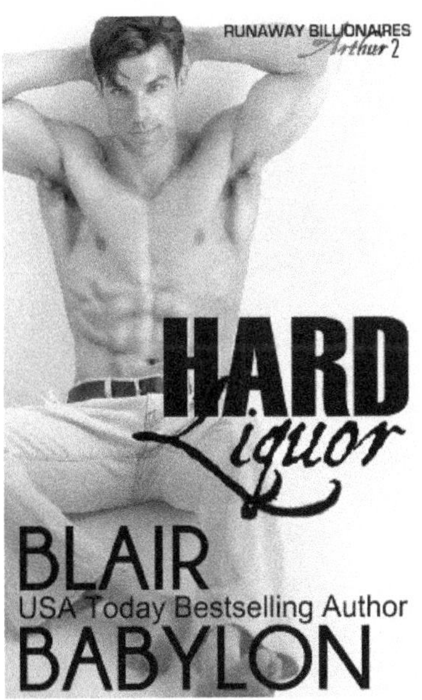

When you need a stiff drink, it had better be hard liquor.

Check your favorite bookstore for
Hard Liquor (Runaway Billionaires #3, Arthur Duet, Part 2).

Trial lawyer Gen has managed to corral that randy colt His Lordship Arthur Finch-Hatten, the Earl of Severn, at least as far as anyone knows. In public, he seems to be behaving himself, but she's kind of gotten involved with her client in a way that the Bar's Ethics Committee would totally not approve of. With Arthur's impending trial in the House of Lords and the constant backstabbing in her law office, the last thing Gen needs is for Arthur to whisk her off to Paris for the social
~~~~~~~~~~~~

wedding of the century to schmooze the people who will decide his fate.

Gen has broken all the rules, and she could very well end up with a broken heart.

She needs a stiff drink, and it had better be hard liquor.